AGNES

AT THE

END

OF THE

WORLD

AGNES
AT THE
END
OF THE
WORLD

KELLY MCWILLIAMS

LITTLE, BROWN AND COMPANY
New York Boston

Copyright © 2020 by Kelly McWilliams
Map illustration © 2020 by Tristan Elwell.

Cover art copyright © 2020 by Tom Bagshaw.
Cover design by Marcie Lawrence and Jenny Kimura.
Cover copyright © 2020 by Hachette Book Group, Inc.

Little, Brown and Company
Hachette Book Group
1290 Avenue of the Americas, New York, NY 10104

Visit us at LBYR.com

First Edition: June 2020

Little, Brown and Company is a division of Hachette Book Group, Inc. The
Little, Brown name and logo are trademarks of Hachette Book Group, Inc.

The publisher is not responsible for websites (or their content) that are not
owned by the publisher.

Library of Congress Cataloging-in-Publication Data
Names: McWilliams, Kelly, author.
Title: Agnes at the end of the world / by Kelly McWilliams.
Description: First edition. | New York : Little, Brown and Company, 2020. |
Audience: Ages 12+. | Summary: "Sixteen-year-old Agnes must escape a cult
and a Prophet as she attempts to save the world from a pandemic"— Provided
by publisher.
Identifiers: LCCN 2019031178 | ISBN 9780316487337 (hardcover) |
ISBN 9780316487306 (ebook) | ISBN 9780316487856
Subjects: CYAC: Cults—Fiction. | Brothers and sisters—Fiction. |
Epidemics—Fiction. | Religion and science—Fiction. | Love—Fiction.
Classification: LCC PZ7.M47885 Agn 2020 | DDC [Fic]—dc23
LC record available at https://locn.loc.gov/2019031178

ISBNs: 978-0-316-48733-7 (hardcover), 978-0-316-48730-6 (ebook)

Printed in the United States of America

LSC-C

10 9 8 7 6 5 4 3 2 1

For Clara Bailey Mullen

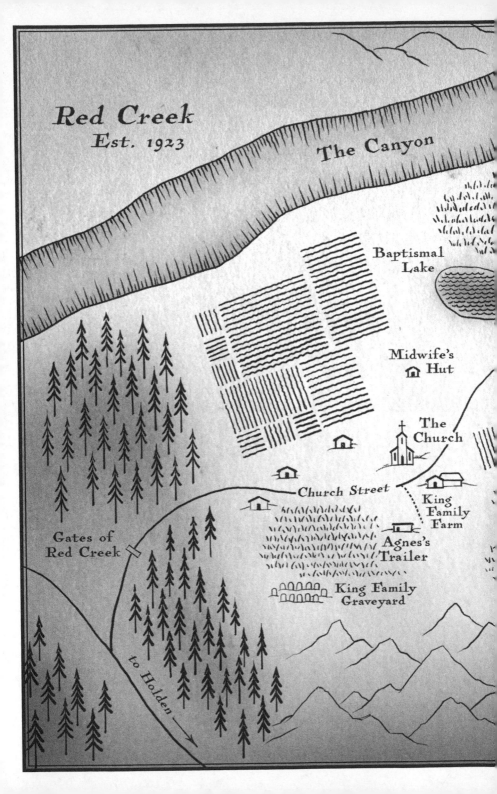

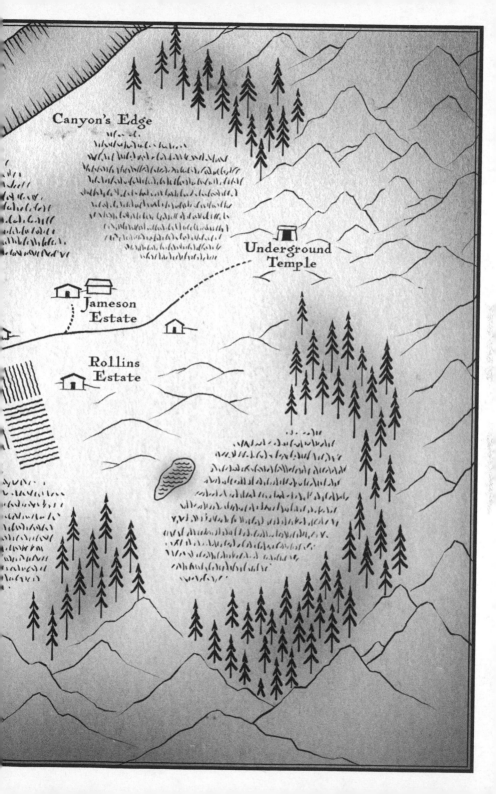

PART ONE

PROLOGUE

Once, a girl lived in a double-wide trailer on ranchland, beneath a wide white sky tumbled with clouds. The Prophet, a scowling crow of a man, presided over everyone and everything. When the girl wasn't praying or busy with chores, she'd spin in meadows dancing with bees and dandelions, until Father called her name from the porch: "Agnes, back in the house!"

Run.

In Agnes's world, secular music was forbidden, as was television, radio, and all technologies of sin. She wore homemade dresses that draped every inch of skin, though they were far too hot. At twelve, boys and girls were forbidden to play together, and the Prophet called the children *little sinners* with a sneer.

Nevertheless, Agnes loved her world. Loved the meadow and the rocky canyon and the hawks that screeched overhead, winging impossibly high.

One day, the meadow spoke. She was dancing when the hum rose up through the bottoms of her feet and into her small, little-girl bones.

It was like a song. An old song. She pressed her ear to the ground and listened. Rocks pulsed, stones echoed, and clouds, trees, leaves rustled with melody. The girl smiled, her heart full, because God had opened her ears. He'd scratched the earth with His fingernail and revealed a hidden world.

The girl was too young to see the danger in being singled out in a land where the Prophet expected his faithful to march like paper dolls, arm in arm, and all the same.

Perfect obedience produces perfect faith.

In Sunday school, Mrs. King asked the children if they remembered to pray.

"I don't need to pray," said Agnes. "Because God is singing, everywhere, all the time."

Children snickered. Their teacher swiftly crossed the room. She grabbed Agnes's arm, her face purple with anger, and stretched it across the desk. Then she slammed a Bible's spine across the girl's knuckles, over and over, until the middle knuckle of her right hand cracked like a nut.

Pain exploded up her arm. She knew better than to scream.

The woman bent and poured poison into her ear. "Insolent child. Only the Prophet hears the voice of God. Lie again and I'll show you real pain."

That night, hand throbbing and swollen, the girl told herself she didn't hear the sky singing or the earth humming. That she'd never heard such lovely, evil things.

Never. *Never.*

Perfect obedience produces perfect faith.

Agnes pretended so hard not to hear that one day, she didn't. The world went silent, all song snuffed out like a candle flame.

When she returned, hesitant and barefoot, to the bee-spun meadow, she heard nothing.

Nothing at all.

AGNES

Sickness is punishment for your rebellion.
It must be corrected by prayer alone.
— PROPHET JACOB ROLLINS

A gnes, are you in rebellion?"

The question startled her like a rifle's crack in the dark. Agnes froze with her hand on the trailer's doorknob, her backpack slung over her shoulder. It was a quarter to midnight, and her fifteen-year-old sister was sitting bolt upright in bed, staring hungrily at her.

Agnes's pulse throbbed in the hollow of her throat, beating a single word: *Caught.*

She'd been sneaking out the last Saturday of every month for two years, and she'd never been seen before.

Such an obedient daughter, the matrons always said.

No one would ever suspect that such a sweet, hardworking girl regularly broke one of Red Creek's strictest Laws—*no contact with Outsiders.*

It was an act for which she could be banished, and she never would've risked it if her brother's life weren't at stake. Luckily, her family were deep sleepers. But some sound—or dark intuition— had woken her sister tonight.

Are you in rebellion?

Agnes shut her eyes, dreading the truth.

She'd always wanted, more than anything, to be *good*. Would God understand she'd never wanted to break His Laws?

Would the Prophet, if he ever found out?

"You can tell me," her sister coaxed. "I won't condemn you. I'm the only one who wouldn't."

"Please, Beth," she pleaded. "Go back to sleep."

Beth was already standing, shivering barefoot in her white nightgown. Her eyes shone lambent in the dark, and Agnes felt a cold wash of fear. She was well acquainted with her sister's stubbornness.

Oh, why couldn't she have slept on, like all the times before?

"Wherever you're going, take me with you."

"It's too dangerous."

Beth's eyes flicked over the living room. "I don't care. I'm bored to death here. Please."

The twins rolled over in their cot. Agnes held her breath, but the younger girls didn't wake. In the far corner, a crucifix nightlight illuminated Ezekiel's sleeping face.

For as long as Agnes could remember, she and Beth had shared everything—a bed, a hairbrush, their dreams.

Everything, except this. Agnes's only secret, too dangerous to share.

Beth's eyes lit up. "Is it a boy? Is that it?"

Agnes pinched the bridge of her nose. She loved her sister dearly, but people whispered she was trouble waiting to happen. They whispered that she was impulsive, spoiled, vain, and exactly the sort of girl to lead an innocent boy into the shadow of the valley of death.

But Agnes loved her too much to believe it.

"No," she said miserably. "I'm not meeting a boy. Why would you even ask me that?"

Beth cocked her head, calculating. "If not a boy, then what on earth—?"

Agnes's cheeks burned. She hated living this shadowy double life—the lies breeding ever more lies, the constant shame like a ball of fire in her chest.

She met Beth's too-pretty eyes, green as lake shallows, and nearly confessed.

I have no choice, she wanted to say. *I sold my soul two years ago. If I hadn't, we'd have buried Ezekiel in the meadow.*

Yet to save his life was a grave-deep sin, and so it must be her cross to bear—hers, alone. As much as she loved her sister, she knew Beth wasn't strong enough to carry that burden for long.

To save her brother's life, Agnes bit her tongue.

"If you *are* in rebellion, I understand," Beth insisted. "Don't you know I have doubts, too? Lately, I think Red Creek is—"

"*Stop,*" Agnes whispered fiercely. She'd had enough of her willful younger sister for one night. "It's none of your business where I go!"

Beth rocked back like she'd been slapped. Then a chill settled over her fine features, an icy mask of rage, and Agnes trembled despite herself.

"Everyone always says you're so faithful," Beth bit out. "But it's all lies, isn't it?"

"Beth." She willed her to understand. "I'm trying my best."

And not everything is about you.

Agnes glanced at Ezekiel clutching his stuffed toy Sheep, then quickly looked away.

"You think I'm a child." Beth's voice smarted with hurt. "But you can't keep me in the dark forever."

"Don't tell," she said urgently. "Hate me if you want, but don't tell."

"Fine." Beth turned her back, digging under the mattress for her diary. "But I'll never forgive you for this. *Never.*"

She scribbled furiously in her book, sheltering in her own little world.

Beth, I love you, Agnes wanted to say, but didn't. *Beth, I'm sorry.*

She glanced at the clock, and her heart contracted. It was nearly midnight. She didn't have much time.

Quietly, Agnes pushed open the trailer door and slipped into the evening air.

The night smelled of lavender, dust, and danger.

—⌇—

Agnes always met the Outsider in the King family cemetery, at the bottom of the hilly meadow that sprawled like a green carpet from their porch, unrolling all the way to the forest's edge. The graveyard marked the boundary she absolutely couldn't cross. The end of her world, before the wild Outside took over.

Holding a flashlight and blue picnic cooler, she hurried towards the small collection of headstones that rose from the ground like rotten teeth. The grass was velvet, the moon a white slice.

The Outsider wasn't there.

Stomach knotting, Agnes sank among the graves to wait.

The King family had lost five children. The stones read: JERE-MIAH, STILLBORN. ANNABELLE, STILLBORN. NOAH, STILLBORN. And JONAH. And RUTH.

Ruth had been a beautiful baby, and Agnes would never forget her funeral. The little wooden casket and how the baby's tiny fingers curled inwards like petals in a bud. The Prophet said God's will had been done when the fever took the child, and Agnes believed him. But she ached for the baby and for her mother, whom all of Red Creek blamed. It was a sign the woman had earned God's wrath that so many children had died, and a judgment she had no choice but to accept.

In the graveyard, an electric certainty struck Agnes like lightning. Keeping Ezekiel alive—administering his shots, checking his blood, praying he wouldn't collapse when she wasn't there to revive him—her head swam with the mountainous, unholy difficulty of caring for a child so ill, all on her own.

She should *walk away*. Go home, confess, and beg God's forgiveness. If Ezekiel fell sick—died, even—well, it wasn't her place to interfere.

But she was glued to the earth. She loved her baby brother with her whole soul, and she'd rather lose her chance at heaven than see him so sick again.

"Agnes?"

She spun around and saw the Outsider coming towards her. A middle-aged woman dressed in her cotton nurse's outfit. Her hair frizzed a halo around her head, and her lips were richly painted. Her skin was darker than any she'd ever seen before—an umber nearly black. The Prophet would call her a child of Cain, a member of a race damned long ago. But Agnes struggled to see her that way, carrying as she was a cooler full of lifesaving medicine in a hand spangled with rings.

Her name was Matilda, and two years ago, she'd saved Ezekiel's life.

And thrust Agnes into this endless, living nightmare.

"Sorry I'm late." Matilda paused, catching her breath. "It's chaos at the hospital. Have you had much trouble here?"

"No trouble, ma'am."

She blinked. "No sickness? Nothing strange?"

Agnes didn't know what she was talking about and didn't care. She wished Matilda would just get on with it, so she could get back to her world and forget all about this.

Or try.

"Oh, sweetheart, you're pale." Matilda touched her shoulder. "Everything okay at home? You can tell me, you know."

Agnes looked away, blinking back tears. It would be so much easier if she could hate the Outsider. But Matilda was gentle, motherly, and Agnes had yearned for a mother ever since her own had taken to her bed. Maybe Matilda knew that. Maybe she was only playing a role. Didn't the Prophet say Outsiders would try to trick you? That they'd hide their wickedness until it was too late?

"Do you ever wish you could leave this place? Go to school?"

Agnes bristled. "I *do* go to school. On Sundays."

Matilda frowned. "I mean a real school, with other kids. A public education."

"I'd hate that more than anything." Agnes caught herself, lowered her voice. "Outsider teachings are against our faith."

Matilda smiled sadly. "You're a good girl, trying to keep faith and care for your brother, too. But Agnes, obedience and faith aren't the same thing."

"You don't like us." Agnes felt increasingly defensive. "But we're following God's word."

The nurse shook her head. "Just think about it, okay?"

Outsiders are devious, the Prophet always said. *Trust them at your peril.*

Agnes glanced back at her trailer, small on the hilltop. Every minute she spent in the cemetery she risked everything. If someone caught her, she might never see her siblings again, and the kids were all she'd ever had.

When daylight came and her brother had his medicine, Agnes swore she'd think of the Outsider as little as humanly possible.

"Insulin for thirty days." Matilda's tone turned businesslike. She handed Agnes a blue picnic cooler.

It felt heavy in her hand—sinful. In exchange, Agnes passed her the empty one. Also, the piece of folded notebook paper she kept in her breast pocket: Ezekiel's diabetes log.

In it, she tracked his blood sugar, carbs, and activity. Her chest tightened while Matilda read it over. Agnes was supposed to keep Ezekiel's blood glucose between 80 and 130, and she tried her best. But despite constant vigilance, his log showed peaks and valleys as mountainous as Red Creek itself.

Matilda's eyes softened. "Fluctuation is normal. You're doing a fine job. Let me guess. You're probably dreaming in numbers now, right?"

Agnes managed a wan smile, thinking of the carb-counter book Matilda had given her two years ago. She'd practically memorized it.

Matilda held her eyes. "Agnes. If he lived in the world, your brother could have all the power of technology keeping him alive."

Yes, she thought sadly. *But what of his soul?*

Matilda sighed, resigned. "Where do you keep his insulin, anyway?"

Agnes chewed her lip, knowing how bizarre it would sound. "I bury it in my garden. Deep, where the earth is cool."

Matilda looked shocked. "Well. I guess you can't keep it in the fridge. You're right that I don't like what I've heard about this place. But I do like *you*."

Agnes fought the urge to be flattered, which was only weakness, plain and simple. Quickly, she zipped the cooler into her backpack.

When she looked up, Matilda was frowning again, and Agnes's stomach clenched.

"Listen," Matilda said. "I can't make it next month. I'm taking on more hospital shifts."

She froze, remembering Ezekiel's first crisis. How close death had come.

"Sweetheart, I'm sending someone else. My son. Danny."

Her son?

Was she insane?

She opened her mouth to protest, to tell Matilda that she couldn't under any circumstances sneak out at night to meet a *boy*. God would surely destroy her for that, if Father didn't first.

She heard Beth's voice, rebelliously eager: *Is it a boy? Is that it?*

Inwardly, she groaned. But the Outsider was already fishing in her purse for car keys. She left her alone and dazed among the graves.

Beneath the stars, Agnes bowed her head to pray.

God forgive me.

The Prophet was right about Outsiders. They tricked you with kindness, and nothing they said was as simple as it seemed.

If she had to meet a boy in the dark next month—a faithless, Gentile boy—she'd bring Father's gun along with her.

In the meantime, she'd bury her secret deeper than the insulin cooler. She'd pretend she'd never met Matilda or witnessed the miracle of her medicine. When she administered Ezekiel's shots, she'd watch the needle with only half her mind, keeping the other half pure and clean.

Every day, she'd be so faithful that God might overlook this trespass. Might even decide it was finally time to cure Ezekiel.

What a miracle it would be, Agnes thought fervently, trudging up the steep hill. *If God took his sickness away.*

2

AGNES

Until marriage, stay chaste. Treat the other sex like snakes.
—Prophet Jacob Rollins

At dawn the next day, Agnes drew Ezekiel into the bathroom and carefully locked the door. She drew up her skirt to unstrap the glucose meter from her thigh, wincing as the tape tugged at sensitive skin.

Solemnly, Ezekiel extended the third finger of his left hand for her to prick.

The sinful screen flashed. His morning blood glucose—a safe 95.

She recorded the number in his log while he played silently with his stuffed Sheep. Then she prepared his basal insulin. With a steady hand, she plunged the syringe into his arm.

"Thumbs-up if you feel high today, okay?" she said. "Thumbs-down, if you feel—"

"Low, I know." He chewed his lip, pouting. "But Agnes, why should I?"

She frowned. "Why signal me, you mean?"

He shook his head vigorously. "I mean, why am I sick? Why is God mad at me?"

Her chest tightened. "Oh, Ezekiel. I truly don't know."

His features firmed with resolve. "I'll pray extra hard in church today. I swear."

Tenderly, Agnes kissed his forehead—her own body burning with grief and guilt.

"Our secret, remember," she reminded him.

He nodded. "Our secret."

Thanks to the Outsider, he had enough insulin to survive another thirty days.

In the kitchen, Beth speared Agnes with a look so meaningful it bordered on sinful.

A look that said, *You'll regret keeping secrets from me, sister.*

"Mary, go brush your teeth!" Agnes shouted, ignoring her. "Sam, help your sisters tie their shoes. I mean it."

If they didn't hurry, they'd be late for church.

Bells tolled and the screen door slammed. They followed Father to Red Creek's dusty road, joining a procession of other families on their way to the white clapboard church. On the first of July, the air shimmered with unrelenting heat.

Only Agnes's mother stayed behind. She never went to church anymore—never went anywhere. Father lied, told their neighbors she was infirm. In truth, she indulged the sin of despair, staring blankly at the bedroom ceiling, day after day.

She only came out to shower when everyone slept.

Agnes had discovered her once, her frail mother standing in the hallway, her hair lank and damp. She wished she'd never seen her mother scuttle back to her room. It was the first time she'd laid eyes on her in weeks.

Afterwards, Agnes made a point of staying in bed when she heard running water.

Father often wondered aloud when the Prophet would gift him with another, better wife. A real helpmate, this time.

"It's a great blessing I have Agnes to keep house," he told approving church matrons. "Honestly, I don't know what I'd do without her."

The road was more alive on Sundays than on any other day. Agnes loved to see three hundred of God's faithful in their starched collars and hear all the children's voices rising high. And there were plenty of children. Most Red Creek families were bursting at the seams. The Prophet himself had twenty-one children and eleven exalted wives.

Father hadn't been so lucky. Agnes and Beth wondered, beneath the bedcovers, what marked him for such misfortune.

"God must've told Prophet Rollins that Father isn't ready to take another wife," Agnes said. "Maybe there's some stain on his soul?"

"I don't want another mother, anyway."

"She could help with chores," Agnes pointed out.

"Or she could be spiteful," Beth replied. "And cause more trouble than she's worth."

The words made Agnes squirm, because they sounded like rebellion. God would give them another mother or not, just as He would give them away in marriage or not. But Beth had always struggled with her woman's role.

I made the right choice, keeping Ezekiel's secret to myself, she thought. *Perfectly right.*

On the road, Agnes held Ezekiel's hand, and Ezekiel cradled his Sheep. Sam hurried to catch up with them, cheeks ruddy under the high desert sun.

"Will the Prophet preach the Rapture today? I want to hear about fire and brimstone and what will happen to the Outsiders!"

Sam couldn't get enough of avenging angels with flaming swords.

A smile touched Agnes's lips. "The Prophet will preach what God wills."

"But the Rapture is so exciting! I wish the apocalypse was happening today."

Ezekiel tugged Agnes's hand, her cue to bend so he could speak into her ear.

"I don't like the Rapture sermon," he whispered gravely. "It gives me nightmares."

"Only Outsiders need fear the Rapture," she whispered back.

"And the rebellious, right?" Ezekiel squinted, anxious. "Won't they be struck down, too?"

Moonlight on the King family gravestones. A syringe in her hand. And Beth asking, *Agnes, are you in rebellion?*

Unsettled, Agnes entered the church.

The building had been constructed in the time of the Prophet's grandfather, with pews to seat the three hundred people of Red Creek. No windows—the Prophet said earthly light was a needless distraction. An enormous cross hung from a wire, twisting slowly on its bearings. The bronze symbol made her anxious, looking as if it were always about to fall. She soothed herself that the wire was strong.

She glanced at Ezekiel, alive by the grace of a dozen broken Laws, and swallowed.

What if *her* wires were faulty? What if she was the one about to fall?

She opened her well-loved Bible with shaking hands. It fell open to a familiar passage:

I have gone astray like a lost sheep; seek thy servant; for I do not forget thy commandments.

"Amen," she whispered while the cross twisted this way and that.

After the sermon, the girls filed into one annex, the boys into another.

Agnes's eyes lingered on Ezekiel's thin back as he disappeared behind the boys' door. She'd stuffed his pockets, as usual, with homemade granola bars in case his blood sugar dipped low. She told herself he'd be fine, that God would watch over him. But her stomach twisted anyway.

In the girls' room, Agnes pulled out her notebook to copy the name of the lesson scrawled on the chalkboard—*Why Perfect Obedience Produces Perfect Faith.*

Beth yanked Agnes's braid and passed her a folded paper.

"I wish you wouldn't pass notes," Agnes murmured irritably.

But their Sunday school teacher hadn't arrived yet. The other girls were busily chattering, enjoying their time away from chores.

The note, written in Beth's bubbly cursive, was short and sweet:

I forgive you.

Agnes looked into her wide green eyes, surprised. Beth smiled so graciously that Agnes couldn't help but smile back. Her sister had a good heart. Of course one single secret wouldn't come between them.

Beth turned away, and Magda Jameson tapped Agnes's shoulder.

Agnes felt an inwards curl of disgust.

Magda was Red Creek's most vicious gossip. She was prone to mincing, fussing, and looking down on anyone whose father owned less land and fewer livestock. Though Agnes braced herself, nothing could've prepared her for the lash of Magda's poisoned tongue.

"I heard your sister's been tempting my brother Cory."

Her pencil clattered to the floor. "What?"

Magda wrinkled her nose in distaste. "Everyone says she's utterly shameless. Practically in rebellion."

Agnes wanted to shake her for saying such a thing. Girls had been shunned, humiliated, *banished* for less.

"That's vile gossip and you know it."

Magda only smirked. Agnes was grateful when Mrs. King marched into the room, angling her hips between rows of identical desks.

"Well, girls? Who'd like to share her summary of the sermon?" Mrs. King's eyes roamed across their faces and, finally, with a cruel glittering, fell on hers. "Agnes? Will you?"

Her stomach dropped.

Since childhood, she'd dreaded public speaking.

She looked helplessly at her hands. On her right was the ugly broken knuckle, never properly healed. She didn't blame Mrs. King for breaking it. Her methods may have been harsh, but Agnes had dearly needed the correction.

She *had* spoken blasphemy, claiming to hear God—but never again.

Mrs. King sighed. "Well. I see the cat's got her tongue."

The other girls tittered, and Agnes could've died.

"You know she can't answer in front of everyone." Beth's voice rang clear as a bell. "So why do you keep calling on her?"

Mrs. King's face darkened. Agnes held her breath.

Rebellion, her heart beat. *Beth, are you in rebellion?*

"If you object to how I run my class, you can leave it," spat Mrs. King. "I'm sure the Prophet will be happy to see you in his office."

Fear buried itself in Agnes's chest like an arrow. Beth *must not* choose this path. Didn't she know what was at stake?

Punishment. Exile.

And worst of all, the wrath of God.

A long, tense pause, while the other girls watched, curious as crows.

"I only mean, it seems unfair," Beth said—but repentantly enough.

Agnes slumped with relief.

"Careful, young lady," Mrs. King warned her sister. "Now. Who will summarize?"

Magda's hand shot up, and Agnes grimaced.

"The sermon was on the role of the sexes." That mincing voice, sickly sweet and taunting. "The Prophet says that until marriage, girls must keep themselves pure and chaste, and treat men as if they were snakes."

Beth laughed, a punched, angry sound.

Mrs. King whirled. "Who's laughing? Raise your hand."

Beth stared innocently at the chalkboard. No girl proved brave enough to point a finger. But the damage was done, her reputation further sullied.

Agnes squirmed, underlining the lesson's title over and over: *Why Perfect Obedience Produces Perfect Faith.*

Then came a bitter rush of guilt. Beth was toying with rebellious urges—Agnes saw that quite clearly now. For years, she'd been entirely focused on Ezekiel's illness. But all along, something dark and equally dangerous had been happening inside Beth.

She remembered her sister saying, *If you* are *in rebellion, I understand. Don't you know I have doubts, too?*

At the first opportunity, Agnes promised herself she'd speak to her sister. She hoped it wasn't too late to stop her from doing something stupid, or dangerous, or both.

3

AGNES

Women are wholly incapable of interpreting God's word.
—Prophet Jacob Rollins

Sundays are a day of rest.

Fortunately for the people of Red Creek, however, God Himself had revealed to the Prophet that women could still perform housework.

For Agnes, that meant mountains of laundry followed by the dull, repetitive work of ironing. Afterwards, she and Beth baked crackers for the week ahead. If they had time, they tackled mending—loose buttons, torn hems.

Today she planned to corner Beth while the crackers baked. Father had gone to his Scripture meeting. If she sent the kids outside, they could talk—really talk—alone. But when it came time to heat the oven, her sister was nowhere to be found. Not in the living room or the bathroom (where she often lingered before the mirror), or in the meadow.

While Agnes searched, her throat tightening, the twins, Mary and Faith, perched outside the screen door, practicing their reading.

"*M* is for Mary, the Mother of our God," they recited from a tattered workbook. "And *N* is for Noah, who saved the Naughty world."

Beth disappeared sometimes. Probably, she was only scribbling in her diary at the forest's edge. But she'd never abandoned Agnes on a busy Sunday before. Glancing at the laundry heaped on the kitchen table, she frowned.

"*O* is for Obadiah," intoned the twins, "who hid the prophets from Oppression."

"Have you seen Beth?" she asked Sam.

He glanced at her, face troubled. "Something's wrong with Ezekiel."

Panic swooped in on black wings. "Where is he?"

He pointed. "He said he was too tired to come up the hill. I called him a wimp, but—"

It was low blood glucose, had to be. Agnes felt inside her pockets, where she kept hard candies, each fifteen carbs exactly. She brushed past Sam and raced outdoors, pulse throbbing in her temples, glucose meter cutting into her thigh. She found her little brother slouched beneath a tree. Deep circles had etched themselves around his eyes. He looked like a puppet whose strings had been cut.

"Agnes?" he slurred.

"Here." She handed him a candy. "Eat this."

With her back turned to the trailer, she reached under her skirt and unstrapped the meter for a check. She'd assumed he was low, but still the number shocked her.

65!

If Sam hadn't warned her—if he'd passed out, all alone . . .

Try not to scare him, Matilda had said. *But understand, a low could kill him faster than you'd believe.*

"Why didn't you eat one of your granola bars?"

"Tommy King took them," Ezekiel whispered.

Agnes shuddered, hating that little bully. But her feelings weren't fair. No one but her and Ezekiel knew anything about his dangerous illness.

It had all started when Ezekiel was five years old. Suddenly, he couldn't get enough to drink. He hogged the bathroom all day and wet the bed every night. He grew as sinewy as a starving lamb.

"You're praying to God, aren't you?" she'd asked while tightening his leather belt around his disappearing waist. "You're asking for forgiveness, for Him to make you well?"

He'd opened his mouth as if to answer, and viscous, black vomit spilled out.

Vomit that smelled of acid and, very clearly, of death.

Terror had seized Agnes then. She'd screamed for her mother, who stumbled bleary-eyed from her bedroom. She'd taken one look at Ezekiel, her last baby, trembling in Agnes's arms, and did what only a woman raised Outside would ever think to do.

Called the hospital.

"Don't send an ambulance," she'd said curtly into the phone. "The neighbors can't know." A pause. "Yes, we're in Red Creek. No, we aren't allowed to leave."

Matilda, the nurse on the phone, volunteered to come herself.

By the time she arrived, Agnes's mother had retreated back into her bedroom. So it was Agnes who learned that Ezekiel had something called type 1 diabetes, and that he'd die without insulin, no matter how hard she prayed. It was Agnes who arranged for Matilda to visit every day whenever Father was out, until she'd wrestled Ezekiel's blood sugar back under control.

In a week's time, Ezekiel was playing outside with Sam and

the twins again, and Agnes understood what she must do—what she must *sacrifice*—if she meant to keep him alive.

She couldn't bear to watch him suffer. Not him, the baby of the family—and, since his mother had abandoned him as an infant, her baby, almost.

In the meadow, Agnes shook away that dark memory and fished a granola bar out of her pocket.

Ezekiel took a bite, chewed, and dissolved into hiccups and sobs.

"Ezekiel," she said, alarmed. "What's wrong?"

"Tommy King."

She scowled. "Don't worry. I'll speak with his mother. I'll—"

Ezekiel shook his head. "No. Agnes, he said there's sickness among the Outsiders. Plague!"

Instinctively, they both looked east. The Underground Temple lay that way—a hidden bunker, where the faithful would one day shelter from the apocalypse.

Hadn't Matilda said something about sickness? About taking on extra shifts?

Agnes kept her voice carefully neutral. "Where did Tommy hear that?"

"He heard it from his father," Ezekiel whispered. "He said the Outsiders are dying and we'll all be in the Temple soon." The color drained from his face. "He said we'd better not be afraid of the dark!"

Agnes rubbed his back in rhythmic circles. "Don't get upset. Remember, your blood sugar—"

He cried ever harder, and what could she say to soothe him?

She only knew what she believed, in her heart's core.

Gently, she prompted, "Do you know why the Prophet's grandfather chose this land for us, so many years ago?"

"Because he was persecuted," Ezekiel mumbled.

"That's right. The Outsiders believe plural marriage is wrong. So he found a land far from the wicked, with a forest protecting it on one side and a canyon on the other. And that's where we stay."

"Except when we need something from Walmart." He brightened at the familiar story. "Like shoes, or crayons."

"Exactly. There are lots of sicknesses Outside, Ezekiel. And violence, thieving, and adultery. But as long as you're in Red Creek, the Prophet will keep you safe."

Ezekiel wiped his eyes. "Promise?"

Her baby brother, so small and trusting. She held him close, inhaling his scent.

"The Rapture won't be a surprise. The Prophet will warn us, because God will warn *him*. I promise, you won't hear it from Tommy King first. Now, let's get you inside."

Wending her way to the porch stoop with Ezekiel's hand in hers, Agnes truly believed her own words. There was *always* chaos among Outsiders, because they chose to live in sin. But Red Creek was just the opposite: a land of peace and order. Even if sickness raged elsewhere, Agnes knew the Prophet would protect them. As long as they remained here, they'd be safe.

Under the wide white sky, Sam and the twins whooped and laughed, gleefully playing the Apocalypse Game. In the game, two children—the "angels"—chased after "sinners." When they caught them, they pierced their hearts with an invisible blade.

Mary shrieked, "Down, blasphemer!"

Sam crumpled, gripping his chest in imaginary agony.

The evening bell tolled. The sound spread like ink through the darkening sky, and Agnes's heart plummeted. Beth had been missing far too long. It was nearly sunset, the meadow's edges tinted red, and Father would be home soon.

In the meadow, the game burned on, blazing with make-believe brimstone. Agnes kept her eyes on the horizon, feeling obscurely frightened.

A crow lighted on their trailer's tin roof, claws clicking. Her hands clenched into fists at her sides.

Where are you, sister? Oh, Beth, where have you gone?

4

BETH

Endure hardship without complaint. Your reward awaits you at life's end.
—Prophet Jacob Rollins

After suffering the longest, most boring Sunday school lesson imaginable, Beth lingered with her family in the church lobby just long enough to catch Cory Jameson's eye.

She was wearing her favorite prairie dress—a pale blue that felt like wearing the sky—and had loosed a few locks of hair, the better to highlight the gold flecks in her eyes. She'd also viciously pinched her cheeks to bring out the blush. While technically she wasn't breaking the Law—*no painted faces or unbraided hair*—she felt no compunction about bending rules that struck her, increasingly, as senselessly unfair.

Nosy matrons shot her sidelong looks, but it was worth it to see Cory's jaw drop, ever so slightly, at the sight of her. Pride straightened her spine—a rare sense of power, like a firework going off in her chest.

Cory winked, and she winked back.

Their signal.

A smile broke over his face like a shaft of sun through parted clouds. He was easily the handsomest boy in Red Creek, and all the girls mooned over him (except Agnes, of course). Better still, Cory's father, the powerful Matthew Jameson, had declared that he'd be a great patriarch one day, the inheritor of his lands. Cory was Matthew's seventh boy child, but like Joseph in the Bible, he was the favorite. And everyone knew it.

Watching him slip away, Beth smiled like a satisfied cat. Then she caught sight of her *oh-so-dutiful* older sister, who was showing the young Mrs. Hearn (a fourteen-year-old new mother clearly on the verge of tears) how to swaddle her baby.

Beth's heart squeezed small as a pomegranate seed. The truth was, she'd been thrilled to catch Agnes sneaking out last night, because Agnes rebelling meant Beth was free to tell her everything—about Cory, and about her own rebellious thoughts—without fear of disapproval. She'd even allowed herself to hope that they'd be confidantes again. Beth couldn't think of anything she wanted more.

But Agnes had cut her dead.

It's none of your business where I go, she'd said.

Well. Her sister wasn't the only one with a secret, and Beth, smarting from rejection, meant to indulge her own in full today.

After all, why should Agnes get to have all the fun?

Cory waited for her beneath their juniper tree, at the canyon's edge.

There the earth plummeted into a sunset-colored abyss, a gash yawning wide and vast. When the wild winds swept it, the earth itself seemed to howl.

Most girls feared the canyon, and the coyotes and catamounts that made it their home, but the canyon was the most adventure-some, romantic setting Beth could picture. She loved it.

Only sometimes, like now, the sight of its vastness saddened her. Made her think how small her life was. How suffocating.

But Beth never stayed melancholy long. She took a deep breath, inhaling the scent of warm earth, and when Cory emerged from behind their tree with a rakish grin, she pressed herself against him and kissed him hard.

"Wow," he said when they broke away. "What was that for?"

"I guess I missed you."

Cory frowned, then cursed vehemently under his breath. "What a fucking mess we're in."

She raised an eyebrow. Red Creek's golden boy liked to sling Outsider curses when they were alone. He learned them from the television at the nearby gas station, where the owner let him watch shows for a quarter. He often "borrowed" his father's truck to get there.

Beth felt a tug of jealousy, thinking of the freedoms he enjoyed. Cory's forays were secret, but even if he were found out—well—who wouldn't forgive the golden boy for breaking a rule here or there?

Boys will be boys—especially the golden ones.

Yet Beth often felt she'd been buried alive.

"So, you didn't miss me?"

His eyes blazed in a way that made her belly clench. "I couldn't think of anything but you all week."

"Is that so bad?"

"What we're doing is wrong." She heard the conflict in his voice, the yearning. "Beth, I think we'd better stop meeting."

Though she kept her face serene, on the inside she panicked.

She'd known Cory Jameson since childhood. He'd always accepted her, flaws and all.

And the kissing was lovely.

Sometimes she'd lean against the juniper tree, just letting herself be kissed while he murmured: *I love you, God help me, but I love you.* At night, she'd write all about it in her diary, which she kept hidden beneath her side of the mattress, replaying every delicious moment before she fell asleep.

"You don't mean that."

"I do." He ran a hand through his sun-kissed hair. "I can't keep doing what I know to be a sin. I'll have responsibilities soon."

She tipped her head back to look at him, aware of the afternoon light prettily illuminating her brow.

"We're not hurting anyone. Anyway, if it wasn't a little sinful, it wouldn't be any fun, would it?"

He laughed, and looked more like himself.

"Beth, you're a hell of a girl," he said, surely quoting some secular movie he'd caught on the gas station television set. "But it's the hereafter that matters. We've had our fun, and we've got to start taking eternal life seriously. Before it's too late."

She slipped from his grip, irritated by the mention of the hereafter—that vague concept around which her life was forced to revolve.

"If that's how you feel, then why did you ever want me?"

He winced. "There's no harm in sinning when you're young, as long as it doesn't mean anything. But now it does. We were never supposed to choose each other. We ought to have waited for God."

"Oh, that's only about marriage," she said airily.

"Treat the other sex like snakes," he shot back. "And stay chaste."

"Is this about your father? Did he say something?"

He scowled, trying to decide how much to tell. Now that she felt on the brink of losing him, he looked more handsome than ever.

So don't lose him, she chided herself.

"You know I'm meant to inherit the homestead?"

She rolled her eyes. "Everybody knows."

"Yesterday, Father said God would surely bless me with many wives—as soon as I'm old enough to marry. Can you even imagine what a huge responsibility that is? I'll be a *patriarch*, Beth. And not later. *Soon*."

A burst of pain, swift and sharp. Girls married as young as fourteen, but boys, as heads of households, waited until eighteen.

Cory was seventeen already.

"Is that what you want?" she demanded. "To be a big exalted patriarch with dozens of dull, obedient wives?"

"I want to be a righteous man."

She stamped her foot—she couldn't help it. "Cory Jameson, you're *boring*! You're smart enough to be anything, *do* anything. You could leave, if you wanted. Have a life *Outside*."

The word quivered on her tongue like a breathless dream.

"But then I'd be damned," he said. "If it's here or the lake of fire, I'd much rather stay where I am."

She crossed her arms over her chest and turned her eyes towards the canyon.

What was wrong with her, that she didn't give a damn about being damned?

I just want to live, she thought desperately. *To kiss a boy, see new things, have real friends...*

The tears streamed hot and sudden down her cheeks.

In an instant, poor, conflicted Cory had her in his arms. "Oh, there. Don't cry. Please don't."

She rested her cheek against his collarbone. "I hope you're happy with your dozen wives," she said bitterly. "I hope they're god-awful nags."

He stroked her hair. "Let's not think about it now. As long

as I'm free, we can keep meeting. But you know, if anyone ever found out—"

Beth thought of Agnes—her sister, hoarding her secrets—and cried harder.

"You knew it wasn't forever when we began," he said. "So what's really bothering you?"

"It's Agnes," she cried. "She's been sneaking out!"

He frowned. "Which one is Agnes?"

"It's because she's plain you haven't noticed her," she said accusingly, pushing back. "You know all the pretty girls by name."

He blushed. "Not *all*."

But Beth knew she was right. It was the strangest thing, because to her, Agnes possessed a striking beauty. There was something in the way she held herself. Something in the tilt of her head. Her features were undeniably coarse and square, and yet sometimes Beth found herself unable to take her eyes off her.

She'd always thought privately (and with mild irritation) that to a certain kind of man, her sister would eclipse her entirely.

"Agnes is my elder sister," she said, her voice shifting to irony. "The paragon of virtue."

"Oh, right." Cory sounded amused. When he wasn't in high-holy mode, amusement was his default position towards life. "So, she has a secret boyfriend?"

"I don't think so." Beth bit her lip, pondering. "I don't think she's ever sinned, even inside her own head."

"What do you think she's up to, then?"

She chewed her thumbnail. "I'm afraid she might be doing something *noble*."

"Really? Like what?" As a future upstanding patriarch, Cory was always interested in gallantry. "No offense, but what can a girl do that's noble?"

"I don't know," she snapped, faintly bothered.

For all that the faithful praised Agnes's piety, no one seemed to see what Beth did—that her sister was special.

When she bowed her head for prayers, the craziest thought sometimes leapt into Beth's mind: that Agnes was like an ancient prophet. The thought would overwhelm her like the vapor of a numinous cloud, then quickly pass, and she'd only see her plain-faced sister praying once more. She'd half forget the unsettling suspicion that Agnes was destined for greatness.

Real greatness.

Beth wouldn't mind that she was destined for greatness, if only she'd share it. But last night, Agnes had slammed a door in her face.

And why? Hadn't she always tried to be a good sister?

Beth broke away from her bleak thoughts and looked ardently at Cory, enjoying the way her gaze made him blush to the tips of his ears.

Despite his grand intentions, he was helpless to resist her.

"Let's not talk about Agnes anymore," she whispered.

Cory groaned, quickly conquered.

Under the juniper tree, they kissed until they were starved for breath, utterly consumed by their shared fire at the crimson edge of the earth.

5

BETH

The bell tolled at sunset. Beth remembered: *I've got to get home.*

She pressed away from Cory, feeling the vise grip of panic.

It wasn't just that Father would punish her if she were late for prayers. On this holy day of chores, there was one task that only she could perform.

Their mother—who Cory had explained might be *depressed*, according to a commercial he'd seen—refused to take food from anyone but Beth.

"She'll be starving," she muttered to herself.

"Who?" Cory's lips looked bee-stung.

"Never mind, we'd better run."

He glanced at the sun, barely clinging to a lavender sky, and blanched. They clasped hands once, then broke away, hurrying in opposite directions.

Beth raced through the far pastures, where the scent of

manure assaulted her senses, and past the brackish baptismal lake. She cursed the heavy prairie skirt she clutched in one hand, while on the other side of town Cory sprinted unencumbered. She decided to cut through the western fields to avoid being seen on Church Street. Then she followed the green forest line to her own meadow and the hill that led her home.

She hoped to just beat Father, but dreaded Agnes's cutting disappointment. Would she scold her in front of the kids? Or simply refuse to speak to her at all?

No one knew what a pain it was to have a perfect older sister. No one knew—

She slowed at the top of the hill, sighting Agnes on the porch stoop. Her sister's arms were wrapped about herself like she was trying to keep out the cold. She looked exhausted, ancient.

Beth stepped onto the porch, automatically stamping her boots on the mat. Red canyon dust betrayed where she'd been. She froze midstamp.

Agnes displayed not a trace of anger or disappointment or even grief. She smiled kindly, with only the hint of a question in her eyes.

A look that said: *If you want, you can tell me. If not, I understand.*

No reaction could've made Beth feel more like slime. Her stomach turned in on itself, contorting with shame.

"Dinner's on the stove. Mother's waiting." Agnes hesitated. "I'm so sorry that chore always falls to you."

The screen door smacked behind her, and she was gone.

Beth doubled over, groaning her frustration.

Oh, why couldn't Agnes shout and scold like other sisters? Why did she have to be so damned *forgiving*?

Insufferable. Infuriating.

Her sister, whom she couldn't hate for loving so.

Their mother was born an Outsider.

Years ago, she'd come to Red Creek in search of a more spiritual way of life. Red Creek didn't usually permit strangers onto the land, but their mother was persistent. Then Father fell in love with her and vouched for her purity of spirit. She'd already given birth to Agnes and Beth when it became clear she'd never fit in at Red Creek. In theory, she'd embraced their Laws; in practice, living among them was torture to her.

"I always thought she'd adjust to our ways," Father had once told Beth, rubbing his bearded jaw bemusedly. "But she never did. She believed her opinions should matter as much as a man's, and never understood that you can't argue with God's Law."

Beth loaded a tray with homemade macaroni and cheese— Ezekiel's favorite. Only the noodles were whole wheat now, which Agnes claimed was healthier. She was obsessive about caring for the baby of the family. Beth couldn't help the rusty jealousy that hooked her heart. After all, Agnes didn't care what *she* ate. Didn't even care to ask where she'd been all afternoon.

Not that Beth owed her an explanation.

She walked the short hallway to the trailer's back room, hardly aware that her hands were shaking, rattling the dishes balanced on their tray.

Once upon a time, Beth had loved being her mother's special favorite. But as the years went on, her feelings had spoiled. Father claimed Beth was the spitting image of her mother when she was younger, a fact that disturbed her deeply. What if she'd inherited some kind of Outsider curse? What if that was why she was so unhappy living here, among God's chosen?

She shook her head, clearing the doubts and fears, thick as cobwebs inside her skull.

I'm not in love, and that's the main thing.

Cory couldn't break her heart, as Father had broken her mother's. She swore she'd never let herself love him so much that it destroyed her.

But she did love her family.

Even in her most selfish moments, her love for Mary, Faith, Ezekiel, and Sam remained like an inner ocean, sometimes ebbing, sometimes swelling—always there. And how could it be otherwise? She remembered the kids as toddlers, when they'd wandered about the trailer like clumsy bumblebees. She'd heard them speak their first words.

Mama, Sam had said, back when their mother was well.

May-ee, said Faith, and *Fate*, echoed Mary.

Aggie, cooed Ezekiel.

But love in the Prophet's land was a treacherous thing, unstable as dynamite.

Beth took a breath at her mother's door and knocked.

A wheezing whisper. "Beth? Is that you?"

Beth glanced back, and her eyes locked with Agnes's. She hated her sister's compassion—the way she tilted her chin, encouraging her.

Hated it and needed it, because Beth loved Agnes like the parched earth thirsts for rain. Her first word had been *Aggie*, too.

"Yes, Mother. It's me."

Beth swam through shadows to her mother's bedside, her eyes slowly adjusting to the dark. There were only two other pieces of furniture in the room: a nightstand with the phone on it—for emergencies and for Father—and a dresser with an Outsider record player. The turntable was always loaded with *Amazing Grace*. Her mother had brought other records, but Father had broken them over his knee when Beth was five, because the lyrics were secular.

Music of the damned, Father had said. *Trust me, this hurts me as much as it hurts you.*

Her mother had kept the broken pieces of those tracks, and the record player balanced on their sharp, daggerlike remains. Seeing them always made Beth shiver, because they looked like an accusation.

And like regret.

Her mother hauled herself upright and patted her tangled, unwashed hair. Beth winced to see the mirror of her own glossy locks so badly neglected.

"I was pretty like you once, you know," her mother snapped, pettish with hunger. "I had the most beautiful hair. . . ."

Beth's chest ached.

Her mother used to tell stories about the Outside.

From her, Beth had heard wonders the others could never dream of: all about amusement parks and shopping malls and movie theaters. She'd learned about televangelists and soap operas, public high schools and monogamy. She'd even learned about other faiths her mother had tried before finally landing in Red Creek—the Moonies and the Hare Krishna.

These days, there were fewer stories and more hazards. She had to be careful. Her mother's tongue, like hers, could cut like razor wire.

"Macaroni and cheese."

Her mother stared at the steaming food, her eyes hollows.

Desperately, Beth wished for the canyon. For Cory's warm touch and the wind in her hair. For *life.*

Get in and get out. No need to linger.

Her mother's hand shot out of the dark, gripping her wrist with surprising strength.

"Mother!" she gasped.

"It's time for you to leave this place, daughter. Time for you to run."

Beth held her breath, shocked and afraid.

"They'll want to marry you soon. Chances are a patriarch already has his eye on you. Don't fool yourself that it will be some handsome boy you could come to love—the young ones never get the pretty girls, and even when they do, they turn hard fast. Like your father." Her mother smacked her chapped lips together. She'd chewed them until they bled.

"The Outside is better, safer. Everything the Prophet taught you is a lie."

Beth couldn't remember the last time she'd heard her mother speak so many words together. So many *forbidden* words. The Prophet would say she was a snake hissing in Beth's ear. The Prophet would say she was a demon.

And Agnes—she'd tell her to gird herself from this spiritual threat with prayer. But suddenly, Beth couldn't recall a single verse or psalm.

Her thoughts pitching and churning, she tried to back away.

Her mother dug her fingernails into the skin of her wrist.

"If you find some money, you can check into a motel in Holden. One of those with a little pool. Stay until you find a job."

She let go and Beth stumbled back.

"You have roses in your cheeks," her mother said. "Your

foolish sister is already lost, but you—you can still be found." Her tone turned black and cold as road ice. "Get out, my dear. Get out while you still can. . . ."

Beth fled the room like she was chased and took shelter in the arms she knew were always open to her.

"My God, your heart is pounding out of your chest!" Agnes said.

"It's Mother." Beth spoke into Agnes's collar. Her sister smelled reassuringly of work—of sweat and sunshine.

"What did she say to you?" Agnes demanded.

Beth shook her head. It was too painful to tell.

The trailer had gone eerily silent.

Embracing, Beth and Agnes were like a lodestar for the other kids, who slowly came to wrap their own small arms around them. They didn't understand all that went on in this house—not even Sam—but they soaked up its grief like sponges. Sam tucked his head against Beth's rib cage, and Ezekiel clung to her leg. Mary and Faith cried softly, frightened to see their elder sisters upset. Their hands tugged at the waist of Beth's dress. She repressed a vain thought—*It's my favorite, don't tear!*—then let herself be enveloped by the only people in the world who could ever know what it was like to lose a mother as they had.

Agnes's cheek pressed against hers. They held each other like shipwreck survivors, and time melted away.

When Beth pulled back, her face was damp. "I'm still mad at you," she whispered.

Agnes winced. "I know."

It's time for you to leave this place. Time for you to run.

There was so much vast life she yearned for but could never, ever have.

Because of *them*. Because of love.

She watched the kids scatter to their books and games, her anger cut with sadness and grief. Her feelings layered in a dizzying array of colors, like the layers of canyon rock.

"Beth, I need to talk to you. About Magda. What you said about rebellion—" Agnes began, but Father blew through the door, looking stern as a minor Abraham.

Time for prayers.

6

AGNES

A man with many wives is holiest in the eyes of the Lord.
—Prophet Jeremiah Rollins

In the evening, Agnes always prayed for the same things: for Ezekiel to be cured, and for God to forgive her weakness. For strength to take care of the kids, and for her mother to be peaceful. That night she added a special word for Beth. *Let no secrets come between us.*

Most Red Creek children never liked sitting through prayers, but Agnes delighted in it. On her knees, she felt very near to God—or as near as any girl could be. It was like lingering in the well between the world and dreams, and she thought she could pray for hours, even days, like the Biblical prophets of old in their desert caves.

But of course, women could never be like those holy men. Not with children and chores to tend to. What a silly fantasy.

Too soon, Father dismissed them to bed.

"Good night, children," he said curtly, his words loaded with the implication that he had far more important things to think of—manly, patriarchal things. But he had a soft spot for Agnes and remembered to give her a small, wry smile.

Their faces were alike: all square jaw, coarse skin, and large brow. Agnes thought those features became him best, but being plain had never bothered her. She could walk past the mirror for weeks without ever truly noticing the shape of the girl reflected there. Whatever worth she had was on the inside, and whatever beauty hewn, she hoped, of spirit.

The children brushed their teeth and washed their faces—one at a time, in the mildewed bathroom—while strains of "Amazing Grace" wove through the air.

Sam went rigid when the song began. Of the little kids, he remembered his mother best. Agnes worried about him. Worried about all of them. A constant pang of *not enough*.

At bedtime, she had a few quiet words for Ezekiel, who feared the dark. As always, she rubbed his back in circles and pointed out the glow of the crucifix night-light.

"Look what protects you."

"Yes, but what if—"

"No what if. Be brave. It's time for sleep."

He scrunched his eyes tight. Watching him try to will himself asleep, Agnes had the strong urge to swaddle him up in his blanket and rock him like an infant.

Meanwhile, the record played on.

'Twas Grace that taught my heart to fear, and Grace my fears relieved...

She and Beth unfolded the convertible couch they shared and spread the sheets in practiced unison. Her sister seemed thoughtful, far-off.

What thoughts were going through Beth's head, and where on earth had she been all day?

Agnes had just slipped into her nightgown when Father called from the kitchen.

"Agnes. A moment."

Her mind sped straight into nightmares. Did Father suspect all wasn't right? Had Ezekiel let something slip—about his medicine?

In the kitchen, Father poured himself a glass of milk. Her relief, when he gestured for her to sit, was intense. He'd want her standing for bad news.

"You're a good girl, Agnes. An obedient daughter."

In the bedroom, her mother's record scratched, stuttered, then stopped.

Father cleared his throat, looking strangely unsure. "Last night, the Prophet had a revelation. About you and Matthew Jameson."

Blood rushed into her ears, drowning out the sound of the clock ticking and the hum of the refrigerator. Surely Father couldn't be talking about *marriage*, because God knew she wasn't ready. According to Mrs. King, He wouldn't match her with a husband until her heart was pure and clean—which it wasn't anymore.

So what was Father talking about?

"It will be a hardship running the household without you. I hope, sometime before the wedding, that you'll find a chance to speak with Beth. You must explain how her responsibilities will grow."

The word echoed senselessly in her ears. *Wedding…wedding… wedding…*

Father took her hand in his rough one. "The Jamesons are a fine family, Agnes. I couldn't be more pleased."

"Matthew Jameson?" she sputtered. "You mean, Cory's father?"

"You'll be his sixth wife. You know, that's a very special number—six." He spoke wistfully. "A man might be at ease in heaven, with six wives to tend him."

The word escaped like a bubble of air. "No."

Father's frown split his brow like a lightning bolt. "What?"

She corrected herself. "I just mean, what if I'm not ready? Not faithful enough?"

Father relaxed. Inside, she knew, he was laughing at her.

"Anyone can see you're the most hardworking girl in Red Creek. Matthew himself admires how you've taken charge since your mother's illness. It's no wonder God showed the Prophet your face in his dream."

Agnes cast about for a memory of her intended but couldn't pick him out from among the shadowy profiles of Red Creek's patriarchs.

Unlike her family, the Jamesons were rich from their ranching, and they lived in the town's finest house: a mansion with views of the canyon. Surely Matthew was a fine man, if God had given him all that—and the idea of marriage itself didn't bother her. She could even imagine a blessedness in being a sixth wife, a bright shining reward for living as God willed.

And yet—

Father's face hardened. "Agnes, are you in rebellion?"

The echo of her sister's words set her hair on end. She looked towards the living room, where the children slept in the night-light's amber glow.

She blurted out, "But who will take care of Ezekiel?"

Father set his glass down. "Beth." He spoke her name darkly, like a curse. "She always was a flighty thing. But she'll just have to learn to do as you do."

She'll just have to learn.

But Father didn't know the half of it.

Could Beth handle giving Ezekiel his shots, and meeting the Outsider at midnight?

Even if Beth could, she was already fifteen. The Prophet might have a marriage revelation for her, too. And Sam, the next eldest, would be a child for a long time yet.

"Listen to me," Father said sternly. "Your union with a good man could change everything for this family. As you know, God never saw fit to give me another wife, because of our family's bad history—and I don't just mean your mother."

Agnes felt nauseated. But she was also curious. Father had never confided in her before. "Is it—something to do with you? Your family?"

Father lowered his voice. "Yes. My grandmother was Sarah Shiner, the founding Prophet's second wife. His favorite wife, for a time. But she slid hard into rebellion. Eventually, she ran from him. Ran Outside."

Agnes had never heard of *anyone* running from Red Creek before.

"She ran of her own free will?"

Father nodded. "And doomed her children unto the third and fourth generations. Sarah Shiner's been the curse on our family for a long time, but I've kept myself righteous, and God sees that. If you marry an esteemed patriarch like Matthew Jameson, God and the Prophet will know we've been redeemed."

Agnes's mind spun, absorbing this story—which seemed to raise as many questions as it answered. For some reason, her mind wandered to the forest at the meadow's edge, the boundary she was forbidden to cross.

When the Prophet's grandfather first came to Red Creek, before farms were built and fields cleared, the faithful were trappers, catching small animals and skinning them for pelts. Rumor had it that traps still littered the forest floor—rusted iron ready to snap at a touch. If you stumbled on one hidden beneath a pile of leaves, it would break your leg in a single, vicious bite.

Family curses. Ancient history.

Agnes felt like she was slowly bleeding to death in the cool, familiar kitchen.

"When's the wedding?"

She couldn't quite bring herself to say *my* wedding.

"Matthew's willing to marry you next Sunday."

She gripped the table until her bad knuckle throbbed.

Sunday. So soon, when what she needed was time.

"Father." She swallowed. "I have a favor to ask."

His eyes narrowed. Her Outsider mother must've begged favors in the past—a newspaper to read, a forbidden pill for a headache— before she'd given up trying.

"What is it?"

"Beth isn't responsible. I need time to prepare her."

God forgive me.

His voice deepened. "Is there something I should know about your sister?"

A trap.

Hastily, so Father wouldn't drag her from bed that very minute, Agnes shook her head. Then for the first time in her memory, she lied to a man of God.

"Beth can't run the household alone. She doesn't know where the kids are in their lessons, or how to starch collars. Just today she burned the crackers, and that's four dollars up in smoke."

In fact, Agnes had burned the crackers. Left alone with her chores, she'd been rushed.

"She can't learn those things in a week?"

Agnes shook her head again, fighting a strange pain—the lies, ripping at her insides. A week was plenty of time to learn to starch collars and bake crackers. But Father himself didn't know the first thing about how the household worked, let alone that Beth had been pulling her weight—more or less, depending on her mood—for years.

With Ezekiel's life on the line, Agnes would snatch any wedge.

"There's more to it. We have schedules to follow, timetables for gardening. I don't think Beth even knows how much of our food is grown."

Agnes sensed Father getting bored. His duty done, he wanted nothing more than to pour himself another glass of milk, unbutton his own starched collar, and go to bed.

"And how long will it take for you to teach her all that?"

She grasped at straws. "A month? Two?"

He drummed his fingers against the table. "God's will, once revealed, should be done quickly. It'll look like you're resisting. And how does that reflect on me?"

God forgive me, but I need more time.

Agnes whittled her voice small. "Mr. Jameson admires how I look after the children. With Mother sick, don't you think he'll understand I must help them?"

"This is a mess of your own making." He scowled, near anger now. "You should've prepared her better."

It was dangerous to press him, but she had to try. "We can't have even a little time?"

Father slapped the table. "You're a special girl, Agnes, but you're not that special!"

Unstoppable tears burst from her chest, surprising them both.

Agnes had lived in harmony with Red Creek's ways her entire life, and she'd never thrown a tantrum when the Laws cinched too tight. But Ezekiel's illness had thrown her off balance, and she couldn't marshal her strength in time.

The words went round and round like her mother's record on

its turntable: *He's going to die, Ezekiel's going to die, God's going to take him and he's going to die. . . .*

"I've been a horrible sister," she said through her hands.

Father looked disgusted, like he'd do anything to stop this tearful, female drama.

"Enough," he said at last. "I can't make any promises. But I'll talk to Matthew. Now clean yourself up and go to bed."

Agnes stood shakily and did as she was told.

7

BETH

Resist not, want not.

—Prophet Jacob Rollins

Beth heard every word about Agnes's upcoming marriage—and terror engulfed her.

She'd known marriage was the ultimate fate of every girl. But she'd built a fortress around the idea that Agnes could be married, cordoning it off with bricks and stone.

What she overheard left her trembling and repentant. All her anger evaporated at the thought that she and the kids might lose the true head of their household, the one who'd mothered all of them.

Beth gripped the bedsheets. Losing her sister and being left to raise her siblings alone ... it felt like the end of the world.

"Agnes," she cried as her weary-looking sister lifted the covers and crawled into bed. "You won't let it happen, will you?"

The sisters clutched each other, shivering like they'd just come in from the rain.

"I tried to buy time." Agnes's teeth chattered. "I had to lie to Father. I hated it."

"Who cares a fig about lying to Father?" Beth whispered intently. "As long as you stay. If you leave—Agnes, it will kill the kids."

Agnes stiffened. "Don't say that!"

"It will. And I couldn't bear it."

They were silent, listening to the sleeping children's breaths, like wavelets breaking on the lakeshore.

Beth pulled back enough to see her sister's face. Shock had shattered her firm, familiar features. In her eyes was a look of stunned disbelief.

Agnes hadn't truly believed she could be married, either.

Beth felt like she was falling—tumbling from the red edge of the canyon—and not even Cory could catch her.

If I don't do something, I'm going to lose her.

Red Creek girls had a way of disappearing into marriage. Once acquired like furniture, they rarely ventured beyond their homes. Married, Agnes would stop attending Sunday school, and then she'd be too busy with her domestic duties to socialize. Beth would glimpse her in church, maybe, or on the road to church.

She'd be a ghost.

"You can't marry," Beth said decisively. "I won't let you."

"It's God's will. The Prophet saw it in a dream."

She shook her head forcefully. "Agnes, why would God destroy Mother like He did and then also take you? Why would He persecute our family? If He's righteous, then *why*?"

Agnes looked incredulous. "Don't you remember the Book of Habakkuk?"

Beth didn't. Nor did she think it was fair for Agnes to belt her with theology.

"*The vision awaits its appointed time,*" her sister quoted. "*But the righteous shall live by His faith.*"

Beth ground her teeth. "What. Does. That. Even. Mean!"

"It means that faith is meaningless when life is easy. Beth, God doesn't owe us any answers. He never did."

The sisters locked pinky fingers beneath the covers—their secret sign since they were small. Beth sighed. She regretted messing around with Cory that afternoon, when she might've been with the one she loved a thousand times more.

"Agnes, what if—" She paused, gathering thoughts she'd never quite admitted even to herself. "What if your marrying isn't God's will?"

She'd never courted rebellion so plainly. It scared her, made her long to retreat into the shell of her old thoughtless indifference. It was so much easier to simply accept the way things were, and so very painful to start asking why.

Agnes peered at her. Beth's face burned under her sister's scrutiny, and her tongue went dry. She sensed Agnes's beloved faith raised before her like an iron shield.

She forced herself to press on. "Can't you see there's something wrong with this place? Look what it did to Mother. Look what it's doing to *you*."

"That's blasphemy," Agnes warned. "You're risking your soul."

"Enough with the souls! I'm sick to death of hearing about them. I'm sick to death of—of—oh, let me show you!"

Ablaze, she dug beneath the mattress for her diary. This was her moment. Her chance to convince Agnes of what she'd guessed, though never dared speak—Red Creek wasn't as holy as it pretended to be.

If you find some money you can check into a motel, her mother had said. *One with a little pool. Stay until you find a job.*

Such a vague dream! Find money—how? And a job—what could she do? Her mother's words were so much vapor, and she couldn't abandon her family for a puff of air.

Now the truth streaked like a comet, bright and clear. Maybe she wasn't strong enough to run alone, but—

They could run together.

She and Agnes.

They could run and take the kids.

She brandished her diary, hymnal thick with a cross on the cover. In fact, it *was* a hymnal—but a misprint, and all the pages inside were blank. She'd found it in church years ago and taken it home. Inside, she'd made a list. An inventory so shocking, she'd almost torn it out.

She flipped quickly through the pages. She was flushed, sweating beneath her nightgown.

"There." She jabbed the page. "Read that. Then tell me it isn't horribly unfair."

"Beth—"

"Just do it."

Agnes squinted.

THE LAWS ACCORDING TO RED CREEK

BOYS

1. Wear starched collars, long pants, closed-toed shoes.
2. Attend sermons three times a week.
3. Marry according to the Prophet's revelation.
4. Don't watch television, listen to the radio, read Outsider newspapers, or listen to secular music.

GIRLS

1. Don't leave Red Creek unattended by a man.
2. Cover every inch of skin.

3. Don't paint your face or adorn yourself with jewelry.
4. Don't talk to boys who aren't your brothers.
5. Don't cut your hair. Hair must be worn in a braid.
6. Don't wear red.
7. Don't drive a vehicle.
8. Don't meet the eyes of a patriarch.
9. Don't question your father, mothers, or the Prophet.
10. Don't entertain jealousy towards sisters or sister-wives.
11. Don't seek to ease the pain of menstrual cramps.
12. Don't love your own children more than any others.
13. Don't tempt men with flirtatious looks.
14. Don't prevent the birth of children with Outsider medicine.
15. Don't keep money or buy goods without permission.
16. Don't steal attention from your husband or father.
17. Don't watch television, listen to the radio, read Outsider newspapers, or listen to secular music.
18. Never speak to Outsiders.
19. Never, ever complain.

"See?" Beth crowed, triumphant. "Red Creek hates us. It hates us and it's *wrong*."

Beth hung on her sister's silence, desperate to find the smallest crack in her obedience. The slightest window.

"The Prophet says women are weaker," Agnes said. "He says the Laws exist to protect us from ourselves."

Beth snorted. "But what do *you* think? You don't believe it, Agnes."

For a moment, she feared Agnes wouldn't answer.

"I think faith asks more of women," she said at last. "I don't always like it. Sometimes I feel life crushing me. But the Prophet has always protected us. Why would I doubt him now, only because my path is hard?"

Beth could've screamed.

"Agnes, you're already in rebellion! If the Laws are so sacred, why do you break them? Why do you sneak out at night? *Where do you go?*"

A complicated flicker of emotions played across her sister's face, and Beth allowed herself to hope. Agnes wasn't lost, as her mother claimed. Nor was she the brute animal Red Creek wished her to be. Underneath it all, she watched. She saw.

"Oh, Beth," Agnes moaned. "I have to tell you everything, because soon it will be your cross to bear. If I tell you where I go, will you swear to stay faithful? To try?"

Beth's heart thundered in her ears. She sensed a filament stretched between them, a fragile line of trust. Her sister would reveal her secret—then Beth would marshal all her love and ask her to run.

Pinky fingers clasped. "Tell me," she begged. "Please don't shut me out."

A scream rent the air, waking the kids and churning the trailer into panic.

Ezekiel was having a night terror.

No, she thought when Agnes shot out of bed. *Not now, Ezekiel. Not* now.

Jealousy cramped in her belly as she sank back against her pillow.

"Ezekiel," Agnes whispered. "You don't have to worry. Everything's just as it should be. The Prophet is in his watchtower. Nothing is wrong."

The passion that had swept Beth moments ago cooled like the embers of a dying fire, leaving only the bitter scent of despair behind. Listening, she realized how futile it would be to try to convince her faithful sister to run. Agnes might see more than she told, but she still belonged to Red Creek, body and soul.

Everything's just as it should be. Like a lion claims its prey, the Prophet's Laws had claimed her.

A tear slipped down the side of Beth's nose.

Agnes would be married. And Beth wasn't brave enough to run alone. She'd never see the Outside. Never dress in flattering Outsider fashions or style her hair as she liked. She had no destiny. No adventure would light her dull, toilsome life.

I still have Cory. That's something.

Her sister came back to bed, whispering her name.

But Beth, feeling worse than she'd ever felt—surely worse than *anyone* had ever felt—feigned sleep.

"Another time, then," Agnes said.

She spoke as if the filament between them hadn't already snapped.

As if the time left to them could do any good.

8

AGNES

Treat not with Outsiders, for God hath set them in a slippery place.

—Prophet Jeremiah Rollins

Matthew Jameson agreed to wait six weeks to marry Agnes. "He prayed on it, and God wants to help our family." Father warned, "Whatever happens, don't waste this gift of time."

By mid-August, Agnes knew, she must have her affairs in order. But time flew, and though she prayed constantly, God never revealed what to do about Ezekiel. Worse, her only backup plan—Beth, who she now suspected was in full-fledged rebellion—was giving her the coldest of cold shoulders, icing her out at the worst possible time.

Agnes's patience for her sister dried up like a riverbed in summer. How dare Beth let her bad attitude get in the way of providing for the kids? Couldn't she see that Sam, the twins, and Ezekiel needed her more? Needed them both?

Beth will come around. She must.

And, she told herself, a tinge frantically, there was still time for a miracle.

God could cure Ezekiel. And when He finally did, she wouldn't have to keep secrets anymore or lie to Father. She could finally be free of this stifling, suffocating mask.

She could finally be *free*.

—⌇—

Two weeks before the wedding date, Agnes snuck out of the house to meet the Outsider's son. If Beth heard her creep out of bed, she kept her peace. But Agnes believed her sister slept. Beth's rib cage lifted rhythmically beneath the sheet.

Agnes had planned to take Father's gun, but in the end, she felt too cowed to break into his shed and brought only the empty cooler and a flashlight with her across the meadow.

The moon was swathed in smoke-black clouds, and she struggled not to trip making her way downhill. She stole looks over her shoulder, half expecting to see Father following. If he found out she was meeting a boy so soon before her marriage, he'd kill her.

Agnes waited a long time among the gravestones. Stars were trapped behind clouds, and she couldn't count a single one.

Maybe the Outsider won't come.

If he didn't, was it a sign?

She spotted a shadow making its way uphill. A boy with a cooler in hand.

A rush of nerves, and her hands balled into fists. She could still run away, even scream.

But because of Ezekiel, she knew she wouldn't.

The boy raised his arm, a tentative greeting. He took great strides, drawing close enough that she could see him clearly.

The Outsider was *big*. Broad across the chest and surprisingly tall. She fought the instinct to run. His skin wasn't as dark as Matilda's but still duskier than anyone's in Red Creek. He wore Outsider clothing—jeans and a T-shirt—and gooseflesh covered his bare arms. A heavy-looking backpack hung from his shoulder. He took in the stones, the meadow, and the silver trailer up above through the lenses of thin-framed glasses.

An Outsider boy, here, in the flesh . . .

She held out her hand for the new cooler, hoping he would make their transaction fast and painless.

"You're Agnes, right?" He spoke just like Outsider teenagers at Walmart, in that casual, easy rhythm. "I'm Danny. My mom's told me a lot about you."

Then nothing. Waiting for her to speak.

Well, she wouldn't. Talking to an Outsider boy was a much graver sin than talking to his mother, and what's more, she didn't want to.

As he looked her over—the prairie dress, her braided hair—a flush crept up her neck. She longed to crawl back into bed and pretend this was nothing but a bad dream.

"I told her it wasn't safe to meet outdoors. What with—" He glanced behind him at the forest, shouldering his backpack and shuddering. "It's crawling with them, you know."

She followed his eyes to the cluster of trees at the base of the hill and barely kept herself from asking, *Crawling with what?*

He read the question on her face and looked alarmed.

"You've seen the Nest in there, haven't you? You should burn it. I mean, it's big as a house. Scary. And you know Nests attract the really dangerous ones."

Agnes stared, trying to shape his words into sense. Was he talking about a bird's nest? They had hawks in Red Creek, but their nests weren't that large. And why would they burn one?

Big as a house—scary—

Nonsense. It must be.

The boy cleared his throat. An arc of freckles made a starry bridge over his nose. His glasses gave him a permanently skeptical look.

For all his size, the Outsider boy struck her as gentle. He clearly didn't spend his days like Red Creek boys did, working in the fields. He did something else. *Was* something else.

"The thing is, my mom says I have to make sure you know about the Virus. But it'd be pretty extreme if you didn't. Everyone knows."

A memory jostled loose.

Tommy King said there's sickness among the Outsiders, Ezekiel had said.

The boy waited for her to answer, and as the pause lengthened, she couldn't think of a way to dodge his question without being insulting.

"Your mother said something about sickness among the Outsiders," she murmured.

"Among the—" He stopped. "Oh. *We're* the Outsiders. Well, I hate to break it to you, but the Outside isn't that far away. And the Virus is everywhere. It's infected hundreds of thousands of animals and people. These last few weeks have been...a nightmare."

The boy fidgeted while Agnes stood mute, thinking he was wrong. The Outside *was* far. For all it had to do with her, it was a million miles away.

"Oh my God, you really don't know a thing about it, do you?" He adjusted his glasses. "My mom said you don't go to school. But what about computers? Do you have those?"

"No."

"Newspapers? Smartphones?"

She shook her head, and Danny let out a long, low whistle that made her dart a glance at her shoes.

"Wow. I really didn't believe my mom about this place. I mean, I believed her, but...wow."

He stared at Agnes like she was some kind of exotic bird. "You've really never used a smartphone?"

Annoyance flared. "They're against the Laws."

He pointed to the cooler. "This is against the Laws, too, though, right?"

She flinched. "Can I have my brother's medicine now?"

"One last thing." God, he was tenacious. "My mom says that if your people aren't taking precautions, you need to keep your brothers and sisters indoors. Or something might get them."

Keep the kids indoors? Just that night they'd been running across the meadow, happily playing the Apocalypse Game. It was perfectly safe.

Her eyes narrowed. "What do you mean, *Something might get them?*"

"Infected creatures are really aggressive." He stole another look at the trees. "They'll come right out of the forest if they see something they can catch. Look, my mom wants you to call her. She gave me a phone to give you. There's a charger in the cooler." He ran a hand through his hair. "People are saying it's the end of the world."

The words were like a dagger thrust between her ribs. She knew by his tone he was only using an expression. But in Red Creek, the end of the world was a threat all too real.

She tipped her chin. "I don't believe you."

He shifted. "Okay. But please take the phone. You might need help someday."

He extended a black device, the likes of which she'd never seen. Their phone back home was a chunky thing, with a coiled wire plugged into the wall. Nothing like this sleek, metallic slice of peril.

The wind whistled, and Agnes shivered.

Sickness, a Virus, creatures coming out of the woods. The idea that the Prophet couldn't protect God's chosen...ludicrous.

When the Rapture came, the Prophet would scream it from the watchtower. When the Rapture came, God would warn His people and spare them from the flames.

"I can't touch that." Bolstered by faith, Agnes met his eyes unflinchingly. "For one thing, I think you're lying. Or deluded. Or both."

She could hardly believe her boldness. Even Beth would be impressed.

His eyes hardened. "My mom would tell you the same thing if she were here. Is she a deluded liar, too?"

"Thank you for the medicine," she said stiffly.

"Agnes, wait." His manner softened, became apologetic. "I didn't mean to offend you."

"Why do you care?" she asked, honestly curious. "What am I to you?"

He blinked. "I feel like I know you. My mom's told me what you do for your brother. How hard it must be for you."

How hard.

Slowly but surely, something unfurled from a mysterious place in her chest. *Gratitude.* Her family, as much as she loved them, treated her like she'd never tire, never break. Like she was made of stone instead of flesh. It shocked her, this feeling that someone understood the shape of her life.

She shook off the unexpected emotion. "I'm sorry if there are problems in your world. But none of this has anything to do with me."

She was already turning to go when she heard it.

The humming.

At first, it was the ghost of a sound—the vibration of a bell right after it ceased ringing, like a metallic keening, gently thrilling along her skin. But then the sound grew stronger, tunneling into her bones, mournful and terrible like nothing she'd ever heard— yet somehow, oddly familiar. She didn't just hear it, she actually felt it, like whispers across her skin. She glanced up at the cloud-swathed moon to make sure she was still here, in a world still real.

She was. It was. And her spirit soared, because her first thought was of God.

The sound was unearthly, hymnal, but nonetheless real. Peaceful, like she wasn't standing with the Outsider boy at all, but back in her trailer, deep in prayer.

The hum emanated from the forest.

She glanced towards its massive darkness, and just knew.

Danny watched her. He didn't hear anything. To him, the night remained silent.

How could he not hear?

"Are you okay?"

Without thinking, she held a finger to her lips, listening harder, leaning into the dark.

Strangely, Agnes felt like the humming sound had been there all along, the way the stars were still there, though obscured. She just hadn't been listening until now.

She studied the Outsider boy. For the first time she let herself wonder: What if he were telling the truth?

She spoke slowly, cautiously. "What did you say was out there?"

He blew out a breath. "Danger."

The sound was filling her up. Prying her open. She couldn't

guess why he didn't hear, but something *was* out there. She was sure. And it bothered her, the thought of something lurking in the woods—something the Prophet surely must know about, as God's emissary on earth.

"If it was really dangerous," she said, "our Prophet would've warned us."

Danny frowned. "Are you sure?"

Agnes felt suddenly nauseated. As the sound hummed around her, blurring the lines that once were so clear, Agnes saw herself for the first time through an Outsider's eyes.

To Danny and Matilda, the Laws of Red Creek weren't her shelter.

They were her prison.

It's a test, she thought wildly. *God sent this boy as a test.*

"Take the phone. Please. My mother says she'll pay through the summer. If you're ever in trouble, all you have to do is tap her name. See?"

He tilted the mobile phone's lighted screen, showing her.

Agnes almost walked away then, leaving him holding that sinister device.

But the humming sound remained, plucking at her ribs.

Agnes, are you in rebellion?

Impulsively, she snatched the phone, pocketed it. Then, with the cooler in hand, she started back uphill, too shaken to say goodbye.

Danny said, faintly, almost sadly: "Goodbye, Agnes."

She kept walking.

The sound—she'd heard something like it before, but *when?*—stayed with her until she reached her trailer.

When she touched the cold metal doorknob, the humming ceased quick as light.

She pressed her back against the wall, breathing hard. The sound couldn't be the same haunting she remembered from childhood, when all the world seemed to sing. It wasn't possible.

She flexed her hand, gazing down at the broken knuckle.

She thought, *It can't be.*

9

AGNES

Who is worthy to receive the Lord's holy messages?
The head of house and prophets only...
—Prophet Jacob Rollins

Sunday, again.

At dawn, Agnes buried the phone in her garden beside Ezekiel's insulin cooler.

All was silence. In the cold gray light, she could almost believe she'd imagined the otherworldly humming. But the phone, so slippery and black, was a concrete reminder.

She never should have accepted it, but it was only a momentary stumble. If she buried her sins deep enough, she wouldn't have to think of the Outsider boy or his wild tale ever again.

At church, despite her best efforts, her mind wasn't easy. She struggled to shut out little things, like how the patriarchs huddled together before the service, whispering urgently.

Or how the Prophet's sermon specifically condemned—for the thousandth time but with uncommon force—the reading of newspapers and the keeping of radios.

"One day soon the Outsiders will fall," the Prophet bellowed from his pulpit. "And we will shelter in the Underground Temple. Until then, we trust in our perfect faith. Amen."

Agitated, Agnes tapped her foot against the hardwood floor.

Surely the Prophet had good reason for keeping them in the dark, if indeed he did. Surely it was better to swallow her curiosity than indulge a sin.

But Lord, it was hard to keep steady today. The events of last night—and the Outsider boy—had set her mind to rattling like a rainstorm shuddering a windowpane.

"Let us pray," intoned the Prophet.

For the first time in her memory, Agnes's eyes batted open while the others bowed their heads. She thought: *But the sound, oh, God, the sound.*

If she hadn't known better, she would've said it was God's voice she'd heard.

She fought not to think: *The glory of God thundereth.*

And fought not to think: *Mine ears thou hast opened.*

It was the deepest possible sin—wasn't it?—to entertain the idea that God would deign to speak to her, when everyone knew only patriarchs and prophets were fit to receive divine guidance. Her eyes met Beth's over the heads of the faithful. A charge leapt between them, and a question appeared in her sister's gem-green eyes: *What's wrong with you today?*

But this time it was Agnes, consumed by her own inner turmoil, who looked away.

10

BETH

Cherish this holy community, for it is your only bastion
against the heat of hell.
—Prophet Jacob Rollins

At the Kings' after-church gathering, Beth leaned against the wall of the dairy barn, struggling to imagine her life after Agnes's wedding in two weeks' time.

No matter how she sliced it, that life looked miserable.

In the pasture below, her siblings—all except Ezekiel, who'd gone home with Agnes—played the Apocalypse Game with the ten little King children. Beth, caught in the sticky web of her thoughts, twined her braid around her knuckles and silently fumed.

Did anyone care how much harder her life was about to become? How much responsibility she'd be forced to shoulder, just to keep the kids dressed, fed, alive?

She wasn't sure she could manage it, and Lord knew she'd have no help from anyone.

Then the Jamesons arrived—Cory with his lesser brothers and Magda—and Beth smiled. Smoothing the waist of her prairie dress, she pushed away from the wall, knowing whose eyes would find her.

Cory winked and nodded towards the barn, and Beth's belly tightened with anticipatory pleasure.

They kissed in the stifling gloom while the cows lowed. She'd missed the feel of his body against hers, and she kissed him like she meant to drink him.

Then she backed into a spiderweb, felt its sticky tendrils against her neck, and shrieked.

"That's one of God's creatures, too, you know." Cory laughed.

"Maybe so, but I still hate them. Their crawly legs..."

With his sleeve, he gallantly brushed the spiderweb away. "There. Better?"

She thought: Here was a boy who would do anything for her. *Anything.*

"Cory," she said, testing, "next time you go to the gas station to watch television, can't you take me with you?"

"Oh, Beth." His face fell. "Why would you want to take a risk like that?"

In truth, she wasn't even sure she wanted to go—it *was* a grave risk, and Father would belt her if she were caught Outside. Anyway, soon enough she'd be too busy with chores to even dream of meeting Cory.

I'm going to have to change my whole self, from the inside out. No more quitting chores. No more distracting the kids when it's time for lessons. No more fun at all.

She sighed. The future unfurled itself before her, bleak as a yellowed scroll.

"Cheer up." Cory touched her chin. "I brought you a present."

She brightened. "You didn't really."

"Damned if I'm lying." He made a show of fishing in his pants pocket for a wad of crinkled pink tissue paper, which he presented with a courtly bow.

She tore into the paper with abandon. "Lotion! Vanilla scented!"

"Vanilla is your favorite, right?"

She threw her arms around his neck. "Is it from Walmart? From"—she gasped at the delicious forbiddenness of it—"the cosmetics aisle?"

A smile tugged his lips. "The very same."

"How did you convince your father to buy it?"

"Father wouldn't condone the frivolity, you know that."

He rolled his eyes at the foibles of the forbidding older patriarch, but Beth found herself thinking of Agnes. What frivolities would Matthew forbid her when she was his wife?

"Beth? Are you okay?"

She fixed a smile on her face. "It's beautiful. But how did you afford it?"

"I saved up. It wasn't very expensive, really, but you know how hard it is to get paying work around here. Mr. Hearn gave me a dime a day to mow his western field. Took me twenty days to afford that little jar. See how sunburnt I am?"

Twenty days.

She bit her lip, overwhelmed by romance. It was just like Jacob slaving seven years for Rachel. But she had to be careful. If she fell in love with Cory, she'd only set herself up for pain. And with Agnes soon to leave, she had enough of that already.

"Thank you, Cory." She pocketed the jar of smooth, white cream. Surely the most luxurious thing she'd ever owned.

"Keep it somewhere secret," he instructed. "It's not quite makeup, but almost."

"You bought it because you think I'm vain."

"No," he teased. "But if anyone had a right, it would be you. Beth, you're the prettiest girl I've ever seen."

"Even on the television? The Prophet always says the really pretty, bad Outsider women are actresses."

"Prettier than them." He grinned. "I'm lucky you ever looked at me twice."

She pulled him to her, reveling in his words. So what if she and Cory weren't forever? She could still be happy in this moment now, savoring the scent of him, the weight of his hands on her waist. To be so admired... it was what she'd always dreamed.

And then, very quickly, it all went to hell.

She heard the soft crush of hay beneath a booted foot. She swiveled her head to find Magda Jameson staring avidly at them.

A furnace burst to life in Beth's chest. The stupid girl had no reason to be in the Kings' dairy barn. She'd wanted to catch them—catch *her*.

Cory leapt backwards. "Magda, what are you doing here?"

But Magda didn't answer. She only covered her smiling mouth with her hand—pretending a deep, shocked disapproval— and slipped out the way she came.

A moment of stunned silence.

"Damn it!" Cory paced the hay-strewn floor while the cows blinked dull eyes. "That girl can't keep her mouth shut."

Beth blew out a breath. "Cory, she's your sister. She wouldn't want you to get in any real trouble, would she?"

He stopped pacing and stared at her, eyes icy. "She won't tell a patriarch, if that's what you mean, but her tongue is like an adder's. She'll spread rumors."

"Rumors." The tension in her shoulders eased. "Well, what do rumors matter? People will believe what they want anyway."

His voice dropped low. "Not just people. *Our* people. The faithful. In this town, nothing's more important than a man's reputation. My father, my brothers—they'll whip me out of the house for this. Beth, I could lose my inheritance."

She gaped. "Is that all you care about? Your *inheritance?*"

"I'm sorry," he said, subdued. "I know your reputation matters, too. That's why we'll have to stop. No more meetings. No more—" He colored. "You know."

Beth's heart froze over, realizing that this golden, beautiful boy was breaking up with her. Cutting her loose like a kite. She could actually feel herself floating up and away.

"Beth?" he asked anxiously. "You know my feelings—well, my feelings haven't changed. You know that, right?"

He was staring at her. Still conflicted. But his conflict wasn't her problem anymore.

"Cory Jameson, I think you're chickenshit," she hissed. "You taught me that word, and of all people on earth, it fits you best. You're breaking up with me? Fine. Don't ever speak to me again. I mean it. Don't *ever.*"

She stayed long enough to register the cramp of pain in his eyes, then went to find her siblings.

It wasn't until the fresh air struck her that she began to gasp, hyperventilating.

Cory didn't love her as much as she'd thought, and Magda had seen them. She *knew.*

Whatever she says, it will only be words. They'll blow over soon enough.

She believed that, yet her belly knotted. She'd have to grieve Cory and her sister both. She'd miss them dreadfully.

In the pasture, teenaged Kings and Jamesons clustered around nosy, insufferable Magda.

Beth's body lurched with shock, seeing how eagerly they

gossiped. She hadn't thought they'd be so avid, hungry as a pack of wolves. Weren't they meant to be her friends?

She made herself keep walking with her head held up, though her cheeks burned. She didn't look back.

At the edge of the field, an image leapt into her mind of a mouse she'd discovered years ago—a bony little creature trapped behind the kitchen range. Unable to wriggle free, it had baked to death between the heated coils and the wall.

What a horrible way to die, she'd thought at the time: *helpless, alone, and in a hell of one's own making.*

11

AGNES

Woman, obey thy husband and father as if they were the Lord.

—Prophet Jeremiah Rollins

Agnes was clipping laundry off the line that afternoon when she heard the humming again.

Beth had taken the other children to the Kings', but Ezekiel had stayed behind. Really, it was for the best. The Apocalypse Game always gave him nightmares.

"Can I pick dandelions up the hill? Can I, please?"

Agnes hesitated. But after a hard day's work the Outsider's warnings seemed silly, misty.

Anyway, the Prophet hadn't said a word about any danger, and surely there couldn't be any harm in letting a child play. She felt sorry for Danny and Matilda, who faced such troubles in their world—but what else did they expect, living estranged from God?

The wind blustered, fluttering white sheets. Her first thought was that the humming was only a gust blowing through the pines, but it grew louder, more urgent, until her blood ran cold.

Keep the kids indoors, Danny had said. *Something might get them.*

Ezekiel. Where was Ezekiel?

She squinted against the sun but couldn't find him.

Instead, she saw a lone javelina, a wild desert boar, wandering up the hill. It came from the forest, and it was small—only an infant. What was it doing so far from its mother?

It sniffed the air, then began galloping in her direction.

Closer, closer. And with every loping step, more bizarre.

Javelina fur was bristly and brown, but sunset colors streaked this creature with coral, copper, and red. It looked like it had been dipped in varnish. The red color seeped even into its eyes.

Shocked, Agnes couldn't move. Couldn't even pray. Javelinas *never* came running at people, and its gait was unnatural, mechanical, like a windup toy.

Demon, she thought. *It looks like a demon.*

It kept running, freakishly determined. Her throat taut, constricted, she couldn't scream. The otherworldly humming crescendoed, and Agnes clapped her hands over her ears. She felt the sound like heat, wave after wave rioting through her body. When the javelina was mere inches away, the humming crested into a deafening shriek.

The creature stumbled back from her as if it'd hit a wall. The world stood still as the javelina stared, stunned by the sound.

Only an instant before it had been aggressive, determined to strike. Now it gawked. She thought it was the humming—the sound blocking it somehow. It was like spectral armor, a cloak that billowed and let nothing evil near.

"Holy God in heaven," she breathed.

As the javelina backed away on marbled hooves, the sound receded to a baleful moan.

They would've stayed like that for a long time, the red-marbled creature and Agnes, gazing at each other in mutual horror, if it weren't for Ezekiel.

"Agnes?" His voice echoed from somewhere uphill.

No, she thought hard at the thing, while the humming floated ethereally around them. *Just look at me. Keep looking at me.*

The javelina's head rotated, owlish and too far. It took one look at Ezekiel and forgot all about her.

"Ezekiel!"

The javelina put on a burst of speed.

Her brother stared, Sheep dangling helplessly from his hand. Agnes bolted towards her garden spade, stuck handle up in the earth, and prayed she could outrace the animal.

She couldn't remember ever moving so fast, but still her heavy prairie dress slowed her, catching at her legs like a net. Finally, she snatched the spade from the ground—God, she'd have killed for a gun—and tore wildly after the creature and Ezekiel. A shaft of sun glinted off the animal's back, illuminating its petrified sheen. Hard. Red. Unnatural.

His eyes were as a flame of fire; and his feet like unto fine brass...

What was she doing, chasing after this red, unholy thing? She should be screaming for someone. For God, or Father, or Mr. King.

Yet she felt the sonic armor all around her, felt she occupied some holy, protected space, so she didn't scream. In a final effort, Agnes slid across the grass, putting her body between her brother and the diseased creature. Just as before, the humming increased, bellowing righteously.

She kicked and heard a bony crack as her boot connected with its snout. The javelina staggered. She looked into the creature's red-marbled eyes, and again and swift as shadow saw fear sweep across those glittering orbs.

It was afraid of her. Why?

The creature gazed helplessly, but Agnes didn't waver. She brandished the spade like a hunting knife and plunged the sharp edge between the beast's head and its spine.

It shivered once, then fell.

The humming ceased.

Agnes wore a pair of heavy gardening gloves to drag the red creature with that awful crystal skin to the forest's edge.

Now she looked closer, she saw its fur wasn't fur at all. The Virus had transformed the bristles into tiny spines, producing that horrifying sheen. Its unnatural carcass seemed enameled, like something from the Book of Revelation.

In the meadow, Ezekiel babbled hysterically about the Rapture.

"A demon means it's the apocalypse. We'll have to go into the bunker. Agnes, I'm afraid of the dark, I'm afraid—"

Exhausted, she dropped the heavy thing she'd been dragging by the hoof. "Listen to me. You're going to keep this secret. Like your medicine."

He recoiled. "But the Prophet—"

Agnes pressed her lips together. Despite his promises, the Prophet had failed to protect them. He claimed to be God's omniscient mouthpiece. So why had she and Ezekiel been exposed to this Outsider sickness? Why hadn't he warned them about animals coming out of the forest? Why had an Outsider boy been the one to warn her, instead?

Something was rotten here.

Someone was lying.

"That's enough, Ezekiel." Mired in her thoughts, she picked up that hoof again.

Sickness, a Virus, the sound.

Ezekiel's insulin—*a sin.*

Secrets, little things, a rotten whiff of lies.

The javelina would've torn Ezekiel to bits if it hadn't been for the hum. Agnes, on her own, couldn't have stopped it. Now her whole body vibrated around a core of white-hot anger, wondering how much the Prophet knew about this threat—the horrible, red-hard disease that had come galloping across her meadow in the middle of the day.

If Danny had spoken the truth, sickness raged everywhere. If the Prophet had read one newspaper, or talked to one Outsider, or even heard the news from God Himself, then he'd been lying to his people. The Prophet always said God sheltered them in Red Creek. But if that weren't true—God, if *that* weren't true—

Her anger simmered.

If she'd learned one thing from secreting Ezekiel's insulin, it was that lies came in packs.

So what else was the Prophet lying about?

"Agnes?" Ezekiel moaned. "*Agnes?*"

At the edge of the forest, the trees whispered an answer she didn't want to hear.

In bed that night, Agnes saw the shining red creature like a vision, and heard the thrilling humming in her mind.

She saw herself, too—not a helpless girl at all, but a woman running to spear a monster, protecting herself and Ezekiel when the Prophet couldn't. Or wouldn't.

She thought of Beth's subversive list of Red Creek's Laws. What if those Laws didn't come from God? What if they existed not to keep them holy, but to keep them in line? She'd held back so many questions for so long. Now they flooded her, irrepressible.

Why was her life harder than a man's?

Why must she always do as she was told?

And why was Ezekiel's life worth more to Outsiders like Danny and Matilda than to his own people?

Her well-trained Red Creek mind tried to shut down her thoughts. *Quiet*, it sneered. *What do you know?*

But her spirit wouldn't accept that, after what she'd been forced to do today.

For years, she'd gritted her teeth through fevers and broken bones, never touching money, attending countless sermons, speaking only when spoken to, washing and ironing, and caring for the kids without complaint, agreeing to marry when ordered to—for God, she'd do all that and more.

But only for God.

Obedience and faith aren't the same thing, Matilda had said.

Faithful, obedient Agnes. The future Mrs. Matthew Jameson.

But what if God wanted her to be more?

And the sound...

"God, was that you?" she whispered towards and beyond the ceiling, her lips trembling.

Before I formed you in the womb I knew you, God told Jeremiah in the Bible, and the words floated into Agnes's soul, clear as an answer.

She slipped out of bed. On the porch, moths buzzed around the faint glow of the lamp, snapping and dying. She picked up her garden spade, determined to unbury all her secrets.

The humming returned as she dug. This time, it didn't

frenetically warn. This time, the earth thrummed contentedly, expectantly beneath her hands.

She dropped her spade, unable to deny any longer that she'd heard the sound before.

As a child, in the meadow.

The earth had hummed a quiet hymn through her feet, and the stars had sung an ancient, silver song.

She'd called it *the prayer space,* envisioning it not as a thing but as a place she inhabited. It was like standing at the holy altar or kneeling for evening prayers. It was the feeling that something holy—something greater—was watching you with patient eyes.

Before I formed you in the womb I knew you, before you were born I set you apart...

Her still-twisted knuckle throbbed with the memory of pain.

A just punishment for blasphemy, Mrs. King had said.

Of course. Because no little girl could have such power in Red Creek, a land where they depended on fathers and husbands for everything—the word of God included. So, Agnes had buried the prayer space deep inside herself. Eventually she'd stopped hearing it altogether.

Until today.

She picked up her spade.

She'd never forget how the prayer space had surged into a heartrending roar when she faced the javelina. The sound had done far more to keep her safe than the Prophet, or Father, or all Red Creek's Laws put together.

She struck Ezekiel's cooler, buried in the earth that kept it cold, but she wasn't digging for insulin. She rooted for the phone Danny had given her, the forbidden device wrapped tightly in a kitchen rag.

Rebellion.

She wouldn't deny it any longer. Though tears streaked down her face, her mourning would have to wait. She looked at the sky, not surprised to hear the stars, singing like they always had.

"God," she said with quiet awe. "It *is* you."

The prayer space, real and true. As for Red Creek...

Furiously, Agnes began to count its lies.

12

AGNES

Technology is the doorway to sin.
—Prophet Jacob Rollins

The next day, Monday, Agnes worried.

The javelina had to be buried, preferably before it began to stink. Thinking of the ugly red carcass hidden near the forest, she dreaded burying it alone. But it was only a matter of time before someone from Red Creek discovered it, and she wasn't ready for that. There was no telling what the Prophet might make of it, and she didn't want the Rapture coming any sooner than it had to.

I have to call the Outsiders.

A craven piece of her still wanted to shelter in the life she'd always known, and in the Laws she'd tried so hard to love. But if God had called her name, then ignoring His voice would be more dangerous than anything she'd ever done.

Agnes, you've got to be strong.

After putting the children to bed, she locked herself in the bathroom and switched on the shower. Then she crouched beneath the sink, praying the running water would mask her voice.

But the phone was tricky, a black rectangle with a single button and a forbidding screen. Agnes fumbled with it so long she began to doubt.

Then an image burst into her mind: the Underground Temple buried in the hillside. The end point of the Apocalypse Game, and of Ezekiel's nightmares, too. The Prophet always said that when plague and destruction overtook the Outsiders, that's where they'd go—deep underground, to await God's will.

But if Red Creek was a lie, it wasn't God's will they'd wait for. It was the Prophet's.

In the cold, dark bathroom, Agnes shivered.

She flicked her fingers once more over the screen and watched it become a harsh square of blinding white light. Squinting, she kept flicking, sometimes tapping.

How did anyone use these little black rectangles for sinning, or anything else, for that matter? Was she simply too backwards? Too dumb to figure it out?

Suddenly, Matilda's name appeared like magic on the screen. She had only to touch it with the tip of her index finger, and the phone began to ring.

"Hello? Agnes?"

Not Matilda's voice. Danny's.

Her cheeks flamed. "Hi." An awkward pause. "I need to speak to your mother, please."

"She just finished a forty-eight-hour shift. She's asleep." His tone changed. "What's the matter? Are you in trouble?"

Never speak to Outsiders. Treat the other sex like snakes.

Agnes nearly hung up.

It would be so easy to give up now. To bury the phone and all her doubts in the ground and marry Matthew Jameson in two weeks. With him, she'd live in a fine house with his children and wives and never make another hard decision, ever again.

To just give up, and become obedient Agnes once more, would be like sinking into a warm bath.

And drowning there.

She took a breath, remembering the humming.

No, not humming. *God's voice.*

"I killed a javelina. I think it was infected. With the Virus you told me about."

Danny's silence rattled her. The Prophet always said that Outsiders were selfish and cruel. Why should he help her?

"Hang on," he said. "I'll be right there."

—◦ᴠᴏ—

Agnes carried a flashlight and two shovels to the Kings' cemetery. She flicked her flashlight on and off while she waited for Danny, trying not to imagine red-marbled animals creeping through the dark.

She couldn't have braved it without God.

Thou art my hiding place; thou shalt preserve me from trouble; thou shalt compass me about with songs of deliverance.

"Songs of deliverance," she said aloud, wondering if the psalmist might've known a prayer space of his own.

Danny met her within the hour. His size startled her all over again—his broad shoulders, his pure height. Something inside her tugged and tightened when his eyes met hers. She was so grateful to see him, she could've wept for relief. But his eyes were badly troubled, raw around the rims.

"Things are getting uglier every day," he explained as they made their way to the forest's edge. "This Virus—they say there's never been a pandemic like it. Already it's spreading on every continent. They're putting military checkpoints in place. Quarantining the hardest-hit towns."

There was so much she needed to know. "What's a pandemic?"

"A disease that spreads around the world."

"How?"

"Your javelina—its skin was red and shiny, right? Like ruby?"

She nodded, thinking of Revelation—in which holy skins shone like gemstones—then repressed the thought.

"That sheen is made of tiny filaments. Infected skin looks smooth as marble, but those filaments bristle, razor sharp. Like shark skin. If you're cut, you'll get sick. A few days of fever, and you'll be just like them—compelled to infect others until you find a Nest. Every species is prone to infection. Birds, reptiles, people, doesn't matter. All they have to do is brush against you."

They'd come to the forest's edge.

Women who cross into the forest will face God's wrath.

Agnes froze, unable to take another step.

"What's the matter?" Danny switched on his flashlight, illuminating the sturdy trunks of ponderosa pines.

"The forest is forbidden. The Prophet says if women enter it, God will strike them down."

He cocked his head. "Do you believe that?"

She looked up at the stars, trying to find her way into that place where the whole world echoed with brilliant sound. The prayer space.

There. Stepping into it was like stepping into her garden. Peaceful, restful, green.

Do you believe that?

"No," she said softly. "Not anymore."

And Danny smiled.

After they'd buried the javelina, Danny taught Agnes how to use the phone more efficiently.

How to turn it on; how to dial his mother's number; his own, which he added. Then he showed her how to connect to the Internet, and how to type questions into a blank space and get a million answers in return.

Miracles. It all seemed like miracles.

"You can read about the Virus, Petra, in the news," he said. "CNN, NPR, the BBC...they're covering it day and night. I can teach you how to use the social sites, too—like Pangaea. That's where people are posting pictures of what's happening."

"How many people are infected?"

"Millions so far, and it's spreading fast."

As he talked, he flicked past photos of infected animals of every kind, and infected people, too. All of them were covered in a red, gem-like shine. Agnes hunched over the screen, forcing herself to look. Once creatures became petrified, they were highly aggressive—*rabid*, Danny said.

"But that isn't the strangest part," he continued. "Once infected, creatures seek each other out. They fuse into these Nests. Look."

She registered people, a crowd, but they stood too close together. Squinting, she saw they'd tangled into a kind of statue. Limbs bent at unnatural angles. Faces and bodies jammed together in chaos. With that hard, red skin, they looked like they'd been turned to stone.

And there were children.

Too roughly, she pushed the phone away.

"I know it's ugly." Danny watched her face. "Usually, Nests are burned quickly. The one in your forest is unusual that way."

Her mind reeled from her first glimpses of the darkness Outside, but what really stunned her were the glimpses of brightness. According to the Prophet, sin had overtaken the Outside long ago, and filth was all you'd find. Agnes saw now that this was an abject lie. Besides Nests, she saw people of all shapes, sizes, and colors, living in lands she'd never heard of, doing a thousand incredible things. She saw gorgeous bridges and graceful buildings, fascinating clothing and children smiling, laughing, or crying. It didn't look like a hell world. It looked like the *real* world.

"Are you okay?" Behind his glasses, Danny looked more skeptical than ever. "You're very pale."

"I'm fine," she lied. "Keep going."

"This is Pangaea."

He flicked open a new screen. A video played. Agnes couldn't tear her eyes from the trio of teenagers, dancing in silly costumes and singing at the top of their lungs. Even through the phone, she felt their exuberance. Wistfully, she placed the tip of her finger on one smiling face.

In Red Creek, Agnes kept a close leash on herself, ever aware of the Laws. But these teenagers were different. They were unafraid.

"Those are my friends, actually," Danny said bashfully. "We made this video last year. Bunch of idiots, I know."

"They're not. They're beautiful."

He grinned at her shyly, and unexpectedly Agnes felt herself fill with gladness. The prayer space had brought her to this moment, and maybe that meant God wanted to show her something greater. Something more. Though for what purpose, she couldn't imagine.

Her vision misted with wonder and gratitude.

"What's wrong?"

"Why are you helping me?" she demanded.

"Hey, I just answered the phone. And like I said, my mom worries. If you ever want to get out of here, you know who to call." He paused, pressed his lips together. "And I want to help people, if I can. I want to be a doctor, one day."

A doctor. Agnes had never even met one.

Reluctantly, she let the screen's light wink out. She thanked Danny, knowing she'd never be able to abandon her family. Though she'd known that truth her whole life, she only now felt an ache taking root.

Regret.

"Agnes," Danny spoke urgently. "Petra isn't going away. If your Prophet isn't taking any precautions against Petra, it might soon become too dangerous to stay."

I need more time, she thought as she picked her way up the hill after they'd said goodbye.

Time to type her questions into the crystal air, and learn the answers. Time to think and, especially, to pray.

Danny had already gone when the white pickup came tearing down the road too late at night.

Barreling towards the trailer.

Agnes tucked her phone inside her dress pocket and dashed around back to climb through the bathroom window. As she hauled herself up, she ripped her palm on a rusty nail. She bit back a cry. If a patriarch caught her outside at night, her pain wouldn't matter anyway.

She didn't feel God anymore. Only heart-stopping, bloodcurdling fear.

Smash. Shatter. Crack!

From the bathroom, she heard boys' voices and the sound of something pelting the trailer. She opened the door just in time to see Father lumbering down the hall in his long-john underwear.

"Who is that? Who's there?"

The kids' eyes were sleep dazed. Father tripped over Sam's toy truck, and Beth made it to the front door first.

She slammed it open. Yelled. Fell back inside the house.

Raw egg smeared Beth's face. She clutched a note tied to a stone, looking more frightened than Agnes had ever seen her.

Oh Beth, she thought, spirit sinking. *What have you done?*

"Give me that," Father snapped.

Beth hesitated, and that's when Agnes knew.

She'd been fooling around with someone. That's why she'd been disappearing. It was the worst thing a girl could ever do, and Red Creek would enforce her punishment with relish. When word got around, the patriarchs could even decide to exile her. If she was allowed to stay, she'd be a pariah.

For all intents and purposes, Beth's life was over.

I've failed my sister.

Father read the note, a vein pulsing in his temple.

He slapped Beth harshly across the face. Then he stormed out of the house, shouting about getting his gun. No one noticed that Agnes's hand bled all over the floor.

The kids were crying, and Beth held herself stiffly as a corpse. The note had fallen from Father's hand and fluttered to the floor.

> *Beth's been whoring with Cory Jameson.*
> *Burn in hell.*

"I'm sorry. I'm so sorry," Beth whispered, unmoving. "I'll be faithful now. I swear."

Agnes couldn't speak. Couldn't even think straight. She could only kneel and hold her sister. She didn't care what Beth had done. She would always be her beloved sister.

"I didn't mean it," Beth babbled. "I just..."

"This is Red Creek's fault," Agnes said firmly. "It's Red Creek that's to blame."

But her sister didn't hear her, lost in the forest of her pain.

13

AGNES

Tend your soul like a garden. Weed out all thoughts that
disturb the spirit of God.
—PROPHET JACOB ROLLINS

Agnes had never seen Father so angry.

All morning he called Beth evil names, his words raining down like blows, and when he was spent, he refused even to look at his second born.

It was called shunning, that cold refusal, and there was no telling how long it might last.

As for Beth, she looked like she was slowly bleeding to death inside. Washing the breakfast dishes, her hands shook, palsied. Uncharacteristically, she ignored the twins plucking at her skirt, begging to play dolls.

"You should've been watching her." Father turned on Agnes. "Both of you will take a water fast. Three days."

Sick at heart, Agnes glanced at Beth, who'd always been too thin, and wondered if her body could take it—let alone her mind.

Later, after Beth had retreated to the bathroom, Sam cornered Agnes. "Is Beth really a—"

"Don't say it," she answered sharply.

His lip quivered at her rebuke. "You don't even know what I was going to say."

Sam deserved some kind of explanation, but Agnes had to tread carefully.

She put her hands on his shoulders. "Any of the words you learned for bad women in church? Don't ever say them. They're more powerful than you know.

"I'll explain it all to you one day, Sam. I swear I will. But for now, let it be."

Unusual for him, Sam nodded and let it go.

Though the atmosphere in the trailer was thick with tension, Agnes wouldn't let the kids play outside. The javelina kept crashing into her mind in a haze of violent red. She brought out the rainy day toys: puzzles and crayons.

"Draw me something," she instructed Ezekiel, who hadn't spoken a word since last night.

Meanwhile, Agnes combed her memory of every conversation she'd had with Beth that summer. Hadn't Cory Jameson's name slipped from her sister's lips once too often? And hadn't Beth tried to tell her, not once but twice, about her crisis of faith?

Regret scraped Agnes's insides. She dearly wished she'd heeded her sister's tentative cries for help. Wished she'd asked her, flat out, about her friendship with Cory Jameson. She even wished she'd gone through her diary.

Anything to spare her this punishment, this shame.

A knock on the door brought Father from the shed and Agnes from the kitchen.

Matthew Jameson stood on their porch in a shaft of morning sun.

Shock rippled through her with dread on its heels. What if Matthew had come to marry her today? What if he took her before she'd had time to prepare?

Her eyes found Ezekiel, who hadn't yet had his before-lunch shot.

Make him go away, she prayed. *Please God, get that man away from here.*

Father led him inside, and Agnes broke into a cold sweat. Desperately, she searched Matthew's face for a clue.

With his snowy beard and craggy, time-worn face, Mr. Jameson looked like he'd stepped straight from the pages of the Old Testament. His eyes, blank as two flints, told her nothing. In their shabby kitchen, his fine clothes seemed absurdly out of place.

Father huffed. "What brings you, Matthew? Can Agnes get you something?"

"Water, please." He didn't so much as look at her. "I think you know what brings me."

Word traveled fast in Red Creek, and his son's name had been written on the cruel note, too—though Agnes doubted Cory would be punished as harshly as her sister. At the kitchen sink, she dared to hope that Matthew had come to break their engagement.

She brought him his water and stepped aside.

"My son assures me nothing happened with your daughter. I prayed on it, and I believe he tells the truth."

"Matthew—"

He held up a liver-spotted palm. "Don't apologize. God sends challenges, but He sends solutions, too."

Father nodded, silenced, and Agnes felt a stab of unease. Though he spoke quietly, Mr. Jameson's voice was laced with power. His will would be done, whatever it was.

"My son's reputation is badly damaged, but I believe I can salvage it by marrying the girl. Beth."

Beth?

He can't, Agnes thought madly, senselessly. *She's too young.*

Her sister stepped into the doorway, her eyes wide with astonishment. Agnes reached automatically for her hand, and they linked pinky fingers. Beth's skin felt clammy, cold.

Father rubbed his jaw. "That's very Christian of you. But are you sure you want her for a wife? She's not innocent in this."

Mr. Jameson's eyes flitted to the doorway, looking through the sisters like they were glass. Agnes remembered Danny's compassion when he'd looked at her—*Are you okay?*—and thought what a bitter irony it was that she'd first experienced masculine kindness from an Outsider.

"In my experience, women settle when taken to wife," Mr. Jameson was saying. "They only need a firm hand. I'm happy to help your Beth shed the vestiges of her rebellion."

The words made Agnes's stomach churn.

Don't agree to it, Father. Don't you dare agree.

While Father thought, his hands folded beneath his chin, Agnes prayed as hard as she ever had in her life. Beth couldn't marry that man. She *must not.*

In Father's slow, yellow smile, Agnes recognized the twisted wire of an animal trap and felt sick. Yes, he'd marry his fifteen-year-old daughter to that flinty-eyed man in place of his sixteen-year-old daughter, if it made his life the least bit simpler.

"How can I ever thank you?"

"No thanks needed. I'll have another water."

Agnes hurried to pour him one.

"And the Prophet?"

Jameson said, "I'll talk to Rollins. I'm sure he'll have another revelation."

Father laughed, and the water glass slipped from Agnes's hand, shattering.

"Foolish girl," Father snapped. "What's wrong with you?"

She risked a glance into Matthew's eyes. Supposedly, he was a faithful man, a believer; yet, he'd spoken of the Prophet's visions like they were lies of convenience. Patently false.

I'll talk to Rollins. I'm sure he'll have another revelation.

While Agnes numbly swept up the broken glass, the men shook hands and left. The trailer door banged behind them, shuddering the aluminum walls.

Among the shards, Agnes struggled to catch her breath. Now she knew for certain: God had nothing to do with marriage in Red Creek. Men wanted what they wanted. It was as simple and vicious as that. But Jameson's words weren't the worst of it. The worst part was that they'd *laughed*.

Agnes tried to catch Beth's eye, expecting to find her outraged. But she only looked colorless, almost transparent, hovering in the doorway like a ghost.

Agnes couldn't dither about praying, or thinking, any longer. They stood in the wreckage of the most dreadful lies—and the men laughed, careless that she'd heard the truth. After years of enforced obedience, it didn't matter a whit to them what she knew. They simply expected her to obey. And the old Agnes would've done just that: buried this little inconsistency in the dark soil of her faith, never to think of it again.

But she'd changed. The Outsiders, the prayer space, the phone...

The girl who obeyed without question was dead, buried in the King family graveyard. Only one thought blazed in her mind now, bright as the polestar:

Virus or not, I have to get the children out.

14

BETH

*Repent with perfect obedience, and yet ye sinners
shall be saved.*
—Prophet Jacob Rollins

Beth flew into a frenzy, collecting everything that reminded her of sin and Cory Jameson.

She threw her hairpins, her barrettes, and even her precious vanilla-scented lotion into the trash, then ripped out the pages of her diary and tossed them into the wastebasket.

"Beth, you don't have to do this," Agnes pleaded. "You're fine how you are."

She whirled. "I'm not fine. Our people want me to *burn in hell.*"

"They're just words. Cruel, thoughtless words."

She wanted to punch something. "I've been out of control, Agnes. Why didn't you stop me, help me? I needed you, and you weren't there!"

"You're exhausted. Let me get you something to eat."

"Are you crazy?" she screamed. "We're supposed to *fast.*"

"Beth, maybe—"

"What's wrong with you?" Beth couldn't remember ever

feeling such rage. Her chest felt pressurized. "Didn't you see the note? Don't you understand?"

Rumors weren't harmless. They were poisoned arrows lodged in her heart, filling her with seeping, pestilent terror. She kept feeling the egg breaking against her face, over and over. Kept seeing that ugly word, *whoring*.

To know herself hated, rejected, despised... it made her want to rip out her rebellious insides and replace them with another girl's. All her niggling self-doubts rose to the surface, stinging worse than Father's slap.

I'm vain and cruel, selfish and cowardly. I'm lazy, always letting Agnes take the heaviest chores and yet resenting her for loving Ezekiel. I've told countless lies, sinned countless times.

Never before had she felt the burrowing anguish of self-hatred, and she'd have done anything—*anything*—to numb her pain.

"I won't be like Lot's wife," she swore. "I won't look back."

But there was stupid Agnes, offering a forbidden glass of milk.

She pushed her sister's arm away, and milk slopped onto the floor. "What happened to you, Agnes? You used to be so good. Who're you now?"

"You don't have to marry him, Beth. There's another way—"

She snapped. "Maybe I should tell Father you've been sneaking out! I bet that would put the fear of God into you."

Agnes's eyes filled with tears, and for half a second, Beth felt sorry, and sorely wanted to fold her sister into her embrace. Then those foul words came rushing back—*Beth's been whoring with Cory Jameson*—and her pain came flooding back, too. Her suffering felt so large it left no room for anything else.

"Just go, Agnes. Leave me alone."

Her sister's boots clicked remorsefully against the tile. Then she was gone.

Alone in the kitchen, Beth groaned like a wounded animal. No other sound but the *drip, drip* of the leaky faucet. Even the kids, hiding out in the living room, kept quiet for once.

Her humiliation consumed her.

Suddenly, there was no more ground beneath her feet. No more steadiness; nothing to hold on to. It didn't matter that she'd ever doubted the faithful or their Laws. All that mattered was that three hundred people now wished her ill, and she felt their judgment striking her like stones. Her soul shrank, mortally afraid and frantic for shelter. The muscles in her back were steel; her hands rigid claws.

"I only wanted to be loved," she whispered.

Sure, the Laws galled, but she ought to have followed them anyway. She ought to have at least pretended faith, because the consequences of her lukewarm rebellion—this relentless, excruciating *shame*—were too miserable to bear.

She knelt in the kitchen and tried to pray, knowing it was too little too late. No peace followed her stumbling attempt at faith.

But all was not lost.

Matthew Jameson had extended his hand. All she had to do was take it.

"A patriarch's wife," Beth said out loud.

And not just any patriarch. The best and wisest of them, excepting the Prophet. If she married the second holiest man in Red Creek, she'd be safe again.

Safe.

For who would dream of reproaching her then?

From one heartbeat to the next, Beth changed her destiny. She decided to marry him.

Immediately, a soothing numbness blossomed inside her like a black velvet flower. She'd never paid much attention in church. So she didn't really know what this new feeling meant.

But she hoped—*prayed*—it was the feeling of redemption.

15

AGNES

Your first allegiance is to your Prophet. Your second, to
God through him. Let your loyalty to your family follow
only in the wake of those.
—PROPHET JACOB ROLLINS

After everyone had gone to sleep, Agnes rescued the torn-up pages of Beth's diary from the bathroom wastebasket.

She tried her best to tape them together without spying on her sister's private thoughts. She couldn't help reading a few snatches, especially when she saw her name.

> I think Agnes is in rebellion....
>
> Agnes is ignoring me again. She loves Ezekiel more than me....
>
> Father says getting a tattoo is the evilest thing a girl can ever do. Now I want one more than anything....
> Is that normal?

Agnes crouched with her head in her hands. If only she'd opened up about Ezekiel's illness...if only they'd kept confiding in each other...

Before Ezekiel was born, she and Beth would lie in the purple meadow grass, their pinky fingers linked, watching the fireflies flicker like low-hanging stars. They believed nothing could break the bond they shared.

Nothing.

But, of course, Red Creek finally had. The home they'd trusted to shelter them had torn them asunder.

Only one living person had any inkling of what she was going through.

Her stomach tightened, remembering how he'd smiled at the forest's edge.

With the shower on full blast, Agnes switched on the phone, fumbling with the small, disappearing keyboard before sending her first text. It looked like a blue balloon, loosed into a miniature white sky.

> Hello Danny. It's Agnes.

His reply was lightning fast, and Agnes's whole body thrummed, because it felt like a miracle. Danny had seen her blue bubble and sent his own through the electric air.

> Hey! What's up?

> I don't think I can be in Red Creek anymore.

A long pause. Too long. Agnes stared hard at the screen, willing words to materialize.

> Are you ready to talk to my mom?
> She can help you get out.

Was she *really* ready?

> I have five brothers and sisters. I can't just leave.

> Are you sure?

She was. The kids were too many and too big to haul out of town kicking and screaming by herself. But if she could get Beth back on her side...

Maybe I should tell Father you've been sneaking out at night. I bet that would put the fear of God into you.

Surely that was only Beth's fear talking. Red Creek had struck her hard. Was it any wonder she still reeled from the blow?

Agnes shivered, drawing her knees up tight against her chest. She needed to think about something else, or she'd lose her mind. She typed:

> Are you really going to be a doctor?

> I want to be. But my internship was canceled because of Petra. Medical schools are shutting down, too. Life is on hold.

She could only pretend to understand words like *medical school, internship,* but she sensed his disappointment even through the phone.

She thought a moment, then typed:

> What's your favorite website?

> Remember Pangaea? Check it out. You're still staying safe, right?

Safe was a word she couldn't recall the meaning of anymore. She started to type, **Thank you for asking**—but stopped, uncertain what her words would mean to him.

With a pang, she wished for Beth. Her sister knew more about boys. She would know whether Danny meant his words tenderly, or whether he was just being polite. And she would know what it meant that when Agnes saw his face, she battled an urge to count the freckles over his nose and know the number of them.

Agnes stared at the screen until the shower ran cold, chilling the air.

> Off to dinner. Take care. Text anytime.

She felt his absence like a physical ache.

Knowing she wouldn't be able to sleep, she scrolled through Pangaea.

Once again, she sensed God wanted to show her something. Wanted her to *see*.

Teenagers stood in front of a great statue in China. A girl sipped coffee in a restaurant. Meals were assembled from outlandish ingredients, and teenagers strummed instruments she'd never seen. A story about a church youth group raising money for the homeless startled her, because the Prophet always said Outsider churches were hotbeds of selfishness and sin.

Inside the claustrophobic trailer, Agnes felt her world expanding with dizzying speed. She couldn't get enough. Beyond Red Creek, there was so much more world than she'd ever imagined. So much more *life*.

But that world was also battling Petra. She caught glimpses of the Virus in fearful messages, prayers, pleas.

Opera House burning. Y can't I stop crying? #PetrifiedAustralia

Auditions canceled, theaters closed. #RIPNYC

Help. Lost cat. Tan, white. #Milly

But Agnes wasn't afraid for these strangers. She believed in their world, with its schools and its scientists. In the end, they'd solve Petra.

She had to believe that, despite the pictures of a burning courthouse, the blazing human Nest, or the articles predicting famine. She'd just discovered Outside; it wouldn't be fair to her brothers and sisters if it was already over.

AVOID CONTACT WITH INFECTED PEOPLE AND ANIMALS, a banner abruptly flashed, blinking a red warning behind the phone's glass. CALL YOUR HOSPITAL AT THE FIRST SIGN OF FEVER.

Hastily, she closed the disturbing message. Shut it down and shut it out.

She wasn't ignoring the Outside's darkness, exactly. She just wanted to soak up a little more hope—a little more good—while she braced herself for escape.

She scrolled back to a story about a teenage sports team.

HUGE TURNOUT FOR STATE CHAMPIONSHIP LAST WEEK!!! TY!!!!

Thou hast set my feet in a large room, she thought with amazement.

She read for hours, and though the bathroom was dark, her mind blazed with color and a glowing, unstoppable light.

16

AGNES

Soon will come a night of fire and brimstone. Outsiders
will atone for their wickedness with blood and pain.
—PROPHET JACOB ROLLINS

Inside out and upside down.

That's what Agnes's world felt like now. What had once been holy—the Prophet and his patriarchs—seemed a horror, and what was once a horror—life on the Outside—now appeared a haven.

How could she have been so blind?

On Pangaea, she'd seen how people looked when they were free, how filled with incautious joy their eyes could be. Mary, Faith, Sam, and Ezekiel might've grown up to be like them one day. Instead they were here, with Red Creek warping them.

I have to get the children out.

The trouble was, they wanted to stay.

"Sam, would you ever want to see Outside?"

"You mean, all the evil and sex and sin? No way!"

"Yeah, gross," echoed the twins.

"But what if it's not as bad as we think? What if there are good people out there?"

"It doesn't matter," said Mary. "They'll all be dead soon. Chicken-fried sinners."

Faith laughed. "Good riddance!"

And then there was Beth. Stubborn, foolish, frightened Beth.

After evening prayers, Father announced she'd be married next Sunday.

In the middle of the night, Agnes pinched her until she couldn't pretend to be sleeping anymore.

"Jeez, Agnes, what is it?"

Agnes propped herself up on her elbow. Demanded, "Do you really want to marry him?"

Beth turned her head so Agnes couldn't see her face. "Yes," she said with surprising feeling. "More than anything."

Agnes bit the inside of her cheek, feeling trapped. A month ago, Beth had flirted with rebellion. Now she acted like an entirely different person.

"Don't you think there's something…suspicious about the way the marriage was arranged?"

Beth recoiled. "You're just jealous because he chose me over you."

Agnes's jaw dropped. "That's ridiculous."

"Is it?" Beth arched a brow.

"I'm not jealous. I'm scared for you."

Her sister's face softened and hope revived. Agnes extended her small finger, and Beth very nearly took it.

But Agnes spoke too soon. "You were right, before. Something *is* wrong with this place. I'm sorry I didn't—"

"Stop!" Beth covered her ears and curled into a ball. "Nothing about me was right before. Nothing! And you should look to yourself. I heard you talking to the kids. You're in rebellion."

Agnes felt as helpless as a bird slamming against a storm

window. She could batter herself to pieces, but Beth was so entrenched in her newfound piety she couldn't see beyond her future as Matthew Jameson's wife.

"I wish you could see yourself as I do," Agnes said. "I wish you could see that you deserve compassion, not punishment."

Beth's shoulders shook, but she didn't speak.

Agnes prayed: *Lord, how can I help them see? Why won't you open their eyes, as you've opened mine?*

She wanted to show them the phone—her own window into the real world. But Beth, in her bewilderment and hurt, was just crazed enough to betray her.

Miserable beyond words, Agnes twisted and tossed in her bed.

On Pangaea, there were no images of girls married to old men.

She'd spent a long time gazing at a young couple, a girl and a boy. The girl had written I LOVE MATT!!! beneath a photo of them smiling outside an ice cream shop. She wore shiny pink paint on her lips and frayed shorts. He wore a cap and a goofy smile.

Agnes drank in the image until her eyes smarted, because the girl reminded her of Beth. If they'd been raised a mile outside Red Creek, her sister might be holding hands with a boy at an ice cream shop, too. She might be posting photos on Pangaea and studying for exams.

But Beth wasn't born a mile outside Red Creek, and instead of enjoying the last years of her childhood, she was living like a penitent, preparing to marry a man old enough to be her father.

Agnes waited until her sister's breath evened out. Then she locked herself inside the bathroom and turned on the shower.

Danny? Is there stuff online about Red Creek?

> Why do you ask?

She could practically see the line forming between his eyes, wrinkling the bridge of freckles across his nose.

> People must talk about us. They talk about everything else.

> True. If you want, you can google it.

She only hesitated a moment.

Links to newspaper articles cropped up in droves.

As did the words: *cult, brainwashing, human rights abuses.*

Agnes's mind reeled as she clicked from page to page.

In Red Creek, Arizona, the "Prophet" Jacob Rollins is a prime example of a malevolent, narcissistic personality who demands his people suppress critical thinking in order to replace their will with his own, one article said. *As of this writing, the Red Creek compound has existed for nearly eighty years. Generations of children have been raised under a harsh, unforgiving system of total indoctrination. The cult is considered "highly dangerous" by state law enforcement…*

She collapsed on the bathroom floor.

I just looked up Red Creek, Danny texted. **It's pretty harsh. Are you okay?**

Agnes wept, feeling like an exile in her own home.

"God gave me a second chance," Beth had been saying all day. "I won't mess it up."

It was upside down and inside out—but Agnes felt exactly the same.

"You'll have to deliver Mother's dinner from now on."

Beth spoke coolly, around a mouthful of pins. Agnes was horrified to find her buried in a pile of old lace. Their mother's wedding dress. Already, the twins were touching it reverently.

"Why me? Why now?"

"I'm too busy with wedding chores. This dress has got to be hemmed three inches, and I want these pearls on the bust."

Panic blossomed in Agnes's chest. She hadn't conversed with her mother in years. "It only takes a minute," she insisted. "You know she prefers you."

Her sister's cheeks pinked, almost as if she were ashamed. But she didn't drop her eyes.

Reluctantly loading a tray with food, Agnes wondered about their mother.

Had she ever tried to escape? Had she ever tried to save her kids?

Oddly, she found herself remembering Sarah Shiner—her ancestor on Father's side. *She* had run from Jeremiah Rollins, but she'd left a son behind. How had she lived with the pain?

"Mother?" she called. "It's me, Agnes."

No answer. She never answered to anyone but Beth.

Luckily, Father had broken the door's lock long ago. Agnes pushed, and the hinges creaked open. The bedroom curtains were tightly drawn against the light. Agnes felt submerged, like she was trying to breathe dark water.

Her mother hauled herself upright, patting her matted, unwashed hair. Seeing Agnes, her eyes lit with fiery accusation.

"I've heard you, you know. Talking to the kids. Feeling them out," her mother whispered. "You're spending lots of time locked in the bathroom, too. Taking lots of showers."

Agnes went white. All those hours reading Pangaea, running water to disguise any sound... She was a fool to forget that her mother might wonder. The dinner tray felt like it weighed a thousand pounds. Trembling, she set it on the edge of the bed, then leapt back, like the woman might bite.

And who knew? Maybe she would.

Agnes tried to imagine her mother's arms holding her as a child or cradling her brothers and sisters. But imagination failed.

"Never thought you'd be the one to run. I always thought Beth."

Fear squeezed Agnes's throat closed, because she knew this could be the end. If her mother told Father...

"Don't worry." Her voice was like wind sweeping through pines. "I won't tell. But I'm surprised. I expected your sister to get the hell out of here. Never you."

Agnes didn't know what hurt more—that she'd always seemed a lost cause to her mother, or that Beth really might be lost.

"You're wrong," she stuttered. "I'm not going to run."

Her mother chuckled dryly. "You will. But you're going about it all wrong, trying to get the kids on your side. That's hopeless. You'll only ever make it out alone."

Her mother came alive, standing, knocking the dinner tray with its sad cup of soup to the floor. She gripped Agnes's arm.

"Promise me you'll run. *Promise.*"

"Mother—" She gazed at the sickly arm that gripped her. There were sores, deep infected cuts where she'd picked relentlessly at the skin. Even her lips were tattered by her own biting teeth. Her mother was destroying herself, bit by tiny bit.

"Don't try to take the children. They're not yours. They're not even mine. They're creatures of the church."

Agnes ripped her arm away and ran.

But the words had been uttered.

You can't take them with you.

Shaking, she told herself her mother didn't know anything,

that she was just a stranger eavesdropping on their lives from the other side of her bedroom wall.

Only that wasn't the truth. And Agnes knew it.

By the time her Outsider mother understood Red Creek's ways, it was too late. The trap had snapped shut the day Agnes was born. Her mother may have wanted to escape, but her children—*brainwashed*—were heavy shackles. They'd weighed her down in rushing waters, and she'd drowned.

She was drowning still.

She'd told Agnes to run. But if she couldn't take the children, what on earth would be the point?

Her mind flashed on Ezekiel as a toddler, looking up at her as she bent to lift him from his crib. Flashed on the twins, dissolving into giggles over a private joke. Flashed on Sam racing across the meadow, his chest thrust out and his head thrown back in delight.

Generations of children have been raised under a harsh, unforgiving system...

She had to get the children out. But she couldn't make it out with the children. It was inside out and upside down.

"God can't mean for me to run alone," she whispered.

She thought again of Sarah Shiner, her great-grandmother, and the only woman she knew who'd escaped. What if she'd left her son behind because she had no choice?

Her back against the door, Agnes slid to the floor.

She heard Beth lecturing Mary in the other room. "The Prophet made a mistake with Matthew Jameson and Agnes, but now he's corrected it, see? Anyway, I'll make a prettier bride..."

17

AGNES

Woman, rest in the knowledge that God has ordained your
husband for you.
—Prophet Jacob Rollins

A gnes wasn't like her mother. She'd struggle and claw for every last ounce of air before she gave in to drowning despair. She swore she'd keep trying with the kids, and keep attending the Prophet's sermons, even when church was hellish.

Truly, it was.

That first Sunday in August, glassy-eyed people waited for the Prophet to tell them what to do, what to wear, and how to live. And Agnes, who'd known the faithful all her life, didn't blame them. It was comforting to believe you lived hand-in-hand with God's will, and that you were one of His chosen. Who wouldn't find solace in that?

She watched Beth anxiously eyeing stern-faced Matthew Jameson. The man never looked at her once—but Cory Jameson did.

Agnes watched him stealing furtive glances, his eyes confused beneath a sweep of golden hair. At heart, he was only a child, too.

In front of her, Mrs. King's needles clicked over a baby's jumper.

The Mrs. Hearns whispered to each other, voices leashed because their husband was liberal with the rod. Magda twisted the ear of a boisterous younger girl hard enough to bring tears to the child's eyes. Mr. Sayles played the half-tuned organ, marching dutifully through the hymn "Be Thou My Vision." When he was done, his wives applauded politely, and he flashed a broken-toothed smile.

A regular Sunday, except for the anger that throbbed in Agnes's bones as she thought how much, and how cruelly, they'd been betrayed—the women and children, in particular.

Did Father and the patriarchs believe their own lies? Were they demons feeding on the faith of others, or simply greedy fools? Mr. Jameson bowed his head to pray, and she thought how much easier it must be to turn your cheek when you had five wives and plenty of children and, even better, dominion over them all.

Agnes studied Sam and Ezekiel, both of whom were meant to be patriarchs one day. Sweet as they were now, how would Red Creek change them? In the end, would they be able to distinguish between truth and lies? And if so, what would they choose?

And then there were the girls—Mary, Faith, and oh, God, Beth—who had no choices.

On Pangaea, Agnes had seen universities, hospitals, schools. If Red Creek had its way, the kids would never know any of that.

As for the Virus plaguing the Outside—well, it couldn't last forever, could it?

The Prophet arrived; the congregation abruptly hushed.

Sam whispered eagerly, "Think he'll preach the Rapture?"

Surrounded by people she'd known forever, Agnes had never felt so alone.

The Prophet wore night-black robes and a silky smile. As always, he oozed confidence and charm and something else—a caginess she'd once mistaken for holiness.

Agnes had seen him take the pulpit countless times. She knew his sweeping gestures better than her own. She could've recognized his lilting, hypnotic voice anywhere, but now she heard it as *a sharp razor, working deceitfully.* His eyes were crow black, glittering in his too-narrow face. He surveyed his people greedily, hungrily.

The Prophet was a liar, but was he evil? Who but an evil man would use a people's faith against them?

His smile grew, and she thought, *Maybe a mad one.*

A *malevolent, narcissistic personality*, the article had said.

Without warning, the prayer space opened up inside her, and she smothered a gasp.

She felt it ripple out, spreading through the building like invisible water, its currents frightfully strong. She looked down at Ezekiel to see if he could feel it, too. He smiled up at her, giving no sign that he felt—or heard—anything.

But Agnes could hear.

She heard the hearts of the faithful thrumming in unison. She heard the stitch in the silty, troubled souls of Beth and Cory. She heard the Bibles humming from the pockets of the pews. Such a shock to find the prayer space even here, ringing in such sharp contrast to the Prophet's falsity.

The prayer space truly is God's voice.

There were no words and no commandments. No shaming rules or crushing Laws. Only this constant singing. This ever-present hum.

It was just as she'd suspected as a child. But why did she alone seem to hear it?

Before I formed you in the womb I knew you, before you were born I set you apart; I appointed you as a prophet to the nations.

"No," she whispered decisively, her horror building. "Oh no. Not me."

That old quote from the Book of Jeremiah—every atom of her upbringing revolted against it, heaving the blasphemous thought overboard.

"People, do you believe the Rapture is near?"

In the prayer space, the Prophet's voice was like icy ground in the midst of green gardens, a place where nothing good could grow.

"Do you believe we'll soon witness the coming of the Lord?"

Shouted assents and murmured amens.

"Do you believe we'll soon descend into the Underground Temple?"

Amen!

"Liars," the Prophet growled, and the faithful fell silent. "Lucky for you, God in His wisdom has sent a sign. A red devil to fortify your faith."

Ezekiel's eyes snapped to hers. Though she'd told him the red javelina was only sick, deep in his mind where nightmares lived, he believed in demons just as he'd been raised to do.

Frightened, his breathing quickened.

Could the prayer space help her?

As a child, she'd never thought to actually use it, as she used her eyes and ears. It was probably blasphemy even to try, but she had to be ready for whatever trick the Prophet planned to play.

Agnes closed her eyes.

The prayer space billowed around her, a protective cloak. She nudged it with her mind, pushing it past its natural edges. Sweat broke out of every pore in her body, and unconsciously she ground her teeth, stretching, reaching.

Miraculously, the prayer space obeyed.

It spread its tendrils beyond the Prophet to the front of the church, and just at the limits of her reach, she heard it—a rising red moan.

The knowledge fell into her lap like a stone tablet: Something frightful would happen here today. Prayer space or not, Agnes feared she'd be powerless to stop it.

Powerless, as always.

"Ezekiel," she whispered. "You're going to have to be very brave. Okay?"

He swayed on the pew. She steadied him.

"What's wrong with him?" Sam asked.

Agnes didn't have time to answer. In the next instant, there was a loud sound—a real-world jolt of metal slamming—that echoed in the rafters and made the faithful jump. Along with the kids, Agnes craned her neck to see the Prophet dragging an animal before the altar with an iron chain.

It was shaped like a dog, marbled red, infected, snarling, and thrumming at the prayer space. A gasp swept the room and Mr. Sayles's hand jittered on the organ. The instrument groaned balefully.

"Behold. The demon!"

The Prophet beckoned for his eldest son, Toby, to take the chain.

Beth murmured, "Oh, God."

"Wow, oh, wow," said Sam, squirming in his seat. Too excited to sit still.

Only Ezekiel knew enough to be afraid. He buried his face in Agnes's arm, and the childish gesture stoked Agnes's rage. The church brimmed with children, but the Prophet cared nothing for them—he never had. The animal growled, the sound low and juddering in its striated throat.

"Outsiders say this dog is sick, but don't believe them," the Prophet crowed. "Thousands of demons like this one now march across the face of the earth. But nor should you be afraid, for they can't harm the righteous. Toby?"

The prayer space flickered, warning again, and more surely than she'd ever known anything, Agnes knew: The Prophet's son was going to set the creature loose.

She jumped up, ignoring the eyes turned towards her. "Beth, help me get the kids out."

"What?" Beth looked scandalized. "No."

"Just do it," Agnes snapped.

"If you leave, everyone will know you're in rebellion." Beth's eyes were wide, her hands clutching the fabric of her dress.

Agnes grabbed her by the arm, ready to force her to stand.

But it was already too late. Toby unleashed the animal and took a quick step back. The dog, now free, eyed its audience warily.

No one spoke as it walked dazedly down the aisle, its marbled claws clicking against the hardwood. Its head swiveled from side to side, taking in the frozen onlookers: the Kings, the Hearns, the Sayleses, the Jamesons. Men, women, and children draped in linens that wouldn't protect them when the mad dog bristled its crystal fur or bared its crimson teeth.

Get up, she thought hard at them. *Get up and run. Get up and go!*

The faithful feared the dog, but they feared the Prophet more. None dared move. Their leader stood at the pulpit watching them with hungry, fevered eyes.

The dog was getting closer. Feet away. Inches. Too close for her and her siblings to run. She could smell its sour smell, like clotted sweat, like death by fever. She couldn't tear her eyes from its shine-slick coat, the color of blood and disease. And the way it moved—jerkily, mechanically...

Agnes braced herself, because the prayer space was above all protective, and in another moment, she knew it would—

Howl.

The sound, like nails shrieking against a chalkboard, exploded behind her eyes. An invisible wall shot up between her and the infected animal. The dog, nearly at her elbow, hit the sonic wall and stumbled back. It studied her, and something crept into those unnatural orbs: a pure, crimson terror.

Just like the javelina, it feared her.

No, not her. *God's voice.*

The Prophet shrieked, "If you are righteous, it cannot harm you! But if you have sinned, your soul will die!"

Across the aisle, Mrs. King dropped her knitting needles with a clatter, and Agnes lost her focus. The prayer space evaporated.

The petrified dog lunged for Mrs. King. She screamed, and chaos broke out. Everyone seemed to be running in different directions. Mothers shouted for children, and children for mothers. The only still point in the riot was Matthew Jameson, sitting straight and calm in his abandoned pew.

"No one leaves!" the Prophet bellowed. "Do you hear me? *No one leaves!*"

Ezekiel took off running, darting and weaving through the crush. Agnes's first instinct was to sprint after him, but she couldn't leave the other kids behind. She grabbed Sam's arm and pushed the twins in front of her, jostling them towards the door and wishing for another set of arms. But Beth pulled Sam away, forcing him to watch, to stay.

Agnes tried reaching for him again, but by then the twins were trying to crawl into Father's lap. Her arms were aching, empty.

Father shouted, "Sit down, girl!"

Panicked, she sought wildly for Ezekiel.

Then the shot rang out.

Prophet Rollins wielded a pearl-handled pistol. A wisp of smoke escaped its muzzle. In the aisle, a dark pool of blood slowly spread beneath the slain dog.

"Three have failed God's test! Three!"

She craned her neck to see beyond the throng.

Her Sunday school teacher, Mrs. King, was bleeding freely and weeping on the floor. The Prophet's eldest son, Toby, shrieked and gripped his thigh.

And Magda Jameson nursed a bloodied arm. The dog had only brushed her, but Agnes's mind flashed back to what Danny had said: Petra spread through broken skin.

Magda would rash, fever, and, finally, turn.

At the pulpit, the Prophet bellowed, "The Rapture has come. The Underground Temple will shelter us from God's wrath. Hallelujah, for the Outsiders will die!"

Everyone in the church was staring at the Prophet, rapt.

But Agnes was done, her stomach sick.

She moved past the twins, searching for Ezekiel. He was curled in a ball in the back, arms wrapped around trembling knees. She picked him up and hurried for the door.

"Who goes there!" The Prophet interrupted himself, and Agnes froze. "What are you doing, girl? What faithless sedition is this?"

He was looking right at her, and except for Mrs. King's pained bleating, the church had fallen silent. Her arms trembled supporting her brother's weight, and her cheeks flamed.

They gaped upon me with their mouths, as a ravening and a roaring lion.

She squirmed under all their scrutiny, but the Prophet's was the worst. Those eyes, glittering spitefully.

"Well?" The word sounded like a gong.

"I—" Her voice faltered.

Everyone stared at her—Father, the kids, the other families—and she felt voiceless, just like in Sunday school.

Conflicted, too, because she was leaving Beth, the twins, and Sam behind. They gaped at her like she was a stranger.

Her whole life she'd been raised to do as the Prophet asked, to do as men asked—but she couldn't, not this time, because Ezekiel, even more than the others, needed her. Stress and fear could wreak havoc on his blood glucose. And he just might be the only one of her family who wasn't too brainwashed to be saved.

She opened her mouth to say, *I'm so sorry, but my brother has to go.*

Only nothing came out. Not even air.

"Sit down," the Prophet ordered, already preparing to ignore her, taking her obedience for granted.

And Agnes wanted to sit. Truly, she did. Because obeying was so much easier than the alternative.

But Ezekiel shook violently, and snot ran from his nose. She could still see the look in the dog's fever-crazed eyes.

And the Prophet was a gun-toting madman who pretended to hear God's voice.

She took one shuffling, pained step towards the door.

"*What are you doing?*" The Prophet roared. "I said, *sit down!*"

His stunned look would've been laughable, if she didn't know she'd pay for this.

She pulled away from his gaze and ran, her boots beating time against the background of horrified silence spreading through the church. Sorrow welled up as she thought of Toby and poor Magda. Both infected now and dying. She wanted to shout for the other kids, but then Ezekiel vomited down the front of her prairie dress.

She struck the church door with her shoulder and gasped to breathe the pine-scented air.

She glanced down at her dress, making sure Ezekiel hadn't vomited the deathly, black fluid she remembered from his first crisis. She exhaled, seeing it was only nervous spit up.

"How do you feel?" She dabbed at his chin.

"Bad, Agnes," he mumbled.

High. As soon as they got home, she'd check his blood glucose and administer a correction shot. Silently, she thanked God for his insulin.

"You'll feel better after your shot," she said firmly. "I promise."

They were alone beneath the sun. None of the faithful would follow them yet. None of them dared.

After all, the Prophet was preaching his greatest, most long-awaited sermon.

The Rapture was here.

18

AGNES

On Judgment Day, we shall shelter in the Underground
Temple, with food enough for four hundred days.
—PROPHET JEREMIAH ROLLINS

Keep going.

Her legs cramped, but Agnes willed herself to hurry. Ezekiel sobbed in her arms.

After the Prophet loosed the dog, Ezekiel ran even before she did. Hope shone inside her, because that meant he wasn't a creature of the church—not entirely. Not yet. Was it insulin that inoculated him? Was it the javelina before? Was it his youth?

Or was there something special inside her baby brother—that same something that had always given him nightmares about the Underground Temple?

Punishment was coming as soon as church let out. If she were lucky, Father would only force her to fast a few more days. Ezekiel had been sick, after all. Truly, he had needed air.

But she'd also disobeyed the Prophet's direct order in front of everyone—flouted the will of God's representative on earth. But what did that matter, now she'd decided to run? She told herself she was not afraid; there was nothing Father or the Prophet could do to hurt her anymore—and yet her heart battered at her throat.

Spying their meadow, she struggled on. Before Father came home, she needed to text Danny. And she needed to talk to Ezekiel—to prepare him.

Please God, let him listen. I won't run alone.

—⌁—

"Demon," Ezekiel whispered. "A demon got Mrs. King."

Inside the trailer, Agnes had wrapped Ezekiel in a blanket. She'd checked his blood glucose and given him a correction shot. Now she rocked him, stroking his duckling-soft hair.

"It wasn't a demon." She wiped his runny nose. "The dog was sick. Like the javelina."

"I didn't tell anyone about the javelina, Agnes."

She beamed. "I know."

"But today, the Prophet said the dog was a demon—"

It was time to tell him the painful truth. "The Prophet *lied.*"

Ezekiel's thumb fell out of his mouth. "He can't lie."

"How do you know?" she asked.

"Father told me, and Mrs. King, and—and *you*, Agnes!"

She winced. "I was wrong. So were they."

He'd stopped shivering, becoming wary. "What do you mean?"

"I mean, I made a mistake. I'm so sorry."

Ezekiel sank back against his pillow. "We're going underground for the Rapture. Right?"

His voice sounded decades older. Agnes could kill the Prophet for frightening him so.

Do you believe we'll soon witness the coming of the Lord?

"Ezekiel. Listen to me. That dog wasn't a demon, and this isn't the Rapture. I won't let you go down into the bunker."

In fact, she couldn't. The faithful kept enough canned food in the Temple for four hundred long, dark days, but not a drop of the insulin Ezekiel needed to survive. It would be his death sentence.

"I don't want to go down there," he whispered. "But won't we burn if we stay here?"

"The Rapture is a lie, and the world won't end like that. It can't."

He was unconvinced. But this was her chance, and Agnes wasn't about to let it slip away. Slowly, in the back of her mind, a plan was falling into place, a path that stretched into the forest and beyond. She didn't like where it was leading, and she didn't like that she saw herself and Ezekiel walking that path alone.

Ezekiel peered curiously over her shoulder as she took out her phone. Last night, she hadn't had time to bury it. All morning, it had been burning a hole in her dress. Immediately, a warning flashed brightly across the screen.

STATE OF EMERGENCY. CITIZENS ARE INSTRUCTED TO REMAIN IN THEIR HOMES UNTIL FURTHER NOTICE.

Fear fluttered in her chest. What did that mean?

She tapped the screen with her thumb, brushing the warning away. She needed Danny.

"What's that?" Ezekiel craned for a look. "What did it say?"

"Shh."

She texted: **Danny, I need your help. Please come get me.**

While she waited for his answer, she flicked the kitchen curtains, looking for any sign of Father. The road was clear, so she showed Ezekiel her favorite Pangaea video, to distract him. The one of Danny's friends, dancing awkwardly and laughing. He watched, transfixed.

"What're they doing?" he asked.

"I don't really know. Would you like to come Outside with me and see?"

His brow wrinkled. "We're not allowed Outside. You *know* that. It's not *allowed*."

> Agnes, I can't. No one's supposed to be on the streets. Soldiers everywhere.

She hesitated. She was asking him to put himself at risk. But what choice did she have?

> Danny, please.

"Ezekiel, listen." Now was the time, terrifying as it might be. "I need you to be very brave…"

And she told him everything.

— ✺ —

Ezekiel listened, and he was brave.

When she left him alone to meet Danny—**Meet at the Nest, or someone might see**, she'd texted—she believed in her bones that Ezekiel wouldn't turn her in.

How will you find the Nest? Danny wanted to know. **You've never been.**

Agnes smiled grimly to herself, knowing exactly how she'd find it. She'd follow the sound.

The prayer space was a powerful sense. It could lead her through the forest, lighting her way with echoes and hums and lilts of bright sound.

But was she strong enough to bend it to her will?

She closed her eyes, pouring her soul into that single effort.

Exhaustion fell on her like a mountain, as if she'd been praying endlessly for hours. But it worked. The Nest's hum clung like a fog to the loamy ground. She trudged across the meadow, following, listening, following.

Soon the leaves above blocked out the light. The hum burrowed into her bones. Traveling deeper into the maze of cypress, juniper, and pine felt like entering some unearthly cathedral made entirely of sound.

God is very close.

She wanted to see the Nest. It was more than just a rendezvous point. The Nest was a slice of the real world, and she needed to know what she was running to.

She lifted her skirt to hop over a creek into a circle of damp earth. Pine needles snapped beneath her boots. Leaves cast spectral shadows on the forest floor and the humming deepened.

Then she saw them with her own eyes.

The Nested crows.

Revulsion rolled over her in waves because there was nothing beautiful about them. They were a rupture. A bizarre ugliness. She was going to be sick, but she couldn't look away. And even if she did squeeze her eyes shut, she knew she would still hear them, in the prayer space.

Because God's voice spoke through them, too.

A chill worked through her as she realized, more strongly than ever before, that the divine didn't only dwell in beauty, but also in pestilence and horror.

Thou hast showed thy people hard things: thou hast made us to drink the wine of astonishment.

"Agnes?"

Danny strode through the brush. Her fear faded. She knew she'd been right to ask him here.

Before them, a hundred birds knotted into a tall, tree-like shape, locked together, yet alive and shivering. Beaked faces, black wings serrated with feathers, and leathery talons interlocking. They'd melted into one another like glass, and she couldn't tell where one bird ended and another began. A red resin glazed their backs. They shivered mindlessly in their crystal trap.

The Nest was something you had to see for yourself, just as you had to break a bone to know real pain. It solidified all she'd thought, all she'd learned. Red Creek was a lie, and all these years she'd been living blind. There was more Outside, much more. Some good. Some bad.

And some—*inexplicable*.

This Nest, she understood from Danny, was something entirely new to the world. And yet, growing up she'd drunk the Bible like milk. She couldn't help but think of Job's leviathan and the description of its red scales: *They are joined one to another; they clasp and cannot be separated.* And she couldn't help but think of God's chariot in the Book of Ezekiel, pulled by crimson beasts with four faces, its shining red wheels rimmed with eyes.

"It's a Virus," Danny said gently. "That's all."

Yes. She knew now that the way she saw the world was just one framework among multitudes. There were many ways to see; countless avenues to understanding.

The thrum of the birds rattled her bones. She stepped back, crunching leaves. The prayer space didn't shriek, but she sensed it on alert. Aware.

She shivered. "They can't hurt us?"

"The Nests don't move. But they do attract others." He glanced back the way he came. "We shouldn't stay long, Agnes."

She'd seen photos of people melded together like those crows. How would it feel to be alive, but not alive? To be twisted up and trapped forever?

Did she really have to wonder? Didn't she already know?

"It's terrible, isn't it?"

He pulled his glasses from his face and wiped the lenses. "Sometimes I think the world is ending. I think..."

Danny's dark hair had grown halfway over his eyes, and he smelled of sweat and fear. It had been brave of him to come.

She whispered, "Was it very hard, getting here?"

He looked surprised that she'd think of him now.

"This last week... I never knew it could be so bad. School's canceled, and we're supposed to stay in our homes, but nobody does. People have to get food somehow, you know? Websites are down, power's out, there's gunfire in the streets..."

The hair stood up on the back of Agnes's neck. "You mean, it isn't safe out there?"

"I know you're thinking of leaving." No one had ever spoken hard words so gently. "But honestly, it might be better if you stayed here."

"What?" Her head reared back.

"Your people aren't rioting in the streets. Buildings aren't burning. Humans aren't yet—" He nodded towards the crows. "You know."

"The Prophet's going to send us into the bunker soon." She spoke quickly, furiously. "And Danny, I don't think anyone's coming out alive."

He ran a hand through the black wave of his hair, looking stricken. She saw him calling on a different part of himself—the analytical, problem-solving part she'd glimpsed in their first meeting. The part that wanted to be a doctor.

"Okay." He stuck his hands in his pockets. "Let's weigh our options."

She'd gotten too close to the crows.

A red beady eye found her, its gaze suddenly animate. The prayer space was shrieking like a kettle, and, for a moment, Agnes couldn't breathe.

Danny grabbed her hand and pulled her to safety. They kept going past the creek, away from the shadowy center of the forest.

"Thank you," she murmured, when she'd caught her breath.

They stayed close, because it felt safer somehow. She could feel the warmth of him. His broad shoulders blocked out the forest dark.

"Agnes, I can't reach my mom," he said. "I haven't heard from her since last night. I'm going straight from here to the hospital to find her."

She looked up at him. In every version of her escape plan, Danny had been there. Solid. Reliable. What would she do if he wasn't?

"You won't disappear on me. Will you?"

"Come with me." His eyes implored her. "You and your brother. But you have to come now."

Now!

Her shock startled him. "Isn't that why you wanted me to come? To help you get away?"

You can't save them.

Yes, she wanted to leave. But now, confusion and doubt took over.

Ezekiel might go willingly. But Beth—she'd ring the alarm if Agnes so much as mentioned running. Without her, she couldn't handle the other kids.

Agnes pictured the bunker, that hatch in the ground, and saw her sister living in the dark, with the rats, the foul air, and Matthew Jameson. She saw Mary and Faith, too small to understand what had happened to them. And Sam still playing the Apocalypse Game—only it was no longer fun, because this time it was real.

I have to try one more time. Or I'll never forgive myself.

But what if her time was already up, and the hourglass empty? What if the Prophet and the patriarchs were waiting for her in her trailer even now, to exile her to the Outside, alone?

"Only one woman ever escaped from Red Creek," she said. "My great-grandmother Sarah. But she had to leave her baby son behind."

Danny was shocked speechless.

"I can't go with you now," she said heavily. "I have to talk to my sister. I have to try to rescue my brothers and sisters."

His face fell. "I read about your Prophet. He's dangerous, Agnes."

She bit her lip. "I can't just leave the kids to die."

"You really think it's death, this bunker?"

A dog on a chain. Blood on the church floor. And the Prophet, waving a pearl-handled pistol.

She rubbed her eyes, thinking of Red Creek's three hundred. "I'm terrified for them."

"How can I help?" Danny asked. "Why am I here?"

He wasn't angry, but there was a thread of sadness in his voice that sounded like *goodbye*.

She glanced through the trees in the direction of her trailer. Earlier, she'd thought she and Ezekiel would be gone before everyone returned from church. But her heart told her she needed to try to save Beth and her siblings, one last time.

She looked at Danny.

In his eyes: heartbreak. He knew how torn she was.

Again, she felt that mysterious *something* inside herself reaching out to him like a grasping hand.

She had one last favor to ask of him. She shocked herself by touching his arm.

"Danny, I need you to teach me to drive. Will you?"

A grin dawned slowly on his face. "Manual or automatic?"

"I have no idea what that means."

He threaded his hand through hers. "We'd better get started, then."

———⌒⌣⌒———

The hike to the car wasn't long. Danny's vehicle was smaller than the Jamesons' truck, gray, and hidden in a glade.

"Let's start from the beginning," said Danny, opening the passenger door. "Sorry it's so crowded in here. I've been collecting medical supplies wherever I can find them. Gauze, disposable ice packs, half-empty cartons of Band-Aids . . . I hope you don't mind."

Agnes didn't mind, but she was surprised to see the back seat cluttered, overflowing with Outsider materials. Some things looked sharp, like Ezekiel's syringes but more complex.

"Don't touch the blood kit. You'll notice my arm is covered in scars. I've been trying to teach myself from textbooks and You-Tube to do things Mom can probably do in her sleep."

She moved a pile of worksheets to sit down, noticing the title of the packet as she did so. ADVANCED CPR, it said.

"What's CPR?"

He slid into the driver's seat. "Cardiopulmonary resuscitation. I'm already certified, but I wanted to brush up. You can't just call 911 anymore." He paused, like he was deciding whether or not to confide something. "I keep having this nightmare that someone's hurt and dying, and I have to figure out how to save their life, all by myself."

Agnes snapped her seat belt's buckle. "Do you? Save them, I mean?"

"No," he said through gritted teeth. "It always turns out I didn't practice enough."

"But you are practicing," she pointed out, and he visibly brightened, adjusting the rearview mirror.

"Good point." He smiled in thanks, and her heart flipped over in her chest.

"Now, watch me start the car. Then you'll try."

Later, Agnes would think two things: that the afternoon she spent learning to drive with Danny was one of the happiest of her life, and that she should've gone with him.

But she waited too long while the sun lowered, and disaster gathered like a storm.

19

AGNES

*In dreams God has revealed to me: It is an abomination for
women to drive vehicles of any kind. Their fathers shall not
teach them.*

—Prophet Jacob Rollins

Trudging up the meadow, Agnes felt lighter than she had any right to, considering the punishment that doubtlessly awaited her. She kept seeing Danny adjusting his glasses. Kept hearing his enthusiasm as she learned to maneuver the car. When she took a sharp turn, his medical supplies had rolled in the back seat, causing her to shoot a glance his way.

She was accustomed to male anger. But Danny's charmed laughter—that was new. Her whole body relaxed at the sound, and despite her grave danger, she felt happy.

His eyes widened like he'd stumbled on something unexpected and delightful.

"Do you know," he said wistfully, "I think this is the first time I've ever seen you smile."

"I'm sure that's not true."

"No," he insisted with touching certainty. "I'm sure it is. I've wondered what it would be like."

Then he blushed, adjusted his glasses again, and launched into a detailed explanation of turn signals.

Her skin still tingled with the memory as she crested the hill.

Father stood in her garden, his arms crossed over his chest. His whole body was taut with rage, but even that could hardly touch her.

Because she had a secret power now.

She could *drive*.

"Agnes, get inside. *Now*."

"Father, I'm—"

"You revealed your true self in church today." His face was white. "I *disown you*. Do you understand me? You'll live in my house and obey my rules, but our spiritual ties are severed. I'll not be embarrassed by you again. Not even in heaven."

She'd expected it to hurt, and it did. But she had more to think of than the loss of his love.

"I understand, Father."

He blinked, taken aback that she hadn't wept or screamed.

"Your Sunday school teacher died an hour ago."

His words pierced her. She swayed. Everything seemed to be happening too fast.

"The funeral must take place in the church, tonight. Your sister's wedding, too."

Oh my God, they're tying up loose ends.

Father nodded curtly, confirming her fears. It was still Sunday—a holy day—and that morning the Prophet had shown them a demon. A *red devil to fortify your faith.*

Matthew Jameson wanted his sixth wife before the Rapture, and Mrs. King must be buried before the end of the world.

They were going to the Temple. And not in some far-off future—*tonight*.

"Help Beth dress," Father said, voice clipped. "We don't have much time."

She needed to text Danny—beg him to come back. She needed to dig up Ezekiel's insulin, grab Father's keys to the truck, and pack a bag. So much to do and she didn't know where to start. Her mind skated and slid, every thought slick as ice.

She hurried inside. "Sam? Where's Beth?"

He pointed towards the bathroom, his eyes tired, bewildered. Ezekiel and the twins looked shattered, too. The crimson dog and the riot in church; then the Rapture sermon—it had been the longest day of their lives.

They should be sleeping.

But, of course, there'd be no sleep tonight.

There was still a chance she could save them. Her family didn't deserve to be buried alive. But it all depended on what Beth did next.

With Beth on her side, everything would turn out right.

After all, hadn't they, as little girls, watched fireflies dancing over the meadow and reveled in a love without end?

The bathroom door cracked open an inch. "Agnes, I can't fasten these eyelets. Can you help me, please?"

Her sister wore their mother's faded ivory wedding gown, beaded with false pearls. She shook like a leaf, teeth chattering as if she were freezing on that warm summer night. But she smiled bravely, holding out her little finger, and an electric hope cramped in Agnes's chest as their fingers clasped.

Silently, fervently, Agnes prayed. *God, let her finally see the truth. Amen.*

20

BETH

The time is nigh.
—PROPHET JACOB ROLLINS

Beth drew Agnes inside the bathroom and then drew her close, pressing their foreheads together. Her sister's breath smelled stale and tired.

Where had she been all day? Where had she been when Mr. Jameson—Matthew—had come to tell her they'd be married in just a few hours, and a terror that felt like dying had seized her?

Doesn't matter. She's here now.

"It's finally happening, Agnes. After the wedding, we're going underground."

Agnes looked at her, a puzzled appeal in her eyes.

"I'm not going, Beth. Neither should you. You don't have to marry him. And you don't have to go into the bunker. We can run."

"We can't miss the *apocalypse*, silly." But panic had a grip on her now.

I'll be Cory's sixth mother, she thought out of nowhere.

His father's wife.

And what is a wife? Do I even really know?

"You used to ask so many questions," whispered Agnes. "You used to be curious about the Outside. What happened?"

Beth remembered raw egg sliding down her face. "Everyone hates me. They all hate me so much."

She glanced in the bathroom mirror. Her face looked gruesome, greenish. How could she explain to Agnes that she felt the faithful's hate like a physical thing—like fetters around her throat, her wrists, her ankles?

"We can run tonight," Agnes was saying. "You, me, and the children."

Beth shot a glance at the door. On the other side, she heard Father muttering.

Surely her sister couldn't be serious.

"Agnes, what are you talking about? I'm getting *married*."

Agnes gripped her shoulders. "The Prophet wants to bury us for four hundred days. Do you understand what that means? Four hundred days, Beth! And Magda and Toby are infected. They'll spread the sickness. It will be hell down there, a living hell."

Beth covered her ears. The girl standing before her, eyes blazing, sounded like a stranger. A terrifying, demanding, Outsider stranger.

"Agnes, stop."

"People will die, and you'll be that old man's slave." She spoke in harsh whispers. "And what about Cory? Did you ever love him at all? Do you really want to be his *mother*?"

Beth buried her face in her hands, felt her own tears leaking.

Why couldn't Agnes see that she'd already decided to rip out her heart and replace it with another, one more suited to Red Creek's ways?

And Matthew Jameson was an upright man. Maybe she'd

finally be safe with him. Maybe, even in the bunker dark, she'd have something worth living for.

It was a thin hope. But she'd cling to it. It was all she had.

She gestured to her wedding dress, still only half-buttoned. "Can't you see it's too late?"

Horror filled Agnes's eyes, and for a second Beth wanted to take it back. Wanted to say, *Yes, I'll run with you, of course I will.*

But her gown was very heavy. Weighing her down.

"I love you, Beth," Agnes said. "And I'm sorry—so awfully sorry—for what has happened to you."

The words resounded in the cramped bathroom. Her sister took a single step back, and Beth felt a chasm yawn between them. Dimly, she was aware she'd refused her last chance—but only dimly. Her mind was clouded with wedding lace and the terror of getting what she thought she wanted.

Where could she go but deeper into that numbness that she called repentance?

"Ezekiel can't survive the bunker. I've been sneaking him medicine. Meeting Outsiders with prescriptions."

Beth nodded, barely registering the revelation of the secret she'd longed to know.

"I'm not going into the Temple," Agnes continued doggedly. "I'm leaving with Ezekiel tonight. If you come with me, we can take the kids. We can get them out of here. Give them a life Outside. But I can't save them alone."

Beth touched Agnes's wrist. "I guess I always knew you'd be the one to leave. You're the strong one, Agnes. The one with the—" Her throat constricted around the word *destiny.* "It was always going to be you. But I can't help you. I've made my choice. My life is here."

Confusion and sadness flickered in Agnes's eyes.

How had they lost each other? When had they grown so far apart?

Beth had believed she had no desires left, that she'd cried them all out in this very bathroom, but it wasn't true.

Suddenly, she couldn't stand the thought of marrying without Agnes there to see her. The church would feel empty without her sister in it.

"Come to my wedding," she begged. "I want someone there who really knows me."

Agnes hesitated, then shook her head.

Beth's heart drummed her terror. *My God, she's going to deny me even this.*

"I can't. I have to go now, before it's too late."

She begged. "I'll make sure you have a chance to slip away. It's my wedding, after all." She lowered her voice. "Agnes, please. I'm so scared."

Agnes held her eyes. Finally, she nodded. "Turn around. I'll button you up."

"So, you'll be there?" She craned to meet her sister's eyes.

Agnes winced. "Of course, I will. And Beth." Her hands stilled.

Beth met Agnes's eyes through the mirror glass. They were round and black, all pupil, and her head cocked to one side like she was listening to some sound no one else could hear. The air around her almost seemed to *shimmer*, like heat over the church road at noon.

No. Her heart thudded in her chest. *You're imagining things.*

"You have my blessing, Beth Ann," Agnes whispered—invoking her middle name, their mother's name. "God bless you in your time of need."

The words sent shivers down her spine.

Then Agnes—eyes still vague and strange, head cocked—kissed her cheek.

A burning, electric shock of a kiss. Beth took a shuddering step back like her sister's lips had scorched her.

When she looked back at Agnes, her eyes had cleared.

"What was that?" she demanded, panicky. "What did you *do*?"

Agnes blinked. "What do you mean? I don't have a wedding present. But I wanted to give you something. I'm sorry it's not—well, cloth or china, or something like that." Her voice broke. "But please know you'll always be in my prayers."

The words were so heartfelt they melted Beth's memory of any strangeness.

Agnes had always had that funny habit of cocking her head like she was listening to some mysterious song. The shock Beth had felt when her sister kissed her must have been nothing but static electricity, and her dark, pupil-black eyes only a trick of the light.

Eyelets fastened. Fingers linked.

Then the bells tolled midnight, and Beth breathed in deep, determined to meet whatever the future might bring.

Before dawn, she'd be a patriarch's wife.

21

AGNES

Glory in the Rapture. Glory in the eye of God.
—Prophet Jacob Rollins

The wedding was over in a brutal ten minutes.

What bothered Agnes most was that there wasn't a single flower in the church—not even for Mrs. King's casket. Beth dazzled in white—she was twice as beautiful as any girl ever married there—but no one cared, and no one wept when Father gave her away.

Their mother attended for once, but her face was puffy, her vision unfocused. Did she even recognize her own wedding dress?

There wasn't even any cake.

Beth deserved better. So much better than this.

But she bore up well. If Agnes weren't so heartbroken, she'd feel proud. As she watched Beth hold her head up at the altar, her eyes meeting Matthew's with only the slightest tremor, she realized there'd never been any reason to protect her from her secrets. Agnes would have done anything to go back to that night when her sister asked for the truth, and she'd denied her.

How wrong can a person be, God? How could I have been so mistaken?

After the ceremony, the Prophet summarily gave Mrs. King's eulogy and then, finally, his great announcement. With his arms outstretched beneath his black robe, he looked like a vulture, declaring:

"The Rapture has come at last!"

Agnes gripped the pew's wooden edge, readying herself.

She would kiss the children goodbye, hiding her tears, then slip out with Ezekiel. They'd run for the trailer, grab some clothes and the cooler, then take the truck. With any luck, they'd be half-way to Holden by the time anyone missed them.

With the Rapture breathing hard and fast, who'd care where she had gone?

She glanced once more at her siblings, trying to memorize each of their faces.

Sam reminded her of a string bean, balanced as he was on the verge of a growth spurt. Pimples were already sprouting at his temples. He was full of agitated hope. He quirked a smile at her, then playfully yanked Mary's blond braid.

The twins, half-asleep in the pews, leaned on each other. They looked like porcelain miniatures, little figurines asleep. She bent over their heads and knew with a sudden contraction of her heart that they wouldn't remember her last kiss—they were just too tired.

Father held her mother's hand tightly, his shoulders tense. He would force his wife into the Temple if he had to.

But Agnes didn't think he'd have to force her. Her mother looked exhausted. Spent. Her hair mussed from her bed.

She met Agnes's glance across the aisle.

Was there a tiny spark of interest buried in her numb expression? She'd never know—not if she meant to live.

As for the rest of the faithful, she mourned the women and

children—especially the children. The little Hearns and Jamesons and Kings she'd watched grow. They'd sicken in the putrid air, starved for light and fresh food. But her greatest fear was Magda, who leaned on her older brother's shoulder, panting even in the cool church air.

Agnes swallowed. Magda would be sick soon—petrified and vicious like the dog. But the faithful didn't know that, because they didn't believe in sickness. Only in good and evil, demons and angels.

They'd be sitting ducks.

She took Ezekiel's hand—*don't look back*—and together they headed for the door.

It was bolted. Locked.

Her hand fell away, fluttering helplessly.

"What's wrong?" Ezekiel asked.

Agnes had no words. Only an awful, sinking feeling.

"We go now, tonight." The Prophet's voice tolled like a heavy bell. "Fathers watch your children, and husbands your wives. See that they reach the Underground Temple, for the Devil is working still..."

Agnes turned slowly, fearfully. The Prophet gestured for their attention, but she could only think of Ezekiel.

How he'd looked as a toddler, reaching up to her from his crib. How she'd promised to always protect him.

How for her foolishness, they'd face the rotting dark.

22

AGNES

For this we were chosen. To live, when the filthy and
bloodstained must die.
—PROPHET JEREMIAH ROLLINS

In the pit of night, Agnes and Ezekiel stood on a grassy hill at the top of a staircase leading deep into the ground. They were two in a line of three hundred slowly descending into the Underground Temple.

Agnes wanted to bolt—to run—but her legs were leaden, the muscles impossibly heavy and useless. She heard Ezekiel's breath jagging in her ears, and her own breath, too.

There was no longer any hope of escape.

One by one the congregants descended those stairs. Faithful. Calm. Obedient.

No matter how she willed them to open their eyes—to see clearly just once before it was too late—their gazes were mirror empty, mirror bright. They'd been raised to believe this was their destiny, and that God protected them no matter what. They'd been raised like cattle for this slaughter.

Weeks ago, Agnes would've walked down those stairs without a second thought. Tonight, she was horror-struck.

The Hearns, the Sayleses, and the Kings—except for the already dead Mrs. King—all burying themselves alive in a common grave.

Agnes's family was next in line, with the Rollinses and the Jamesons bringing up the rear.

She hadn't found a single chance to run. Father kept a close eye on his children as they walked from the church, because the Prophet had warned: "Watch the little ones, that they don't succumb to weakness."

Was this really how her life would end? And Ezekiel—without his insulin...

The bunker door was an open mouth ahead of her.

Father descended, holding his wife's knobby elbow to guide her. It'd been years since Agnes had seen them touch.

Resignation swamped her mother's dull, wandering eyes, but when she spotted Agnes, she seemed to wake.

"Beth," she hissed—mixing up her own daughters. "Beth, what're you still doing here?" She shooed her with her emaciated hands. "Get away, get away!"

"Sweetheart," Father whispered into her hair. "Calm down now."

And together, they disappeared into the dark.

Then Sam—oh, Sam!—she groaned, watching him bravely beginning his long-awaited adventure, shredding her soul in the process. She wanted to call out some final words to him but couldn't think what she'd say.

Be brave? He was already brave. *I'm sorry?* He wouldn't understand.

She couldn't watch the twins go. She could only look up at the moon and focus on not screaming. The moon glowed cold, indifferent. She didn't know, dear God, how much grief a body could bear.

Then it was Agnes's and Ezekiel's turn.

She peered down at the twisting, narrow stair. The Underground Temple smelled of cement and stale air. She heard voices—tinny, trapped.

Ezekiel balked, backing into her legs. "I don't want to go!"

Her eyes darted. She could feel the people behind her, a current of bodies prepared to push and prod if she resisted.

Earlier she'd caught sight of Magda in the crush, the girl sickly, shivering with fever. Soon she'd be raring to snap, touch, bite. One would sicken, then another, and another, and then they'd fuse together to feather a fearsome underground Nest.

The faithful thought they were sheltering from the Outsider apocalypse.

But they were so very wrong.

She recalled the psalm: *The heathen are sunk down in the pit that they made: in the net which they hid is their own foot taken.*

"Go on. Your turn." Mr. Jameson spoke impatiently from behind her, with Beth, his beautiful bride, beside him. His beard was full, white. In the moonlight, his eyes were steely.

The prayer space. It will help me.

She dove deep inside herself and tried to find it. But terror overwhelmed her. She couldn't hear anything. No humming. Only a vast silence.

Distraught, her eyes fluttered open.

She should've gone with Danny when she'd had the chance. She shouldn't have let Beth talk her into attending her wedding. Now she'd failed herself and Ezekiel, too.

Shivering and powerless, she felt cruelly forsaken by God.

What had it all been for anyway? The phone, the Outsiders? Her slow, painful awakening? Where was her power when she needed it most?

A wild, unexpected shriek came from behind her.

Beth was having a fit, rolling in the grass, soiling her wedding dress.

"I won't go! I won't go!"

She was kicking and screaming like a tantrummy toddler or a woman gone mad.

But Agnes knew better.

I'll make sure you have a chance to slip away, she'd said.

Tears pricked her eyes. *Oh, Beth. Oh, my sister.*

The patriarchs rushed her. "The Devil's infected her! Hold her!"

The men formed a circle, and the remaining women and children stared—embarrassed, frightened, appalled. Mr. Jameson picked Beth up bodily and hauled her towards the hatch door, knocking Agnes roughly aside. Beth gripped the walls, refusing to be forced.

"What're they doing to her?" Ezekiel moaned. "What're they *doing?*"

"Dang it, she bit me!" Matthew Jameson howled.

All eyes were on Beth, and Agnes had her window.

Her chance.

She backed away slowly at first, working herself and Ezekiel deeper into the dark. One step. Another. Her hands trembled as she slipped into a circle of trees, her arms wrapped around Ezekiel's small, heaving chest.

"Be very quiet," she whispered. "Don't make a sound."

They faded into the shadows. She prayed death wouldn't notice them, that the men with torches wouldn't turn their way.

Mr. Jameson pried Beth's hands from the hatch. He forced her down the stairs, and the grim procession resumed, Beth's screams fading.

Agnes stood frozen, staring at the place where her sister had been but moments ago.

I'll always remember this, she swore to Beth now. *I'll never forget what you sacrificed.*

The Jameson family, one by one, went down into the bunker. The Prophet's twenty-one children, led by eleven obedient wives, went down into the bunker.

None looked back.

The Prophet himself was the last to go. Agnes wondered what he thought, as he stared across the moonlit fields.

Was he hearing some scrambled version of God's voice in his mind? Or wondering where His God had gone?

Then he, too, took the stairs and pulled the heavy hatch closed after him.

Sealing Red Creek's three hundred into the rapturous dark.

23

AGNES

When the Rapture comes at last, there will be no safe
haven in the tortured world Outside.
—Prophet Jacob Rollins

Insulin. Fresh vegetables. Bread, cheese, a change of clothes. Ezekiel's Sheep—don't forget that—and crayons, too. Flashlight, spade. All the secrets buried in her garden—spare meter, syringes, batteries. Socks, car keys, dish soap (who knew why?), and a gallon of milk that would spoil if she left it, spoil like Red Creek because no one was coming back.

The sight of dishes moldering in the sink and Sam's toy truck, forgotten on the floor—*Too much, don't think about it.*

Phone in her dress pocket, but what was she forgetting? Something important. What?

"Agnes?" Ezekiel stood, disoriented and afraid.

"What is it?"

He was staring at the unmade beds. "I don't want to leave them. I don't want to go."

"But, Ezekiel, there's no insulin in the bunker. Remember?"

"The Prophet said the Lord will be there."

Her braid had come undone, unraveling down her back. "It's lies. Only lies."

"I don't care. I want Beth. I want Sam." He was coming apart, crumbling. "Agnes, I want to go back."

"We can't," she said, more sharply than she'd meant to.

Her pack on her back. Keys in hand. There was still time for the Prophet to count his faithful and decide to come after them. She doubted he'd bother, but she couldn't take the risk.

The phone. She typed:

> We're leaving now, Danny. Are you very far away? Can you meet us somewhere?

Ezekiel tugged her sleeve. "Agnes? I changed my mind. I want to go back."

She whirled on him, exasperated. "Ezekiel, you just have to trust me."

He darted for his cot, the safest place he knew.

Agnes scooped him up before he could get there, and he yowled like a cat, beating his heels against her belly. She hardened her heart as she headed out the door—the screen slamming behind them, shocking the aluminum walls. The picnic cooler was beneath one arm, and her brother in the other, her strong muscles straining.

"Agnes, take me back!"

Suddenly, she remembered what she'd forgotten. The important thing.

"Darn it," she muttered, heading back inside the house.

She dropped Ezekiel and went to her side of the bed. She'd hidden what was left of Beth's diary beneath the mattress. It was all that remained of her sister, whom she already counted among the dead. She pressed the book tightly to her chest.

A note. I owe her a note, just in case.

She grabbed a pen, ripped a sheet from the diary, and scribbled, knowing Beth would likely never find it.

Agnes had seen the bunker. She knew it was a tomb.

She heard another door slam—the bathroom, this time—and a fumbling as Ezekiel tried to lock himself inside.

"Ezekiel! Hold still!"

She hurried. He hadn't succeeded in locking the door—it was a bolt lock, and he was too short to reach it.

He sobbed when he saw her.

She lifted him, ignoring his agonized cries. She'd nearly reached Father's white pickup when fear gripped her.

What if the gas tank was empty or the engine was dead?

She opened the door and thrust Ezekiel into the passenger seat before running to the driver's side. Hands shaking, she turned the key in the ignition. The engine started. The tank was half-full.

She breathed out.

She heard Danny's voice say, *Parking brake, then put it in drive.*

Check the rearview mirror but ignore the screaming child.

"Agnes? Agnes?"

Headlights bored holes into the dark, illuminating empty trailers, the abandoned town.

She jammed the accelerator. Beneath her, the truck ripped to life—rushing forwards, defying gravity. A feeling as powerful and frightening as freedom itself. She roared down the road, past the church she hoped never to see again, onto the main road leading to the gate. She was nearly there, nearly escaped, and she tasted freedom on her tongue like something sweet.

Now she thought if she focused hard, she could uncover the prayer space from where it was hiding inside the hovel of her fear.

She couldn't close her eyes while driving, but she could open her mind. She could meditate on peace and prayer and let the sense come alive.

Think big like God, she thought. *Think wide.*

The prayer space exploded awake. It rippled around her, Ezekiel, and the truck, taking in the road and the night sky, singing and calling and whooping for joy like a bird suddenly released from a wire trap.

Driving, she heard the world come alive again, and she held tight to the knowledge that everything was connected and that God was the connection running through everything. The prayer space was inside her and beyond her, too, speaking and chanting and humming sweetly through every seemingly separate particle.

Where have you been? Tears flooded her cheeks. *Where have you been?*

She heard the tight ringing of Red Creek's great, spired gate, wrapped in locks and chains. Their village, closed for the Rapture.

Seat belt? Danny's voice echoed.

"Ezekiel, can you buckle up?" She snapped her own belt into place.

He was crying hysterically. She wished he could feel what she did: the warm glowing rightness of what they'd done to survive.

She wouldn't get out of the truck, couldn't risk that one of the patriarchs had gone topside to find them. She reached across Ezekiel's lap—he slapped at her arm—and snapped his seat belt into the buckle. On the slippery gravel, she lost control of the truck for a moment, and her muscles tightened.

What am I doing? I can't drive.

It's all about confidence, Danny had said. *Check your mirrors. Get your bearings. Don't be afraid of speed. Oh, and don't text and drive.*

Why, oh, why hadn't he texted her back?

She slammed on the accelerator, feeling the truck lurch beneath them. Ezekiel gripped the leather seat belt, eyes wide as they sped towards the gate.

"Agnes!"

"It's a big truck," she said. "We'll be okay."

Letters in rusted iron read RED CREEK in an arch. She focused on the prayer space; the stars, singing silver; and the sky beyond. They should be trapped by now—slowly dying in the Underground Temple—but they weren't.

They were free.

The truck struck iron with a deafening crash, but Agnes didn't dare close her eyes. The gate gave in an instant, and then they were Outside.

PART
TWO

24

AGNES

I had fainted, unless I had believed to see the goodness of
the Lord in the land of the living.

—PSALM 27:13

Agnes sped through layer after layer of darkness on her way out of Red Creek. In the rearview mirror, the iron gates shrank into the night and the church steeple withered to a lonely hillside cross. Ahead, a green sign blared: HOLDEN, 33 MILES.

The truck pitched as she hit the gas—wanting, needing, to fly. The prayer space was with her, thrumming inside her chest like a second heart. She was deeply relieved to still hear God singing in everything. Part of her had been afraid that the prayer space would vanish the instant she left home.

Trees whistled as she flew down that road, and the asphalt glimmered in the moonlight, whispering infinite possibilities beneath the rubber of her tires.

She'd finally made it out, but new fears washed in like cold water on a tide. Where would they go? What would they do? And would Ezekiel ever forgive her for saving his life?

In the passenger seat, he clutched Sheep and wept pitifully.

Agnes waited it out, her damaged knuckle whitening against the wheel. She'd had no choice. It was run or die.

He hiccupped. "Where are you taking me?"

"Somewhere better," she promised. "Somewhere safe." He didn't need to know that she had no idea where that might be.

"What about Sam?"

She blinked rapidly, fending off tears. She couldn't think about the other kids now. She had to focus on driving, on getting them far away from the bunker's hungry maw. She still felt it tugging like a magnet, threatening with every heartbeat to pull them back in. After so much terror, it was impossible to believe they'd truly escaped, and panic coursed through her veins.

The bunker steps, the people of Red Creek urging her down, down—

She leaned harder on the gas and the hill crested. A moment too late she realized she was going eighty. *Too fast.* Her stomach dropped as the truck lifted into the air. They thudded at the hill's bottom with a nerve-jangling jolt, and Ezekiel lost it.

"I want to go back! Take me back! Take me *back!*"

"Calm down. Your blood sugar—"

He pointed an accusing finger. "If you don't take me back, you're going to hell, Agnes. You're going to *hell, hell, hell!*"

She winced. It didn't mean he wouldn't thank her one day.

Compulsively, Agnes checked the rearview mirror for headlights. There was nothing but darkness behind, and despite her fears, her rational mind knew the mirror would stay dark. To the Prophet, one little boy and a rebellious girl weren't worth the trouble—not now that the Rapture was at hand.

They skidded again. If she didn't get hold of herself, she was going to crash, and if she wrapped their truck around a tree tonight no one was coming to save them. She'd seen such a thing once before, when one of the Hearn boys went joyriding in his father's truck. He'd struck a tree and wound up with a crushed windpipe. The people were too faithful to call an ambulance, but it probably wouldn't have mattered. He'd died within the hour.

She made herself slow down, then stopped the truck on the side of the road. She needed to catch her breath, still her shaking hands. Ezekiel beat his heels against his seat, howling like a hellcat. She ignored him.

In the pitch dark, the highway lamps were empty glass eyes. Danny said the power had been out for weeks, but Red Creek ran on generators, and she hadn't been prepared for the reality of true night. In the parked truck, it was hard to keep her spirits up. The idling engine ticked like a clock. Even with Ezekiel beside her she felt very much alone. More than anything in the world, she wished Danny were with her now.

She scrambled for the phone in her dress pocket, needing to reassure herself it was still there. She breathed a sigh of relief when she felt its weight in her hand. Ezekiel studied the black device, his arms wrapped tightly around himself. He wasn't screaming anymore. Just rocking, back and forth. The stars appeared frozen beyond the windshield, silver needle points in the black fabric of the sky.

"I want to go home."

"We can't," she told him. "Everyone's already inside the bunker."

"We should be there, too."

"Why, Ezekiel?"

He looked at her like she'd grown a second head. "Because God wanted it."

"No. The *Prophet* wanted it. And he has nothing to do with God."

His face twisted. "You're lying! Take me back!"

"You'll die if I do. You don't want to die."

"I want to go to *heaven!*"

The word flamed from his mouth and scorched her. Heaven was something Agnes hadn't thought of in a long while. She'd been too busy trying to save her family. Now doubt pricked her heart. Was she absolutely, 100 percent certain she was going the right way? That heaven wasn't lost forever behind them?

The prayer space hummed a warning, and she looked up to see a stag crossing the road. Its coat was red marbled in her headlights, its eyes stony and unafraid. It slowed as it neared.

Ezekiel whispered, "See? A demon."

But Agnes didn't see that at all. She saw a poor, sick creature sniffing the air, then deciding their truck was only metal and not worth its time.

She remembered the Book of Habakkuk. After the prophet's home burned to the ground, his faith scrambled on like a deer finding its footing even in desolate, dangerous places. She prayed hers could do the same.

Illuminated by the headlights, the stag twitched its crimson tail and trotted away. Stone hooves echoed on asphalt. The prayer space waited until the deer disappeared, then fell quiet.

No, she didn't doubt her choice. Dark as it was, the Outside could never be as bleak as the fate she'd left behind. She just needed a safe place to get her bearings, that was all.

The phone rang then, and Agnes and Ezekiel both jumped.

"Hello?"

A crackle. "Agnes?"

She couldn't believe it—Danny. Thank God. "Danny, we just left Red Creek, and now I don't know where to go. Are you at the hospital? Can we come see you?"

"Not—"

He broke off, and for a terrifying instant that felt like free fall, he was gone. Disappeared into thin air.

"—but my mom already left to go after me, very dangerous on the—"

"Who's that?" Ezekiel asked, curious in spite of himself.

She held a finger to her lips. "Danny? I can't hear you."

"—make it to the Third Municipal Library? We'll be here for—"

Suddenly, another voice on the phone. Strong. Authoritative. Even the airwaves obeyed that voice, and the reception evened out.

"Agnes? This is Matilda. Do you have a road map? You'll find Gila's library marked."

Agnes reached across Ezekiel to open the glove compartment. The closure dropped open like a mouth, and she riffled clumsily among the documents.

"Agnes, dear? We can't stay on the line."

Deep in the glove box, she found a yellowish, weather-beaten road atlas.

Relief. "Yes! I have a map."

"Good," said Matilda. "Keep your phone charged. We'll see you soon."

Ezekiel calmed when he understood they were going to meet Matilda. Agnes didn't know how much he remembered of her, but he must've felt some reassuring connection to the woman who'd saved his life.

She gave him the job of navigator and that helped, too. By the shine of the overhead light he traced the intertwining roads—Agnes never would've guessed a world could contain so many—to a town called Gila.

"We'll go back to Red Creek soon," Ezekiel told her in a tone she didn't dare contradict. "We'll go back for Beth and Mary and Faith and Sam."

Gila's library was located on the outskirts of the city, well past Holden—or anywhere she'd ever dreamed she'd be. Agnes resolved to drive through the night, because she felt safe inside the truck, and even safer on the move. Trees rushed past the window, dark shadows blurring. She kept focused on driving—braking at stop signs, scanning the horizon.

Then Ezekiel asked, "Where are the other cars?"

And just like that, she panicked again. Because Ezekiel was right—the road was too empty. With so many millions of Outsiders living in the state, shouldn't someone else be traveling, even at night?

Millions are already infected, Danny'd told her, *and lots of people are running for the coast. Arizona's emptying out.*

"The Rapture," Ezekiel mumbled. "That's where. God's punishing them."

"Not every Outsider deserves to die." Agnes willed him to understand. "Lots of them are perfectly good."

Ezekiel's face was glum. "The good ones are all in their bunkers, I bet."

She sighed. "You didn't want to go down into the bunker. Not when you were standing right there. Remember how dark it was?"

He sniffed.

She spoke gently. "It's not the Rapture. I promise we'll find other people soon."

But they didn't. The night grew older, and she felt an eerie, overbearing silence hovering like a vulture. Terror bled into exhaustion, and she wished she could crawl into a hole and sleep for a year. But she had to keep driving, despite her nagging fear that they'd fled too late. That the world she'd worked so hard to reach was already gone.

Another fluorescent sign: LEAVING HOLDEN. GILA 60 MILES.

Agnes pressed the gas pedal, determined not to let the empty, endless miles rattle her. Even if Holden was completely abandoned, it was just one town. Just one place. In Ezekiel's hands, civilization's map was sweeping, and somewhere they'd find a home among those squiggled lines. The Outside world was vast, and they'd only just arrived.

Sixty miles to the library, she mouthed. *Only sixty miles to go.*

25

BETH

*I am forgotten as a dead man out of mind: I am like a
broken vessel.*

—PSALM 31:12

There was nothing holy about the bunker; nothing sacred
about the dark.

Beth knew that within seconds of being forced down those
stairs. At first, her fight had been for show, a ploy to buy Agnes
time to slip away. But then, as her husband raged, as he pushed
and prodded her more like livestock than a bride just married
in the sight of God, something snapped—and Beth struggled in
earnest.

She didn't want to go down into the Temple.

So she fought. Slapped and kicked, bit and roared.

She would've kept fighting forever if it hadn't been for the
heavy pop of her shoulder, the red explosion of pain as it came free
of its socket. Even then, she'd thrashed as well as she could in her
wedding lace, running on pure terror. If she'd had the strength,
she'd have killed Matthew Jameson for just one more breath of
clear night air. And she'd have run, like Agnes, as far and as fast as
her legs could carry her.

As for her newfound piety?

Now that it was too late, it was crystal clear: She owed these people nothing. For the last few weeks she'd lulled herself into a Red Creek sleep, but down here, she was wide-the-hell-awake.

A single bulb was the only light swinging at the bottom of that horrid flight. The bunker smelled cellar damp, and little kids wept in their mothers' laps. She didn't have time to notice anything else, because Mr. Jameson was barking about the Devil's influence and spitting words like *quarantine*. Pained red stars shot across her eyes and she couldn't parse it all, but he wanted her kept away from his other wives and kids, she understood that much.

His voice—her husband-of-a-night's voice—was riddled with disgust.

New Beth, the post-egging Beth, wanted to cringe and beg and die of shame. But Old Beth had finally woken up, and she thought, *Right back at you.*

"Put her with the other sinner," someone said, and before she could blink, she was thrust into a closet.

Poor dying Magda was there, and Beth's shoulder pain, of course, but precious little else. Not even light.

For a while, she beat the door with her one good fist. Exhausted, defeated, she slumped.

I made a mistake.

Or, as Cory would say: *I fucked up.*

And boy, had she ever.

Dark. Horribly dark.

She'd thought her eyes would adjust, but hours passed, and the darkness remained heavy, thick. Beth's left arm was useless, a throbbing weight at her side. The way it hung from her shoulder nauseated her.

She marked the time in sermons—she could hear the Prophet preaching on the other side of the wall, reciting those apocalyptic exhortations they'd all heard so many times before.

She heard the one about the Outsiders blazing in fire and brimstone and dearly regretting their earthly sins. And the one about the chosen people, descending into the Underground Temple. The Prophet barely even took a breath before launching into the discourse about the pale horse—*"And he who sat on it had the name DEATH, and killed with sword and with pestilence and by the wild beasts of the earth."*

She rested her head against the door as muffled words washed over her. An arm's length away, Magda wept.

And wept and wept.

"What did I do to deserve this?"

"Spread rumors about me, for one thing," Beth snarled, trying to rub some feeling back into her left hand. "Convinced those boys to egg my house."

Magda cried harder.

Beth regretted her words. The girl wanted a sharp smack in the face, maybe, but she certainly hadn't earned her brush with a demonic dog. No one deserved that.

Beth couldn't see Magda through the dark, but she could hear fever chattering her teeth. The Prophet said demons couldn't harm the righteous, so if Magda were hurting now, she had no one to blame but herself. It was like dream logic. Old Beth had never quite believed in curse by stomach flu, or damnation by sniffle. But she hadn't questioned it as much as she should have. Sometimes, it was just easier to go with the flow than to fight the red current.

At least, until the current threatened to swallow you whole.

Beth tapped her forehead against the wooden door, unintentionally disturbing gauzy spiderwebs. She hated spiderwebs. Hated the dark, too. Screams smoked in her throat and she was sure that after another hour, she wouldn't be able to swallow them. And if—*when*—she did scream, it'd be torture for the twins and cannon fodder for the patriarchs.

Do you hear? they'd say. *Those are the shrieks of rebellion, the mad wailing of the demon...*

Magda moaned, and Beth jerked, jostling her dislocated arm. Sweat broke out all over her body. Flush against her skin, the wedding lace began to itch. How many hours had she spent sewing on those stupid faux pearls?

Magda will die in this closet, she realized. *But what about me?*

A selfish thought, but then again, she'd never wanted to be a saint. She'd only ever wanted to have friends who laughed with her, and a sister who loved her, and someone cute to talk to when loneliness spiked. And for that—and, maybe, for blind stubbornness, too—she'd been doomed to this.

Not fair. Not freaking fair.

"I've had word that one among us has broken with our faith," the Prophet droned. "She fled the sanctuary tonight and took an innocent with her. We will pray for the child's dying to be painless. But for the girl—I'm told her name was *Agnes*—we pray for eternal destruction and unending pain. *Amen.*"

Beth nearly laughed out loud.

Jesus, *Agnes*. She'd made it out.

Of course she had. Things always worked out for her sister. Fierce pride coursed through her, and in the shadow of that pride lingered jealousy, dark and chilled. Jealousy had a shadow, too—and it was rage. Beth gripped that emotion like a drowning woman grips a floating branch.

"How could you leave me and the kids?" she murmured into her hands. *"How could you?"*

But she already knew. Agnes would do anything to save Ezekiel.

And it was Beth's own fault she'd wound up here. Her own fault that Sam and the twins must face the dark, too.

But Beth refused to bear the brunt of the blame. That belonged to the Prophet, and the patriarchs, and the horror that was Red Creek at its heart.

Murderers, she thought. *Murderers!*

Having seen the bunker for herself, Beth felt positive no one was meant to see the light again. The cold, damp bunker, already smelling ripely of human waste, was a mass grave.

And maybe she deserved to die, for being foolish enough to believe marrying Matthew Jameson would make her safe.

Staring into the impenetrable dark, Beth ground her teeth and swallowed her screams.

Silence. The people had been ordered to sleep, to *save their strength for the coming of the Lord.* In the hush, Magda's small movements were a lot louder—and she smelled a lot worse. Her stench reminded Beth of the mouse carcass she'd discovered behind the range ages ago, only stronger. And, unlike the mouse, she could talk.

"I'm changing," Magda rasped. "My skin—it's feels *tight.* I'm scared, Beth."

If she were Agnes, she'd be holding Magda now, trying to comfort the dying girl. Agnes wouldn't hesitate—hadn't hesitated either to pick up the dead mouse, saving Beth from having to dispose of it. Her sister did things like that out of kindness and unthinkably vast reserves of love, but also because that was simply who she was. Who she'd always been.

Think. She needed to think.

If God hadn't reached out and personally cursed Magda, then it all went back to the dog. The dog brushed Magda, and if Magda touched Beth—well, she didn't know what would happen, but she had a feeling it wouldn't be kisses, giggles, and a barrel of laughs.

She scooted closer to the door, cradling her bad arm and ignoring the guilty hammering of her heart. She couldn't risk touching Magda because there was still a chance she'd get out of this, somehow.

Wasn't there?

You're a survivor, her mother had told her once. *Not like Agnes.* You're *the survivor.*

Her mother might've been wearing that hat ass backwards, as Cory would say, but could she have spoken truth? Didn't Beth want, more than anything, to survive? To see the sun again, to feel the breeze, to smell the scent of vanilla, or anything other than Magda's awful stink?

Beth did. She very, very much did. All at once it was alive again, that part of her soul she'd shut down when a flying egg struck her face and words leapt out at her like rats—*Beth's been whoring with Cory Jameson. Burn in hell.*

They'd tried to kill the best, most world-loving part of her. But guess what? They'd failed. They'd praised the Lord, taken their shot, and missed. Now fair was fair, and it was her turn to play. She made a conscious effort to calm herself—*deep breaths,* Agnes always said, and it was so *annoying* how she was always right, even here—and set her mind to saving her own life.

She needed light, water, and to get the hell away from Magda. But before she could even think of those things, she needed to fix her arm. Somewhere, she'd heard foxes caught in a trap would bite their leg off rather than wait to die.

Well, she was at least as tough as a fox. Or had been once.

Carefully, she took a nip of her sleeve between her teeth. The old material ripped easily. She needed her skin bare. She couldn't take the chance her hand would slip when she tried to shove her shoulder back into place—she wasn't sure she'd have the stomach to try it twice.

She tore the sleeve free at her collarbone, ignoring the wave of dizziness that flushed up from the pain, and then, remembering all the reasons she didn't want to scream, rolled the fabric into a ball.

"Oh, Magda," she said, before stuffing the dirty dress sleeve into her mouth. "You'd better pray for me. Because this is *really* going to hurt."

26

AGNES

Our soul is escaped as a bird out of the snare of the fowlers:
the snare is broken, and we are escaped.

—PSALM 124:7

Hope burned in Agnes's chest almost unbearably bright. She'd driven these unfamiliar roads in the dark, and here was the dawn she'd earned, dawn in a town called Gila.

GILA—according to the map and the welcome sign.

What a beautiful, foreign-sounding name. After breathing Red Creek's suffocating air, she craved everything exciting and new.

So this is Outside.

On her way into town she'd recognized a post office, restaurants, a stable, and a school. It was all shuttered and abandoned now, with ominous flyers peppering the sidewalk like autumn leaves—REPORT SIGNS OF INFECTION IMMEDIATELY, DON'T WAIT!— but the Outsiders would get Petra under control soon. She was sure of it. Then the people would return, and Agnes and Ezekiel could set about making Gila a home.

She parked outside the library. She'd spread the map over her brother's sleeping form. He was muttering something, tortured even in dreams.

"Ezekiel." She nudged him awake. "We're here."

"Where?"

"The library, remember? We've come to meet our friends."

She helped Ezekiel out of the car. He stumbled, lurching clumsily, like running from the bunker had aged his poor soul.

"Sam," he insisted. "I want Sam."

Grief rumbled up from between her ribs. "I know. Be brave."

He wiped his runny nose with his sleeve.

"Now, wait," she said. "Before we leave the truck. What are you forgetting?"

Confusion clouded his face. "To pray?"

She shook her head. "Your insulin cooler. Now that we're Outside, I need you to be responsible for it. You're old enough to understand: It's life or death."

He reached into the back seat and tucked the cooler under his arm.

Then, together, they gaped at the old brick library building.

It was larger than their church, stately. On the lawn, an American flag flapped in the wind. A symbol the Prophet had hated enough to describe in detail. A weathervane spun at the roof's apex. It looked like some kind of dark bird, a grackle or a crow.

"Can I wait in the car?" Ezekiel asked.

"What? No," she said. "We're here to find a new home. Like the Hebrews out of Egypt."

"The Hebrews never saw the promised land," he reminded her. "They ate manna in the desert and then they died."

Okay, that was true. "I oversimplified. Their children's children made it home."

"And is that us?"

She stiffened because she didn't know. Beyond the faith that had raised them, who were they?

"Come on, Ezekiel. Let's go."

Hand-in-hand, they tackled the granite steps that led to the library's double doors.

She raised her fist, preparing to knock. Before she touched wood, the door creaked open, startling them. An Outsider stood at the threshold. Not Danny. Not Matilda.

A stranger.

Face-to-face with a brightly pretty girl in shorts and a strappy blue top, Agnes knew she should say something, but the sight of bare shoulders had stunned her silent. *Sinful.* A dire, Red Creek thought.

She was also thinking, *Danger.*

Ezekiel yanked her hand, urging her back to the safety of Father's truck.

"Are you Agnes?"

Her name in the Outsider's mouth—but where were Danny and Matilda? Had this girl done something to them? Stabbed them in their sleep?

She smiled, showing off the whitest, straightest teeth Agnes had ever seen. She couldn't read the stranger's smile, because Outsider manners were so alien. She didn't look like a murderer— her shiny lips candy pink—but who knew?

On the Outside, Agnes felt helpless as a child and resented it.

"Danny said you might be coming. He's walking the perimeter with Matilda, checking for infected. Want to come inside?"

It sounded sane enough—Danny and Matilda, keeping them safe. Only Ezekiel's eyes pleaded, *Don't make me do this.*

She glanced back down the rural road, debating. She wished someone were here to tell her what to do. But if she ever hoped to live among the Outsiders, she must get comfortable making decisions for herself.

On their family trips to Walmart, Father had always ordered them to avert their eyes from Outsider women. Flashes of color and bright white teeth were all she knew of them. Now free from Father's control, she could look more closely.

Despite her garish clothes, the stranger's eyes were mild, a pleasant maple-syrup color. She was Agnes's age, only thinner and more coltish. And she looked nice. Like she'd help you fold your laundry, maybe, or bake you cookies.

Outsiders are devious as snakes, whispered the Prophet.

Get out of my head, she thought back.

"We'll come inside. Thank you."

It felt like triumph to say it, but when she tried to step through the doorway, Ezekiel jerked her arm again.

Looking into her brother's anxious face, she thought of the prayer space. Wouldn't it warn her if danger was near? She slipped into it, briefly closing her eyes. It was getting easier. Some mysterious spiritual muscle grew stronger with every use.

Gila's quiet washed over her. She sensed a lawn behind the library and beyond that the dry rustling not of ponderosa pines, but of cacti and mesquite. Somewhere to the north, she heard the steady thrum of rushing water.

She also sensed a Nest. It ringed the town in a semicircle, vibrating and humming like Red Creek's crows, except this Nest was human, composed of dozens upon dozens of people. She could hear the shivering, human shape of them.

She tried to ignore her mounting dread. Nests couldn't hurt you directly—unlike the walking creatures. If what Danny had said was true, half the Southwest had likely Nested now.

And Gila could still be a good place. A safe place.

She only wished she could convince Ezekiel of that.

"I want to go home," he insisted, while the stranger looked on. He clutched Sheep to his chest, his eyes wide.

Agnes swallowed. "I know it's odd to be with Outsiders, but—"

"I want Father. I want Sam."

"We can have a fresh start here. A new life. Maybe, one day, you can even start school."

This was a dream, fragile as spun sugar. She voiced it quietly, like a prayer.

"I don't want to meet Outsiders! I just want to go *home*."

"Will you trust me, Ezekiel?" She felt desperate. "Please."

He stared at her. For a horrifying instant she pictured him bolting down the stairs and running headlong into the desert.

The Outsider interrupted. "Hey. Do you guys like macaroni and cheese?"

Ezekiel cocked his head.

"It's his favorite," whispered Agnes.

The girl put a hand on her hip and her top rode up, revealing another inch of bare skin.

Sinful, Agnes thought again, and hated herself for it.

"We're having macaroni for breakfast, because we're fresh out of oatmeal. We're happy to share."

Ezekiel studied Agnes, who kept her face carefully neutral. He had to learn to make decisions, too.

He marched inside the library like a condemned man, but at least he was moving forwards, not looking back.

The Outsider girl caught Agnes's eye and winked.

Thank you, she mouthed, and the girl shrugged. *Don't worry about it*, the gesture said.

It was a small moment of understanding between them, fleeting as a summer breeze. But to Agnes, crossing the threshold of

Gila's Third Municipal Library with her brother, his insulin, and all her hopes in hand, it meant the world.

———— ✺ ————

"It's not the right color," griped Ezekiel, staring down at his macaroni.

"Really? It's Kraft's," said the girl, who'd introduced herself as Jasmine.

Jazz, for short.

Her boyfriend, Max, hunched beside her. Even slurping his macaroni, he was easily the most attractive man Agnes had ever seen. He made handsome Cory Jameson look like a muddy sneaker. She'd have blushed if he'd so much as looked at her, but he showed no interest in anything but eating.

She blinked down at her food, which *was* shockingly orange—a neon, artificial color. She dipped her fork into her bowl, chewed, and swallowed.

"It's amazing."

She looked straight at Ezekiel, willing him not to be rude. Hunger got the best of him, and, doubtfully, he tasted his first bite. Then he smiled, his own sweet, boyish smile, and a knot inside her chest released.

They ate in a makeshift kitchen, an alcove that had once been an office, complete with filing cabinets and wire wastebaskets. The Outsiders had filled it with gadgets—hot plates, a coffee machine, a water filter—and turned a cabinet on its side for a table.

"There's no electricity, of course," Jazz explained. "But Matilda has a battery-powered camping stove with outlets. We use it to charge our phones, power the coffee machine, stuff like that. You can charge up, if you want."

"For what good it will do," Max mumbled through a mouthful of orange.

Agnes looked questioningly at Jasmine.

Jasmine jerked her thumb at him. "Max is convinced cell service will black out any day now. But as long as the towers stand . . ." She trailed off, looking suddenly anxious. "Anyway." She shook off her pall. "No one really knows what will happen, so it's better to look on the bright side, right?"

Right.

But Agnes felt like she was drifting in some surreal dream. Everything about their surroundings was just a little *off*, from the slick, shiny floors, to Jasmine's pierced ears, to Max's very un-Red-Creek-like slouch.

Strangest of all, though, was the library itself.

When Danny mentioned it, Agnes had pictured Mrs. King's small collection of instructional volumes—N *is for* Noah, *who saved the* Naughty *world*. But more books packed this building than she ever could've dreamed of. Both she and Ezekiel gaped, but the Outsider girl chattered away like it was nothing.

Thousands of books. *Thousands.*

Now Jazz poured herself a cup of coffee. She offered Agnes one, but she declined. Her nerves were shattered as it was.

"We got here a few days ago." The Outsider girl seemed determined to keep the conversation going. "We walked all the way from Arid and hooked up with Danny and Matilda by accident. Lucky thing, because we were all out of food. How do you know Matilda? Did you drive far?"

Agnes took a break from eating, not sure how much to tell.

Handsome Max gazed sleepily at them. His oversize T-shirt was emblazoned with the inscrutable phrase MODEST MOUSE.

Agnes was quiet a touch too long and the Outsiders exchanged a glance.

"We came from—up near Holden," she hurried to say. "We've never been to Gila before. How many people live here?"

"Is that a joke?" Max barked. "Obviously, we're the stragglers. Everyone is long gone."

Long gone.

Agnes suppressed a shiver.

She'd done her best, as they sped past barns and water towers and abandoned single-family homes, to imagine a future here. But it unnerved her that silence draped over everything, heavy as a wool blanket.

They ate manna in the desert and then they died, Ezekiel had intoned.

Also unsettling: In the corner of the kitchen someone had heaped a mountain of emergency supplies. Canned food, tents, flashlights, sleeping bags. Everything you'd need to sleep and travel rough. Everything you'd need if the world were ending.

Dread licked her like a frost, cold. "So—" she couldn't help asking. "When will everyone be back?"

Another fast, unreadable look.

"Didn't you hear about the evacuation?"

While Ezekiel scraped his bowl, Agnes struggled with the word. *Evacuation.* She only had the shadow of a guess for what it might mean.

Jasmine's eyes widened. "Oh my God. You're from Red Creek, aren't you?"

How did she know?

Was there something in her face that separated her from normal people—or possibly, something in her eyes?

"I wrote a report on fundamentalist cults for school," Jazz continued. "I read about the clothes you wear."

Agnes glanced down at her prairie dress, sweat stained and wrinkled after their long night, and touched the messy plait of her waist-long hair. So different from the girl's cropped boy cut.

Max, now grudgingly interested, raised a chiseled eyebrow. "What happened? Infection smoke you out?"

The bunker flashed before her eyes. She felt tears rising, but Ezekiel beat her to it, erupting into helpless, quaking sobs. He was seven years old, exhausted, and headed for a full-blown tantrum. In a moment, she knew, he'd be writhing on the floor.

"Shh, Ezekiel, shh."

"I want to go home," he hiccupped. "I want to go home, I want to go home!"

As the Outsider teenagers looked on, a horrible idea sprouted in Agnes's heart: *Wherever you go, Red Creek goes with you, and you'll never escape, not truly.*

Then Matilda appeared in the doorway, wearing pale green scrubs and a rifle slung over her shoulder. Ezekiel spotted the nurse who'd saved his life—his mother's age but looking at him with such tenderness—and his tears stuttered to a stop.

He flew wordlessly into her arms.

"Zeke, baby Zeke." Matilda enfolded him. "You made it. You're here."

Agnes stared at the two of them, her hand at her throat. Then she jumped up and threw her arms around the older woman, who smelled of lavender and good clean soap. Matilda wept, but tried to hide it, looking anywhere but directly into their faces.

She didn't think we'd make it, Agnes realized. *She thought Red Creek would catch us and kill us, as it was meant to do.*

Or failing that, the red creatures.

"Where's Danny?"

Matilda pulled back, her face grave, and terror crept up Agnes's spine. Watching, Max and Jasmine snapped alert.

"Was it an infected? Are they here?" Max's voice rumbled darkly.

"No, nothing like that, just the flu. He's checking his temperature. He'll be along."

Agnes shifted, agitated. Danny was the Outsider she knew best, and the intensity of her fear shook her. She couldn't imagine this Outside world without him in it. If he were gone—

"Agnes?"

She whirled like she expected to see a ghost, but it was Danny: a little worn, a little thin, but the same. A starry bridge of freckles over his nose.

And he was grinning.

To her sleep-deprived eyes, he looked like the opposite of the bunker. The opposite of the dark. She had to clench her fists at her sides to keep from running into his arms—a ridiculous, and ridiculously indecent, urge.

Having only ever seen each other in the land of her captivity, their meeting at the Third Municipal Library felt electric. In her mind, she imagined the bright sound of iron breaking.

"I knew you'd make it." He beamed at her. "I *knew* you would."

Then he tumbled into a chair, coughing like he'd die of it.

27

BETH

*For the enemy hath persecuted my soul; he hath smitten
my life down to the ground; he hath made me to dwell in
darkness, as those that have been long dead.*
—Psalm 143:3

Magda Jameson was changing.

Beth had been trapped in the small closet for almost twenty-four hours with nothing to eat or drink. Since she'd popped her shoulder back into its socket, the thirst was an ever-present voice in her head, threatening to drive her insane.

In the perfect dark, she saw only shadows, but still she knew exactly where Magda was—the girl was emanating heat like the coils of a stove. All night she'd shivered with fever, thrashing and writhing before she finally stopped moving entirely. She went so still Beth assumed, with guilty relief, that she'd finally died.

But she wasn't dead. Beth flinched at a dull, raking sound, like teeth grinding. Wide-eyed, she watched as the shadows in the corner tightened into a predatory crouch.

Magda—or the creature who'd been Magda—wasn't turned inwards towards her agony any longer.

Beth froze, thinking of the dog in church—how its nails

clicked against the floor, how it lunged with snakelike speed for Mrs. King. The Prophet shot the dog, but with no one to stop Magda, what would happen? Would she just pass on her disease and leave it at that? Or would she keep biting and biting? Would she swallow what she bit?

Outside their prison door, the Prophet ceased sermonizing, and that was a piece of luck, at least. It would've been too easy to crawl inside his reassuring words—*demons can't harm the righteous*—and fall back into the Red Creek sleep. Hours ago, she'd crunched her shoulder back into its socket and hadn't fainted when white pain blinded her. All that would be for nothing if she didn't keep fighting now.

Then Magda made a noise—an inhuman growl—and Beth flattened herself against the door.

Please tell me I imagined it.

A scratching against the cellar's wood floor. The Magda creature shuffled hesitantly closer, then nearer still. Beth saw the shadowy outline of her head bending down—horror of horrors—to *sniff Beth's toes.* Beth whipped her legs beneath her wedding skirt.

Magda's head snapped up. Her eyes were two smoldering points in the dark.

Beth's breath was ragged.

Sam once asked if you could die in a nightmare—keel over from fear alone. She'd told him no, but now she wondered.

"Magda. Don't come any closer. I'm warning you."

A pathetic threat. But there must've been some spark of the girl left inside that shell, because Magda settled back onto her ankles.

Keep talking. Better keep talking.

"Look, I'm sorry about Cory. But it wasn't fair to get your

friends to call me a whore. That really hurt. Made me feel like I was rotten inside, even though I never did anything. *Not anything.*"

Some of her words were whispers, some were shrieks—and at least two were a bald-faced lie, because she'd done plenty with Cory Jameson.

But it didn't matter. Magda was listening.

"I didn't realize until your father tried to tear my arm off, but the words he and the Prophet use—*righteous, holy, demon, whore*—they're worse than lies. They paint everything black and white and destroy what's in between. They make you feel so ashamed you'd do anything to feel clean again." Beth hadn't taken a breath since she'd started talking, and now she had a spinning, drowning feeling.

"Girls marry who they say and crawl into the bunker when they're told. But, Magda, it's a trap. Agnes knew. She—"

Magda growled again. Beth stopped talking. The intensity of the creature's stare told her it was no use. She was going to die in here.

The thing, once Magda, was going to kill her.

I want Agnes, she thought. *Dear God, I want Agnes.*

Even in the moment before a bloody death, her sister would've remained steady. She'd get that wise look on her face—that look like she was seeing layers deeper than anyone else. Beth would've clawed out her own eyes to feel Agnes's comforting presence beside her now.

The creature started to tremble, almost vibrate, and, facing death, Beth began to remember. She remembered Agnes staring over her garden while the air shimmered like heat around her, and Agnes bowing her head in prayer. She remembered Agnes weeping, arguing, then agreeing to stay in Red Creek to attend Beth's wedding, knowing full well the risk she took.

Agnes.

In the grips of dreamy terror, she knew a strange, unsettling truth. She couldn't say how—she had no evidence—but it was a kind of faith. Pure and true.

She knew: *This Magda-monster couldn't harm Agnes.*

Hadn't she felt something before her wedding? Hadn't she sensed some kind of—*power*—in that shocking, electric kiss?

You have my blessing, Beth Ann. God bless you in your time of need.

God smiled on her sister. Beth had always known it, deep down. If she were here, she'd be like Joseph in his coat of dreams. Untouchable.

But Beth wasn't.

The creature was readying to lunge.

Beth threw herself against the door. She beat it with her fists, screaming, "Let me out! Help!" She slammed with her good shoulder, but the wood never gave.

It was too late to pray but Beth tried anyway. She got as far as *God who art in heaven* when the door swung open, and a hand clapped over her mouth.

Someone pulled her into the bunker's great room—the single bulb painfully bright to her light-starved eyes—and pressed her back against the door. On the other side, Magda strained to break free.

"Help me push!"

"Cory?"

"Push," he hissed.

She was incredibly strong, this altered Magda, and they struggled to contain her in grim silence. Beth's foot slipped in sawdust, and the door yawned open. She scrambled back, adding her weight to Cory's.

The door slammed shut.

Cory's hands trembled as he shoved the key into the lock. The bolt took, and Magda went wild behind the door. Beth dearly wished she'd never heard the sound of her nails, snapping and breaking against splintering wood.

Cory stared. "Is that my sister?"

She touched his arm, shaking. "Not anymore."

"Toby's like that. Getting sicker every hour." Cory inhaled, straightened. "Everyone's sleeping. Be quiet and stay low."

He dropped to a crawl. She followed him into a cavernous maze. Their breath was earthy down here and her knees chafed against roots and stones. Cory seemed to know his way around. She'd never been so happy to see the dirty soles of a pair of shoes in her life.

They turned into a narrow tunnel. Cory switched on a flashlight, lighting a room packed with canned preserves. Unlike in the tunnel, they could stand. Silver spiderwebs clotted the crevices between jars, but Beth was so thirsty she didn't care. She snatched a jar off the shelf, unscrewed the lid, and drank deeply of peach juice. Her throat convulsed until she drained it. The syrup a sweet relief.

"My mothers canned most of this," Cory whispered. "Food for four hundred days."

Beth fought a wave of pain, her bad arm screaming after their crawl. *Don't think about it, not until we've gotten out.*

But did Cory even *want* to get out? Since those boys called her a whore, she'd avoided Matthew Jameson's son like the plague. Maybe he didn't mean to escape. Maybe he'd simply been unable to stomach the thought of her becoming Magda chow.

She looked into his eyes for a clue, and the longing in them disconcerted her. Eerily, his eyes were the spitting image of his father's—only Mr. Jameson had never longed for Beth.

Throughout the wedding service, he'd glanced down at his wristwatch or over his shoulder in the direction—she realized now—of the bunker. It made a kind of sick sense. After all, he'd waited decades for the world's end, for the one spectacular moment that would prove his life a righteous one. When the time was finally at hand, he'd gazed after it like a lover. Like Cory gazed at her now.

She wiped syrup from her mouth. "What's your plan?"

"To rescue you, then beat the Christ-hell out of here."

"I thought you wanted to be a patriarch with eleven wives," Beth shot back.

His face twisted. The reality of the bunker, the awful dark, had changed him, too. "Ignorant little shit, wasn't I?"

She agreed, but it wasn't the time to hassle him.

"How do we get out?"

"I know a way."

No one opposed them as they crawled through a rising, narrowing passageway. The people, exhausted, were sleeping. No one had thought to establish a guard—after all, who would want to escape into the fire-breathing Rapture?

"Look." Cory pointed at a small emergency hatch buried in a dark tunnel.

They both stared, breathing the earthy air, for longer than was wise.

"My sister would try to find the kids," Beth said numbly. "Get them out."

She felt, rather than saw, Cory look at her. "Is that what you want to do?"

God help her, but she didn't. Terror had pitted her heart, hollowed it. She pushed away the image of the children's faces, wondering if she'd one day regret this choice.

"We can't go back," she said. "They'd catch us, for sure."

"I tried to convince my brothers that what was happening to you and Magda was wrong." Cory coughed. "Unholy, even."

"And?" she whispered.

"They said, 'Two wayward girls aren't worth your soul.'" He sounded broken. Lost. "I think—I think I'll never see them again."

She took his hand. Squeezed it. He surprised her by reaching out, brushing a dirt smudge from her cheek with his thumb. Then he fumbled with the hatch and pushed it open.

Beth gasped fresh air in huge, grateful gulps. It was sweeter than peach juice. Sweeter than anything.

Cory climbed through and she followed, tripping over her dirt-caked wedding dress. She was aching to run and not stop until they reached Holden.

With a metallic *snick*, the hatch closed on their old lives forever.

They bolted for the trees.

Cory was fast, but maybe because of what she'd seen Magda become, Beth was faster. In the dark shelter of the forest, she held her bad arm close to her chest. *Don't look back.* In the trees, she felt her horror of a marriage close on her heels, and a red death, too. She sensed Magda and Matthew and the faithful's harsh judgments. She felt egg sliding down her face and the wind muttering, *whore, whore, whore.*

A mind-numbing *snap*, loud as a gunshot, stopped her in her tracks.

"Beth!" Cory howled, and she knew in her marrow what had happened.

Cory Jameson had triggered one of Red Creek's rusty, half-hidden traps.

She looked back. There was a dense patch of shadow between them, and that night, no moon to light betrayal.

I could just keep running. I don't have to stop.

A shameful thought, but there it was. She didn't have to stop. Later, when guilt fell deeper than shadows, she could tell herself she hadn't heard him cry out—that they'd been separated in the forest. After growing up in Red Creek, she knew how to believe what lies she needed to survive.

She hesitated a moment longer. Then she thought of Agnes—Agnes, and her unshakable love—and couldn't abandon him. She cradled her arm on the way back to Cory, and when she saw him doubled up in the undergrowth, she began to cry—but not for him. She'd been close, *so close*, half a mile, maybe, from the road. But close wasn't going to cut it, in the end.

"I think my leg's broken."

He was caught in a mouth filled with iron-sharp teeth, and she didn't know how to get him out. Even if she did, the unnatural crook of his leg told her they weren't going anywhere tonight. And he was bleeding into the forest loam. She could smell the copper tang.

She looked once more, longingly, into the shadows, then faced the cruel iron trap as she tried to shake the feeling that Red Creek had done them in at last.

You *could* die in a nightmare, you really could.

She only wished she could tell Sam.

28

AGNES

For a thousand years in thy sight are but as yesterday when
it is past, and as a watch in the night.

—PSALM 90:4

Danny had fallen sick sometime in the middle of the night, he explained while Matilda put Ezekiel—whom she off-handedly called Zeke—down for a much-needed nap.

"It's just a bug, probably caught it from Mom," Danny said. "She was working night and day there for a while. Typical, really."

Though the library was warm, he huddled inside his wind-breaker. Agnes didn't want to badger him with questions—but there were things she needed to know.

"Where did everyone go?"

"California, or Las Vegas." He adjusted his glasses. "There are military outposts all over the Southwest."

"We should all be somewhere like that," Max put in bitterly. "My town was a holdout, and wouldn't you know it, the Burn Squad blazed it down."

Pain blossomed in Jasmine's face.

Agnes wasn't the only one dealing with the ghosts of a ruined past, and she chided herself for her selfishness. It was new, extending her compassion to Outsiders and seeing them for what they were: real and human and capable of suffering, as she was.

"They killed people, this Burn Squad?" she asked.

"They're sickos." Max stuck a toothpick in his mouth and chewed it.

"It started with burning Nests," Danny explained. "The government sanctioned them for containment after the evacuation. But some of the Squads went rogue. Some of them decided it was more efficient, or more fun, to burn whole towns." He examined his hands. "Even with living people in them."

Agnes shuddered, picturing red licking flames, a Rapture of a different kind.

Danny took a long drink of water, and she remembered something she'd only barely registered on her journey from the high desert—with its towering pines and clear, cold air—to this parched lower region.

"Where are all the birds?"

The Outsiders blinked at her, and she tried again. "I just mean, I didn't hear any birds singing this morning. Is that normal?"

"Agnes, have you never been—" Jasmine started, but Danny cut her off, gesturing excitedly.

"If there are still uninfected birds in Red Creek, it's got to be about the last place on earth," he enthused. "All over the world birds have been hit hard. Scientists say it's an environmental disaster in the making."

"Hang on," said Max. "How many infected do you have up in Red Creek? Infected people, I mean?"

Agnes could only think of Magda Jameson and Toby, the Prophet's son. "Just two. And only because the Prophet wanted people hurt."

Max slapped the table. "If we've got to stay in Arizona"—at

this he shot Danny a very dirty look—"that's where we should be. In freaking Red Creek, where there are still freaking birds!"

Agnes felt cold. She glanced at Danny, because he'd seen it. He knew.

"Trust me, Red Creek is the last place we want to be." He returned Max's look with frank dislike. "There's a madman in charge."

Max rolled his eyes, and Danny pulled a face she'd never seen him make before.

Agnes leaned away.

Something is different about him on the Outside.

As the Outsiders continued their conversation, she tried to put her finger on what had changed, and decided it was the way he acted with the others. Though they'd only met a few days ago, the Outsiders already had more in common with one another than they ever would with her. She didn't understand half of what they were saying, and she tried to keep a mental list of new words so she could look them up later. Who was Stephen King, where was Reno, and what were laptops? What was Jonestown, and what was a vegetarian (Jasmine was one)? And what on earth did CDC and EPA stand for?

She told herself she shouldn't hope to be one of them, but only among them. Close, but never touching. And maybe that was all right.

Considering how her body reacted when Danny was near, maybe that was better.

Danny reached for a napkin and wiped the sweat from his forehead. He was shaking.

Max had noticed, too. His eyes narrowed. "What was your temperature?"

"A hundred and two, but it's not—"

Max pushed his empty bowl away. "Take your shirt off."

"It's not the Virus," said Danny. "So just cool it."

Max laughed, an ugly sound. "Would you tell us if it was?"

"Not everyone left on this planet is a selfish jerk, you worthless—"

"Enough." Matilda returned, looking tired. "I know you're on edge, but there has to be some trust. If we're going to stay together, I mean."

Her eyes were challenging, and for a long moment, Max held them.

Then at last he shoved his hands sullenly into his pockets and looked away.

Agnes felt dumbfounded. She'd never seen a woman wield that kind of power. Back home, even the mothers of teenage boys mostly let them rule. They were still men, after all.

"Ignore him." Jasmine's tone was streaked with anger. "Of course we want to stay with you. Where else would we go?"

"That's what we've got to discuss."

Max stood abruptly. "Are you all completely addled? It's a mistake to stay with that Nest so close. Something's bound to happen. Any fool can see it."

"Max, what's your alternative?" Danny demanded. "Would you prefer the military outposts? Where do *you* think it's safe?"

Max met Agnes's eyes for the first time. She sensed the vast pain his anger hid, the suffering that echoed in the belly of his soul. Tragedy had struck him when he was still, essentially, a child, and he felt bitterly wronged by it.

"If there are still birds in Red Creek, *she* might've just run from the last safe place on earth. Maybe it's worth it to join a cult, if it means we don't wind up infected."

"Max," Jasmine snapped.

"It's okay." Agnes could tell that Max itched for a fight. Any fight. "But we have infected creatures there, too. A javelina almost caught my brother."

"But no infected *people* means our chances would be—"

"It wouldn't be worth it," she said simply, truthfully. "To risk meeting the Prophet. He's mad. There's no telling what he might do, even now."

Max set his perfect jaw. "Whatever. I'm going back to sleep. Let me know what you guys decide."

"I think that's best." Jazz spoke coolly. "You've been very rude."

He left them, and the Outsider girl rolled her eyes in exasperation.

In sixteen years of life, Agnes had never seen such a bizarre interaction between men and women. She filed it away, to play it over in her mind later.

"Listen, Agnes." Matilda tapped her lower lip with two fingers— a tic she recognized. "There are things you need to know."

"Can it wait?" Danny interjected. "She's dead on her feet."

"I'm afraid it can't," Matilda said. "You've got to know, Agnes, that there's almost no population left in Arizona anymore. Only Burn Squads roam the desert now. And I don't know, maybe we stayed too long…but then, if we'd evacuated, we wouldn't have been here for you and Ezekiel."

Beside her, Danny twitched.

"No running water, but there's a well nearby," she continued, ticking points off on her fingers. "No gangs or thieves we've seen so far. Most people think the military havens are safest, but I've heard awful stories about violence in the camps. Then there's the journey to consider. Gasoline is scarce, and I wouldn't want to travel on foot."

"Even better," Danny cut in. "We haven't seen many active infected in Gila, and the library's boarded up tight. I think if we just stay put..." He coughed. "Sorry. I feel like death."

Matilda patted her son's arm. "Our best shot is to hunker down until the CDC gets a handle on Petra. There's a vaccine in the making, I heard, and... other plans..."

Her eyes wandered in a way that wasn't reassuring, at all.

"Matilda." Agnes tried to stop herself even thinking it, but fear had sunk its claws deeply into her. "Is this the end of the world?"

Her head snapped up. "No, dear, don't be silly. It's an epidemic, and a bad one, but the world's seen those before."

"Like the Spanish flu," said Danny hoarsely.

Great. Something else she'd never heard of. But she felt bolstered by their certainty. What a sick irony it would have been, if she'd stumbled into the arms of the Rapture after all.

"Civilization will recover. We only have to wait." Matilda smiled at her. "And here's as good a place as any, if we're going to be stragglers."

That word again. *Stragglers*. Was that what she and Ezekiel were now?

A look flitted across Matilda's face, reflecting all the burden of being the only adult responsible for many children. A feeling Agnes knew well.

Her eyes settled on Danny. "You. Rest."

Agnes's heart sped, watching him stand, revealing his astonishing height. She knew that next he'd look at her, and all their Red Creek familiarity would be in his eyes—and their new distance, too.

"I'm really glad you're here," he said.

"Me too."

He opened his mouth. Closed it. It was strange to see such a large boy so tentative. All her life Agnes had been a workhorse, but he treated her like a little lost kitten, frail and delicate. All at once, Agnes wanted to cry.

"I was afraid—" He stopped. "Well. I was afraid."

Jasmine tilted her head, watching them quizzically. Then Matilda made Agnes the best offer she'd had all day.

"I bet you're exhausted, sweetheart. How about we find you a sleeping bag?"

As soon as the words left Matilda's mouth, Agnes's eyes were already drooping.

———————

Matilda led her through the stacks to a narrow storeroom.

The door was ajar, and she could see Ezekiel inside, sleeping with his cooler beside him. Quietly, Matilda opened its lid and slid a few blue plastic ice packs inside.

All you had to do was snap them, and magically, they became cold.

She smiled at Agnes, whose eyes were wide. "At least you don't have to bury it in your garden anymore. Rest well, dear."

A sleeping bag piled with pillows looked like heaven. Someone had left out candles and bottled water.

Ezekiel was out like a toddler, Sheep flush against his chest.

But Agnes didn't sleep right away. She waited a few quiet moments, listening to the Outsider's receding footsteps, then snuck back into the lobby.

She wanted another look at that astonishing collection of books.

She wanted to hear what sounds they made, in the prayer space.

She closed her eyes, searching for that special place inside that was wiser than herself alone. She found it, like a gem on the lakeshore, and let its light spread through the library, rippling out. She stood stock-still a long time, listening to a sound like pages turning, crisp and autumnal, and a sound like many voices singing in hushed chorus.

The Prophet always said Outsider books were filth, but to Agnes the library felt like a church. A place where people came in search of truth.

She pictured the Outsiders who'd come here before Petra took hold, the men and women and children moving quietly through the shelves or sitting reading at the long metal tables. Such joy. She'd only ever read printouts of the Prophet's sermons, two or three preachy picture books, a hymnal, and the Bible.

But there were thousands of books here, every one of them singing an earnest melody, agreeing, contradicting, and bickering with one another. It all combined into a symphony of unimaginable complexity. A web of knowledge and learning both ancient and new. A song as timeless and as vast as God Himself.

Think of all I might've learned if I'd been allowed in a place like this.

She backed into the dust-soaked shadows, feeling an invisible wound opening.

She hadn't known, and she couldn't shake the feeling that she'd run Outside too late, and among the rustling whispers, she felt lonely, sorrowful, and ashamed. But Ezekiel still had a chance. She poured all her faith into picturing him as a learned Outsider, like Danny with his medical books.

She shut the storeroom door.

They'd be safe in Gila. All day long, Ezekiel could read and learn, readying himself to join the world. When things finally settled, she'd have done more than just save his life.

She'd have given him a better one.

29

BETH

Surely he shall deliver thee from the snare of the fowler,
and from the noisome pestilence.

—Psalm 91:3

Of all the places in all the world, the church where she'd married Matthew Jameson was the last Beth ever wanted to see. But it was the building nearest to the forest's edge and Cory couldn't stand. She'd dragged him by his armpits through the undergrowth, scraping his mangled leg across fallen branches and rutted stones. It took an hour that felt like years—an hour she'd never forget as long as she lived, punctuated as it was by Cory's screams.

She had no choice but to use her bad arm, a torture with every motion. Pain spread into her chest, neck, skull. Her vision grayed. She feared she'd pass out, leaving Cory to bleed to death. But she didn't pass out.

In the end, her face was dirt smeared, her wedding dress a rag. She was covered head to toe in her boyfriend's drying blood, and even yet, she was still standing. Who could've guessed she had such strength of will inside her? All her life, she'd been flighty

Beth, pretty Beth. But there was more substance to her than met the eye. More strength, more darkness—and more rage.

On Red Creek's abandoned street, quiet but for Cory's pained gasps, she stared at the church's wide-flung doors—in their hell-fire hurry, the faithful had forgotten to shut them—and shook with fury.

"What the hell was it all for?" she demanded of the church. "What the hell reason could there be for stuffing your own people inside that awful bunker? What sense does it make?"

Cory swallowed convulsively. "The Rapture—"

She exploded, gesturing to the calm sky, the undisturbed street. *"What Rapture? Where?"*

"Please," he groaned. "I'm dying. I know I am."

Beth looked into his pain-dulled eyes, and her anger cooled. Cory hadn't run because he'd stopped believing in the Prophet's God—he was still talking about the Rapture, even now.

No, he'd run because he loved her, truly loved her, and the proof was that he'd been willing to brave a Rapturous hellscape for a chance to save her life.

It was a stunning thing, that kind of love, and Beth thought she'd probably never feel it herself. She was just too selfish. But she could pay Cory back by helping him see another dawn. And if she wanted to do that, she had to think carefully, because every choice was going to matter.

"Beth, I want you to know—"

"Shut up a minute," she interrupted. "I need to think."

He shut up, and she tapped her bottom lip with a bloodstained finger.

The church—safe or not?

None of the faithful would notice they'd gone missing until

morning. Then it was a coin toss whether they'd bother to send out a search party or simply start praying for the destruction of their souls.

And there were supplies inside. Bandages in the basement, maybe. At the very least, she'd have clean rags and a stove to boil water.

With a pang, she wished for Agnes.

If you come back, I'll forgive everything. Just don't make me do this alone.

But Agnes wasn't coming back.

It took forever to get Cory across that road. Moaning, he struggled like a fish on a line, and she kept glancing at the wide-mouthed church doors that never seemed to get any closer. Her back ached, her shoulder screamed, and her dress caught underfoot. Cory kept trying to unburden his soul. But she refused to stop and listen, because that would mean admitting he wasn't going to make it.

Eventually he passed out. Though his body felt heavier, Beth's heart lightened. The sound of his heavy-breathing pain had been too much, especially when she remembered the sounds he used to make when they kissed at the canyon's edge. Those sounds had been heavy, too, but they were rough with pleasure, not pain.

My marriage was supposed to be consummated last night, she realized as she pulled him across the threshold. *I was supposed to be his father's wife.*

An alien thought, like a memory from another girl's life.

Inside the church, she noted the dusty footprints of the faithful, the bronze cross. Air whistling through organ pipes made a ghostly, incomplete sound.

Beth let out a breath. Cory was bleeding, her mouth tasted of ash, and she couldn't bring herself to shut the doors behind her. After the bunker, she might never close a door again.

She settled Cory into the third pew; his pant leg was sopping black with blood. She needed something, anything, to stanch the bleeding.

Think carefully. Don't let your feelings get the best of you.

She repeated this to herself as she headed for the basement stairs.

A rusty tooth had snapped off in the shredded muscle of Cory's thigh. While Beth clumsily tried to clean it, he woke screaming.

"Holy hell," he shouted. "Christ on a bike, just let me die."

"Quiet. Someone might hear."

He cackled. "Who? Everyone we know is waiting for God."

Her shoulder blades itched. She glanced towards the wide-open doors. Outside, the wind blew like it was any other summer night, whipping up the scents of wildflowers and prickly pear.

In the church kitchen, she'd found towels, soap, a paring knife, a pot to boil water, and duct tape. After she'd washed the wound, she shredded the towels. Blood pulsed in oily gushes from Cory's leg, his hair was matted with sweat, and by the maudlin look on his still-handsome face, he was becoming delirious.

"I love you, you know that?" he mumbled. "I've been in love with you for years."

"Sure, I know."

But it worried her that he felt he had to say it now.

"Love you so much. More than anything. I was so blessed." An edge of recrimination crept into his voice. "But then you married Father. Never even spoke to me first. And I was ready to run away with you."

Beth said nothing, ripping duct tape with her teeth and laying strips out in a row.

"But you wouldn't give me the time of day, because you don't love me, do you? You never did." He sobbed once. "Jesus, don't squeeze so hard, I just want to die!"

She studied his face, knowing what he'd have her say. Another girl might lie to him. Heck, Agnes might lie; it was kinder. But Beth was done shaping her life to anyone's wishes but her own.

"You're right, Cory Jameson, I don't love you." She leaned back, the duct tape strung between her hands. "But I like you enough that I'd never lie about it. That's something."

She thought he smiled, but it was hard to tell. She picked up a steel-gray strip of tape. His eyes rolled back. He fell unconscious again.

This time Cory stayed out.

Once she was sure she'd stopped the bleeding, she went looking for something to occupy her mind. If she stayed still longer than a moment, memories of the bunker flooded her. She considered trying to sleep—God knew she needed the rest—but that was a fool's errand if there ever was one. So she channeled her energy into shamelessly breaking into the Prophet's private office. And why not? He didn't deserve privacy, after what he'd done.

The lock was easy to break. A solid crack with a wooden broom handle was all it took.

Inside, it was just so depressingly male. Leather books, a smoky smell, and in dawn's gray light, a stag's head mounted gruesomely on the wall. Dead, glassy eyes tracked her as she moved cautiously about the room.

I can touch whatever I want, because he's not coming back. Maybe not ever.

Papers cluttered his desk—maps, blueprints, and dozens of

newspapers with headlines: VIRUS THREATENS CITY, AUTHORITIES AT A LOSS; UNCONTROLLED EPIDEMIC; EVACUATIONS ORDERED.

Beth glanced through the papers, but they didn't much interest her.

What she wanted to know was what had happened *here*. Why had the Prophet condemned his own people to darkness and, probably, death?

In her mind, she heard Mary, Faith, and Sam. They were crying out her name.

She hunched over, thrusting her head between her knees. After a moment, the nauseating guilt faded to a dull roar. But her anger redoubled.

Furiously, she slammed open the Prophet's desk drawers— letter openers, used gum wrappers, a plastic flyswatter—and finally uncovered a leather-bound book.

A *diary*.

In fact, there were two diaries. Handsome, old-looking volumes with sprawling cursive inside. She remembered all the hours she'd spent recording every taboo, secret thought in the pages of her own journal, and felt a flare of excitement.

Brazenly, she settled into the Prophet's fine leather chair. The stag watched her.

Beth read breathlessly. The history of Red Creek was contained in those books, and she was astonished that she'd never heard any of it before. But then, Red Creek was about the end of history, not history itself. Why tell the stories of the past if it would soon go up in smoke?

The story began with the first diary, which didn't belong to the Prophet at all, but to his grandfather Jeremiah. She read on the edge of her seat, because she recognized this tale. Or some of it, anyway.

And she wasn't at all surprised to find that all roads led back to Agnes.

Agnes, at last.

My name is Jeremiah Rollins, the book began. *When I was small, the earth, and the trees, and the very stars began to sing...*

Beth froze, remembering way back to early childhood, when Agnes used to tell her strange stories—about *sounds*, of all things. She used to tell her about the hum of the earth. About how rocks and stones sang differently from soil, how soil and water combined into a murky, muddy moan. How clouds whispered and sunshine chimed. She'd assumed it was a game, a fairy tale invented to amuse her.

And eventually, Agnes grew up—and the stories stopped.

But some thoughtful part of her always wondered if Agnes really could hear those things—and if, just maybe, she still did. Beth had remembered every bit of those fairy tales, storing away memories like a squirrel gathers nuts for winter.

Now winter had come, and she knew every word was true.

Agnes was a prophet.

A *real* one.

And maybe Jeremiah Rollins had been, too.

"Holy shit." Beth cursed in honor of the now-unconscious Cory, her hands clenched into claws around the diary's leather spine. "Holy shit, holy shit, holy *shit*."

30

AGNES

The heavens declare the glory of God; and the firmament
sheweth his handywork.

—PSALM 19:1

On her third day Outside, Agnes woke early with a strong desire to brush her teeth.

She wandered into the makeshift kitchen and found the water filters dry as bone.

It was Max's turn to ferry buckets from the well, but she wasn't surprised to discover him lingering inside, watching a movie. She'd quickly discovered that Outsiders weren't accustomed to physical labor and would avoid it at all costs.

"I have a headache," he explained without looking up from his phone.

At the library, there were plenty of chores to be done. The well needed visiting twice a day, and Matilda insisted the water be boiled, then purified with iodine. They washed laundry by hand and had to get creative with the cooking, with few supplies and only the battery-charged camping stove for power. They took an anxious daily inventory of all they had, from candles to the last can of beans, and periodically Danny and Matilda—who always carried her rifle—patrolled the area for red creatures.

The chores were light compared to Agnes's duties at home, but the Outsider teenagers complained ceaselessly. In a way, it was refreshing. They didn't seem to think God—or a patriarch— would smite them for it.

In other ways, it was annoying. Like when she really needed, more than anything, to wash her face and clean her teeth.

Wires dangled from Max's ears. She could just hear the pattering of tiny movie voices, whispering make-believe dramas. The phone's screen flashed with kaleidoscopic colors.

She'd had no idea how attached the Outsiders were to these devices. And this despite the fact that the Internet was down, cell service spotty, and the social media sites long since shuttered. Max watched pre-downloaded movies, Jasmine played a vast collection of video games, and Danny constantly piped music into his ears while he hunched anxiously over his medical books.

"Ezekiel and I can go for water," Agnes said shyly.

Max eyed her while the movie flickered, not bothering to remove his earbuds. His handsome face was vulpine, his eyes black and wide. He and Jazz were both seventeen. It was hard to believe, because Agnes knew fourteen-year-old wives with more gravity than the two of them put together.

"Jeez, that'd be great," he drawled, half sarcastic, as always. "But you'd better take the rifle. You were incredibly sheltered, before. Have you ever even *seen* a walking red person?"

Agnes ducked her head, thinking.

Should she tell him that she was safer outdoors than anyone else at the library, because she'd been for some unknown reason graced with the power to hear the sound of every rock and stone and red creature?

Should she tell him she believed she heard God's voice, and that it protected her when infection was near?

No. Even the people of Red Creek, primed as they were to see God's face in every shadow, wouldn't believe a story like that. And the Outsiders were troublingly quiet on the subject of God. The prayer space must remain her secret.

"Don't worry about me," she said.

But Max wasn't listening. He'd already disappeared back into his movie, his eyes transfixed.

The well was a quarter mile away. Before the world turned upside down, it had been a curiosity, nothing more. A flyer read: MAY 21ST: LEARN ABOUT GILA'S HISTORIC WELLS! Fortunately, the cobbled relic still provided potable water.

Agnes carried two buckets down the path, marveling at how far the sky stretched without a forest to curtail it—a view of gold sand and white-blue air in every direction—while Ezekiel trotted beside her.

At the library, her brother's moods followed a mysterious rhythm. Sometimes he was perfectly content to trail Matilda like an adoring shadow. Other times, he sniped at everyone.

Agnes understood. Sometimes she felt so grateful to be Outside, she wanted to sing for joy. But in the mornings she woke with a scream climbing the rungs of her throat, certain she'd been forced down into the bunker after all.

For Ezekiel, today was a bad day.

And this time, he was harping on sweet, cotton-candy Jazz.

"She's indecent," he said primly, plainly referring to the way she dressed: in shorts and tank tops and strapless dresses.

"She just dresses like all Outsiders do. You'll get used to it."

"I won't." He kicked a pebble. "I won't because God hates it."

"All those Laws . . . they're just made up. Remember?"

He glowered. "She looks like a Jezebel."

"Be nice. They're our new friends."

"They're Outsiders."

She looked down at his agitated face and spoke very clearly, so he wouldn't forget.

"Yes, Zeke." She used Matilda's nickname for him, because she could tell he liked it. "But we're Outsiders now, too."

Confusion clouded his face, and he nearly stumbled. A little boy caught between two worlds is never steady.

But he was young. He'd adapt.

Gila's hot, dry air felt like sand, scraping her face. In the low desert, thorny plants ranged, determined to grow despite the lack of water or shade.

Gray cobbles led to the well. Her buckets clanked as she set them down. Then she rolled up her sleeves to work the pump. Zeke sat on the well's opposite side, pressing his back against the coolness of its stones. She heard him scraping the dirt with a twig, doodling.

She'd already filled one bucket when something caught her eye. Inside the lip of the well, someone had painstakingly etched letters in the rock.

She hung her head upside down, pressing her ribs against the cobblestones to read:

THERE IS NO GREATER SIN
THAN TO DENY GOD'S GIFT TO YOU.
J. ROLLINS, 1922

She gasped and gripped the edge to steady herself.

The Prophet's name was *Jacob* Rollins, but he hadn't been born in 1922, when the etching was made.

He hadn't been born—but his grandfather, *Jeremiah* Rollins, had.

Coincidence?

Rollins could be a common surname. Maybe the well had been built by someone completely unrelated—a John or a James?

Yet her skin prickled, thinking how deeply ironic it would be if Red Creek's founder were responsible for the life-giving water they drank every day.

In his travels before Red Creek, had Jeremiah Rollins ever lived in a place called Gila?

Ask the prayer space.

"Agnes?"

"Hang on a second, Zeke."

He sighed dramatically, but she ignored him. This was important. She stood on her tiptoes looking over the dewy edge of the well, listening to the *plunk*, *plunk* of water dripping into the abyss. With blood rushing to her head, she closed her eyes and opened her heart.

She heard: the blue-white sky roaring to life above her and the parched earth rasping, thirsting; a red coyote, dully wandering in the far desert valleys; Gila's human Nest shimmering to the west; Zeke's heart beating.

And the etching, beckoning.

Eyes closed, Agnes reached into the cool dark well to run her fingers over the letters.

An electric shriek ran up her arm, the feel and sound of a human being—a *girl*—crying out in abject pain. In the prayer space, the sound shot up her spine and into the base of her skull, lodging like a needle.

A face flashed before her eyes, one she recognized from old photographs.

Red Creek's founding Prophet, Jeremiah Rollins.

He'd been here, in Gila. And he'd hurt someone. A girl.

She leapt out of the prayer space as fast as she could. She stumbled back, tripped, and fell hard onto the sand.

"Agnes!" Zeke rushed to where she lay trembling. "You fell, Agnes. You fell down!"

She opened her arms to Ezekiel and held him against her chest.

"I'm okay." She rubbed his back. "I only tripped."

But her mind wandered away from him, thinking how harrowing it was that Red Creek's first Prophet had been *here*, in her haven on the Outside. What did it mean that of all the desert towns, she'd come to this one—and seemingly by accident?

There are no accidents anymore. God's eye is too much on you.

Shivering, she felt in her bones that this was true.

"Look." Zeke pointed into the distance. "Someone's coming."

Jazz hurried their way, her sandals slapping against the ground. Her tanned legs glowed under the sun. Spotting them, her face contracted with worry.

"Oh my God, are you hurt?"

"No." Agnes stood, fighting dizziness. "I'm okay."

"She *fell*," Zeke insisted, surprising Agnes by addressing the Outsider girl directly—and asking, in his way, for help.

"Let me see." Jazz took her hands as if she and Agnes might dance, looking her over from head to toe.

Her cheeks burned with mild embarrassment. "Really, I'm fine."

Jazz turned to Zeke. "Good news. I think she's going to live."

Did Ezekiel almost smile—at the girl he'd called a Jezebel?

"I'm glad I ran into you." Jazz's smile dazzled. "I'll help you carry the water."

On the path back to the library, Jazz stole curious looks at her.

"I can't believe you're really from Red Creek," she said quietly, so Zeke couldn't hear. "I told you I wrote a report for school? It's like a strange dream, meeting you."

A *strange dream.*

Agnes shivered again, glancing over her shoulder towards the well.

Jazz couldn't contain herself any longer. "What was it *like*? I mean, did you know girls who were married, with sister-wives? Did you really have to pray for *hours*? Did you stockpile food for the apocalypse?"

Agnes had expected to be dragged into darkness by such questions. But she only laughed, amused to find an Outsider so curious about her rural, mouse-brown life.

"Yes, we stockpiled food and prayed. And we practiced plural marriage." She paused. "My sister became a sixth wife."

Jarringly, she remembered the twins, so sleepy on Beth's wedding day, who wouldn't remember her final kiss. How were they now? Were they suffering even as she laughed with a stranger?

"I lost my sister, too," Jazz said. "My whole family, actually, when the Burn Squad came. After, Max and I just ran. We would've starved if we hadn't found Matilda. We slept for days, you know, when we first got here. We just—slept."

Without thinking, Agnes set her bucket down. Jazz looked stunned but pleased when Agnes hugged her, trying to sop up some of the Outsider's raw pain.

Zeke had stopped walking to witness this embrace.

Baffled as he looked, she was glad he'd seen it.

Jazz patted Agnes's hair in a happy way, her color high.

"So, what's the deal with you and Danny? Are you guys—you know—together?"

Agnes's jaw dropped. "What makes you ask that?"

"Well, for one thing, the way you *look* at each other."

Agnes hadn't thought much about boys—or men—back home. She'd always been too busy, too worried sick to let herself feel. Even engaged to Matthew Jameson, thoughts of men and women together had barely brushed her mind.

But now...

Well. Zeke wasn't the only one struggling with how to be, Outside.

She cleared her throat. "He's been very kind, that's all."

"Ah." Jazz didn't press her. "He's good-looking, in a funny sort of way. He's very tall."

Agnes turned her head to hide her smile.

Danny *was* good-looking—in a funny sort of way. And he was undeniably tall.

As they walked in companionable silence, Zeke trailing behind them, Agnes wondered if Jazz had just crossed over the line from Outsider stranger to friend.

31

AGNES

He brought them out of darkness and the shadow of death,
and brake their bands in sunder.
—PSALM 107:14

The boys were shouting in the makeshift kitchen. Fighting, arguing. It sounded rough.

Jazz had peeled off to practice her yoga on the granite steps, a discipline that seemed to consist of contorting her body into odd shapes with animal names. Agnes wished she'd stayed to watch her—that she and Zeke weren't overhearing this ugly fight.

They stood outside the door with their buckets sloshing water, unsure of what to do. Angry male voices reminded her of home. Agnes resisted the urge to chew her nails.

"She just got here, how could you give her your chores?" Danny yelled. "What the hell is wrong with you?"

"Why are you jumping all over me?"

"It isn't safe out there, that's why, and she's got a little kid with her."

Zeke shot Agnes a dark look. He didn't appreciate being called a little kid.

"We haven't seen any infected," Max said. "What could happen?"

"Anything could happen. And you know she isn't like us. She doesn't *know* anything."

Agnes's first instinct was to turn away, pretend she hadn't heard. But then she'd be acting just like the girl she'd been back at Red Creek—the pale creature who took orders and tried to stay out of everyone's way—and not the new girl she hoped to become.

Agnes might not have read as many books as an Outsider, but she'd known to run from the bunker, hadn't she?

More important, Ezekiel was watching. His eyes saying, *See? Listen to what those heathens think of us.*

Agnes steeled herself, then opened the door. "Leave him alone, Danny. I offered to go."

Max rolled his eyes. "*Thank you.* That's what I've been saying."

Danny stared at her, eyes bloodshot, puzzled, and angry.

Well, she could be angry, too. In Red Creek it hadn't been allowed, she'd been forced to act sweet and easy as milk. But here, she didn't have to let things go.

"I'm not weak like you think," she told Danny. "You complain because there's no air-conditioning here? Back home, we *never* had air-conditioning." She ticked her fingers. "Or dishwashers, or washing machines, or instant noodles with powdered cheese. I was on my feet twelve hours a day. I think I can handle a trip to the well, thank you very much."

Both boys looked chastened. Agnes pushed past Danny on her way to drop off the buckets, and Zeke fell into step behind her.

"Agnes—" Danny started.

But Zeke shot him a look of utter disdain, and the Outsider boy fell silent again.

Strong as he'd seemed before, Zeke looked lost at dinner. His eyes never focused, and he showed no appetite, even for macaroni. Watching him, Agnes frowned.

Danny tried to draw him out. "Hey—would you like to learn to suture a wound? I have a *human arm*—well, a plastic one—in my backpack just for practicing. What do you think?"

Danny looked at Agnes for approval, but she wouldn't meet his eager eyes. She kept hearing him say, *She isn't like us. She doesn't* know *anything.*

But she appreciated that he was trying with Ezekiel. She nudged her brother. "Well? What do you say? Would it be neat to learn how to stitch up a wound?"

Zeke stared sadly into his bowl, just as if he hadn't heard.

A sharp pain pierced Agnes's heart, knowing how much he'd lost. *I'll never be able to make it up to him. Never.*

"Do you have a favorite movie, Zeke?" Jazz asked. "Did you ever watch any... television?"

Jazz colored quickly, remembering Red Creek's strict rules.

"No," he said bleakly. "Movies are sin."

"Wait a second," Max chimed in, much to Agnes's irritation. As much as she liked Jazz, she wasn't a particular fan of her boyfriend. He struck her as disrespectful and lazy. "Are you telling me you've never seen any of the Batman movies? Superman? Spider-Man? Aquaman? Captain America? The Avengers?"

Zeke shook his head, a cautious gleam in his eyes.

"Holy cow." Max slapped his forehead. "The real sin is that a guy like you has been deprived of the classics his whole life. There's so much we've got to catch you up on, dude."

Agnes fought the urge to pinch the bridge of her nose, wishing Max would at least try to speak to him like the child he was. She'd understood only half the words that came out of his mouth, and Zeke would surely understand fewer.

Zeke's eyes narrowed. "Batman—is that like Satan?"

Matilda's fork froze halfway to her mouth, and all heads swiveled to Max. Agnes held her breath.

"Well." The Outsider leaned back in his chair and stuck a toothpick in his mouth. "Batman *does* live in a cave underground, but his whole thing is, like, fighting for justice for the oppressed. He's more of a badass savior figure, if you know what I'm saying."

To her utter shock, Zeke nodded avidly. "A savior. Like Jesus?"

Max roared with laughter. "Jesus in a leather bat suit? You know, maybe. But the thing about Batman is, he doesn't have any superpowers. Just loads of cash and a burning desire to save the innocent citizens of Gotham." Passion enlivened Max's face. "Does that make him more or less relatable to regular joes like us? That's the question."

Agnes caught Danny's exasperated eye roll.

But Zeke was staring at Max like he was the second coming. "How come you know so much stuff?"

"I've just seen lots of movies, that's all." Then, suddenly shy, Max added, "If you want, I can show you one after dinner."

"Oh, I don't know if—" Agnes began, but stopped.

Zeke was smiling.

Grinning so bright and wide, he might've been back home in his trailer, talking to Sam. Agnes bit her lip, torn between hope and grief, promise and loss.

Matilda winked at her. *This is a good thing*, she seemed to say. *Let the boy grow.*

Agnes looked at Max with fresh eyes.

Danny coughed. "Hey. There's that cat again."

An orange tabby had wandered into the kitchen with a hungry look in his eyes, his fur matted.

Jazz punched Max lightly on the shoulder. "I *told* you I didn't imagine him."

"Poor thing must've been hiding," Matilda said. "I guess someone forgot to take him when they evacuated."

Zeke leapt to his feet. "Who could forget *him*? He's beautiful!"

The cat made his way straight towards Zeke. Pets were never allowed in Red Creek. Zeke eagerly extended his hand to pat that dust-covered head.

"Do cats like macaroni? What's his name, anyway?"

"He's not wearing a tag," Matilda said. "Would you like to name him?"

Zeke sucked in a breath and Agnes hid a smile. He wouldn't be able to hold out against the Outsiders for long. Their world was just too interesting.

"Benny," Zeke announced. "His name's Benny."

Danny's eyes found Agnes. She nearly smiled at him, before she remembered him saying, *She isn't like us.*

His hopeful smile dropped away.

Matilda set down her fork. "Now, I have to ask. How much insulin do you and Zeke have left?"

Zeke stiffened, and Agnes squeezed his shoulder. "Enough for a few weeks."

Matilda sipped her water. "Mercy Hospital is operating some fifty miles west. In a few days, we should pool our gas and drive there."

Agnes picked nervously at a scab on her palm. "You're sure they'll have his medicine? They won't run out?"

Matilda nodded. "Last I heard, they're in it for the long haul. Someone's got to look after the stragglers, after all."

"You're diabetic, guy?" Max asked Zeke. "Which type?"

"He's type 1," Agnes answered for him.

Type 1, she understood from Matilda, was an autoimmune disease. The nurse had told her many times that it was no one's fault. Not hers, or Zeke's, or even God's.

Zeke, who'd never actually heard the word *diabetes* before, just blinked.

"My cousin was diagnosed type 1 in college," Max continued. "No problem, except he'd always wanted to be an astronaut, and I guess people with diabetes aren't allowed in space."

"What's an astronaut?" Zeke asked.

Again, looks flew around the room, and Danny winced. Agnes tried not to look too curious—she didn't know what an astronaut was, either.

"Uh—you know," Max said. "The guys that walk on the moon."

"There are men on the moon?"

"People, anyway," Jazz mumbled. "Sometimes."

Zeke's face reddened. He looked furious, disbelieving, and betrayed. Agnes knew what he was feeling. People walking on the moon ... it was such an unbelievable story. If these Outsiders were lying, how could he laugh with them again? And if they *weren't* lying—well, that meant he'd been denied the wonder of knowing people walked on the moon. In a way, that was worse.

Agnes's hands played in her lap, wanting to help—to save him—but she couldn't. She didn't doubt that Outsiders could walk on the moon if they wanted to, and, vaguely, she thought one day she'd like to hear all about it. But not tonight. The world was growing too fast as it was.

"You're lying," Zeke snarled. "There can't be people on the moon because God would never, ever let it happen! The Prophet said so—not *ever!*"

The sermon on the evils of technology. Agnes could recite it verbatim. According to the Prophet, Outsiders pretended they possessed powers that God would never allow them to have. Such as the power to travel among the stars.

Agnes moved to take her distraught brother into her arms, but Matilda beat her to it. She hugged the stuttering, crying boy and whispered in his ear.

"I think it's time for Zeke to go to bed," Matilda said calmly. "But maybe we'll read a bedtime story first. How does a book about the moon landing sound?"

The Outsiders looked expectantly at Agnes, waiting for her to decide. Danny held especially still.

She isn't like us.

He'd said it, and it had hurt, but it was also the truth.

"You can read to him," Agnes whispered. "Anything you want, as long as it's true."

When Zeke was gone from the room, she fixed her eyes straight ahead while the Outsiders shifted around her, uncomfortable. Telling herself, *I must not cry. I must not cry.*

Miraculously, she didn't.

When Agnes turned in to bed that night, she discovered Zeke curled in his sleeping bag with a book clutched to his chest. Sheep had been sentenced to spend the night on the cold floor.

Curious, she raised the camping lantern: *The Moon, For Kids!*

It must've been Matilda's way of proving that Outsiders

weren't liars, and that, impossible as it sounded, people really had walked on the moon.

In thick white suits and glass helmets, apparently.

Zeke's eyes snapped open. "Agnes?"

Behind her, the door creaked on its hinges. Benny.

Zeke sat up. "Can he sleep with me? Please?"

Agnes smiled. "You'd better ask him."

The cat mewled expressively.

"He wants to stay," he said firmly. "Just, shut the door. In case."

"Oh, Zeke, what if he has to use the bathroom, or something?"

"He can use the bucket."

She didn't think cats worked like that, but her brother insisted. Still, she was pleased to see him embracing an Outsider habit— even a messy, furry one.

"All right. But promise you'll sleep."

He bundled the cat into bed. Agnes smoothed the blanket along his sides. It was just like at home, except it was terribly quiet without the other kids rustling, talking.

For years she'd looked after her siblings like a mother, tying shoes and kissing bruises. Her throat burned, knowing what it must've been like for them when she disappeared.

At first, they wouldn't have believed it. The twins would've held more tightly to their cloth dolls. Confident, methodical Sam would tell them not to worry, that they'd probably just gotten separated. He'd wander among the other families, asking, *Have you seen Agnes? Have* you? He wouldn't believe the King boys when they said she wasn't there. He'd think they were just pulling his leg.

The other kids—they'd believe in her.

They'd believe, right up until the moment the Prophet commanded them to pray for the destruction of her soul.

She buried her face in her hands.

Zeke's eyes opened. For a crazy moment she thought he understood her pain. But he was still a little boy, overwhelmed with the work of shedding his home like a skin.

"Agnes, why did Father lie about the moon?" For him, this was the lie that unraveled everything.

She sighed. "Maybe Father didn't know."

"Did the Prophet know?"

She hesitated. "Zeke. The Prophet lied to us. *All* of us. He knew."

He looked battered, and her chest ached. "You miss your brother and sisters, but that's okay," she whispered. "Missing is a way of loving, too."

"You don't miss them," he accused. "Not as much as me."

"Every minute I'm thinking of them. But I've got to think of you, too. Your future."

He said nothing.

"Remember Matthew?"

A long, stubborn pause. Then, *"Blessed are those who mourn,"* he recited leadenly.

"For they will *be comforted,"* she urged. "You still have your faith. That you get to keep."

Benny nudged his small skull into the palm of Zeke's hand, begging to be petted.

"We're never going home again."

Not a question. A statement.

"There's nothing to go home to," Agnes answered.

She blew out the lantern and snuggled into the sleeping bag with him, *The Moon, For Kids!*, and Benny, whose eyes glowed yellow in the dark. For a long time, Zeke cried in that quiet, muffled way you learn when you grow up in a trailer full of people.

Their little tin home—it was a million miles away, as remote as the moon.

She pictured it on the hillside, abandoned and empty.

Blessed are those who mourn, for they will be comforted, she repeated to herself, drifting into troubled dreams. *Blessed are the pure of heart, for they will see God.*

32

BETH

Woe to him that buildeth a town with blood, and
stablisheth a city by iniquity!
—HABAKKUK 2:12

Y ou're a fool, Cory Jameson," Beth said, after he'd proclaimed, for the thousandth time, that he was going to hell for his betrayal of the Prophet.

His head rested in her lap. He rolled his blue eyes up to her, his look full of naked hurt. She'd snapped, but it wasn't entirely her fault. They'd been trapped in the church for three days, huddled between the pews and eating only what she found in the basement: watered-down wine, stale crackers, moldy cheese. She could've gone out for more, but Cory couldn't bear to be separated even for a moment—not since the smell of rot had started billowing around him like a cloud of death flies.

For three awful days, she'd tried everything to help him. She'd washed his wound with soap and vinegar, but still the edges had curled, turning sickly green. When the veins beneath turned black as ink, she'd poured boiling water over the lesion, deafening herself to his agonized screams. She'd nursed him as well as she could, but it hadn't mattered.

His fever persisted. He was clearly dying. She couldn't blame him for not wanting to face the end alone.

"Why am I a fool?" he demanded.

She gestured helplessly, knowing she couldn't tell the truth. It hurt to have your faith shattered—hurt like dying, and he was already doing that. Why should she make his last days more painful?

At least the kids never knew. The thought hurtled towards her like a meteor, unstoppable. Whatever happened to them after she and Cory left, they never had to wonder if their whole lives were built on a foundation of lies.

Cory snorted. "I don't understand what's wrong with you. You've been cruel and moody even though *I'm* the one who's hurt. I don't know where you get off acting like—"

"I hate this place, okay?" she shouted, and his eyes widened. "I hate this church! I can't breathe, knowing—"

"What? What do you think you know?"

It was a challenge, and it worked. Thinking about the kids when she tried so desperately hard not to had pushed her over the edge.

She exploded. "A hell of a lot more than you! I mean, so you broke the Laws of Red Creek. Who cares? They were only invented to torture us."

"Beth—" Cory warned.

"Don't say it," she hissed. "Don't tell me to get ahold of my *weak woman's soul*. I read the Prophet's diaries and his grandfather's. Those awful men have been lying to their people for almost eighty years."

"You did *what*?"

She colored slightly. "I wanted to understand how Jacob Rollins could trap the faithful in that—that *tomb*. Cory, I don't think they're ever coming out again. It's only a matter of time before Toby or Magda spread their sickness."

She hated the pictures her mind painted. Sam with gem-hard skin, and the twins—

Stop, she ordered herself. *Stop or you'll scream.*

"They're waiting for God," Cory said. "It's the opposite of dying. I should know."

She forced herself to look into his face, which had shrunk down to his bones. She remembered the first time they'd kissed at the canyon's edge. How vital and golden and downright *cheeky* he'd been.

"I want to be a faithful man," he'd told her while the desert wind teased his hair. "But not just yet."

Then he'd kissed her, striking a match that sent sparks flying throughout her body. They'd been unable to part until sunset, when the cold forced them home, and after that, they'd been unable to keep away.

In the church, a strange mix of yearning and sorrow made her head swim.

"Cory, Red Creek isn't what you think."

The diaries were tucked inside a knapsack she'd found. She felt the hate inside those pages, smoldering like coals.

"Then tell me."

"Are you sure you want to know?"

In his silence she sensed an opening—a hairline crack in his faith. But odds were she'd never get through to him. There just wasn't time.

I'm so lucky I don't love him.

If she did and he denied the truth of her story—as surely he was going to do—her heart would shatter.

"You can't interrupt me, not for anything. No matter how

crazy it sounds. If you say one word, Cory, I won't speak to you for the rest of your life."

A long, awkward pause.

"I don't mean because you're..."

Cory looked at her. "You can say it."

"Well." They locked eyes. "We both know you're dying."

"True," said Cory, shooting her his sexiest grin.

Beth caught another confusing vision of the boy he'd been—exasperating, irritating, irresistible—and felt like crying.

Don't think of the past and don't think of the kids. Don't think about what will happen after he dies—how then you'll be truly alone.

She stoked her courage and began.

"A long time ago, there was a young trapper named Jeremiah. He was charming and handsome, but poor as dirt. He managed to find himself a wife, a farmer's daughter who followed him all over the West while he sold pelts. But he'd always believed his destiny was to become a Prophet, because he'd been born with a special power."

She risked a glance at Cory. His face was impassive.

She continued. "The power was—weird. He could hear the earth humming and the stars singing. He kept it secret because he didn't want to sound daft. More than anything, he wanted to be respected, feared...and revered."

Beth could picture him: this young Prophet with a budding power exactly like her sister's. She saw how the air must've shimmered around him, how he would've been charming, entrancing when he tried.

Not that Agnes ever tried to be charming. She was too good—too *responsible*.

"In any case, nothing remarkable would've happened in Jeremiah's life if it hadn't been for a girl, the daughter of the constable in a town called Gila. Jeremiah worked odd jobs. Fence building, roofing. He was thirty-two. The girl was only fourteen, but he fell in love with her anyway. When he couldn't stop wanting her, he decided God wanted him to steal her."

Beth's voice grew wispy, thin. She could slide so easily into that girl's skin and feel what she'd felt.

"He kidnapped her in the middle of the night. Knowing her father would stop at nothing to hang him, he ran. But he had a problem. No Outsider church would allow him to marry the girl, because marrying more than one woman is an Outsider crime."

Cory huffed. "But we know better, right? Plural marriage is God's will."

"How do you know?" Beth demanded. "Other than because the Prophet told you so, over and *over* again?"

"It makes people feel holy," Cory said. "Men and women."

"No," she snapped. "It makes *men* feel holy and women feel worthless. What does it feel like when a woman is told that one man is worth six of her? Speaking as a sixth wife, I can tell you. It feels like hell."

Cory jerked as if she'd stabbed him. A shadow crossed his face and Beth's bones felt heavier.

She'd wanted Cory passionately. But she'd married his father. According to church rites, she'd be married to him forever. Even in death.

"I'm sorry I interrupted. Please don't stop."

She raised her finger. "One free pass. One."

He nodded, acquiescent.

"Anyway. Jeremiah convinced himself that God wanted him to marry this girl, but God was just an excuse. Hearing the earth, the trees, the stars—it twisted him. Made him selfish and entitled."

From a young age, I knew I must be the greatest man alive, he'd written.

"Jeremiah managed to evade the law. Eventually, he found his way to a place where the earth sang louder than anywhere else. A powerful place."

This part she could picture, too. Young Jeremiah, smiling at the fantastical sight of a land protected by the forest on one side and a canyon on the other.

"Jeremiah performed his second marriage ceremony on the ground where he planned to build his church." Beth swallowed. "The girl's name was Sarah Shiner. Though she cried, begging to go home, what she wanted never mattered."

She was an insignificant creature, but beautiful. Her greatest sin was in failing to see my power for what it was—a sign that God upheld my will.

Cory kept still.

"But here's the clincher. Sometime during their wedding night, Jeremiah's power disappeared. He couldn't hear the earth humming, even when he got down on his knees. The stars didn't sing. Marrying Sarah, he'd transgressed against his gift. For that, his power abandoned him—though he never saw it that way.

"He took out his frustration on Sarah. Eventually, she couldn't take it anymore. Years later, she fled like Hagar into the wilderness. Jeremiah vowed that all her descendants would forever suffer her disgrace.

"For decades Jeremiah prayed for his power to return while he amassed ever more wives and followers. But the earth never made another sound.

"In his final years, he was rotting from the inside out. From the way he wrote..." She spread her hands, a helpless gesture. "In the end, Jeremiah went mad."

She looked meaningfully at Cory.

"The point is, God never spoke to him directly. Not once in all his life. And Jeremiah remained, until his dying day, a miserable, hateful man. He considered driving his people over the canyon's edge or forcing them to take poison...but he didn't. He clung to one last hope: that one of his sons would be born with the power he'd lost."

Her voice fell to a whisper. "They never were. But a *grandson* was. His name was Jacob Rollins."

Cory let out a breath. She stole a glance at his face, worried that he'd fight rather than hear his Prophet maligned. To her surprise, he looked sad.

She felt sad, too. But the truth begged to be told.

"Just like his grandfather, Jacob set about becoming the most entitled, horrible man he could—keeping up all of Red Creek's lies and adding some of his own. For all I know, he even believed them. Men, it seems, convince themselves of what they want to be true.

"Jacob kept his power a long time. Then he started beating one of his less obedient wives—his fourth wife—and the power disappeared. He'd squandered it, like his grandfather before."

She dropped her eyes, feeling suddenly tired.

"Beth, look at me."

Stomach churning, she remembered all the times she'd avoided looking at him: in the days after she'd been called a whore, and then again, on her wedding day.

Now she felt desperate not to run—or deny, evade. She looked at him squarely, like Agnes would've done.

His mouth twitched.

She blinked. "You're not upset?"

"I read the diaries while you were sleeping," he confessed. "So, I already knew the story." His voice hardened. "Those 'Prophets' were a couple of filthy bastards."

She shoved him. "Why did you make me tell it, then? Why did you make such a fuss?"

"Beth, you know better than anyone that I never could stay faithful, much as I wanted to. I think...because, deep down, I always knew there had to be something wrong with any place that would keep us apart. I used to have god-awful nightmares...

"But when I woke up, I'd think, *Perfect obedience produces perfect faith.*" He licked his lips. "I needed to hear someone say, out loud, that the Prophet lied." He looked tenderly at her. "I should've known it would be you who finally said it."

She bit her lip. "Did it help, hearing it out loud?"

"I'm still scared of hell," he said. "I can still see the lake of fire, clear as day."

She almost said, *Give it time.* But time was the one thing Cory Jameson didn't have.

"I worried you wouldn't believe me because you're a man," she admitted. "After the Prophets, I thought all men might be destroyers at heart."

"The Prophets were mad," he said vehemently. "That crap about magic powers and hearing stars—obviously, they were out of their fucking minds."

"Cory," she said slowly. "That part was true."

He scoffed.

Beth knew how crazy she sounded. But she remembered all the ways her sister was different, how she'd told her stories about mystic, impossible sounds.

"I mean it," she said. "My sister heard the stars, too."

He twisted around to face her. "Who? One of the twins?"

She gaped. How had Agnes gone unnoticed for so long in a place that claimed to be a haven of spiritual wisdom?

"No, *Agnes*." She spoke the name like a prayer. She could've sworn that the church snapped to attention. Listening.

And who knew? Maybe it was.

"Okay, okay," Cory said. "The Prophets certainly believed in their powers—and what the hell, maybe that's why their hold on the faithful was always so strong. But, Beth, you left something out."

She glanced away, because she *had* dropped one detail from her story. Considering his situation, she'd thought it kinder.

Leave it alone, Cory. Just leave it alone.

"Jacob's power was different from his grandfather's." Cory stared steadily at her, making her feel guilty and a little afraid. "Unique."

"It doesn't matter," she said, panicky. "He lost it, remember? It's gone."

It was coming like a train wreck. The twist in Cory's face and the helpless suffering in his eyes. He'd been strong as long as he was playing his game, trying to wring the truth from her like water from a cloth. But now the truth was out. The game over.

"If what you're saying about Agnes is true..." he mused. "Then Jeremiah *could* hear the stars, and the Prophet—our Prophet—could heal with a touch. He wrote all about it in his book." His voice broke. "He could heal me. Couldn't he?"

The Prophet's words came back to Beth: *The power to heal belongs to me and to God. I thereby forbid my people to receive a cure from any other source.*

What a cruel Law the Prophet had written, forbidding medical help. And all because he wanted to make himself feel more powerful—more godlike.

Beth had never seen him heal through faith. But when people were ill, they still went to the Prophet for his prayers. She'd thought it was only wishfulness. She'd never imagined that he'd once been able to really, truly take their sickness away. Like Jesus in the gospels.

The woman was dying, he'd written in his diary. *But I laid my hands upon her head and they glowed crimson, a blessed, holy color. I watched the pain drain from her eyes. Her sickness, like a demon, cast out.*

"No," Beth corrected Cory gently. "The Prophet can't heal you. Maybe he could have once. But Agnes was the last power in Red Creek, and she's gone."

She didn't mention that Agnes had stopped talking about the sounds she'd heard. Her sister might have lost her power, too.

But she couldn't believe it. If anyone could keep God's favor, it was Agnes.

"What if she came back, Beth?" Cory's eyes darted, desperately searching for the smallest sliver of hope. "What then?"

She didn't think Agnes could heal, or else she'd have cured Ezekiel. But maybe she just hadn't yet learned how. Maybe she was capable of a thousand kinds of miracles, if she tried.

Beth sighed. She didn't want to think of her sister. It was just as she'd always suspected—Agnes was special—but knowing for certain made her twitchy and irritable.

After all, no one ever handed *her* a destiny on a silver platter.

No powers made *her* life any easier. She'd had no choice but to escape from the bunker the hard way, no choice now but to watch Cory die, so slowly and painfully.

And then what? What would she do after?

Why didn't God care what happened to her?

Not fair, Beth thought, watching Cory drift into a feverish sleep. *It's just not fair.*

33

AGNES

Before I formed you in the womb I knew you, before you
were born I set you apart; I appointed you as a prophet to
the nations.

—JEREMIAH 1:5

Agnes woke gasping in the middle of the night from a vision of the bunker turning red—a vision of all her people, with hard, gem-like skins, wrapped in an infected embrace while they shivered like the tower of crows. The image singed her, charred her soul. She'd never been so badly frightened by a nightmare.

She pulled away from Ezekiel, her skin covered in goose bumps. She moved for her pack and Beth's diary, flipping quickly past her lost sister's secrets to the first blank page.

Words gathered in her mind like storm clouds.

But a pen. She needed a pen.

She lit a candle and crept into the lobby. All was silent except for the ticking of a clock. The library smelled, as always, of paper and dust.

In the kitchen, their emergency supplies: dry goods, tents, sleeping bags, extra blankets, backpacks, water. Matilda had prepared for everything. Prepared, even, for some god-awful day when they'd have to lose their library shelter.

Agnes grabbed a pen from a jar and sat down at the table, rubbing her arms against the cold. The impulse to write was so urgent her hand had cramped into a claw. She shook it, willing the muscles to relax.

She scribbled:

> I dream of human Nests.
> So relentlessly do I dream, that I know
> there is a message in them. But, God, what?

Her heart beat hard, thinking of all she'd seen, all she knew.

The church that Jeremiah Rollins had built was supposed to unite people in the solace of togetherness. Instead, it cordoned them off with walls of fear and hate. But the prayer space was the opposite. The prayer space, rich with the power of interconnection, was the light. Slowly, it was painting her a portrait of God. Only in place of brushstrokes and color, its medium was sound.

Holding the pen, her hand began to spasm and shake.

In the Bible, only a handful of people knew God so personally. All of them were prophets.

Is that why I was the one who escaped? Did You save me, so I could be Your prophet?

She wanted to spit out that thought like a bit of rancid food. It seemed too cruel, by far. And yet, ever more each day, the belief hardened in her bones. Between the prayer space and her dreams, it felt inescapable.

But that didn't mean she had to like it.

She tipped her chin to the ceiling, cried: "Just answer me one thing: Why didn't You save the kids?"

Then she dropped her pen and sobbed.

Agnes knew something about prophets, those fearful creatures who left heavy footprints in the Old Testament. They appeared in times of crisis, when relations between human beings and God were strained, and when people grappled with the implications of their existence. Hearing in ways others couldn't hear, prophets interpreted God's messages for the world.

Generally speaking, they were also men.

Lord, she prayed, *You know me. You know I'm not strong enough.*

Then she remembered herself running after the javelina, garden spade in hand. Her belly fluttered with sickly, nervous fear.

"Agnes?"

She looked up, startled to find Danny watching her, a textbook tucked under his arm.

"What's wrong, Agnes?"

She shook her head, wishing he hadn't seen her cry.

He pulled up a chair. "Look, I'm sorry. I was completely out of line, yelling at Max on your behalf. In my defense, it wasn't entirely about you." His lip twitched. "You know, I can't stand that guy."

For a moment, Agnes couldn't breathe. A man had never apologized to her before, and she knew he meant the words with his whole heart. Impulsively, she rested her hand on top of his large one.

"It's okay. I'm not crying because of what you said."

He glanced down at their hands and flushed. But he didn't move a muscle, and neither did she. Astounding, how a little dark could embolden a lonely spirit.

Danny's eyes, as always, held her carefully. "Are you frightened? Homesick?"

"Heartsick," she admitted. "And afraid."

"What can I do?"

She remembered the distance she'd felt between them when she first arrived. How she'd sensed acutely that he'd always be an Outsider, while she'd always be Red Creek's girl. In the flickering candlelight, she knew the distance was illusory. Weren't they both awake and afraid in the middle of the night? Didn't they both feel lonely and uncertain of the future?

"Danny," she whispered. "Do you believe in God?"

He glanced guiltily up at the ceiling. "No. I've been to church. But I never believed."

She blinked, trying to conceive of such a thing. "Isn't that lonesome?"

"Not really." Shadows danced vividly across his face. "I believe in people, and kindness, and in the importance of easing suffering."

She brightened. "Me too. I believe in all that, too."

He nodded, eyes flicking to his textbook. "That's why I want to be a doctor."

Now she understood why he was wakeful. "You had the nightmare again. About having to save someone?"

"If there's some emergency when my mom's not here..." She sensed his anxiety ratcheting up.

"When the time comes, you'll be ready," she told him. "I know you will."

"You really still believe in God?" he asked wonderingly. "Even after Red Creek?"

She smiled. "It's very easy for me to believe. I hear Him everywhere."

"Really?" He raised an eyebrow. "How about here?"

With a start, she realized their faces were very close. If she wanted, she could count the freckles on his nose.

God, is this a sin?

She closed her eyes, slipping into the prayer space. Time stopped, and the night expanded. She heard the gentle whisper of books and the singing moon outside. She heard the Outsiders humming with dreams, and Benny, hoping this new boy was his to keep. All the sounds of rest, and of a brief forgetting.

She heard Danny, too. His heart raced.

She opened her eyes. Something shifted in Danny's face, in the very air.

She was suddenly sure he was going to kiss her.

Treat the other sex like snakes.

The Prophet's words whipped out like a lash. She moved away, scraping her chair loudly against the floor. Danny startled.

"I didn't mean..." she started.

"It's okay," he said too quickly. "I understand."

He grabbed his book and, blushing, stood.

"Danny." She felt panicked, desperate to keep him there. "Can you help me with something?"

Relief smoothed his brow. Helping her, he was on familiar ground. "Anything."

She plucked at the collar of her prairie dress, loath to reveal the depths of her ignorance. "Can you show me how to use the library? How to look things up?"

"Sure." If her ignorance surprised him, he hid it well. "But I should warn you, I haven't used a library to look anything up since elementary school. Everything used to be, well, online.

"What do you want to know?"

God, there was *so much*. Why had she been given the prayer

space? Why had she been allowed to escape her lethal cult only to enter a crumbling, suffering world?

To truly understand, she knew, she'd have to face Gila's Nest. The human one.

Her intuition, once repressed, was a force she was slowly learning to trust.

But she wasn't ready to see the Nest, yet.

"Agnes?" Danny prodded gently.

"I want to know the history of Gila," she said, her mind on the well and the shriek that had erupted inside her—a human shriek. A girl's. "I want to know what happened here in 1922."

34

AGNES

The counsel of the Lord standeth for ever, the thoughts of
his heart to all generations.
—PSALM 33:11

By the time they'd finally pieced together the whole story, dawn streamed liquid through the library windows. Danny took off his glasses, rubbing tiredly at his eyes.

"I'm sorry I kept you up," Agnes whispered.

They crouched in the stacks, surrounded by piles of census data, municipal maps, and yellowed crime reports. Her legs had cramped from being so long tucked under her and her eyes burned with fatigue.

Now she knew whose scream she'd heard at the well, and she couldn't have felt sorrier for that girl. Or more ashamed of the land where she'd been born.

"That's okay. This was—well, *fun*'s the wrong word." Danny smiled wanly.

They both looked down at the arrest warrant for Jeremiah Rollins, who'd kidnapped a fourteen-year-old girl named Sarah Shiner.

"After he left here with his wife and Sarah, he founded my

town. Not to form a new religious community, but to hide from the law. They were going to hang him."

"Yes." Danny trod carefully around her grief. "That's the story the facts support."

Agnes drew her knees up beneath her skirt. "What are the chances that Zeke and I would end up here, of all the towns in the world?"

"One in a hundred?" He shrugged. "We're not so far from Red Creek, after all."

"Danny. Sarah Shiner was my great-grandmother. My father told me about her, just before I was engaged to Matthew Jameson. He said she ran away from Red Creek but left a son behind. That son and all his descendants suffered her disfavor. All that hate—it lasted generations. And she was from *here*."

Danny looked stricken.

Their candles had long since melted, guttered. Dawn painted long, finger-like shadows over the floor of the LOCAL HISTORY section.

"You were engaged?" Danny's voice was strained. "Like, to a grown man? Who?"

She winced. "His name was Matthew. He was a liar who believed himself to be faithful. In the end, he married my sister instead." She saw that he was going to speak—to express how sorry he was—and she hurried on, fearing the weight of his pity. "You would've liked Beth, I think. She was—*is*—very clever, very beautiful."

"Of course," he said earnestly. "*You* are those things, too."

He surprised her into laughing. "We couldn't look more different, Beth and me. It was almost like we weren't sisters at all."

Then her mind caught up with what he'd implied. That she—plain-faced, square-jawed Agnes—was beautiful.

Looking into his careful, seeking eyes, she wondered what he saw that she didn't.

Then sorrow flooded her, thinking of Beth and home. She wiped her nose with her mouse-brown sleeve. "Oh, Danny, what if *this* was why God allowed me and Zeke to escape? What if I'm a kind of witness to the horror of my home? A crypt keeper?"

His face softened. If she reached for him, she knew, he'd hold her against his side.

"Agnes. God didn't *allow* anything. You escaped because you're tough as nails. You escaped because you're you."

His words rang with truth. God allowing this or forbidding that—that was Red Creek thinking. The God she experienced in the prayer space was more complicated. A thousand-fold more nuanced and complex.

"I can't think straight." She pressed her fingertips to her eyes. "I've never been so tired."

"You're here now. Red Creek is behind you."

She swallowed. "It'll never be behind me."

"No, of course not," he hurried to say. "I just meant, don't beat yourself up. You've done a lot."

Yes, but there's more.

And though she couldn't explain it even to herself, she felt increasingly certain that God would soon reveal exactly what that *more* was.

Looking at knowledgeable, rational Danny, she asked herself if she had lost her mind. If just maybe she was hearing sounds when there were none.

She didn't wonder long. Whatever its reasons for being with her, the prayer space was the realest thing she'd ever experienced. To find it, she had only to close her eyes and sink deep.

Inevitably, she knew, God would ask something of her in

return. Wasn't that how it always worked in the Bible? Joseph didn't wear his coat of dreams for free, and Noah wasn't warned of rain just to predict the weather.

Danny contemplated the window in a way that made her pay close attention to what he said next.

"Agnes, I need you to know that helping you escape was the best thing I ever did in my whole damned life. I've gotten a lot of As on a lot of stupid exams. But I've never been prouder of anything than of being there for you."

His gaze slammed into her, stealing her breath.

"You mean that?" Agnes whispered.

"I do. There's nothing like an apocalypse to show you what really matters."

She stared at the same spot on the window that had so fascinated him a moment ago.

"It meant everything to me, too, when you came to Red Creek," she admitted. "Changed everything. But I never could figure out why you tried so hard to help me. I must have seemed like a lost cause."

"Agnes, please look at me."

She did, faintly trembling. Or vibrating. It was difficult to say.

"I don't believe in love at first sight," he murmured. "But seeing you so fierce and determined in that graveyard, with a braid of the longest hair I'd ever seen—I'll tell you something. It gave me one hell of a crush." He laughed deeply. "Honestly, it was like getting hit by a train."

Her mouth dropped open, years of repressed and stifled feelings stirring.

To hell with the Prophet, she thought. *I'm dying to kiss him.*

Then she remembered Sarah's tragic story, and her suspicions about her own destiny.

She couldn't kiss him. Not until she understood who—or what—she really was.

Danny broke eye contact first, began collecting the old papers, books, documents.

"You should get some rest. I'll clean up."

She was too exhausted to argue.

After a few steps, though, she glanced back.

She quickly counted the freckles over his nose.

Fourteen.

35

AGNES

You will seek me and find me when you seek me with all your heart.

—JEREMIAH 29:13

That morning, while Zeke watched superhero movies in the kitchen with Max, Agnes prayed.

She prayed so hard she began to weep, her face a mess of salt and wet. She didn't know, at first, whether she prayed for guidance—or for mercy.

"God," she said. "I know you want me to visit the human Nest. I know that like Jeremiah's well, it's only waiting for its chance to speak." She exhaled. "But I don't want a destiny, please. I only want to be an Outsider, unafraid and unattached."

She pictured Danny's face, how close they'd come, last night, to kissing.

And hadn't she earned a moment's respite? A moment's peace?

If God took over her life, she could be many things—powerful, sainted, wise—but never that one thing she'd always been denied.

If God took her life, she'd never be *free*.

On her knees, she felt untethered, adrift. The shock of so much newness had collapsed her. The Outside, the strengthening prayer space, even her near-kiss with Danny had drained her. But worst of all was the thought—curdling into certainty—that she'd come to Gila to become a prophet.

A hateful idea, not least because it still tasted, to her Red Creek tongue, of blasphemy.

And yet. She couldn't deny that she knew things she shouldn't—couldn't—know. Huge, painful, unwieldy things.

She flinched, recalling the sound of Sarah Shiner's scream in the prayer space.

That *shriek*.

"God," she whispered. "If I can't change Your mind, then tell me clearly. Who am I supposed to be? What do You want me to do?"

A tentative knock on the door. "Can I come in?"

Jazz.

Agnes straightened quickly, wiping her swollen eyes. "Yes. I'm all right."

The Outsider took one look at her face and hurried forwards. "No, you're not. Oh, Agnes." Jazz wrapped her tanned arms around her neck. She smelled of cinnamon. "I understand completely."

"You do?"

She nodded vigorously. "You're caught between two worlds. But I can help you."

Agnes looked skeptically at her. "You can?"

"Did you know I used to keep butterflies?"

Agnes shook her head, bewildered. What did butterflies have to do with anything?

"Monarchs." Jazz's words turned melancholy. "Every spring, I'd raise them from caterpillars. Max thinks I'm crazy, but I really, honestly believed . . . that they told the future."

Agnes couldn't hide her smile.

Jazz blushed, hurrying through her speech. "Really. Like, if ten of twelve were healthy, I was going to have a great year at school. But if only six made it out of the cocoon, I'd get injured at cheer practice and have to sit the whole season out."

"What happened last spring?"

Jazz looked away. "The spring before Petra, a parasite infected my cocoons. They took weeks too long to hatch, and when they did—wasps came out."

Horrified, Agnes looked more deeply into Jazz's syrup-colored eyes. Was it possible that signs and symbols had guided the Outsider girl to this place, as the prayer space had guided her? Was it possible that God had brought their unique little group—Danny with his science and his nightmares, Matilda with her motherliness, Jazz with her eccentricities, and Max with his superheroes—together for a reason?

Her pulse leapt into her wrists, knowing exactly what she'd have to do to answer that question—see the human Nest—but she still wasn't ready to do it.

The idea of giving up her own life in service of something illimitable . . . not to mention the idea of seeing Nested *people* . . .

Jazz grabbed her hand. "Come on. I know just how to make you feel better."

Agnes had no choice but to follow the excited girl through the stacks to the BIOGRAPHY section, where she slept with Max.

She was startled to see only one sleeping bag spread before two pillows. She felt seared, thinking of Danny—and quickly stopped herself thinking.

"This is my stuff." Jazz's luggage overflowed. A rainbow of blouses, dresses, hair ribbons, and shoes. She plucked from the pile—jean shorts and a lavender top.

"Agnes, you need a change. A big one. And I think this is your color."

Looking at those insubstantial clothes, Agnes's cheeks burned. Surely Jazz couldn't be serious?

A memory slithered out of the shadows. She was six years old at the watering hole—with the Jameson boys, and just as naked. Father had screamed at her.

If I ever catch you naked outdoors again, I'll kill you.

Only now Father wasn't here. Maybe Jazz was right that she needed a change.

The Outsider girl turned her back, giving her privacy. Agnes took a deep breath and let her dress fall to her feet. She zipped up Jazz's shorts and pulled the top over her head, waiting for the transformation—but nothing happened. Though dressed, she felt utterly naked. Beaming, Jazz guided her to the storm window.

Agnes stared sadly at her reflection in the thick glass.

She didn't like to see her skin so exposed—it was like seeing a tree stripped of its bark. Her thoughts remained trapped in Red Creek's hateful net, but it wasn't only that.

This isn't my future.

Change was coming, yes. But she was never meant to be an Outsider.

"I'm sorry," she said. "It just isn't me."

Jazz's smile slipped. "Really? You're sure?"

Agnes was.

"You really do look wonderful." Jazz, reflected beside her in the glass, paused. "Wait. Will you try one more thing?"

Agnes nodded. She'd try a hundred different garments if it made her new friend happy—but her final decision would be the same. She was no caterpillar, capable of blooming overnight. She was only and always herself.

Jazz darted to her bag, returning with a scarlet satin ribbon, shiny and startlingly bright.

Agnes gasped.

"Your hair is incredible. It must be waist length? Maybe you could tie it with something colorful. What do you think?"

Stunned, Agnes let the Outsider's deft fingers undo her braid. She closed her eyes, remembering back to her earliest childhood, when her mother used to plait her hair.

Jazz began threading ribbon through her braids. Agnes wasn't sure she'd like it until she saw her reflection.

Her eyes, her face, were strong, serious, determined. Somehow the bold ribbon emphasized those qualities. Once she would've reprimanded herself for vanity. Now she nearly preened. She knew her poor sister, ever fond of the mirror, would approve.

Jazz clapped her hands. "You like it. I can tell."

"Thank you," she breathed. "I'll wear it always."

And especially, she thought, *tonight, when I go to see the human Nest.*

This token of love from an Outsider was the final piece of armor she needed.

The shining scarlet—that vibrant, forbidden color—reminded her of what she'd been through to come so far. And she couldn't help but wonder what she might be capable of, if she pushed herself only a little further.

In the mirror, she saw at last the beauty Danny had claimed to see. A beauty mixed with strangeness and, most strikingly, with strength.

In the mirror, Agnes lifted her chin.

The hour had come to learn what God would ask of her, here on the Outside.

36

BETH

Man is like to vanity: his days are as a shadow that
passeth away.
—PSALM 144:4

Cory's screams drove Beth into the street on their sixth day living inside the abandoned church.

Terrible screams, like stakes piercing her heart.

"I'll be back," she told him. "I'm going to find medicine. I swear, I'll come back as fast as I can."

His hands clawed the altar cloth they used for a blanket and his eyes bulged in their sockets. He didn't look like the boy she'd kissed at the canyon's edge. He hardly looked human.

He'll die tonight.

Outside, she gripped her elbows and tilted her face towards the white, indifferent moon, wishing herself blameless.

It was undeniable: Cory was dying because she'd been too foolish to flee Red Creek when she'd had the chance. He was dying for her mistakes.

Her legs tensed, yearning to *run*. To race into the night and never look back. But she couldn't—not now.

"Don't mess this up, Beth," she scolded herself. "It's almost over. Don't ruin it like everything else."

She adjusted the tattered lace of her wedding dress around her waist—her starved hips bony compass points—brushed her sweat-damp hair from her face, and hurried in the direction of the midwife's hut.

She would sell her soul for medicine, for something, anything, to temper Cory's pain. She'd tried calling the hospital from the landline in the Prophet's office. She'd tried over and over again, but the phone only rang. It felt bewildering, like a punishment. She imagined spiteful Outsiders ignoring her, laughing at her because she called from Red Creek.

The birthing hut was her last hope. It was against the Laws to ease the pain of childbirth, but were the midwives as faithful as they seemed? Or had someone secreted a bit of Outsider medicine for emergencies?

The hut was a quarter mile down the road. Off the beaten path, so people couldn't hear the labor screams. She pushed open the thick, wooden door—like a cellar door, almost—and shut it behind her.

Inside, darkness and horror.

In Red Creek, giving birth was God's punishment for being female. The air reeked of eucalyptus, lavender tincture, and human fluids. Mothers were expected to birth on an earthen floor. Cold seeped through her shoes as she walked. There were lanterns at the entrance, in case of midnight labors. She lit one and raised it over vats and buckets for catching blood.

Horrible.

Her skin crawled at the thought of touching anything in this dreadful place, but she was determined to help Cory.

Furiously, she emptied jars of crushed thyme and minced

sage, looking for hidden pills, secret bottles. She ripped through the drawers of the desk—cheaper and smaller than the Prophet's—and riffled through a pile of moldering linens. She upended baskets of grisly tools—forceps and clamps and knives—desperately searching.

Nothing, nothing, and more nothing.

Outside, wind gusted, howling.

"What were you—sheep?" she screamed at the absent midwives. "How could you follow every stupid rule?"

She slid down the wall, collapsing, despairing.

The room smelled of blood. She caught sight of herself in a full-length mirror, and her reflection shocked her. She looked ghostly in her filthy wedding gown. Her eyes hollows, her hair unkempt. The beauty she'd prized so highly had gone. She hardly recognized herself.

In the mirror, she saw her mother.

For the first time since the bunker, she let herself cry. Bawling, weeping like a child.

She felt cold—dreadfully cold. Her arms ached for the warmth and comfort Cory was no longer able to provide. They ached to hold the twins, the sweet little girls who loved to nuzzle into her embrace. If she closed her eyes and wrapped her arms around herself, she could almost feel them.

Almost.

With a sob, Beth opened her eyes and spotted something on a table.

A heavy book. A *legendary* book.

The Book of Begats.

She blinked, surprised it hadn't disappeared into the bunker along with the midwives. Red Creek's families were large, their genealogies multibranch and confusing. To keep lineages straight, every birth was recorded in that one great volume, like the section of the Bible that read like an interminable list: *and Isaiah begat Methuselah, and Methuselah begat Ezekiel*... and on and on, forever.

Chewing nervously on the split ends of her hair, Beth perched on the edge of the bed, examining the leather tome more studiously than she did any of her Sunday school work.

Red Creek's births and deaths webbed over dozens of pages. Her mind crowded with names and faces, with ghosts and memories and dreams. Her lantern flickered, casting odd shadows, as the names of the dead or dying scrolled past.

Somewhere near the back of the book she found her own family. Her mother's name was marked with an X. Written beside it was a single word: *Outsider.*

She traced her family's lineage back to the first of the Rollinses—to Jeremiah and his second wife. That second wife's name was scratched out as if Jeremiah had meant to erase her, but Beth knew her already.

She was Sarah Shiner, the girl he'd kidnapped from the Outsider town.

Sarah Shiner, her great-grandmother.

God blesses runaways. She remembered those words from the Old Testament. Even though Hagar ran from Abraham, He'd blessed her and her son, Ishmael.

Beth's thoughts swirled.

Two women in her family had successfully fled Red Creek: Agnes and Sarah. Though it pained her to think beyond Cory's death, she couldn't help but wonder if that meant that she, like Agnes, had a destiny waiting for her Outside.

For the first time since the bunker, she closed her eyes and prayed.

God, are You watching me? God, are You there?

It might've been her imagination grasping wildly for comfort. But in the dark, she had the sharp, distinct feeling that she was— and *was not*—alone.

Cory was still, too still beneath the altar cloth.

Seeing him, every muscle in her body weakened.

God forgive me. I wasn't here.

"Cory." Beth groped her way to his side. "Cory, can you hear me?"

She placed a hand on his chest and felt it rising, falling. But she sensed death hovering like a specter, looking over her shoulder into the face of the boy she'd very nearly loved. The boy she should've loved, if it hadn't all gone so wrong.

A tear rivered down her face.

She was sure he was too far gone to speak. Then, after what felt like ages, he did.

His mouth worked, but the words were bubbles on his lips— thin puffs of breath.

Jesus, Agnes, she thought frantically. *I could really use some help.*

"It isn't over," he whispered, his voice dry as autumn leaves. "For every flood there is an ark. For every exile...a prophet."

He was delirious. Babbling. She put her hand over her mouth to stifle a sob.

When his eyes rolled up into his head, she didn't shrink or scream. She rested her palm on his sweaty forehead and waited for the convulsion that would end his pain.

His back arched. She leaned forwards to hear his final words.

"It can't all be for nothing." He ground his teeth. "It can't, it can't!"

"Shh," she soothed. "Be peaceful, Cory. It's all right."

"It's not all right! We left them to die. They're all dying, down there." The muscles in his neck stood out like ropes. "Agnes must come back! Agnes *must be here!*" He clutched her hair with shocking strength. "Bring her back. Promise me you'll *bring Agnes home.*"

He went limp.

Beth rocked back on her heels, a jealous terror pounding in her head. It was awful and wrong and unutterably selfish to feel this way as Cory lay dying, she knew that—she did.

Still, bitterness consumed her. She'd never forget that, in the end, even the boy who loved her didn't want her, or ask for her, or say her name.

In his final hour, he wanted Agnes instead.

37

AGNES

The Lord will rise up . . . to do his work, his strange work,
and perform his task, his alien task.
—Isaiah 28:21

Once again, Agnes was sneaking out in the middle of the night.

Not out of her trailer to meet a boy—but out of the library.

She went to meet God.

She packed her bag with Beth's diary, her phone, and one of Matilda's flashlights. She kissed Zeke's cheek (thinking, *Just in case*), then strode quickly through the library halls, praying she wouldn't wake anyone.

How would she explain herself to Danny or Matilda, if she did? Even Jazz, with her firm belief in the divinatory power of butterflies, would think she'd fallen off the deep end.

She followed the cobbled path, remembering the message inscribed on the lip of the well in 1922: *There is no greater sin than to deny God's gift to you.* She despised the patriarch who'd etched those words. But might the message still be true? Though she'd only been a child, she *had* denied God's gift. After Mrs. King shattered her knuckle, she'd almost smothered the prayer space for good.

In the Bible, sin didn't just mean hurting other people. From Deuteronomy on, sin was any life lived out of harmony, and out of tune, with God.

Her footsteps faltered. She was terrified.

Only in the prayer space would she find the strength to carry on. She stepped into it, opening wide and deep.

Minutes passed, punctuated by the click of her boots. Beyond the well, the cobblestones became a dirt path, then the path, too, disappeared. Nothing but saguaros and boulders marked the desert outskirts. The human Nest had nowhere to hide. The stars sang above, the earth below, and in between...

The sight of the Nest tore her inner world asunder.

The tower of crows was one thing, but these were *people*.

She guessed that sixty men, women, and children with shining hard skins were clinging tightly together. *Petrified*. They trembled like a great tuning fork.

Agnes held very still. Then she touched the ribbon in her hair, drawing strength.

She stepped closer—it was a Gordian knot of legs, arms, red glowing eyes. It was impossible to pick any single person apart. They might have been made that way. Shaped from the beginning into a many-eyed statue.

When the wind swept their crystal bristles, those bristles stirred. When the light of her flashlight disturbed a red-marbled eye, it blinked.

Her knees weakened, wobbling.

"God," she whispered. "Why am I here? What do you want me to see?"

She closed her eyes, leaning hard into the soundscape. She heard the emotion and passion underlying God's song. She heard sadness and pathos; grief and regret.

The humming was, and had always been, a mourning song.

If God was the source of the Virus, *punishment* was far too crude a concept. *Mystery*—that was closer. Just as all suffering had always been mystery, Petra was the shivering embodiment of suffering's most unfathomable depths.

And God suffered with these people. He *grieved*.

"Teach me," she begged. "Tell me what it means."

The prayer space swelled around her. The many-faced human Nest vibrated in the moonlight.

Her knees gave way and Agnes fell. Gravel stuck in her palms. Tears dropped from her chin and into the red dirt as she wept in Gila's desert—grieving, along with God, for the world.

Something made her look up.

The face closest to hers belonged to a little girl. It might've been Faith, her little sister, with her hair tied back into a ponytail—but it couldn't be. Yet she knew this small, gem-hard creature was a relative of hers.

Sarah Shiner's descendant, born on the Outside—her daughter's granddaughter.

It was no accident Agnes had come to Gila. She'd been brought here, to see *this* child's face.

This is the moment. It's coming now.

Her mouth never moved, yet the girl spoke.

From *inside Agnes* she spoke, but the voice was really God's, still and small yet somehow thunderous. It was the first time He'd ever spoken to her in words. Her throat dried up, and her muscles tensed with fear. A sudden, mortal fear, like she'd once felt looking into the yellow eyes of a catamount.

Oh my God, she thought.

There will come a test of your righteousness, the still voice said. ***If you fail, your journey ends. If you succeed, you will usher in a new age.***

This was what she'd expected and feared—the prophetic call. Noah had one, and Ezekiel, and Isaiah, and Jeremiah, too. Their whole lives had hinged upon a few words, shouted or whispered or roared from a mountaintop.

Her life would never be the same.

Then, silence. The message had been uttered; the die cast. There was nothing anymore to hear but the Nest, and the earth, and the whirling, windswept stars.

Agnes stood, smoothing the pleats of her dress to still her shaking hands.

Then, compelled by some force beyond herself, she leaned towards Sarah Shiner's descendant and kissed her red bristled cheek.

"God bless you." The very words she'd spoken to Beth. "Bless you in your time of need."

She stepped back, touching her lips.

A mistake.

Had she made a grievous mistake?

Agnes's skin hadn't been pierced. She hadn't been exposed to the infection. She wondered if the prayer space had protected her.

A test of your righteousness.

The human Nest shivered. What could such a test be?

And what did it mean, that her journey might end?

The prayer space, she realized. *I could lose it.*

She fingered the scarlet ribbon, trying to believe herself strong enough to work God's will as a girl, not as a man, and as a stranger in a strange, infected land.

It wasn't until she stepped out of the prayer space that she heard the out-loud sound of someone coming. Of *many* coming from the west, in gravel-crunching trucks.

A dozen headlights poured across the desert with stinging brightness. In the distance a car horn blared, and the trucks, dark on the horizon, were coming fast.

Agnes's stomach clenched.

There's almost no population left in Arizona, Matilda had said. *Only Burn Squads roam the desert now.*

Agnes picked up her skirts and bolted for the library. Images of fire and rapturous destruction teemed in her mind. And Max and Jazz had lost one home to a rogue Squad's flames already.

"Oh no," she murmured. "Oh *no*."

She prayed she'd reach the others in time.

38

AGNES

*And he said unto them, "Render therefore unto Caesar
the things which be Caesar's, and unto God the things
which be God's."*

—LUKE 20:25

It was Jazz's wails Agnes would never forget—her wails and the
sound of Max trying to calm her in the library's gloom.

Matilda and Danny bickered in the kitchen, loudly disagree-
ing over what they ought to do. Agnes stayed with Ezekiel and
Benny in their room. Ezekiel curled up in her lap and lodged his
thumb in his mouth.

The Burn Squad had come for the human Nest—Agnes
understood that much. If they were anything like the Squad that
razed Jazz's home, they'd burn the whole town along with it.

Zeke regarded her solemnly. "Are we going to have to leave
this place, too?"

Dread curled in her belly. "I don't know."

He buried his face in the cat's fur. "I thought you said this was
our new home."

Agnes didn't know what to say. *Home* was what she wanted

more than anything, the safety and the permanence, but God kept ripping it out from under her like a rug.

A door slammed, and Agnes jumped. Someone had left the library.

"Come on, Zeke."

"No." He held Benny. "It's scary out there."

"I need you to be brave."

How many times would she have to speak those words before they were finally safe?

They met the others in the lantern-lit lobby. Jazz remained hidden in the stacks.

"My mom went to meet them." Danny ran his hand through his hair. "She thinks she can convince them to leave us alone."

"That's nuts," Max hissed. "They're murderous, those Squads. We've got to get out of here, right now."

"Just wait. Wait a second." Agitated, Danny adjusted his glasses. "They might be more reasonable than the Squad that—"

"*Reasonable?* Are you kidding me? We could be *on fire* any minute!"

Danny's eyes flashed. "My mother put me in charge. Understand?"

Max scoffed. "Why? Because Dr. Know-It-All knows best? My girlfriend is fucking *traumatized*, and you're standing here telling me—"

Zeke shrank against Agnes's side, and she felt a spark of anger. Zeke had been frightened enough for one lifetime. She wouldn't let them fight like this in front of him.

"Quiet, both of you." Agnes turned to Danny. "What exactly is your mother's plan?"

He covered his mouth, stifling a hysterical laugh. "She went— oh my God, it's so crazy, but so *her*—"

"She went to invite them for breakfast," Max spat. "Friggin' breakfast."

"Your mother did the right thing." Agnes feigned certainty. "The hospitable thing. I'll put the water on to boil. Zeke." She looked at her brother. "Can you set the table, please?"

Danny looked incredulous. "Are you sure he should be here?"

Zeke silently beseeched her, not wanting to be sent away.

"Danny," she snapped. "Chicken soup. Heat it up, okay?"

"And what's my mission, Sergeant Red Creek?" Max drawled sarcastically. "Mac and cheese?"

From the stacks, a gut-wrenching sob.

"Yes." In a way, this wasn't so different from dealing with the kids back home. Her voice softened. "But first, check on Jazz."

Even inside the library, the Captain of the Burn Squad wore aviator sunglasses—a dark, visor-like shield. He was a mountain of a man, taller even than Danny. Like all Outsiders, his smile was unreadable, a white slash. At his throat, he wore a cross that spun the candlelight into gold.

"Thanks." He coldly eyed the steaming banquet they'd prepared—chicken soup, macaroni, and powdered milk. "But I can't stay."

"Won't you sit, at least?" Matilda gestured to a chair.

He shook his head. "My men are waiting."

Jazz never made it into the kitchen. Max said she couldn't bear the sight of his uniform—a black, flame-retardant jacket with silver shoulder patches. Up close, the patches were clearly duct tape: the mark of a makeshift militia, hastily thrown together at the end of the world.

No one had to tell Agnes the Captain planned to burn Gila to the ground. She could smell gasoline on him, see the fire in his eyes.

But maybe Matilda could convince him, change his mind. Agnes clutched at the hope.

"My understanding is that you want to stay, correct?" He removed his black gloves, revealing hands laced with pale burn scars.

Matilda crossed her arms over her chest. "Yes. The library is safe."

"Wrong," he boomed, and Agnes flinched. "There's a Nest along your perimeter. It's got to be blazed."

Agnes touched her lips, remembering the girl she'd kissed.

"Nests are everywhere," Matilda insisted. "There's no place we could go where we wouldn't have to live with one."

The muscles in his neck tautened. "What about the military outposts? You heard the evacuation orders. It was foolish to plant yourself here." His eyes flicked around the room, and when he spoke again, his voice dripped disdain. "And with *kids.*"

"The roads..."

"Are unsafe, yes." He flexed his scarred hands. "Luckily, we're not just cleaning up wreckage. We're also collecting stragglers."

Max huffed, and the Captain spun on his heel. "Something to add, son?"

Max paled. "I don't—" He glanced at Zeke, as if drawing courage. "I don't believe you. You people murdered my family."

Danny glared daggers at Max.

But Agnes watched the Captain.

He was the one on whom everything depended: their home and the existence of the human Nest. The final resting place of Sarah Shiner's great-granddaughter.

He eased his sunglasses off slowly, revealing silver scars that crowded his eyes like crow's-feet. "I'm sorry to hear that. We had noble intentions, but not every Squad stayed on mission. Not every captain respected policy."

Matilda held up her hands. "Captain, we're taking precautions—"

"How? For all you know, the Nests could wake up one day. Turn on us in a flash."

"It's not a war." Matilda's pitch climbed. "It's an epidemic."

"More like a war." His voice had roughened, turned gravelly as the desert outside. "But we're on *your* side. We can protect you. See you to safety."

"This place is safe," insisted Danny. "We haven't seen any walking red creatures. They must all be Nested already. Why can't you leave us alone?"

The Captain shook his head, looking for all the world like he regretted the necessity of burning Gila to the ground.

But Agnes didn't think he really did.

Watching him, she thought Matilda was right. He saw himself as a soldier in a mysterious war. True belief ran through his veins like poison, and true believers were always the same.

"Policy is, we burn."

Matilda blanched. "There has to be some way to file a complaint—"

"All due respect, but that's the old world you're thinking of. If you want to travel with us, I'll need your decision now."

Agnes sagged. How could this happen? God watched over Gila. Didn't He?

"Well, kids." Matilda dropped the words like an anchor. "What do you think?"

Danny took Agnes's hand, their fingers twining, gripping in a room smelling of gunpowder and lighter fluid. Warmth traveled up her arm.

"I've heard things I don't like about the military outposts," he said. "Too many guns, not enough food—"

"That's right." Max sounded relieved. "We're better off on our own. Anyway, Jazz wouldn't—she'd never—"

"I see," the Captain said flatly. "And where do you plan to go, alone?"

"Mercy Hospital," Matilda answered quickly. "It won't take long by car."

"Ah." The Captain slid his glasses back onto his face. "I'm afraid that's no longer an option."

Matilda's false smile fell away. "What?"

"The gas in your vehicles has been requisitioned by the Burn Squad, under Ordinance 2.81 of the state of Arizona. We've already siphoned your tanks."

"So, you'll give it back now." Max's voice quavered. "Right?"

The Captain considered him. "No."

"Are you kidding me?" Max was nearly shouting. "I mean, is this a joke? What are we supposed to do? *Walk?*"

"I believe I've laid out your options quite clearly."

Agnes felt desperation rising like bile. Walking or driving, she didn't care how they got to Mercy. But burning the Nest, any Nest, was wrong. She could feel it.

She opened her mouth to say something—*anything*—then closed it. What if the Squad's arrival wasn't a mistake? What if they were never meant to stay here?

She remembered: *There will come a test of your righteousness.*

She felt the blood drain from her face, and Danny shot a fast, concerned glance at her.

"If you've made your choice, I'll need to see some identification," the Captain said.

"Why?" Matilda demanded. "You're not the law."

"We like to know who we're dealing with. Hand them over."

The Outsiders moved smoothly for their wallets, but Agnes had never owned one. The Captain studied one ID after another, giving a sharp nod to each.

Then, expectantly, he turned to Agnes and Zeke.

"I don't have a driver's license." She tried not to squirm under his scrutiny.

"Learner's permit? School ID?"

"No."

The Captain eyed her. "Where are you from, exactly?"

"Red Creek."

He snapped to attention. "What's the news up there? Anyone need our help?"

She gripped Danny's hand, too hard. *Help.* Where was "help" the night the Prophet condemned his people to the bunker? Where was "help" when Agnes and the kids were growing up unschooled or when her fifteen-year-old sister was married off?

She stared at him, so flooded with anger she couldn't speak.

Zeke piped up. "If you go to Red Creek, they'll shoot you to death."

Beside her, Danny stilled.

The Captain knelt stiffly in front of Ezekiel. "What do you mean by that, son?"

Agnes strained to hear him. "They hate Outsiders. More than anything."

"I see. And do you hate Outsiders?" The Captain's head swiveled, hawk fast, to Agnes. "Does your sister?"

"My sister *loves* Outsiders, but mostly, I think they're weird." He brightened. "I like the movies, though. *Batman's* my favorite."

The Captain chuckled and held out his hand. Gravely, Zeke shook it.

Agnes exhaled.

"Vacate the premises by noon tomorrow." He stood. "You won't want to stay any longer than that."

Danny and Agnes walked him to the door, and he left in a swirl of gasoline fumes. Realizing their hands were still linked, they glanced at each other in embarrassed surprise. But there was no time to mutter apologies and excuses.

From the kitchen came the wrenching sound of Danny's mother weeping.

They stood rooted in place, listening while steadfast Matilda broke down.

Danny turned to Agnes, his face riven with worry. "It wasn't supposed to be like this. I brought you here because I thought it would be safe. For you, for your brother."

Her heart softened, because he was apologizing to her again—this time, for the state of the whole Outside. She wrapped his hand in both of hers and held it beneath her chin. His smell had become familiar, comforting.

"I know, Danny."

"Do you?" He peered at her. "The world was never like this, before. Never so uncertain."

Agnes marshaled all her faith. "It will be safe again, one day. I believe in you Outsiders, you know."

Danny smiled gratefully, if sadly, at her. "You have more faith than anyone I've ever met," he said. "I'm starting to think it's some kind of superpower."

Agnes squeezed his hand, but inside, she wondered if she could bear to lose another home. If the wound, so soon reopened, would ever have a chance to heal.

39

AGNES

I answered thee in the secret place of thunder.
—PSALM 81:7

The next morning, while the others finished packing, Agnes returned to Jeremiah's well, to say goodbye.

What she really wanted was to see the little girl in the Nest one last time. But focusing her power, she sensed the Squad members had already assembled there. She heard every invading footfall, every excitedly beating heart. They were going to incinerate the Nest, the library, the entire town.

In the prayer space, she couldn't even hate them for it. They were God's creatures, too.

She pressed her belly against the well's stone lip, bending to read the message again. *There is no greater sin than to deny God's gift to you.*

Feeling like she'd swallowed a mouthful of hot, black sand, Agnes began to cry.

Hard as the Laws of Red Creek were, they promised that if you followed them, God would always support you, protect you, love you. But the still, small voice had spoken to Agnes, its message resoundingly clear. From now on, God would no longer be her port in a storm. From now on, He'd be something very different: the force that moved her, challenged her, pushed her even to the breaking point.

She'd read the Bible. God didn't ease the way for His prophets. More than one of them had wished he'd never been born.

A twig snapped behind her. She spun around.

The Captain stood on the path, his hand hovering over his gun. "What are you doing out here? And alone?"

She tipped her chin defiantly. "Saying goodbye."

"You're so attached to this infected place?" He looked around, sniffing the air. "It reeks of them."

"I only smell wind and air."

"Lucky you." He paused, staring. "Are you armed?"

"No."

He frowned. "You'll get yourself infected, or worse."

She'd meant to keep a stony, dignified silence. Instead, she found herself pleading, "Captain. Don't burn the Nest."

He stood stoic, watchful. The cross at his throat winked in the sun.

"It's a sin against God," Agnes said tremulously. In a way, she knew, she was delivering her first prophecy. "I think, one day, you'll have to repent of it."

"According to your creed, is saving humanity a sin?"

"Our creeds are the same. At least underneath, where it matters." She flushed, hearing herself. "And burning the Nests won't save humanity. The people in them are alive, in their own way. That means something. Don't you think?"

The Captain gazed at her from behind his aviators for a long time.

Shouts carried from the outskirts of town—the voices of his men, jubilant. Agnes smelled smoke. She imagined the face of Sarah's great-granddaughter, melting in the flames.

Agnes was only human. She wanted to rail, rage, shake her fist at God.

But He'd been very clear. If she failed the coming test, she'd lose the prayer space and the protection of His care—her and Zeke's only real protection Outside. So she took a deep breath and resolved to begin the painful work of accepting the mystery of suffering—whether petrified or soft flesh, it was all the same.

She thought of Job: *Behold, he taketh away, who can hinder him? Who will say unto Him, What doest thou?*

"The nurse has made up her mind," the Captain said at last. "But your brother is only a child. You should come with me."

Agnes knew he thought he did a kindness. "Thank you. But we'll be fine."

He glanced pointedly up at the sky. "You know a storm's coming. Don't you?"

She nodded.

"There's no safety net out here, no one to call if you're in a fix." He stepped closer. "Look, this is against policy. But if anything happens, you can reach me with this."

He held out a chunky black device with a wobbling antenna. A radio, she guessed.

Agnes let his arm hang. "I won't need help from you, Captain."

"It's a hard world, Agnes," he said gruffly. "Aren't you afraid?"

"Why do you care?" Agnes asked, without rancor.

He rubbed his stubbled jaw. "I had a daughter, you know."

She winced. "Is she . . . ?"

His face convulsed. "Every member of my Squad carries a radio. This one is yours."

Agnes frowned, taking it. "I don't even know how to use this."

He put his hand over hers. "Press the button. Here."

The radio chittered with static.

"For the next three days, we'll be rounding up stragglers. If anything happens during that time, press the button. Easy."

"Thank you." Agnes didn't know what else to say.

The Captain nodded, turned, and continued down the path. He was going to meet his Squad and destroy what remained of Gila, as God had destroyed Gomorrah.

Agnes stuck the radio in the bottom of her pack. It was noon, and the sky was already darkening with smoke.

With an effort of will, she turned her mind to the test.

She knew she couldn't afford to fail.

Everyone was assembled on the steps, supplies heaped on their backs in hefty backpacks supported by metal poles. Matilda had imagined this possibility—that they might be homeless at the end of the world—and prepared with tents and sleeping bags in rain-proof fabrics.

Danny had a backpack waiting for Agnes. She would carry her share of the food and camping supplies, too.

With pride, Agnes noticed that Zeke had remembered his cooler.

"I'll take that now," she told him. "But it's still your job to remember it every morning. We can't lose it anywhere. Understand?"

He nodded, fretfully chewing one of Max's toothpicks.

"Agnes, are you ready to go?" Matilda asked.

She wasn't ready. She had no idea why God wanted them on the road, what He had planned, or how much more they'd lose before the end.

But she answered, "Yes."

It stormed twice on the road where no birds sang.

The first was an ash storm. Gila was on fire.

As the fire grew, smoke blotted the sky. Buildings, books, and Nested people were burning. The wind swirled gray specks into their mouths.

Agnes wept silently for the little girl in the Nest.

Don't worry about me, she heard a voice whisper in her mind. *You gave me your blessing. Remember?*

But what could a blessing matter now?

"Cover your faces!" Matilda shouted, passing out rags. "Smoke inhalation can kill."

"What about Benny?" Zeke called. Matilda didn't hear him at first. He screamed it again, louder. "What about Benny?"

Originally, they'd planned to stuff the cat into one of their backpacks, but Zeke had refused. Now Benny rode on his shoulders, slung around his neck like an ugly, orange scarf.

"He'll be fine!" Matilda cupped her hands to yell. "We'll be out from under it soon."

Agnes hoped so. The prayer space felt wild, out of control. It shot ahead of her, pressuring, demanding, *Hurry up, hurry up!*

I'm not the one in charge anymore. The thought shivered across her mind. *Maybe I never was.*

The second storm came near nightfall. Matilda was so anxious to get to Mercy Hospital she hadn't allowed them to stop except for water breaks.

"Every minute we waste out here, we're risking our lives," she said. "Infected creatures, thieves…"

"We know, Mom," Danny grumbled, his hair gray from the ash. "We get it, okay?"

The rainstorm didn't start slowly, but came thundering, sudden and hard.

Matilda ordered Max and Danny to plant stakes for tents. Benny yowled, struggling on Zeke's neck. The boys fought to raise shelter, but they couldn't do it. The rain was too harsh, and lightning ripped the sky.

In the midst of it all, God spoke. That still, small voice again, clear as a glassy lake. But not without its sense of danger.

A cave. You'll find it in the wash ahead.

Agnes stumbled, and Jazz caught her elbow. "Are you okay?"

She wasn't. The breath in her chest felt dagger sharp. She'd never get used to hearing God speak in words.

Nor did she dare disobey.

"Watch Zeke!" she shouted. "Don't let the cat get away from him."

"Where are you going?" Jazz called after her.

"To find shelter!"

She left Jazz with her mouth hanging open. Asking, *Where?*

While the Outsiders struggled, Agnes pushed the prayer space as far as she could. A headache pierced her temple. The prayer space grew stronger every day, and conjuring it now felt frightful, like playing with fire. But what choice did she have?

Her power led her to a steep hill, and to a rain-swollen ravine, now running briskly as a river. She pushed a tendril of hair out of her eyes, listening hard.

There. She heard the cool echoes of a limestone cave, hidden by brambles below.

"Danny! Matilda!" she called excitedly. "Look over here!"

Thunder cracked, juddering her bones. Blue lightning shattered the sky.

Breathe, she told herself. *Just breathe.*

Her test, she knew, would take place down by that cave, tonight or tomorrow. A powerful shiver worked through her, chattering her teeth and rattling her bones.

What on earth was she doing, putting herself at God's mercy, knowing full well what horrors He was capable of?

Wind roared, and a powerful sensation of vertigo surged through her. She felt she stood on destiny's cliff, seconds away from falling, tumbling down.

40

BETH

Beth guessed if she were going to reach out to God again, ever in her life, it would be now, while she held a dying Cory Jameson.

She felt dry inside, listening to his labored breathing. Too dry, even, to cry. But though he couldn't hear, she wanted to say something to him. Wanted to tell him, maybe, not to fear the lake of fire, or that he might soon meet his brothers, in heaven. This moment before the gate opened between the worlds must not pass unmarked, she felt. Cory mustn't slip away without a final word of friendship—or, better yet, of love.

But you don't love me, do you? Cory had said. *You never did.*

Her heart ached fiercely, and she was running out of time. She'd opened her mouth to speak not knowing what words would come, when the deep, unexpected voice of a man startled her.

"It's open."

Matthew Jameson.

Beth froze.

What was her husband doing, outside the bunker? And what did it mean for her brother and sisters?

"It's probably nothing," Mr. Hearn said.

And Beth was galvanized. Patriarchs were coming, her husband among them. How long did she have before they found her? A minute? Less?

She supposed Matthew had loved Cory as much as he was able, but if he'd gotten his way, he would've made his son into another monster. He didn't deserve to see him again—not even as he lay dying.

She set her teeth and slid her arms beneath Cory's shoulders, dragging him just as she'd dragged him out of the woods. If someone came inside now, she'd be caught. Her only chance was to move fast.

"Feels haunted," said Mr. Hearn.

"Yes," Matthew said, heavily. "It does."

Beth hastily slid Cory down the aisle, heading for the basement door.

From outside, she heard a crushing sound, someone collapsing an aluminum can in his fist. She had no idea how she was going to get Cory down the basement stairs.

"Matthew." The voices were inside now, echoing in the rafters. "I think someone's been living in here. See that?"

Shit. Shit, shit, shit.

She'd left their blankets and supplies behind.

Look, God, I'm not sure I like you very much and I'm positive you don't like me. But if these patriarchs don't find us, I promise to reconsider our whole relationship.

It was possibly the sorriest prayer anyone had uttered in the history of the world, yet she drew some kind of strength from it. She managed to sling Cory's arm over her shoulder and navigate his weight with her hip, pushing and guiding him down the stairs almost like he was walking. Her arms strained and sweat bulleted every bare inch of her skin, but she was doing it.

At the bottom of the steps, her vision swam.

The dark. It felt just like going down into the bunker.

The sound of footsteps made Beth glance up, sharply pulling a tendon in her neck. Cory was slipping lower. Soon his weight would be too much.

Any moment now, Matthew Jameson was going to open the basement door.

The storage pantry. There wasn't much room, but it was their only chance.

The door at the top of the stairs opened with a stuttering creak.

Beth threw herself and Cory inside.

It was hard to say what was more terrible—the tight, enclosed pantry or the sound of her husband searching for them.

Such a waste to expend this energy trying to hide, Beth thought sadly, such a waste because *of course* he was going to check the pantry. Had she been expecting a miracle, or was she just plain stupid, or what?

Her hands sought Cory's face. She felt his cheek, her eyes straining against the dark. He was cold as ice.

A bang in the basement. "Darn it!" barked Mr. Jameson.

As he shuffled around the room, she realized she had one advantage. Like every other man in Red Creek, he'd never been in the basement kitchen before. But Beth had spent hours down here, baking baptismal cookies and funeral cakes under the stern direction of Mrs. King. The pantry was slight, no more than a cupboard tucked between the range and the wall, and he might not realize it was there.

He really might not.

He was close enough now she could hear him breathing.

Oh, why couldn't he just leave her alone? All she wanted was to grieve for the dying boy in her arms.

"Cory?" Matthew whispered, and Beth went rigid. "Cory, if you're there, I'm not angry. I want you to know that." His breaths, closer. And his voice, tender as she'd never heard it.

"If you're here, please answer." His voice cracked. Was he— sobbing? "Maybe we did wrong, angered God somehow. I don't know. But the faithful are so very sick. Red and hard, like demons. I had no choice but to flee. I want you to know that."

Beth held her breath, her throat thick. She'd known in her heart the bunker was a death sentence. Yet hearing the words aloud shattered a hope she hadn't known she still held. She covered her mouth with her hand, her elbow resting on poor Cory's sternum.

My family. She bit her lip until she tasted blood, to keep herself from wailing. *My family.*

"You always were my favorite child, Cory. Well. Wherever you are, I hope you know you'll always have my blessing."

Matthew came closer, closer—then backed away.

He hadn't discovered them. A moment later, she heard his footsteps climbing the stairs.

You'll always have my blessing.

It rang a bell, those words. They rang deep in the open wound of her soul—that echoing, grief-struck place.

Sam and the twins, sick unto death. And Cory, blood poisoned in her arms.

Blessing, blessing.

When she was sure he'd gone, Beth pushed open the pantry door, letting its rusty hinges whine. In the dark, with the only sound the roaring of blood in her ears, she thought of Agnes, who'd blessed her, once.

You have my blessing, Beth Ann. Her sister had spoken in the strangest voice—deep and low, almost sacred. *God bless you in your time of need.*

Beth touched her cheek where her sister had kissed it, thinking she'd never been more in need than she was now—never more alone.

When she took her fingers away, a miracle. Her own slender fingers glowed, physically *glowed*, like small embers. Soon color and heat consumed her whole hand. She realized with a start that she wasn't breathing.

"My God," she whispered.

Her hand shone translucent, reddish, like she'd pressed the head of a flashlight against her palm and flooded her skin's tissue with light. Only no external source was responsible for this radiance. No source, anyway, that Beth could see.

But I laid my hands upon her head and they glowed crimson, a blessed, holy color, the Prophet had written in his diary. *Her sickness, like a demon, cast out.*

Agnes hadn't entirely abandoned her, after all. She'd left her with this blessing, and it was powerful. Was it really so unbelievable that a miracle could happen in this church? Was it really so strange that her sister might still be protecting her, even now?

Maybe. But she cared for Cory too much to let him go without a fight. Caring for him in this church was the best thing she'd ever done. The most selfless, loving thing.

And she had nothing left, anymore, to lose.

"I love you, Cory," she whispered.

The words weren't true until they struck the air like a match, and then, there was nothing truer. All of a sudden, she could feel God—or something like Him—hovering in the air. All her heart's spaces filled with love for the boy in her arms, and for her lost sister, too. Hadn't she always suspected that Agnes's quiet, calm love was vastly more potent than all the Prophets' hate combined?

All she had to do was imagine her standing there.

Agnes.

For the first time in a long time, Beth wasn't afraid.

She placed her glowing hands over Cory's thigh, over his festering wound. She braced herself for nothing. Or, just possibly— *please, God*—for something huge.

41

AGNES

But your message burns in my heart and bones, and
I cannot keep silent.
—JEREMIAH 20:9

Sunday morning. Exactly one week since she'd run away. Agnes opened her eyes in the cave where they'd sheltered, sensing her time had come.

I could lose the prayer space today. I really could.

Her heart sank like a stone, contemplating the unbearable loss. She turned towards the light streaming through the cave's entrance, soft and misted after the rain. She hoped to face her test before the others woke.

But God, she'd never been so afraid. Not even standing at the bunker door.

Jeremiah Rollins. I know what your test looked like.

Seeing Sarah Shiner, desire overwhelmed him.

Jacob Rollins. I can guess your test, too.

The Prophet was rumored to be a harsh man, especially when it came to his less obedient wives.

But for herself, what would temptation look like? What bright, shiny apple would God hang from His forbidden tree?

"Agnes? Where are you going?" Sleepy-eyed Zeke sat up under the cave's low ceiling, arms wrapped tightly around Benny.

"There's something I have to do," she whispered to him. "Alone."

She motioned to the others, still sprawled sleeping across the limestone earth. Danny used his backpack for a pillow; Matilda clutched the barrel of her rifle. Max and Jazz curled into each other, as Mary and Faith used to do.

"Something secret?" He was suddenly alert. "Can I come, too?"

She wished she could take him. There was something unutterably lonely about going to face her mysterious God.

But she shook her head. "Not this time."

He looked warily at the streaming sunlight. "What if there are red creatures outside?"

She leaned down to kiss the top of his head. "I'll tell you a secret. Red creatures are afraid of *me*."

His eyes widened. "How come?"

She winked. "I'll tell you as soon as I know."

And that's when Agnes realized that, come hell or high water, she meant to succeed. The prayer space had become as precious to her as her own life, her own private font of miracles, and so, she determined that she wouldn't lose it. Not for anything.

She slipped away, tiptoeing out of the cave's narrow mouth. A steep slope pitched from their shelter to the muddy ground below. She clambered down carefully, knowing she could easily break a leg from that height if she fell.

She expected to feel dawn's chill and the drizzle of what remained of last night's rain. But she felt nothing. Not even air. Because she wasn't in the muddy ravine.

She was in Sunday school, facing the dusty, green chalkboard. Staring at Mrs. King's broad back, just as if she'd never left home.

Is this real? Is it a dream?

Chalk screeched and her stomach dropped. That sound was too real for any dream.

She glanced back, looking for the cave—but there was only the schoolroom wall. A broken pipe in the ceiling dripped, and the air smelled of rotten fruit.

Her Sunday school teacher's hand moved quickly, looping cursive letters. Then she stepped back, hand on hip, to examine her work.

Why Perfect Obedience Produces Perfect Faith

Agnes prayed Mrs. King wouldn't turn around, because she was *dead, dead, dead*. The dog had attacked her in the church; she'd succumbed to the fever. She couldn't be standing here, writing with chalk.

Agnes opened her eyes.

Mrs. King turned, grin sly. "Agnes," she said coldly. "You're late. *Sit down.*"

Titters of schoolgirl laughter. She looked dazedly for her customary chair. There it was at the front, but Beth's place beside it was empty. Sweat collected at her hairline as she made her way, hip knocking against a desk's sharp corner.

"Clumsy," Magda hissed.

But you're dead, too. Or Nested.

The weight of the past was crushingly heavy, a hand forcing her down. She sank into her desk chair—sank deeper than she'd expected. The desktop was level with her collarbone, just like when she was a little girl.

Small, useless, and insignificant.

A future wife—and nothing more.

Mrs. King crossed her arms over her bust. She'd never stopped smiling her sly, toothy grin. "Now take out your books."

Automatically, Agnes groped for her book bag—and it was there, real, solid, and familiar. Without taking her eyes off the dead woman, she unzipped it and placed a heavy book on her desk. Mrs. King marched furiously towards her, and finally Agnes looked down at what she'd assumed would be her Bible.

Danny's textbook.

In her panic, she knocked the book open. It flopped to chapter seven: AN ETIOLOGY OF JUVENILE DIABETES.

Mrs. King snatched the book up before she could move. She scanned the pages.

What was she doing with a text like this in Red Creek? What was she *thinking*, reading medical texts at all? It was against the Laws to dabble in such magic.

"Please," Agnes squeaked. "It's a mistake."

"This," Mrs. King snarled, "is a mortal sin."

With shocking strength, her Sunday school teacher tore the book in two.

"What's that in her hair?" Suddenly, Magda's hands tangled in her braid, yanking her neck backwards. Agnes squirmed, struggling to get free. Magda's fingers closed around the scarlet ribbon Jazz had woven through the strands, and she tore.

Agnes cried out.

Magda backed away, grinning and holding the ribbon and snatches of mouse-brown hair.

"Blasphemer," sneered Mrs. King.

A nightmare. Just a nightmare.

She moaned, bowing her head towards her desk.

You're not in Red Creek anymore. You ran. Reading Outsider books is not a sin. You've seen a library and a new town and made new friends....

But deep down, she didn't believe it. Nor could she believe that God had ever singled her out. Inside, she felt empty, chilled.

"Stretch out your hand," Mrs. King commanded.

Though every nerve in her body screamed at her to run, Agnes flattened her right hand on the desktop. Around her, the other girls talked, laughing like nothing was wrong.

Fear writhed in her stomach as Mrs. King raised her Bible high.

"What is God, Agnes?"

"God is love."

Slam.

The pain, so immediate—and so familiar.

"What is God?" Mrs. King demanded again.

Like the little girl she'd once been, Agnes whimpered. But she couldn't lie about her faith now. She couldn't tell her accuser what she wanted to hear: that God was the judge, the destroyer, the whisperer in the Prophet's ear.

Mrs. King raised the Bible over her shoulder, preparing to strike again.

"Connection!" she gasped desperately. "The thread that runs through everything!"

Slam.

She felt her knuckle give way, a sickening, flattening *crunch.* She swallowed, and her mouth tasted of bile.

"One last chance, Agnes. What. Is. God?"

She couldn't remember.

She'd known God once—she'd even believed He'd spoken to her at Gila's human Nest. But all that seemed a fantasy.

The prayer space.

Agnes swayed in her seat.

How had she so quickly forgotten the power that protected her? Closing her eyes, she searched for it.

"What are you doing?" Mrs. King snapped. "Look at me, right now!"

Agnes ignored her.

At first, she couldn't hear anything.

But reaching for God, she remembered that this was a test, and understood that she was here to prove that Red Creek hadn't broken her, that her new faith was stronger than the ghosts of her past. Terror lapped at her insides, but she didn't give up.

She grasped her power. Her hands heated with a fire hotter than any she'd ever felt; the backs of her eyelids glowed crimson. Her heart hammered in her throat but she didn't back down. Nor did she dare open her eyes.

Think about God, wide and deep.

"What is God, Agnes?"

She shouted at the top of her lungs. "He's a sound, you witch! A sound in the prayer space. The song of redemption!"

Agnes opened her eyes and saw Mrs. King and the schoolgirls for what they really were: a snarling pack of infected wolves.

"God is *sound*, a song that lives in everything."

Crimson-eyed wolves, their tongues lolling, stared at her.

Wolves. They were only sick wolves all along.

Agnes shouted, "He's singing even in you!"

And like that, she had it. The strongest hold on the prayer space that she'd ever experienced. It gave way to a feeling so vast and powerful she lost the sense of her own body, her own skin. Now she *was* the air, and trees, and those poor infected animals, too. The layers of the world peeled backwards, revealing the truth.

With a tremendous upwelling of joy, she understood God as

she never had before, as a fluid, flexible substance, like the prayer space itself.

The Prophet had always described a bearded man in the sky, but He wasn't like that. She didn't even have any sense that He was male. Her impression of God was more like her impression of water, breath, or thought. Something you could lasso, use, push, and stretch—if it let you. But ask nicely, because it was dangerous, too. Elemental and vicious, passionate and old.

She looked up at the sky.

Thank God. The sky.

"Agnes!" Matilda screamed from the mouth of the cave, her rifle at her shoulder. All the Outsiders stood behind her, looking down—and Zeke, too, his face white with terror.

"Agnes, get back! *Right now!*"

It was like a voice calling from another world. She exhaled, watching her breath curl and steam in the air, still dewy with past rain.

She knew what they must see: a dozen gem-hard wolves circling her, snapping their jaws, their bloodred teeth. The others couldn't understand that they snapped and snarled with anxiety, menaced as they were by the prayer space.

She gave her power a little shove. The wolves yipped, falling over their heels. She felt sorry for them. These creatures had once been formed of fur, gristle, and bone, but Petra had replaced all that with a sheen the color of rubies.

With a snap, Matilda cocked her rifle.

"Don't!" Agnes shouted. "You don't have to hurt them."

"Agnes," shouted Danny from the cave's height. "This is crazy! Come back here."

"Watch, Danny. Just watch."

She took a step forwards and the trembling animals stepped back. They moved all at once and all together. She did it again and again. Soon the wolves were keening, their crystal skin bristling. Then, they fled.

Agnes was sweating, overheated. Her right hand throbbed, the knuckle broken. The scarlet ribbon dangled freely from her unraveling braid.

All at once she knew why red creatures feared her.

I'm the antidote. Somehow, I'm the cure.

"*Yes!*" Zeke whooped. "I told you she was safe! Demons can't hurt the righteous!"

She grinned, because for the first time, she *felt* righteous. And more than righteous—powerful.

Matilda tried to grab him. "Zeke, don't!"

But he was already sprinting downhill.

He ran towards Agnes and the wolves, his faith in her shining like a beacon. He'd tucked his insulin cooler under his arm.

Agnes's mind was clear, her happiness complete. The wolves had retreated, and the prayer space was hers to keep. In a moment, she'd have her brother in her arms. Joyfully, she laughed.

Ezekiel had nearly reached her when he tripped over a mud-slick stone.

He went sprawling. The cooler flew out of his arms, flipping end over end in the open air.

No.

It struck the earth at the unluckiest angle, bouncing back into the air. It careened from rock to ground, and there was nothing she could do to stop it.

In horror, Agnes clapped her hands over her mouth, forgetting the pain of her crushed knuckle. The plastic latch broke open.

More horrible still was the unmistakable sound of those crystal vials shattering into so many bewildered shards of glass.

Out of the corner of her eye, she saw Danny running towards her. Running fast.

She'd passed the test. The prayer space hadn't abandoned her.

But Ezekiel's medicine—

It was gone.

PART
THREE

42

BETH

*Petra showed us painfully and by necessity: As long as
we draw breath, we are all capable of miracles.*
—AGNES, EARLY WRITINGS

Beth's hands stopped glowing as color rushed back into Cory's
face. His eyes batted open and tears streamed down her
cheeks.

We saved him, Agnes. We did.

"A miracle," Cory breathed. "My leg. It feels—"

"I know, Cory Jameson, I know."

He ran his hands over his thigh, his face luminous with wonder. His wound no longer oozed pus or smelled of death. Miraculously, his skin had woven itself back together without leaving so much as a scar. He sat up, bent his leg forwards and back—then started laughing uncontrollably, laughing from the center of his belly, loudly and fully.

"Can you believe it?" His laughter was contagious, and Beth laughed with him.

"No." He wiped the tears from his eyes. "I really thought I'd bitten it."

"Look." She poked his thigh. "Like it never happened."

He jumped, bounced on the balls of his feet. Then he sank back down onto the dusty basement floor and opened his arms.

Beth kissed him, staggered by his life, his strength, and for a warm moment, their troubles melted away. They lay on the dusty floor, kissing and loving until their lips were swollen, chafed.

"Oh, Beth," he spoke into her hair. "How's it possible?"

"Agnes gave me her blessing," she whispered. "She said, *God bless you in your time of need*. I got chills like the words were—"

"Powerful." Cory looked awestruck.

She whooshed out a breath. His father and Mr. Hearn had left the church only a short while ago, but Cory didn't know a thing about it. He hadn't heard Matthew admit that their people had sickened. He didn't know everyone they'd ever loved had already been lost. Every muscle in Beth's body rebelled against the necessity of telling him the truth, but he had a right to know.

"Cory." She cupped his face in her hands. "Listen to me."

His face was painfully innocent. "What?"

"They're dying," she said. "All our family."

She told him everything she knew. Told him how his father had proved himself a coward, running from the bunker, from Red Creek. And she told him, though it felt like chewing broken glass, that his brothers and mothers were dead or dying.

After, he cleared his throat. "You know what we have to do now, right?"

"Leave," she said decisively. "We need to get the hell out of Red Creek."

He looked at her, shocked and offended. "No, Beth. Of course we can't go."

"Why not?"

He was still looking at her like she'd kicked a puppy. "Because your sister is a prophet, that's why. An immensely powerful one. Beth, she can save them. All of them."

She closed her eyes, feeling the blood pulse behind them. A monstrous effort, not to imagine the twins turning red, or Sam vicious as Magda had been.

"Cory." Beth felt shattered. "Agnes isn't here."

"So, we'll bring her back."

"You don't know what it was like, watching you die. I can't spend another night here." She sought for a way to make him understand. "This is a bad place. A cursed place. Can't you see that? Nothing we do here could possibly do any good. I just want to leave. Start over."

"You said something, while I was dying." Cory spoke sternly. "Something about loving me. Was it true?"

An hour ago, she'd seen death in his blue eyes—she *knew* she had—but all his boyish life had been redeemed. She had her sister to thank for that; her sister, and her sister's God.

"Yes," she admitted. "I do love you."

"Then prove it. Help me bring Agnes home. Jesus, Beth, help me save your brother and the twins. They don't deserve to die in the dark."

She groaned, knowing he'd already won. Worse, hope was building in her body at an alarming rate. What if God had some plan for her still? What if she could save her family? Wouldn't it be worth it, then, to stay?

"What makes you so sure Agnes can save anyone?" Beth demanded. "What makes you so sure even she can do any good?"

"She saved me, didn't she?" Cory said. "She saved me through you."

Beth chewed her thumbnail, thinking. Agnes wouldn't have

left Red Creek without leaving some way to reach her, just in case. A number, a mailing address, a clue.

But it meant going back to her trailer, and she'd rather leap from the canyon's edge than face the memories that festered there.

Cory took her hand. "My brothers, my mother..."

His skin—so warm, so undeniably healthy. A *miracle*.

"All right," she snapped. "Let's try. But I don't like this, Cory Jameson. You'll owe me."

"Of course." He shot her one of his knee-weakening smiles. "Don't you know it, sweet Beth? I owe you my whole life."

43

AGNES

Never deny the God you feel to be real. That feeling is your
heart; it is all you have.
—Agnes, Early Writings

The Outsiders couldn't get out of the ravine fast enough. On the precipitous, scraggy climb to the road, Jazz stumbled twice, cutting her palm on a stone. Blood snaked down her forearm, ringing her wrist like bracelets, but she never stopped moving, never stopped climbing. Matilda ran awkwardly with her rifle, but she was quicker than she looked, and Max carried Zeke in his arms like a bride. Once, Agnes paused to look back down at the broken glass sparkling at the bottom of the wash, but Danny kept her going, his hand hovering beneath her elbow. In the eyes of the Outsiders, Agnes recognized pure, animal terror.

Seeing the red wolves, they'd all seen fever, petrification, and imminent death.

All except for Ezekiel, who'd trusted her too much.

On the roadside, Matilda bound Agnes's injured hand with thick gauze, immobilizing it.

"A dirty break," she kept mumbling. "That, my dear, is a very dirty break."

Agnes's hand looked alien, swollen to the size of an eggplant and just as purple. It had been rebroken at the third knuckle—the exact wound she'd sustained as a child. Through shock's gauzy veil, she was insensible of the pain.

She kept thinking: Had Ezekiel really lost it? *All* his insulin? Was it really gone?

Agnes brushed Matilda off as she tried to stand, but the earth and the sky switched places. She lost her footing and fell hard.

Pain went off like a firecracker, knuckle to wrist to elbow. She clutched her arm to her chest. Above her, Matilda faded in and out of focus.

Inside Agnes's heart, God spoke once more. His words, bright and clear, resounded between her ears like thunderclaps.

Your test is over. Now return to Zion.

Zion? She wanted to scream. *God, if I knew where the promised land was, wouldn't I be there already?*

Then—*whoosh*—her candle went out.

Agnes woke inside a blue nylon tent. It was brand-new, and the air smelled plastic.

Matilda's face hovered over hers, frowning. The prayer space had burned through her insides like wildfire.

She tried to sit up, but Matilda pressed her back. "You need to rest."

"Zeke's m-medicine," she stammered. "We need...we have to..."

"Zeke's with Max. I just checked him; he's fine. It's you I'm worried about."

Matilda helped her swallow a few pills—*ibuprofen.*

"Sounds like a Hebrew name," Agnes croaked.

Matilda chuckled. Then she performed Agnes's first-ever physical.

Strange objects appeared in Matilda's hands: a stethoscope for listening to her heart and lungs, a blood pressure cuff, a fancy thermometer. A rubber mallet and a pulse monitor that clamped onto her finger. Matilda measured, frowned, double-checked, then took down the numbers in a little wire-bound notebook, muttering results.

Agnes heard Zeke's laughter beyond the tent and lurched with panic.

"Matilda, how will he eat? How—"

"Hush. We're almost done." Matilda made one last note, then looked at her squarely. "Tell me exactly what happened out there. Leave nothing out."

Agnes bit her lip. She hadn't mentioned the prayer space to anyone—not even Zeke.

"It's okay," Matilda soothed. "I would never judge you. You know that, right?"

She dearly wanted to believe these Outsiders would always accept her, whatever happened. Hadn't Jazz felt free to tell her about her butterflies? Hadn't Danny admitted his nightmares? And Max—hadn't he always expressed his affection for Jazz without fear of retribution?

Agnes truly believed this Outsider world was a better, gentler place than the one she'd left behind. But still, she held back.

Matilda waited, patient. A perfect silence stretched between them like a length of dark fabric. They might've been the only two people on earth.

Something shifted inside Agnes's chest. God, what a relief it would be to share her inner world with someone else, to divest herself of her last, and heaviest, secret. In many ways, the prayer space was the most important thing about her.

"I call it the prayer space."

Matilda cocked her head. "Why?"

"I hear things. Sounds no one else can. It feels like praying, but deeper."

"What kind of sounds?"

"The ground hums. Stars sing. I hear people's hearts beating. I think—"

Tears blazed in Agnes's eyes, but hadn't she learned by now that the best course was to always speak the God's-honest truth?

"I think I might have discovered my own religion," she whispered. "Or remembered it. Something." Her face burned. "The God I know, He's different from the one the Prophet preached."

Matilda nodded. "Tell me about that."

"You swear you won't think I'm crazy?"

Matilda's eyes were steady. "I was there, remember? I saw you with the wolves. I saw...something. We all did."

In Agnes's heart, floodgates opened.

"God was never the man in the sky the Prophet used to preach." The words tumbled out of her. "And He definitely isn't a Him. God is just...interconnection. I hear *sacredness* running through everything. Whether we hear it or not, another world is singing all the time. Even in petrified creatures. *Especially* in them, because God wants us to notice. Learn something." She winced, knowing how egomaniacal she sounded. "I think I'm supposed to discover what that something is. And relay the message. Like a prophet does."

A wayward wind rattled the tent and brought into their silence the scorched smell of desert. Agnes imagined the Prophet sneering at her half-baked religion, her mushy, ill-defined faith. What, no Laws? No rules? No threat?

With surprisingly little effort, she pushed his image away.

"I'm so proud of you," Matilda finally said.

Agnes startled. "Proud?"

"When we first met, you were brainwashed. Do you know what that means?"

She nodded, thinking of the Internet articles she'd read about Red Creek.

"It can take a lifetime to recover from a cult experience. But you've constructed a new belief system for yourself, and that's wonderful. It will help you heal. But…"

Matilda fiddled with her pen, and Agnes tensed.

"Sweetheart, I don't know what to make of your sounds or the way those wolves behaved. But if you're not careful, this prayer space will kill you."

Her words were like a punch in the gut. "*What?*"

"Whatever happened today, it shot your heart rate sky-high and hit you with a one hundred five–degree fever. You nearly died. Agnes." Matilda's eyes held hers. "The prayer space, whatever it is, you can't use it. You have to stop."

Stop. How could she stop? The prayer space was her calling. God's gift to her.

But what if it was also a curse?

She'd read the Bible. Nothing in a spiritual life was free. Noah gained a boat but lost his home; Jeremiah wished for death; and Moses never saw the promised land. The prayer space might be a gift, but who could say how much of herself God expected in return?

Your test is over. Now return to Zion.

She picked at the gauze wrapping around her hand, feeling uncharacteristically irritated.

Where was Zion, that everlasting metaphor? Could her message be any *less* clear?

"There's one more thing." Matilda's voice, suddenly brisk and professional, dragged her back. "Your hand. I have to ask if there's any chance you've done this to yourself." Her eyes weren't unkind, but nor were they unwary. "Do you ever think about hurting yourself, or hurting others? It's important you answer truthfully."

Agnes slumped.

So Matilda didn't believe her, after all.

Despite what she'd witnessed, the rational part of her *had* decided that she was delusional. Agnes could try to explain how her knuckle had been broken in a vision, but what would be the point? Their worldviews were incongruous shards, pieces that would never fit together. She'd be explaining until the stars fell from the sky.

"God tested me," Agnes said, flatly.

Matilda's face remained a cautious mask. "I thought your God was more loving, more *gentle* than the one you left behind."

Agnes stifled a laugh. *Gentle!* Yes.

But God contained multitudes—or He wouldn't *be* God.

She quoted the psalm. *"He looketh on the earth, and it trembleth: he toucheth the hills, and they smoke."*

"Sweetheart," Matilda said finally. "I'm choosing to believe you. Don't make me a fool."

"Hello?" Danny called. "Are you almost done? Can we say hi?"

Matilda touched her shoulder. "Are you ready?"

Agnes nodded.

All at once the tent was crowded. Zeke made a beeline for her lap, Max and Jazz sat almost on top of each other like always, and Danny settled cross-legged on the ground at her feet, looking drawn and anxious.

She feared she'd horrified him—that she'd horrified all of them.

"I'm sorry," she burst out. "Please believe I'm really, truly sorry."

Silence. Zeke froze, his arms around her neck.

"Sorry?" Max barked. "Are you kidding me? You *saved* us from those wolves. They could've trapped us in that cave."

She blinked. *Max wasn't angry.*

Now that she looked closely, she saw that none of them were. There were no glowering faces, no quick-fire hatred or righteous distrust. They were giving her the benefit of the doubt. She'd never felt so safe among other people before. So safe or so loved.

"I didn't save you," she said. "I *endangered* you. I'm the reason those creatures showed up in the first place. It was a kind of test." She looked down at her hands. "I'm sorry."

"Agnes, can you look at me?" Danny asked. "What test? Who was testing you?"

"God, obviously," said Jazz.

Agnes blinked, surprised.

Danny shook his head. "Sorry. But I don't believe in God."

Max's lips curled upwards in a smile. "Me neither, but I'm starting to reconsider."

Matilda cut in. "Why don't we let Agnes tell us the story in her own words, from the beginning?"

The beginning. It seemed centuries ago.

Don't hate me for not telling you, Danny.

Agnes held Zeke, inhaling his childish scent and trying not

to think of the future, or what the loss of his insulin might mean. The story was what mattered now.

She began:

"When I was a girl, I used to hear the earth humming. When I looked at the sky, the stars would sing..."

44

AGNES

*The mystery of illness has been with us since the
beginning, but the Virus forced us to look into its eyes
and know its name.*

—AGNES, EARLY WRITINGS

The sun set as Agnes finished the story of how God came to
speak to her.

Her arms tensed around Zeke. He slept hard in her lap while
the Outsiders stared at her with varying degrees of disbelief and
confusion. She tried not to look too closely at any one of them;
their stunned silence sufficed. She thought heavily of Jeremiah,
the loneliest prophet in the Old Testament—the one who no one
ever believed.

But Agnes already had a great deal of practice being lonely.
She didn't need converts and she'd endure anything, as long as
Zeke was safe.

Only, he wasn't safe anymore. It was past dinnertime, and
without a bolus or a basal rate, she didn't know how on earth she
was going to feed him.

His body doesn't make the hormones it needs to survive, Matilda had said when they'd first met. *You can't pray him healthy. Without medicine, he'll die.*

In the tent, the memory gutted her.

Zeke can't die. He can't.

"Matilda." She sensed a blackness encroaching. "Matilda, what're we going to do—"

The nurse lanced Zeke's finger while he slept, then flashed the number Agnes's way.

"Look," she said. "He's all right, sweetheart. He is."

"He has to eat eventually," Agnes murmured.

"Yes." Matilda nodded. "We'll feed him protein. Beef jerky won't raise his blood glucose. Max, will you put him to bed? We'll check him again in an hour. And every two hours after that."

Agnes felt light-headed. When Zeke was first diagnosed, she'd had to check him every two hours. She'd gone weeks without a solid night's sleep, creeping through the trailer so the other kids wouldn't wake. The very idea filled her with memories of panic, guilt, and fear.

Taking Zeke from Agnes's arms, Max shot her an encouraging— if puzzled—smile.

Jazz bent to whisper in her ear, "I believe, you know. I believe every word."

Then Danny, Agnes, and Matilda were alone in the tent.

Danny, meet my eyes. Danny, will you, please?

He looked down at his hands. Instinctively she'd known her story would affect him most. After all, hadn't he wanted to kiss her once?

She refocused. "Before we had insulin, he nearly died, Matilda."

"Yes, but this is different. We'll keep him carefully controlled. As long as he stays regulated—"

A nightmare of an idea sprang to mind. "He vomits when he's afraid."

Matilda shook her head sharply. "It's very important that doesn't happen. We've got to prevent dehydration, minimize stress."

Danny spoke up. "The hospital. Can't they send an ambulance?"

Don't send an ambulance, her mother had once said. *The neighbors can't know.*

Agnes shivered.

"I've been calling," Matilda said. "Their phones must be down. I'll keep trying."

Agnes straightened, nerves buzzing. "So, we walk. We just keep going and hope we get there in time?"

"Walking will help lower his blood glucose." Matilda removed the pen from behind her ear, fiddling with it. "Listen, sweetheart, I know you're frightened. But there's no reason he can't survive the next few days."

"You really think so?" Agnes whispered.

"Yes. I do."

"Matilda," she asked suddenly. "Do you believe in God?"

Danny looked sharply at her.

"Sure, sweetheart." Matilda shrugged. "More or less. But we won't need Him. Not once we reach Mercy."

Fear crashed over Agnes in jagged waves.

Now return to Zion.

But where on earth was that?

God. She screwed her eyes shut, and in perfect silence, her mind screamed. *I want to be faithful, but where?*

⌀

Agnes checked Zeke's blood glucose, then went to find Danny.

He was keeping watch for red creatures that night, while the embers of their campfire slowly died. It was a lonely job, but someone had to do it. They couldn't forget that the desert brimmed with danger.

"Agnes?" Danny sat on a fallen branch near the fading fire, Matilda's rifle in his lap and a textbook spread out before him— reading, to keep awake.

As she approached, he closed his book quickly. But not before she'd gotten a good look.

He read: AN INTRODUCTION TO PSYCHOLOGY.

Agnes had a guess what *psychology* might be. "You don't have to hide that. I expected you'd be skeptical."

He reddened. "You know, there's some evidence that most psychic experiences have a basis in neurology...."

She sat beside him, cradling her throbbing hand. "I don't know what any of those words mean, Danny. What I do know is that my experiences have a basis in God."

That made him laugh, at least.

"I told you in the library, remember," she said. "I told you that I hear God all the time."

He threw up his hands. "I just thought you were flirting with me."

She blushed. "That, too."

His eyes danced upwards, scanning hers. "Why didn't you tell me before?"

She leaned against the tree trunk, its bark rough and reassuring against her lower back.

"I suppose I knew you wouldn't believe me, and it's so lonely, to be disbelieved." She studied his profile. "Do you really think it's all in my head?"

"No," he said hurriedly. "Of course, not all. The wolves... maybe you have some kind of immunity...some kind of repellent, antiviral factor..."

"Or maybe," she said gently, "it's like I said: I talk to God."

The stars were whirling, her skin tingling. His whole body strained towards hers—she could feel it. But could two people of such different faiths ever really understand each other? Love each other, even?

"Did you want to kiss me back at the library?" she asked.

"Well—" He flushed. "Yes."

"Do you still want to kiss me?"

"Agnes, can I see your hand?" They were nose-to-nose now. "My mom doesn't understand how it could've been broken. Neither do I."

She swallowed, held out her wrist. In the fading firelight, he unwrapped the bandages, revealing the crater of her third knuckle and the bruises, spiderwebbing out from there.

"Oh, Agnes." His voice broke. "Whatever's going on with you, it's too much. Too hard."

With every fiber of her being, she urged him to understand. "This is my path. I wish you could travel it with me." She paused. "More than anything, I wish you still felt like you did before."

"You can't know what I feel," he scolded her. "God can't tell you that, too."

"You're right. I'm only guessing."

"Don't." He wrapped his arms around his knees. "I'm my own person, not some puppet in God's play, and *neither are you*. Agnes, a martyr complex isn't a good thing. It's—"

"I never said I was a martyr. A prophet is completely different."

He took an exasperated breath. "Define *prophet*. Can you do that?"

"You think I'm claiming to be something I don't even understand?"

"Schizophrenics often claim to be messiahs," he said. "Hundreds every year. But if you're schizophrenic, it's *not your fault*. It's a sickness, I would still love you—"

Anger flared in her chest at his blind obstinacy. "Did you forget about the wolves? Did you forget—" She stopped suddenly, mind reeling.

Helping you escape was the best thing I ever did in my whole damned life, he'd told her back at the library. And if that wasn't love, what was?

She looked at him again and saw not a stubborn boy, but a terribly frightened young man with his heart on the verge of breaking.

"A prophet is not a martyr *or* a messiah," she said. "In the Bible, God appoints a prophet to interpret His word in times of change. Their most important job is to keep God alive through history. To explain how His teaching still applies."

Danny peered at her, relief pure and plain on his face. "Is that all?"

She hesitated, sifting for the truth. "Sometimes, they have other tasks."

He nodded, blew out a breath. "Other tasks aside, what you're describing is like a preacher or a college professor."

She stifled a laugh behind her good hand. *College professor? Really, Danny?*

But who cared what framework he used to understand her life, as long as he was trying to understand?

"Danny, I wanted you to kiss me in the library. But I wasn't ready then." She paused, thinking of the test, when she'd announced the meaning of her God to her ghosts and to herself. "I am ready now."

Her bandage lay coiled at his feet. Her arm was still awkwardly suspended between them.

He bowed his head and tenderly kissed the crook of her elbow. She gasped.

"That didn't hurt, did it?"

"No." A tremor worked through her. "It was perfect."

"Interpreting the world in times of change," he murmured. "Okay."

He kissed her elbow again, then the side of her shoulder, then her neck.

And then he was kissing her mouth and Agnes was kissing him firmly back, trying to fill all her lonely, frightened places, her ache in the night.

She couldn't wrap her arms around him like she wanted to; she couldn't put both hands on his broad back. But as the kissing went on, the pain in her hand mysteriously began to fade—a phenomenon for which she had no doubt Danny could provide some medical explanation. Yet, as she began to be able to touch him, hold him, she thought their kissing made them more spirit and less flesh. More breath, and less indifferent air.

Mindful of Matilda's warning, Agnes never stepped into the prayer space. But she believed that if she did, she'd hear wonders and miracles in the heat that built between them.

As they melded together, she fought the urge to say, *amen.*

45

AGNES

God's mysteries will frustrate you, terrify you. Let other
people be your rock. They all must face the mystery, too.
—AGNES, EARLY WRITINGS

Zeke's blood sugar rose and fell, too quickly, all night. By morning he'd breached 400, a shocking high, and Matilda was terribly eager to get him up and moving. Without insulin, only exercise could lower his blood glucose.

"Why don't you two walk ahead while we pack," Matilda chirped with suspicious brightness. "Then you can test him again. Okay?"

"I'm not a baby." Zeke clung to Benny like the orange cat was his only friend in the world. "You can't talk about me like I'm not here."

Matilda and Agnes exchanged anguished looks. Crankiness had become a familiar signal of high blood sugar over the years. Losing the ability to treat him with a swift and simple shot felt like losing a hand.

"Drink some water." Agnes pushed her canteen on him.

"No. I think I'm going to be sick."

"Deep breaths." She rubbed his back in circles. "You'll feel better once we start walking."

If they were lucky, they'd reach Mercy by foot in three days. And maybe the hospital was what God meant, when He told her to return to Zion?

Mercy and *Zion* weren't quite synonyms, but they were close.

Agnes checked her own pack. Without insulin, her few supplies were more meaningful than ever. There was the ketone test, Matilda's extra meter, and a spare set of batteries. Extra test strips. Extra syringes, too—though they were useless without medicine.

"Come on, Zeke," she prompted him.

"I want to wait for Max."

"Sorry." Agnes fought to conceal her frustration. "But we can't."

She grabbed Zeke's hand and tugged him along. Out of the corner of her eye, she caught quick movement: a hawk, winging in the distance.

Fear seized her.

What if it was infected?

Despite Matilda's warning, she stepped into the prayer space, letting it billow like a quilt over the yellow-orange desert.

"Your hand is warm," Zeke said.

He was right, and unease twisted in her belly. Hurriedly, she scanned the desert, letting her power wander like curious fingers over its lunar surface.

There were red creatures in the distance—in the prayer space, she could hear them like screams. She sensed infected lizards, pronghorns, hawks, and foxes, but all far away, for now. The desert looked empty to the naked eye, but in reality, it bristled with infection.

With sweat dripping into her eyes, she sensed no urgent threats. Still, they shouldn't wander too far from Matilda and her rifle.

With relief, she shut the prayer space down, letting it dim and cool and die.

After they'd walked a while, she knelt to prick Zeke's finger again.

390. He was lowering, thank God.

"You're angry I dropped my insulin," Zeke said sullenly. "You're all mad at me. Right?"

She blinked. "Why would we be mad at you?"

He kicked a pebble with his shoe. "I'm too much trouble."

"Zeke—"

His eyes sparkled, overbright. "God loves you, and that's why He gave you superpowers. But He hates me, Agnes. That's why He made me sick. I know I was supposed to die a long time ago. I prayed as hard as I could—but God never took my diabetes away."

"Stop." Agnes felt ill. She'd had no idea how deeply these thoughts coiled inside him. "Ezekiel, I need you to listen. God isn't simple, like the Prophet led you to believe. He's large and unknowable and complex." She swallowed. "If God gave you your diabetes—and I'm only saying, *if*—He didn't do it to hurt you."

Zeke cocked his head. "Then, why?"

"The same reason He gave me my superpower, as you call it. He gave you your struggle to make you more *you*. More than that, we'll never understand."

He mulled it over under the white eye of the sun.

"Agnes," he said at last. "Am I going to die?"

"You're going to feel very sick," she said gravely, knowing these were some of the most important words she'd ever spoken. "But you'll keep walking, because you have to, and because I believe in you. And in three days, you'll have insulin again."

The others had caught up with them. Seeing Max, Zeke's face split into a smile. He adjusted Benny on his shoulders and went to walk beside his favorite Outsider.

Agnes looked at Danny. She yearned to bury her face in his neck. But of course, that would hardly be appropriate now.

He smiled at her. "Did you two have a good talk?"

"Yes." She sucked in a breath. "But I'm afraid."

Surreptitiously, Danny took her hand. "We don't have far to go, now."

Three days would bring them to Mercy.

God willing, it would be Zion.

46

BETH

*If Petra taught us anything, let it be this: Inside our worst
nightmares burns an ember of redemption.*
—AGNES, EARLY WRITINGS

Inside the trailer were the scattered remnants of Beth's broken
life: toys, sofa, table, Ezekiel's crucifix night-light—all covered
in silvery dust. In the kitchen, the refrigerator hunched dark and
silent in its corner. Cory opened it, then covered his nose.

"*Je-sus.* That's some rot."

He tossed spoiled meat into the garbage. Beth hurried to help
him, vaguely embarrassed by her poor little impoverished trailer.
Cory, of the wealthy Jamesons, had never seen it before. But she
tripped over Sam's toy truck, crushing the plastic beneath her
boot.

With her hands braced against the dust-silky kitchen tile, she
struggled hard against her rising tears—and against something
else. Something darker.

In the church, her grief for her family had been theoretical,
a mist of memories and dreams. In her trailer, sorrow was real.
Even for Father, whose spare belt lay coiled in a corner, she felt
immense sadness.

And Beth had always so hated sadness. It caused her to tighten, contract—and the tightening gave way to an ugly, self-protective fear. She couldn't stand this trailer or the memories that clogged it. She'd rather peel her own skin off than spend another moment here.

Light filtered thinly through shuttered trailer windows. Beth went to the pullout sofa where she'd slept with Agnes. Their bed looked too small now. Cramped and sad. She dug furiously for her diary but wasn't surprised, really, to find it gone. Cory came to stand beside her, still nervously rubbing his thigh.

"Agnes took my diary," she said numbly.

"Why?"

"I guess she thinks I'm done for."

"Did she always underestimate you?"

"What do you know about it?" She spun on him. "*You* couldn't pick her out of a crowd."

He raised his hands placatingly.

"Do you know I considered asking her to run away with me *months ago?*" She glowered at their rumpled sheets. "But I never asked, because I was afraid she'd say no. I was a coward."

"You wanted to run? Just the two of you?"

"I wanted the kids to come, too. Ezekiel, Sam, the twins."

"You never thought of asking me?" She heard the hurt in his voice, so raw and clear.

Beth flushed, because the truth was, she'd never even considered asking Cory to run with her. She'd just assumed he was too faithful.

"I'm sorry," she mumbled. "I didn't know you that well."

"No?" He sounded so miserable she couldn't look at him. "I thought I knew you."

She swallowed hard, then drove her hands back under the mattress.

Searching, digging.

And there, in the diary's place, was the note she'd always known—in dreams, anyway—that Agnes would've left, just in case.

Her pulse leapt into her wrists as she held it up to the dying light. Dust motes twirled and spun.

> Dear Beth,
> Have a cell phone. Long story. Phone number is 555-9801.
> Love, A

Agnes's Sunday school cursive looked uncharacteristically messy, evidence of her hurry, her frantic fear. Beth looked towards the bedroom where Father kept the dangerous things.

Like rifles.

Mad mothers.

The phone.

Only Father ever used the landline. He'd call Mr. Hearn asking about odd jobs, or what he should bring to the Easter potluck, or where he could get a cheap price on a used truck.

"No one's paid any bills this month," Cory worried aloud. "What if—"

But Beth was already hurrying into the bedroom, rehearsing what she'd say to her sister while adrenaline coursed through her veins.

Agnes, you've got to come home. I think you can save them, the twins, Mother, Sam. . . . If you'll only come back, you can save them all.

She picked up the black receiver. It felt slick and frightful. Forbidden. The dial tone moaned balefully into her ear.

What if Agnes didn't answer?

What if she'd already made a new life on the Outside and refused to jeopardize it by returning to this cursed place?

I sure wouldn't, if I were in her shoes.

Beth's nose was runny. She swiped at it with her forearm and stared at her mother's ratty curtains. Broken shards of secular music were still stuffed beneath the record player, like the jagged pieces of a broken heart.

"Beth? Beth, can you dial?"

She gasped, strangling on the canned trailer air. Then she banged at the buttons, clumsily hitting all the wrong numbers. Her fingers felt thick, useless. She couldn't do this obvious and simple thing—dial her sister's number.

She couldn't.

Cory put a hand on her shoulder. "Agnes will come back, you'll see. Then everything will be all right."

"Do you really believe that?"

His eyes looked older. In these last weeks, he'd changed.

What about her? Had she changed, too?

In the woods, I almost let him die, she thought sickly. *What kind of person would do that?*

Deep in her soul, she worried she was still that same horrible, unworthy person. She'd done good, looking after Cory. But what if that was just varnish over the same old paint? What if she didn't deserve Agnes, or her blessing, either?

"There's no point calling." Despair choked her. "No point at all."

"Beth," Cory said. "She's your sister. Have faith."

With the tip of her index finger, she punched the numbers, then held the slick receiver to her ear. Cory pressed his stubbled face to hers, listening as the phone rang.

Come on, Agnes, I don't know how much time the kids have left.

And rang.

Come on, Agnes!

And rang.

47

AGNES

*You can blame God for the red tragedy, but will that bring
you any closer to understanding?*
—Agnes, Early Writings

In the dead of afternoon, Agnes's phone buzzed urgently in her
dress pocket. After a five-mile walk through suffocating heat,
they'd pitched their tents to get a break from the blistering sun.
Agnes rested beside Zeke, but she couldn't sleep.

His blood glucose: 529.

That afternoon, she'd begun to see misery in his eyes, a
canyon-deep exhaustion. It was pitiful, watching him try to hide
his pain. She knew all his tells.

Though walking would improve his blood sugar, Max had
carried him piggyback for the last two miles, because he'd begun
to stumble.

But Agnes wasn't afraid. She *wasn't.*

By now, she understood enough about the workings of fear
to know that she couldn't afford to open the door to it, not even a
crack. Once fear got a toehold, it would rip the door off its hinges.

Buzz...buzz...

Puzzled, she frowned. How could she be getting a phone call? Everyone she knew in the world was already here.

For a moment, silence. Maybe she'd imagined it?

Buzzing sounded again. She *was* getting a phone call.

She struggled to her feet. Her ankles felt like someone had beaten them with a lead pipe, and Danny'd had to yank her boots off her road-thickened feet.

And the heat. Agnes had lived in it all her life, but she'd never suffered in it. Never been exposed to it hour after dauntless hour. Every inch of her skin hurt. She felt like a soft, fragile, white-bellied creature that some devil had scrubbed with sandpaper.

Fully awake now, she scrambled in her pocket for the phone. If the racket woke Ezekiel, who so badly needed rest, she'd scream.

She didn't recognize the number; but then, Danny's or Matilda's were the only numbers she *would* recognize.

She thumbed the screen. "Hello?"

Garbled static.

"Is anybody there?"

Buried in that white noise, a small, panicked speaker. A woman? A girl?

Though it was impossible, she thought it might be—

Her phone went dead. A hunk of cold metal pressed against her ear.

She slipped out of the tent and into the blazing sun, heading for the camping stove and the white plastic cords.

"Hey." Jazz was watching for creatures, the rifle in her lap. "What's up?"

"I have to charge this, but my hand—"

"Here." Jazz took the phone from her bandaged grip. "I'll do it."

Agnes sat shakily. The phone blinked, drinking power.

"Agnes." Jazz spoke out of the blue. "I have to know. Is the prayer space really God?"

Startled, Agnes looked into her syrup-colored eyes. She sensed some hidden danger here. The idea of preaching like the Prophet preached—in ignorance—turned her stomach sour. But could there be any harm in telling what she truly believed?

"*I* believe the prayer space is God."

Tears spilled down Jazz's cheeks. "Does that mean—" Her eyes turned hungry. "Is my family in heaven, Agnes? *Are* they?"

Her skin crawled, but wasn't the question inevitable? Eventually, someone was going to ask her to explain mysteries beyond her ken, and she had to make a choice: between giving comfort and telling the truth.

For a long, tightrope walk of a moment, Agnes wanted to give comfort. Wanted to tell her yes, the family you love is in heaven, waiting for you. She knew it for fact. But she couldn't, because the God of the prayer space always demanded truth.

"I'm sorry. I don't know."

Jazz's eyes hardened. "What? Aren't you a prophet, or something?"

Agnes felt sick. "Please don't look at me like that. I can't be—that sort of prophet."

"What sort?"

"The kind who claims to have all the answers. In my experience, they're liars."

"But that's the whole thing with you, isn't it?" Jazz said bitingly. "You *don't* have any experience—in the real world—but still you get more answers than the rest of us."

Back at the library, Agnes never would have guessed she'd one day be fighting with sweet Jasmine. But then, the road, so unforgiving and hard, was like another world.

"Jazz, I know you're frightened—"

Agnes's phone flicked on, and for some reason, she pictured her sister. *Beth.* Could it have been her voice on the phone?

Agnes leapt up, ignoring the forsaken look on Jazz's face. She unhooked the phone and dialed the mysterious number back.

The call trilled only once before she heard a firm, final *click.* Then a woman's voice spoke smoothly into her ear.

"Your service provider regrets to inform you that as a result of the ongoing emergency, cell service will be discontinued indefinitely. For more information, tune into your local broadcast. Goodbye."

The unfamiliar Outsider words numbed her. "There's a problem with my phone."

Jazz smiled tightly. "Didn't charge?"

"I was trying to call someone—" *Yes, and who* was *it?* "And a recorded voice cut in."

Jazz's smile curdled. She went to the tents, rustling, calling. Soon everyone was up from their nap, except for Zeke. Danny's eyes were bleary. Max chewed a toothpick. Matilda sat on a log, rubbing her bare, swollen feet.

"It finally happened," Jazz told them. "Cell service blacked out."

Agnes still didn't understand what that meant, but phones leapt like magic into the Outsiders' hands. They were all trying to make calls, tapping away at their screens.

Matilda put hers on speaker, and Agnes heard the same recorded message.

Her friends unraveled.

"It could be temporary," Danny insisted.

"Like hell." Max paced the campground. "This is it. The end of the goddamn world!"

"Hey." Matilda clapped her hands, schoolteacherly. "This

doesn't change anything. We'll reach Mercy soon. Then we'll be safe."

Return to Zion.

But Agnes didn't like the glazed shock in the Outsiders' faces. They needed these devices—their very working presence helped them keep a kind of faith.

"It won't last forever," Danny was saying. "Once the outbreak is over—"

Jazz turned to him, eyes raw. "When will it be over? It's already been forever, so when? My family and friends are dead. We're traveling with a girl who's some kind of saint and bad things *still* keep happening to us. What did we do to deserve this?" She'd reached a breaking point. "How much more suffering are we supposed to take?"

"Jazz," Agnes said. "You'll wake Zeke."

Jazz whirled on Agnes. "This is *your fault*. Everything that's happened since you came. I wish we'd never met you. I wish you'd never come!"

Max jerked as if to restrain her, but in the end no one moved.

Agnes blinked, feeling lost. Could this really be the same girl who'd welcomed her so warmly when she first arrived? The girl who raised butterflies and wove a satin ribbon into her braid?

Without thinking, Agnes slipped into the prayer space. She heard the baleful buzz of Jazz's fear. The Outsider girl felt abandoned, forsaken, afraid. She didn't mean to be hurtful. She just needed something to believe in.

"Jazz," she said. "Can we talk, alone?"

Max stepped between them, his eyes round with fear. "Agnes, she didn't mean—"

Max is afraid of me. They all are, a little.

Agnes ignored him and drew Jazz into the shade. In the shadows, her fine-featured face might have been Beth's.

"You know none of this is my fault, Jazz," Agnes said. "You know I'm just like you."

"Sure, except God speaks to you." A bitter laugh. "God looks out for you, tells you everything you need to know. And what do you do? You hoard it all for yourself."

Agnes felt hot, flushed and ashamed. "I don't know nearly as much as you think. I don't know what's going to happen. I'm just trying to survive."

The Outsider wiped her eyes, examined her nails. But Agnes saw the old Jasmine—the kinder one—peeking through the shadows.

Jasmine's eyes swept up. "You're really in the dark, same as us?"

"Every human person is in the dark."

The wind blew hard, and small stones rolled through their campsite.

First the Virus, then the library, then the cave; Zeke's medicine, and now the problem with the phones...the chain of events reminded her of Revelation. At the end of the world, disaster followed disaster—hail, plague, then fire—and didn't stop for anyone. Not for sweet baby brothers or scrappy sisters. Not for Outsiders with hearts of gold. Disasters kept arriving and they didn't stop until they flattened the earth.

In her heart, she knew Beth had tried to call. That meant that she, like Sarah and Agnes before her, had escaped.

But there was nothing Agnes could do to help her, reach her. Nothing, except—

"Jazz," she said. "Will you pray with me?"

The Outsider girl rubbed her tired eyes. "I don't know. Will it help?"

"Try it and see."

They linked hands while the sun beat down.

They prayed, and hoped, and prayed.

48

BETH

*Any nonharming belief is ultimately protective, a defense
against despair.*
—AGNES, EARLY WRITINGS

Beth was awake yet dreaming.

She was in a cheap motel room in Holden, snuggled
beneath a comforter with Agnes and the kids. She'd finally mustered the courage to ask Agnes to run, and now they were hiding
out, frightened but hopeful. The plan was to sell Father's truck
and buy a plane ticket to Texas or Nevada, whichever was cheap-
est, then get a job at a laundry while they sent the kids to school.
Sure, the kids weren't all on board yet—Sam in particular was
surly, ever threatening to run home to Father—but they'd adjust.
They were already adjusting.

The twins made friends with the family next door. Ezekiel
begged to try foreign foods he'd seen on TV. Sam, though he
wouldn't admit it, was curious about school, science classes, sports
teams, and—*eww, gross*—girls.

Yes, in time, the kids would be fine. Meanwhile, she and
Agnes, shorn of their prairie dresses, were spinning dreams and
making plans. Agnes would get her GED and Beth would travel

on a round-the-world airplane ticket, stopping at a beach some-where to get her belly button pierced. Maybe she'd even talk Agnes into getting a tattoo. Something to commemorate the day they'd found the courage to run. The day they became Outsiders and apostates and refugees and dreamers.

The day their new lives had begun.

But that, of course, was just a dream.

"Beth? Are you all right? *Beth?*"

Cory was shaking her.

She rubbed at her eyes, still holding the phone to her ear, lis-tening to the flat dial tone.

She'd left a voice mail, but it wouldn't matter. Even if she left a million messages, Agnes was never coming home. Why would she, when she was already free?

"Beth, sit down," Cory said anxiously.

She slumped on the edge of her parents' unmade bed, trying to get hold of herself.

"Listen to me," Cory insisted. "Agnes is going to get that mes-sage and come home."

"No," Beth said frostily. "She won't."

"How do you know?" he demanded.

"My sister always thinks about what's best for Ezekiel," Beth snapped. "Do you think he'd be better off coming back here? Do you?"

Cory held her cold hands. "You're losing faith. We'd better pray."

She snatched her hands away. "To who? To what? I *told* you this place was cursed."

He touched his leg. "The miracle—"

"For all we know, the Devil did it."

Cory's face twisted with shock and horror, but Beth wouldn't take it back.

Better to forget the whole experience in that church—Agnes's blessing and the incomparable feeling of power—and crawl back into her shell of selfishness. She'd survived Red Creek a long time that way.

It was no use waiting for Agnes to call. It was time to admit that the kids were dead—or worse. Red Creek was dead—and truly, running was the only sane thing left to do.

She stood. "I'm going to shower and pack a bag. I suggest you grab some of Father's clothes if you're coming with me."

His mouth dropped open. "Agnes is going to call you back on this phone. If we leave, she'll have no way to reach you. We can't go."

"Watch me."

On the way to the bathroom, she was already peeling off the disgusting wedding gown. Shedding it like an itchy, scaly skin.

49

AGNES

Human beings have always needed reminders that God
isn't like us; that His thoughts are utterly alien. One look
at a human Nest screams that this is so.
—AGNES, EARLY WRITINGS

O n the third day, Ezekiel refused to get up and walk.

"I'm aching," he whispered. "I can't."

His blood glucose: 598.

"That's diabetic ketoacidosis," Matilda said, blanching. "But look, we're nearly there. If we can only..."

Max whipped the toothpick out of his mouth. "Want to ride piggyback, little guy?"

"Are you sure you're strong enough?" Agnes asked. Max had thrown out his back carrying Zeke the day before.

He shrugged, lifting the child. "I guess I'd better be."

Agnes marveled at the change in Max. Could this really be the same Outsider boy who'd been too lazy to ferry well water back at the library?

That day, Agnes, Zeke, and the Outsiders made better time than anyone had thought possible, forcing their legs to keep moving despite their exhaustion and the relentless heat. The endless shimmering asphalt seared Agnes's eyes, and she felt welts rising on her cheeks, vicious sunburns. But Zeke was feeling better, bit by bit. Drinking water, even talking again. And they'd seen no red creatures, which felt like a blessing: like God had decided to ease their path now they'd nearly reached the end of it.

"Come on, Max! We're almost there!" Danny called.

Weakly but playfully, Zeke slapped Max's chest. "Yeah, Max! Giddyup!"

The Outsider let out a pretend whinny and put on a burst of speed. Sweat drenched his Modest Mouse T-shirt, but he never once complained.

Beside Agnes, Danny grinned triumphantly. They were going to make it. Soon, they'd be safe. Already, relief emanated from Matilda's shoulders in great waves.

"Do you think we'll have showers at Mercy?" Danny wondered. "Hot water, even?"

"Don't get your hopes up, kid." Matilda gasped for breath as the hill steepened. "The best you can expect is a bar of soap and a sink."

"I'll take it. I'm filthy."

"Too right," called Max. "Ezekiel, doesn't Danny stink?"

Her brother smiled a pale smile, and then they reached the hilltop.

Agnes's heart faltered, stuttering.

There was no hospital.

No Mercy.

Where the building should've stood, there was nothing but blazing rubble scattered over a desolate field.

Agnes felt like she'd been clubbed across the middle with a

sledgehammer. This must be a sunstroke hallucination. What she saw... It was impossible.

She closed her eyes, then opened them.

"Oh my God." Danny reached for her hand. "It's gone."

It was no hallucination. There was nothing but waste, destruction, and ruin. Small fires still danced in the rubble.

Her mind turned sloppy and encumbered, her thoughts like quicksand.

Think.

Matilda hadn't been able to reach Mercy on the phone, but none of them had anticipated anything like this. Not even the Burn Squad, who knew Mercy was their only hope—

The Burn Squad.

Agnes's muscles tensed.

"They set it on fire," Danny whispered. "Those bastards, they—"

"No," said Matilda firmly. "The Captain didn't do this. This mess was made by someone far stupider. Just think of the waste. The medicines, the machines..."

"It was someone with a bomb," said Max. "No gasoline fire could do this much damage."

Agnes clutched Danny's arm. Together, they stared down the long stretch of parking lot at the thousands of pounds of useless rubble where the promised land should've been, still rippling with flame.

Bomb or not, a great building had toppled. Only one corner of it had held, reaching up into the sky like a stone spine ripped from its body. Glass covered the ground below it like a glittering snowpack, and in the remains of a parking structure, giant smoke-blackened letters spelled MERCY.

It was almost like a joke—or a curse—because surely this would've been the largest, grandest building Agnes had ever seen.

No *haven on the Outside,* the Prophet whispered in her ear.

"A Nest must've formed here," Matilda said. "Some band of idiot criminals must've thought the best thing to do was—destroy everything."

No *haven,* came the Prophet's voice, cold as a raven's caw. *No haven on the Outside!*

"I don't understand," Agnes moaned. "What did I do wrong?"

"Oh, sweetheart," said Matilda. "It's not your fault. Just bad luck."

Jazz appeared at her side. "Remember what you said? God is still here. God is still singing. Right?"

In Sunday school Agnes had learned that the word *apocalypse* meant "unveiling." So she'd learned that when the Rapture finally came, the world's true nature would be laid bare.

She saw that the Outsiders' hospital was a wasteland, its earth salted with exploded glass; and her heart was a wasteland, too, sharp with exposed joists and stanchions. She tried hard to understand what mistake she'd made, because in her bones she didn't believe in luck.

This was an act of God, but she couldn't understand it.

Why had God let Zeke's insulin shatter when he dropped his cooler, and where on earth was the home they deserved?

Where was *Zion?*

Max's voice cut sharply into her thoughts. "*Agnes?*"

She turned. "What?"

"Something's wrong." Max slid Ezekiel off his back, into his arms.

Agnes reached Zeke just in time to see him double over, retch, and vomit black bile onto his shoes.

Max took a quick step back, his face misshapen with horror.

The vomit. It reeked.

"I'm sorry." Zeke groped for her blindly. "Agnes, I'm—"

She pulled him against her chest, terror yawning beneath her like a trigger-trap door.

"Roll him on his side!" Matilda hurriedly checked his vitals. "Set him down gently, Agnes! Danny, put up a tent. I need my black bag—"

"Zeke, it's okay." Agnes rocked him like the baby he'd always be—to her, at least.

He trembled against her, and she couldn't help but remember that day long ago, before Matilda, before insulin. The sense of death, so near. And the smell of it.

Zeke held her eyes. Trusting.

Agnes gripped Matilda's sleeve. "What do we do now?"

The nurse looked haunted. "I think you should try the prayer space."

Even secular, rational Matilda was asking for a miracle. Nothing could've frightened Agnes more.

Agnes bowed her head over Zeke.

The prayer space unfurled like an infinitely petaled flower, but what she found in its depths wasn't comforting. No matter how hard she sought God, the prayer space wouldn't answer. She tried until her hands burned, and she felt faint with fever. But no sound came, and her hands refused to glow.

Gently but firmly, the prayer space said, No.

The prayer space was capable of any miracle, she was sure. Why would it deny her this?

"I don't understand," she cried out.

Matilda observed her pityingly. "Hold his hand. We'll have the tent up in a moment, and I'll start an IV. Then..."

The nurse let the words hang, twisting uselessly in the wind.

But holding her brother, Agnes felt her panic fading. A

strange, distancing calm settled over her like a shroud. Mercy still blazed in the field below, and Danny was cursing, struggling with the blue plastic tarp. She smelled late summer on the breeze. Autumn was just around the corner, but Zeke might not live to see it.

He might not live.

And then the sun finally set, leaving the sky an injured, blackened shade of dark.

The end of the world overtaking her at last.

50

BETH

There is rebellion that creates and rebellion that destroys.
Choose carefully.

—AGNES, EARLY WRITINGS

After showers, food, and rest, Beth managed to get a reluctant Cory into the driver's seat of Mr. King's truck. But he wouldn't fasten his seat belt, let alone start the engine. He dangled the keys they'd discovered in Mr. King's shed.

Beth stared daggers at him as insects gathered in buzzing clouds on the hilltop.

She wore her blue prairie dress for the trip, her hair neatly braided. At her feet was a duffel bag packed with her few things: a change of clothes, Sam's broken toy truck (she couldn't bring herself to leave it), and a box of stale breadsticks they'd already half demolished. The truck smelled of manure and oiled leather.

Cory kept very still, watching sunlight glinting off the keychain's cross.

"Well?" she finally asked him. "What are we waiting for?"

Blue eyes met hers, brilliant and hard.

She sucked in her breath, because Cory's expression was every inch as unforgiving as his father's. She'd never seen him look so much like a patriarch before—or so much like the hard man she'd married.

"I'm not leaving unless you *swear* we're going to look for Agnes. You and I both believe she can heal the sick in the bunker. Maybe we'll find her in Holden. Then we can come back."

She threw up her hands. "Agnes could be anywhere. We'd be fools to come back."

"We're fools to leave."

She'd never learned to drive, and pleading with Cory was infuriating. Familiar, too, because wasn't that how she'd always had to handle men?

"God knows I'm scared to death, too," said Cory. "But it isn't right to run. Not when there's a chance of saving our families."

Beth's lips thinned. "Get this through your head, Cory: Agnes. Isn't. Coming. Back. What happened here isn't our fault. How can we be responsible now?"

He stared, incredulous. "Because we're the only ones who know! It's like the Good Samaritan or being your brother's keeper—"

She fumed. "Don't quote Scripture at me."

He gripped the steering wheel, looking ridiculous in her father's oversize spare shirt.

"Don't tell me that miracle didn't change you. You must care about the word now."

"Hmm, let me think," she answered sarcastically. "Nope, still not caring."

Bewildered, he asked, "Why?"

"Because this isn't Bible study, it's *life and death*. We can't sit around waiting for something that might never come. We'll starve if we stay."

"I think she *is* coming."

"You've never spoken two words to my sister! What the hell makes you so sure?"

"*Faith*, Beth!" He struck the dashboard hard enough to make her jump. "*The rebellious dwell in a dry land.*"

"Stop it."

"*They shall fall by the sword: they shall be a portion for foxes.*"

"It was lies, Cory. The Prophet—"

"What about the Bible? Is that just lies, too?"

Fighting with Cory felt like being forced to swallow shards of glass. Beth wanted to beg for mercy—to shout, *Stop, enough!* But she couldn't. Some small, buried part of her was like a growing vine, reaching and searching for the light. For life.

And she knew in her bones—she'd *always* known—that Red Creek was death.

"Our brothers and sisters—they're as good as dead, Cory. You know it. I know it."

Cory's Adam's apple bobbed. He seemed to be searching for some safe place to land, some point on which they might still agree.

"Maybe you're right," he admitted. "But we can still try to do the right thing. Even if it gets us exactly nowhere, we have to *try.*"

Beth bit her lip. "You'd die for a chance? A slim one?"

"Yes."

"Why?"

"Because it's right. *Noble.*"

The sun had nearly disappeared. Soon, fireflies would rise from the meadow grass, and it would be time for the children to play the Apocalypse Game. She could almost hear the twins shrieking, laughing as they gathered grass stains and courted skinned knees.

"I'm sorry," she whispered. "But I won't die for a chance."

Cory's mouth tightened. "Why'd you marry my father?"

The question caught her off guard.

"You knew how I felt about you," he pressed. "So why?"

The memory of the terror she'd felt when the egg struck her face flew up from her heart like a flock of crows, startling her badly.

"I was afraid, all right?" she bit out. "I thought no one could hurt me as long as I was a patriarch's wife."

"You *gave up*." His voice was venomous.

"I didn't have a lot of choices!"

His eyes darkened. "I wanted to save you. But you avoided me like the plague."

"I made a mistake." She couldn't keep the tremor out of her voice. "Now I just want to forget. Please, Cory. Can't we just leave?"

"You're taking the easy way out, making the same mistake all over again. You're abandoning your family."

"Agnes abandoned them first." It appalled her, how petulant she sounded. "It's Agnes you should be angry with, not me!"

He drew back, wintry.

Discordantly, she thought of the canyon's edge and the first time they'd really gotten serious about fooling around.

Are you ready to do this? he'd said, his eyes so sweet, hopeful. And she'd told him, *Yes.*

But her answer was different now. She didn't care if she was being selfish. She wouldn't stay in Red Creek to wait for Agnes. Even for Cory, she wouldn't stay and die.

"I guess you're not the girl I thought you were." Cory dried his eyes on his sleeve. "You can take the truck. But I can't go with you."

Beth stared out the window. She couldn't believe he was

breaking up with her—and for the second time. "What will you do?"

He didn't hesitate. "Pray. And wait."

"Cory," she pleaded. "Don't."

He smiled thinly, then stepped out of the truck.

Beth felt cold, bloodless. Apparently, Cory had already forgotten that he owed her his life. Apparently, he'd just assumed she'd bend to his will when it mattered. The men of Red Creek had always tried to control her, silence her. But Outside, she could build a new life, have everything she'd ever dreamed of.

Except, of course, for Cory Jameson.

It was all so unexpected—the thought of going on without him.

"My sister made it out alone," she said tremulously. "Somehow, she took Father's truck and . . . made it out."

Cory squinted. "Can you drive?"

She tugged nervously at her collar. "Agnes did it. How hard could it be?"

She slid into Cory's seat, and he watched skeptically while she fumbled with the ignition, leaning his forearm against the window well. She breathed in the smell of him, that smell she loved even better than the scent of vanilla, and all at once felt utterly terrified. Her sister was the earth and the stars, but Beth was made of altogether flimsier stuff. And she still wanted Cory, whose love had meant the world.

Tears burned. "I don't understand. How can you not see it's foolishness to stay?"

His blue eyes held hers. "How can you not see it's rebellion to leave?"

Rebellion.

At the sound of that awful word, Beth shifted Mr. King's truck into gear, and Cory took a quick step back.

"You really are your father's son," she spat.

His face crumpled like she'd shot him.

She wanted to take it back, but the truck was already rolling downhill, and she grappled with the wheel. She forced herself to focus on driving, swallowing her last regrets.

Only once did she glance in the rearview mirror.

But Cory was already gone.

51

AGNES

What does it feel like to receive a message from God?
Stand in a deep cave and shout the words you think you
know; then hear them echo back, alien and estranged.
—AGNES, EARLY WRITINGS

In its way, the end was gentle. Zeke grew tired over the course of the day, and then, late that evening, he fell into a sleep from which no one could wake him.

That night, Agnes didn't scream at God or dramatically renounce her faith. Moses could rail and Job could shake his fists and even Jesus might yell at a fig tree, but she...she would simply have to accept it, as women had always accepted such terrible things.

Zeke was dying.

And it was Agnes's job, alone with him inside their tent, to watch him go.

Every half hour, Matilda took Zeke's vitals, frowning ever more deeply, and fiddled with the IV that pulsed water into his body. Otherwise, she left Agnes alone with her grief.

Agnes swore to see this through. To sit at Zeke's bedside with dignity and grace. It was the last, best thing she could do for him.

It was nearing midnight, six hours since he'd fallen asleep. In her mind she heard the Prophet reciting, *Thy kingdom come, Thy will be done on earth as it is in heaven*. She envisioned him anointing her brother with oil.

And who will speak for our brother Ezekiel?

In her head, she addressed the weeping faithful—and Beth, especially. Even in her imagination, she found it hard to meet her sister's eyes. *You couldn't keep him safe?* those eyes said. *You abandoned me for him, and you couldn't even keep him* safe?

Beth wouldn't forgive her for this, and neither would Agnes forgive herself, even if she lived a hundred years. But still she didn't understand her mistake—where she'd gone so wrong.

She thought back to the morning at the cave: the test and the infected wolves. For what had she been tested? If she wasn't meant to save Ezekiel, what was her destiny?

She stroked his cool forehead, singing softly to him. His lips edged white and his eyes rolled with dreams. She prayed they were good dreams—that he was playing in their meadow with Sam, that the twins were playing fair, and that he ran faster than he ever had.

Someone rustled the tent fabric.

"Agnes?" came Danny's voice.

She sighed, thinking, *Not now*. But his voice quaked with worry, and so she set herself aside. "Come in."

He unzipped the tent, letting in a crack of moonlit dark. Benny trotted in behind him, freshly fed. The cat hurried to Zeke's side—his master, prone on a messy pile of sleeping bags—and curled beside his head.

"Guess what Max and Jazz are doing."

Agnes blinked at him, not in a guessing mood.

"They're searching Mercy's rubble, for insulin. They're not giving up. None of us are."

Her lips quirked. Outsiders were indomitable, even when they were clearly beaten.

"Zeke's dying," she told Danny. "What I'm trying to understand is why."

He nodded. "Want company?"

"No, thanks."

"I brought your bag." Danny hefted it. "Your phone, too. It just finished charging."

"Why'd you bother? Service is out."

"Yeah, but you have a voice mail. Jazz noticed. She said you got a call earlier?"

Agnes froze.

Beth. Had she left a message?

She flicked her thumb across the phone's crystal screen, her nerves taut. At first the message was garbled, then the voice became clear. She put her hand over her mouth, astonished.

"Agnes, you've got to come back, you've got to come home!"

Danny mouthed, *Who is it?*

Agnes shook her head, listening hard.

Beth's voice pattered urgently, the words cascading out of her. *"Red Creek needs you. The people in the bunker are sick. Cory and I think—no, we* know*—that you can save them.*

"Do you remember what you used to tell me? You said the earth hummed. The Prophets heard it, too . . . only they thought their power existed only to serve them. They never saw a larger purpose."

A muffled sound. Agnes was mortally sure her sister was crying away from the phone. On the other side of the line—on the other side of the *world*—Beth blew her nose.

"You can save them, Agnes. You have to come back. You can save them all."

The phone beeped. The message had ended.

She'd gotten it wrong.

Red Creek is my Zion.

She'd been going the wrong way the whole time. She stuffed her fist in her mouth to stifle a sob.

Danny knelt beside her and stroked her knees, saying, "Hey, it's okay, you're okay," but she barely noticed him. Beth had sounded so desolate—so lost.

"I wasn't there when she needed me," Agnes cried. "I wasn't there."

"Who, Agnes? Who needed you?"

"Beth!" she cried out. "But, Danny, that's not the worst thing. God's voice . . . it told me . . ."

She couldn't speak for weeping.

She'd always blamed the Prophet for leading the faithful astray, but was it possible that it had all begun with a misinterpretation, as she'd misinterpreted God's directive? Was it possible that faced with the many tones of God's mysterious voice, every human person was primed to hear what they wanted to hear?

Danny stroked her hair. "What did God tell you?"

She took a shuddering breath. "God said, *Your test is over. Now return to Zion.* But I didn't understand, don't you see? Just like the Prophets, *I got it wrong.*"

She gripped Danny's shoulders, her nails digging into his flesh.

"I thought I was supposed to find Zeke a *new* Zion. But, Danny, there's *no haven on the Outside.* That was the only true thing the Prophet ever said. And it was right there in the message, when God told me to *return.*"

"Agnes," he soothed. "You can't blame yourself. You couldn't have known—"

"But I did know!" The words flew out of her, and her hands released him to tug at the ribbon in her hair. "I saw how far the world had fallen. But I was too focused on finding my baby brother a home, when I should have been trying to—to *make* him one. That's what God asked of me, but I didn't listen. In God's eyes, I've been in rebellion ever since."

Beside her brother's placid face, Benny flicked his tail, irritated by the excess of emotion.

"Losing Zeke is the real test," she whispered. "It wasn't the wolves or the cave. God struck Ezekiel to see if I would only use my power to serve myself. Or if I would finally learn that it's not about me at all."

Danny's eyes were wide and pained. "If that's true, Agnes, that's a cruel God you follow."

Looking at her brother, Agnes sagged.

Danny tossed her pack aside to take her in his arms. It was what he'd come for, after all.

The bag, tossed so carelessly, struck a tarp-covered rock with a heavy, metallic *clunk*.

Agnes's eyes widened at a memory.

She pushed back from Danny, marveling. Because though she knew her God was, in fact, sometimes a cruel one, the prayer space had shown mercy.

Mercy, at last.

"Wait. There's one more thing left to try."

Danny's eyes followed hers to the bag he'd cast aside.

Beth, just stay where you are. Beth, I heard you, I'm coming.

"He's *not* going to die," she breathed, and nearly toppled over, grasping madly for the bag.

52

BETH

God's word is a combustible, fragile, infinitely mistakable
thing. Even handled with the greatest care, His words can
detonate in an instant in the palm of your hands.

—AGNES, EARLY WRITING

Driving was harder than it looked.

Beth wished to God she'd paid more attention. to Father's maneuvering. But that girl from before—the girl who'd gone quietly to Walmart and back again, never letting her feelings be known except in her diary—had truly been an indolent creature, completely uninterested in learning to fend for herself.

Driving, Beth told herself she didn't feel guilty for abandoning her home. After all, even if her sister did get her voice message, she'd have no reason to believe she held the fate of Red Creek in her hands. Agnes hadn't seen the miracle in church or read the Prophets' diaries. Why would she think she could heal the faithful with a touch?

In her shoes, Beth wouldn't believe it. She'd think her sister had lost her mind.

She drove past the midwife's hut and the horrible white

clapboard church, steering a little more steadily with a few minutes' practice under her belt.

At last, Red Creek's iron gates came into view.

In Sunday school, Mrs. King used to say her "heart lifted" whenever she thought of their Prophet, and Beth always used to roll her eyes. But now she knew it was a real thing—your heart *could* leap inside your chest.

She was finally going Outside.

The gates loomed larger, coming closer, and she felt a pinch of anxiety.

What if they were locked?

But they were thrown wide open. Broken. A ruptured chain dangled from a hinge, and tire marks zagged the ground.

Agnes? Was that you?

Then, at long last, Beth was on the road to Holden.

33 MILES, a green sign read.

She wanted to sound the car horn, wanted to shout or sing or scream. Instead, she scrabbled with the radio dial, hoping to land on a station playing the evilest kind of secular music—rock and roll. But the truck's radio fuzzed. She wondered if Mr. King had broken it, so his children couldn't channel the Devil on the sly.

The sun slipped below the trees, trapping her in a thick net of darkness. Enclosed spaces still sickened her, ever since her time in the closet with Magda. She'd felt fine a moment ago, when she could see the twilight sky through the window, but now . . .

Why was it so *dark*?

Streetlights ranged on either side of the two-lane road, but every last lamp was blind.

Headlights! How do I turn on my headlights?

"Cory—"

She'd already turned to ask him before she remembered—she'd left him behind.

Her heart plummeted.

She jiggered with the rods on either side of the steering wheel but only set the wipers to swishing, and then she couldn't turn the damned things off. She tried to read the cryptic symbols etched into the plastic, but they only confused her more. She drove erratically, stomach fluttering, squinting to see the road's faint white lines.

"*Damn it.*"

She couldn't turn her lights on—such a simple thing!—and she knew what Cory would say, if he were here.

God's refusing to show you the way.

Even in her head, he was infuriatingly smug. And worse, in this dark, her mind kept wandering back to Magda's gleaming red eyes.

If you knew for sure that Agnes would be back in a week, would you wait?

Yes, of course.

What about a month?

She hadn't given up on Agnes for impatience's sake. She'd given up because Agnes was well and fully gone.

A year?

"Oh my God," she shouted. "Don't you get it? *Agnes is never, ever coming back!*"

And that's when the face jumped out of the dark.

Beth pitched forwards in her seat, saved from flying through the windshield only by the tension of her seat belt. Her forehead careened off the steering wheel and something warm and wet dripped into her eyes. She felt like she'd been punched in the chest, and for a moment, she couldn't remember how to brake. Her feet scrambled for purchase, and she accelerated, lurching forwards.

Something crunched and decompressed beneath her wheels. At last the toe of her boot found the correct pedal, and despite her panic, she brought the truck to a stop.

An all-consuming dread settled on her in the cricket-chirping dark.

Please, God, don't let it be a person.

The map light switched on when she opened the door. The air smelled of pine, burnt rubber, and something far crueler.

Shaking and mangling a prayer, she unbuckled her seat belt and stepped out of the car. She heard what sounded like a birdcall—only her breathing sped up, knowing what it really was.

A human whimper of pain.

The moon barely illuminated the awkward geometry of the body in the road, angled and doubled back on itself in impossible ways.

It was a man. She'd driven over his legs, breaking them, tugging them out of shape. He looked like a marionette some careless child had tossed aside.

She stood over the man on the road, cursing herself for not forcing Cory to come with her. She didn't know what to do.

My first Outsider and I've killed him.

She could go to jail.

Couldn't she? She didn't really know.

"This isn't my fault," she muttered. "It *isn't*." She whirled on the man. "Why were you walking down the middle of the road at night, anyway? What are you, suicidal?"

It was difficult to tell, but she thought she saw his Adam's apple bob once. Regret crashed over her. She knelt to cradle the poor man's head.

Then she recoiled in disgust, gasping, scrambling away.

It was just her luck that the man she'd hit was Red Creek's miserable Prophet, and that he was still alive and watching her with crow-black eyes.

53

AGNES

Sometimes the most dignified thing to do is accept the mystery in all its troubled glory.

—AGNES, EARLY WRITINGS

Agnes had forgotten about the radio, the one the Burn Squad captain had given her. When Danny dropped her pack, it landed in her memory with a heavy, metallic *clunk*.

In the tent, Zeke's breath labored on, Benny blinked his yellow eyes, and Danny vigorously shook his head.

"One, the Captain planned to be in California by now. Two, even if they're still in Arizona, these radios don't have a lot of reach."

"We'll reach him. I *know* we will."

"Agnes, I just don't want you to be disappointed."

"Don't worry." She fumbled with the radio's antenna. "He'll answer."

"What makes you so sure?"

"Faith." She sank her thumb into the plastic button. The radio crackled.

"Agnes," Danny warned. "He's a captain of a *Burn Squad*. Even if he *can* help us, who's to say he will?"

She remembered the Captain's winking, gold cross. The anxious way he'd given her the radio to begin with.

"I believe he tries to do the right thing," she told Danny. "He's just—gotten it wrong sometimes. But then, so have I."

She brought the radio to her lips. "Captain? Are you there?"

The fuzzing continued.

"You have to let the button go," Danny explained.

She released it.

Silence fractured her heart with doubt. She glanced at Zeke. In profile, he looked like Beth. Same cheekbones, same nose. He would be a handsome man one day, if he survived this.

"Hello?" someone snapped. "Who's on this channel? Identify, over."

Danny was at her side in an instant.

"Captain?" She spoke, never breaking eye contact with Danny. "It's Agnes. My brother's very sick. We need insulin. We need you to come to Mercy Hospital."

"Over," Danny whispered in her ear, his breath tickling. "You have to say *over*, so he knows it's his turn to speak."

"Over."

"Agnes." In the Captain's mouth, her name was an entire tragedy unto itself. "I don't know how you're getting such a good signal, but it's too late. We're south of Phoenix, on our way to California. We've got three hundred stragglers in tow. Three hundred desperate people who need our help, understand? Over."

Danny's shoulders dropped a fraction of an inch, and for a moment Agnes felt daunted.

Then the still, small voice spoke.

There's nothing left of California, God said. **They'll die in the desert.**

Agnes nearly dropped the radio.

Danny steadied her. "Are you okay?"

Three hundred people.

Her eyes brimmed with tears. She saw now that returning to Red Creek—the land God had called Zion—was a holy work, generations in the making, and God was invested in every second of it. Even when the patriarchs went horribly astray, God had kept faith in Red Creek and planted a new seed: *her.*

It was her destiny to defeat the Virus.

After all, hadn't she lived her life among hardened, red-marbled human hearts, like Father's and Mrs. King's? Didn't she understand better than anyone how faith and home and family could be twisted into something ugly—something not unlike a petrified human Nest?

"Captain," she said slowly. "You haven't been able to reach anyone in California. Not for days. Over."

A pause. Then, "How do you know that, Agnes? Over."

Danny's eyes were skeptical, cautioning. She ignored him.

"I know because we're like you. We journeyed to Mercy with perfect faith that it would still stand when we arrived. But there was no city in the wilderness. Only rubble." She swallowed, daring to take the greatest chance—and wagering Zeke's life on it. "And I know because *God told me.* You're leading your people into death, Captain. You're going in the wrong direction. You wear a cross, so ask your heart. Over."

Her voice cracked and Danny stared.

"What have you done? The Captain thinks in terms of orders and authority. He doesn't listen to his heart."

She thought of the prayer space and the people who had been set in her path: Jazz, Max, Matilda, Danny. None of them believed exactly in the God of her understanding, but all of them had proved themselves creatures of astounding heart.

And that was no accident. No accident at all.

"Just wait," she told Danny breathlessly. "You'll see."

He looked into her eyes and registered the determination there. With a sigh, he slid an arm around her waist. They both held their breath, waiting.

The radio chortled. "Look, Agnes. I don't know if you're crazy or—or just what. But unless you have some alternative, you're on your own. All of us are. Over."

"But I *do* have an alternative," she gasped into the radio. "I can lead you to a safe place, a land protected by a forest on one side and a canyon on the other. A land the infection has barely brushed. The human infection there has been—contained. It's the safest place in the world for your stragglers. Birds still fly there, Captain."

Danny stiffened.

"You're right that we're all on our own in this world," she continued. "But God has given us a gift, and it was no mistake that we met in Gila. In your heart, I think you know that already. That's why you left me a way to contact you."

She took her finger off the button, feeling suspended over some great abyss.

"Over," Danny reminded her.

"Over."

In the long silence, Benny shook out his rumpled fur, bestirring himself to stand. With a whisper of fabric, he disappeared from the tent into the night.

"This place. Is it Red Creek? Are you certain there's room for three hundred newcomers?"

She closed her eyes, praying. "Yes. I'm sure."

"What's the time frame?" he shot back. "When do you need us? Over."

The tears that brimmed moments ago now traveled down her face. With his thumbs, Danny sweetly brushed them away.

"You did it," he whispered in shocked delight, his face close. "You've saved Ezekiel."

She fought to keep her voice steady over the radio. "Wake your people and come right now with insulin, or it will be too late for Zeke. Over."

"And if he dies in the interim, will you uphold your end of the bargain? Over."

Agnes opened her mouth to answer, and all her strength fled. She realized she hadn't slept in ages, realized that her eyes had dried out in their sockets. She had nothing left.

Gently, Danny extracted the radio from her grip.

"Captain, this is Danny. We still have a deal even if Zeke dies. How far are you from Mercy? Over."

"We might reach you by morning. But understand I won't be pleased if this is some kind of trick. I've got three hundred people depending on me. Put Agnes back on to confirm. Over."

"I can save your people, Captain." Tired as she was, blessed relief expanded inside her, saying the words aloud. "Bring them to me and I'll save them all."

"Over and out," Danny said, his eyes glinting with growing excitement.

"Over and out."

She collapsed beside Zeke. She pressed her forehead to her brother's, willing her thoughts to leap into him. She wanted him to know that he hadn't slipped through the cracks at the end of the world.

"Help is coming, brother," she said. "You don't have to be afraid of the dark."

54

BETH

It's easy to go through life avoiding the questions
that matter most. Chaos forces us to ask: Who am I?
What shape is my soul?
—AGNES, EARLY WRITINGS

The decision to leave the Prophet to die on Holden's road was easy.

He'd sent three hundred gullible faithful and innocent children to their deaths, and Beth had read his diaries. She knew how flagrantly he'd abused his power.

It's hereby forbidden for anyone to wear the color red, he'd said, and what a thrill it had been when three hundred people obeyed his command, bowing down like he was God Himself.

No music, he'd said, and they'd obeyed.

No medicine, he'd said, and they'd obeyed.

Go into the Underground Temple. Finally, he slavered after the biggest high of all. *Even if it kills you, go.*

And lo, it had killed them.

"You despicable man!" She struggled to her feet.

His mouth hung open like a fish's, his face whitening fast. She thought he'd die right then, immediately. But he gasped a lungful of air and reached for the hem of her dress. Disgusted, she swished it away from him.

"Save me, child. Get your parents. Tell them—"

He doesn't recognize me, she realized. *He officiated my wedding, but I fell beneath his notice. He sent me to my death, and still—*

The thought struck her as repulsive. Intolerable.

"Look at me!" Her voice rang out. "Who am I?"

He blinked foggily. She glanced down at his legs and saw that they'd been crushed, like a mouse body in a spring trap.

"You're one of the faithful, praise God! Your name is—"

He paused a long time before his eyes lit with recognition.

"Agnes!" He looked at her with frantic hope. "Aren't you Agnes?"

Beth screamed, drawing breath after breath while the Prophet's eyes glazed with terror. She felt like a wild thing. How *dare* he forget her? Had he ever even bothered to learn her name?

The Prophet's chest expanded and collapsed rapidly, the muscles of his neck straining after every breath.

"You should've prayed Agnes would be the one to find you," Beth spat. "She'd have saved your worthless life. But I won't."

She expected Red Creek's Prophet to argue. To shout or accuse. But he only closed his eyes and began, in rhythmic, watery gulps, to cry.

Beth was determined not to let the sound of this grown man weeping move her. Yet once again she remembered his diary— how intimate it felt to read his private thoughts. Though the Prophet didn't know it, they'd shared something in that church, and with every pitiful gulp of his she felt herself weakening.

I don't understand, he'd written after his miracles dried up. *Why doesn't my God smile on me? What have I done to earn His indifference?*

Vile creature that he was, he'd felt abandoned, heartbroken.

And that was a feeling Beth could understand.

Why doesn't Agnes care? she'd once written. *Why doesn't she love me anymore?*

Loneliness gaped inside her chest like a mortal wound. She'd thought she wanted, more than anything, to see the Outside, but it wasn't true. She wanted her family back more.

The Prophet mumbled something inaudible. She shuffled nearer.

Up close his breath smelled sour. Without his cloak his potbelly was visible, vulnerable.

"You're right." He struggled to speak. "I am worthless. I thought, after the apocalypse, God might smile on me again." He reached for her hand, gripped it. "But God frowned. God *smirked.* He killed them, Agnes. He turned them to reddest stone."

Beth's heart hardened. "But not you, because you *ran.*"

"It was hopeless!" Wild eyes rolled. "They were so sick— nothing I could do—" His fingers tightened around her wrist. "Why not just—"

Beth scraped his hand off like slime. The Prophet Rollins, Matthew Jameson, Mr. Hearn . . . all of them had abandoned their people when they needed them most. She could think of nothing more despicable.

Rollins moaned in dismay, groping blindly for her. Out of his reach, she drew her knees up to her chest and rocked back and forth.

Looking into the Prophet's darkness—his middle-aged, depressingly masculine darkness—Agnes's light shone ever brighter in Beth's memory. Bright as the sun.

She knew with sudden certainty that her sister *would* come back, if she knew how badly she was needed. To return to Red Creek, she'd move mountains.

But even if she never made it home, Cory would wait forever, nobly hoping. That was how *his* light shone.

And what about mine?

She stared at the Prophet's stark white hand. It was still groping for her but jerkily, its movements slowing.

"You should've stayed in the bunker, Rollins. Maybe it *was* hopeless, but you should've stayed."

It seemed impossible she'd ever reach her sister. But in the darkness Beth saw that her life was a string of decisions, of actions and inactions. She'd told Cory truthfully that she'd married his father out of fear. For fear, she'd done a lot of stupid things. None had ended well. In fact, when she considered this last hellish summer of her existence, she felt proud only of the moments when she'd spited fear—when she'd cursed it and spit in its eye.

So Beth knew she'd better drag her sorry self back to Red Creek, pick up the phone, and *try.* Otherwise, what separated her from the patriarchs?

She glanced down the dark road one more time, thinking she'd have to keep dreaming of the wonders that waited Outside— fine clothes, friends, the freedom to make her own choices.

She sighed.

She'd know those marvels eventually, she hoped. But not tonight. Or tomorrow, either.

Grudgingly, she gripped the Prophet's spasming hand, letting him know she wasn't the sort of person who would leave a man— any man—to die on the road alone.

55

AGNES

God bestows no greater gift than the chance to learn from those utterly different.

—AGNES, EARLY WRITINGS

Agnes woke to a great rumbling, a mechanized cacophony: the sound of dozens of trucks rolling over the upturned face of the desert.

The Captain was coming.

Danny's face rested inches from her own. They'd fallen asleep together, their bodies pressed as closely as facing pages in a book.

Carefully, she extricated herself from beneath Danny's arm. They hadn't kissed since the night Zeke missed his first insulin dose. But their bodies remembered. Even in sleep, they gravitated towards each other.

The ground beneath her quaked, quailing at the approach of so many crunching wheels and snarling engines. Agnes had never heard anything like it.

She shook Danny awake. "They're coming. Get your coat."

She thrust her feet into her boots and kissed Zeke's cheek— his skin felt dry as newsprint.

She flexed her stiff, bandaged hand, then left to greet the dawn.

Outside, daylight blossomed over Mercy's ruined field. It smelled like a desert morning, like endless miles of sweeping wind. She and Danny stood at the top of the hill, listening as the rumble became a roar. Trucks chewed ground and engines huffed air. A breeze blew the powerful stench of exhaust their way, and Agnes covered her nose with her arm.

In a moment, the refugee caravan would crest the hill.

"Three hundred Outsiders, and I promised all of them a home," she murmured.

Danny turned to her. "Are you sure you want to go back to Red Creek?"

I can save your people, she'd told the Captain. *I can save them all.*

"Beth's there," she said. "And it's the safest place for the Outsiders. I truly believe that."

Danny's mouth twitched. "You don't have to call us Outsiders anymore. You're one of us."

"You think so?"

"There's no official ceremony, no paperwork to join. You only have to love a few of us."

Something in his voice made Agnes glance up.

Danny peered at her with troubled, rainstorm eyes. Her lower belly tightened, her nerves rising a pitch.

He swallowed. "Agnes, don't you know that I—"

But then the caravan appeared.

The sight took Agnes's breath away. Dozens upon dozens of cars and vans and mobile homes, as well as dark military-style trucks, clambered over the red-and-yellow earth like giant black beetles. They drove in tight formation, and somehow solemnly, like a funeral procession. Agnes couldn't imagine how the Captain had coordinated it. Her insides slackened, thinking what a massive undertaking it would be to get all these people home.

"Survivors," Danny said under his breath. "They're all survivors, like us."

Yes. All of them with stories and memories and grief rolling in on Petra's red crystal tide. And these survivors, she hoped, would one day become the seedlings of a new Red Creek.

The vehicles slowed, fanning out to park in the lot, the fields. Engines shut off. Windows rolled down.

Then people emerged.

Agnes's eyes hungered for other human beings, and she couldn't have looked away if she'd wanted to. Camping chairs materialized, and tents, and yurts. People hailed one another. Shook hands or embraced. Someone fired up a portable grill.

Beth would've loved to see this.

After all this time, Agnes had finally conjured the world she'd dreamed of. A new and better world, bursting with human beings who'd never known Red Creek's shackles. Souls who, like Max and Danny and Jazz, could show her what it meant to be free.

She heard the bright yap of a little dog and saw small children teasing it. An odd tightness spread through her chest, wondering what Outsider kids played instead of the Apocalypse Game.

Ezekiel.

She scanned urgently for the Captain.

"The radio," Danny reminded her.

"Captain, this is Agnes. Do you see our tents? Over."

The calm, smooth way she spoke pleased her, no matter that she felt like vomiting from nerves alone.

A jolt of static. "We see you. We'll be right up with medicine. Over and out."

The words didn't penetrate right away. Then it was like a hundred pounds of stone lifted from her shoulders. She sagged into Danny, inhaling the good, green scent of him. He whooped and picked her up, spinning her around and around.

"Didn't I tell you everything would be all right?" Danny crowed. "*Didn't* I?"

She loved the sound of his laugh, the feel of his chest. And her heart sang like stars in the prayer space because the youngest wouldn't die before the oldest, thank God.

The Captain had brought medicine.

Zeke would live.

Hovering over Zeke, Agnes and Matilda locked eyes.

"Thank you for this."

"Oh, sweetheart, don't thank me." Matilda reached across Zeke's torso to touch her cheek. "It was all you."

Agnes braced herself, watching insulin flow into his IV line. He wouldn't wake right away, but Agnes had nowhere else she'd rather be. She settled at his bedside, her chin in her hand, thinking of all the people who'd worked so hard to give him a chance at life. Eventually, as the afternoon shadows lengthened, she fell asleep.

"Agnes?"

Ezekiel.

His eyes open, his hand in hers. She loved every impulse that animated his fingers, the renewed warmth of his palm.

"Agnes, am I alive?"

She wouldn't cry. Not now. A shaft of light illuminated the tent as Matilda glided quietly back in her nurse's way, to fix more medicine to his IV stand.

"You're alive, and you're going to live a long time," Agnes said. "And Zeke. I have good news."

He raised his eyebrows. In his coma, bones had emerged that she'd never seen before.

"We're going back to Red Creek. To save your brother and sisters, if I can."

"Really?" he whispered. "You mean it?"

"I do."

He closed his swollen eyes, exhausted.

She didn't want to let him go back to sleep, but he needed his rest. And the Captain had brought her a gigantic supply of insulin, the most she'd ever had. Zeke was going to be okay for a very long while.

She listened to the far-off sound of voices rising from the valley below, smelling campfire smoke and dinners cooking. The world hadn't ended after all.

Matilda urged her out of the tent. "Tell them the news, Agnes."

She stepped into the air and found the Captain and the others, drinking from their canteens and talking quietly.

The look on her face told them everything they needed to know. Jazz wept tears of relief, and Max stuck a toothpick in his mouth, chewing contentedly. Danny's wink felt as intimate as a kiss.

The Captain nodded, also pleased, then removed his sunglasses. "My stragglers are frightened, Agnes."

She pulled herself together. "Yes. But they needn't be. Red Creek might be the safest place on earth."

The scrollwork of scars around his eyes tightened. "I need to know you're telling the God's-honest truth. You've made a lot of promises."

She looked into the Captain's exposed eyes. Responsibility and anxiety had tinged them with wretchedness.

Three hundred people. Three hundred lives.

"Captain, I always tell the truth."

"You don't know what these people have been through. They've lost family to the Virus. Lost homes. They're exhausted, hungry, terrified. We have a woman who's about to have a baby. They all need something to believe in, a reason to keep going."

A *baby*, Agnes thought wonderingly.

"Red Creek is worth believing in." She lowered her voice. "God's behind it, somehow."

"I suppose now you'll say *He works in mysterious ways?*" the Captain said dryly.

She smiled. "Usually, He does. But this time the message was clear as crystal. Red Creek is shelter from the storm."

His eyes widened, his expression skeptical and afraid to hope. But the desire for hope was there, and for now, Agnes thought that might just be enough. Outsider or faithful, agnostic or believer, it was the human condition to be faith-starved, searching. The biggest lie the Prophet ever told was that perfect obedience bred perfect faith. Because faith was never perfect. Only the imperfect kind existed, and you didn't reach it through obedience. Sometimes, faith was best discovered in rebellion.

"It's a new world, Captain. We can make Red Creek a kind place, a safe haven for anyone who needs it. We can build the city of our dreams."

He stuck his hand out, but Agnes couldn't shake it, bruised as she was.

Instead, she rose on tiptoes and kissed his stubbled cheek. "God bless you for coming."

He touched the spot she'd kissed, momentarily bewildered.

From below, she heard travelers talking, laughing, their voices uplifted by wind.

"I'd better get back," the Captain said.

When he'd gone, Agnes fell into Danny's arms, and Max's and Jazz's, too. They huddled together, limbs entwined. A deep quiet filled her, peaceful and strong. Within her soul a long-sought puzzle piece had fallen into place, and after all this struggle, all this time, she was finally—*finally*—complete.

A girl made whole in the light of her imperfect faith.

PART
FOUR

56

AGNES

Eventually, each must ask: What am I willing to give to make the world a better place?
—AGNES, EARLY WRITINGS

Agnes wasn't *sure* that the night before she returned to Red Creek would be her last on earth—but she suspected as much.

Matilda had warned her to stay out of the prayer space. But she'd have to use it, to try to save the people in the bunker. She didn't want to die, not when there was so much to live for: a new town to build, her love for Danny to explore, and Zeke growing bigger every day. But if she could trade her life for her family? She'd take that bargain in a heartbeat. It made a kind of elemental sense: Breath for breath. Life for life. Song for song.

But what should she do with the book she'd written in the back pages of Beth's diary? She'd filled every blank space with her thoughts on God, Petra, her experience in the prayer space. And not just *her* thoughts.

Some, she knew by the goose bumps that peaked on her arms, were holy.

Danny. He would keep her writing safe. And if the worst

happened, he would know what to do with it—how to get it into the world.

While Zeke slept peacefully in their tent, Agnes crossed the campground.

All three hundred of her people had raised tents in a grassy meadow on Holden's outskirts. The journey from Mercy had been grindingly slow, two days of dusty travel in trucks and Humvees. The Captain had worn himself out. Now he worried because food grew scarce and the pregnant Outsider neared her time.

Agnes had warned the Captain there wouldn't be an abundance of food in Red Creek—but there would be some, in the houses of the faithful. Scavenging bands could light out from there, to search the Walmart, gas stations, grocery stores.

And, when they were finally settled, they could begin planting fields with seeds of hope. She dreamed of pumpkins, alfalfa, corn—even fruit trees. In a year or two, the land might flourish.

So many tents, spread under the stars. So many sleeping Outsiders. Walking, she loved the glow of the smoldering campfires, the wisps of late-night laughter. Her eyes welled.

Her people.

It would be very hard to say goodbye.

Agnes rustled Danny's tent. When he didn't answer, she let herself in.

"Agnes?" He groped blindly for his glasses. "Is something wrong?"

She sat cross-legged beside his sleeping bag, which smelled pleasantly of *boy*. She'd gotten to know his scent well. Whenever they tumbled from the Captain's Humvee, eager to stretch their legs, they always made straight for a private place—a tree, a ditch, a riverbed—and then there was kissing. Snuggling and cuddling, sneaking around, though Jazz winked and giggled to let her know that she *knew.*

Whatever force attracted them had only intensified as they whispered silly secrets and treasured dreams. They liked, especially, to argue over the existence of God—an almost sinful amount of fun.

If there's no God, who created the world?

Well, there's a theory called the big bang...

You think God can't make a bang?

I'm not saying God can't, just that there's no evidence God did.

What about right and wrong? Where does that come from?

No matter how heated the arguments became, they always ended in more kissing. And that felt like merging, fusing, rejoicing. Sometimes it was like they shared a single, glorious skin.

In the tent, Danny struggled upright. She handed him his glasses—he really was blind as a bat—and he wrapped his long arms around his knees.

"What's up, Agnes?"

She showed him her book. "I've been collecting my thoughts. But tomorrow, I don't know what will happen. I want you to keep this manuscript safe."

Danny's eyes sharpened. "You think you're going to die tomorrow."

The tent rippled in the night wind.

"Matilda told me to stay out of the prayer space," she said, quietly. "But I can't."

"Why the hell not?"

"You heard Beth. She thinks I can save my family. How else am I going to do that, Danny?"

He leveled a challenging stare. "So, your plan is to—what? Resurrect them?"

"They aren't dead. Only Nested."

He threw up his hands. "That's as good as dead, and you know it!"

"Maybe," she said calmly. "We'll have to see."

He rose and began angrily shuffling through his things.

She held the book in her good hand. Matilda had promised that once they were settled, she'd reset the broken bones in her right, so the knuckles could heal properly. But Agnes didn't know if she'd live that long.

"What're you doing, Danny?"

Tubes, wires, pill bottles, needles, rubbery bags, those chemical-blue ice packs. He stuffed them into his pack until it looked ready to burst.

Agnes pinched the bridge of her nose. "Danny. Tell me you'll take care of this book. It's important. Please."

He turned to her, eyes hard. "Does it matter that I don't believe you can help your family? That you might kill yourself in vain?"

"No," she said honestly.

He snorted, exasperated. "Of course I'll look after your book. But you're not going to die."

She narrowed her eyes. "You won't try to stop me, will you?"

He laughed dryly. "Once you've made up your mind to do something, nobody can stop you."

"Then what makes you so sure—"

"Agnes," he said firmly. "You have your faith. Let me have mine."

"You still have the nightmare," she said with realization.

His eyes skidded away. "And it always ends the same."

"Badly?" she asked, more worried for him than for herself.

Compassion was a funny thing that way, a powerful antidote to even mortal fear.

He hung his head. "I'm never good enough. Never fast or smart enough."

She spoke softly. "Your nightmare—it might not have anything to do with me."

"We both know it was always about you."

He sounded so crushed that for half a heartbeat, she regretted the time they'd spent kissing, loving. But if she started regretting something as wondrous as that, she'd loose the thread that unraveled everything. When it came to love, there could be no regrets.

Agnes handed him her book—once, Beth's diary—with a shiver. It felt like handing him the empty cooler, back when she was Red Creek's prisoner.

He moved closer, cupped her face in his hands.

"I love you. I'm *in* love with you. Please say you love me, too."

She pulled away. She did love him, but telling him now, on what might be her last night on earth . . . was that compassionate? Kind?

His face collapsed in sadness and surprise.

And seeing that, she crumbled. From the first, their souls had recognized something in each other. Wrong or not, she couldn't push him away.

She pressed herself into him, letting his chin rest lightly on her head.

"I'm sorry," Agnes said. "Of course I'm in love with you. You've been so patient with me, every step of the way. I never knew a man could be like you: considerate and selfless and kind."

"Not that selfless," he murmured, and slid his arms around her waist.

She kissed him, and it happened again: a powerful merging that shocked every nerve in her body. It was like standing in the midst of the prayer space—only this time, they themselves hummed, vibrating. Sacred creatures, the two of them, together.

A shriek split the air.

Agnes leapt away from Danny, thinking, *Red creatures. What if one had found its way into camp, despite the barbed wire the Captain had put up?*

"It's okay," Danny soothed. "Mom said Amber might go into labor tonight."

Labor. Her whole body stiffened with a half-forgotten fear. Birth meant blood, pain, and—all too often—death. In her mind, she pictured the toothy stones of the King family graveyard.

"Healthy women hardly ever die in childbirth anymore," Danny said, reading her face.

"You mean it?"

"Yes."

She exhaled. "Thank God."

"Thank *science*." He grinned ruefully. Then his face turned serious again. "Agnes. I meant what I said. I'm not letting you die."

"Just keep the book," she said. "Some of it's pretty good, I think."

He reached out, fingered the ribbon in her hair. "I can't wait to discuss it with you, later."

Leaving his tent, Agnes felt the throes of regret for the years she could have shared with him. She swiped at her eyes, rocked by the strength of her feelings. She felt deeply grateful that God had given her a chance to experience this new kind of love, before the end. Though, of course, Danny would say God never *gave* them anything. He'd say they created every ounce of it themselves. In the book she'd written, Agnes had tried to explain that, paradoxically, both origin stories were equally true. It was all in the eye of the believer.

Beneath the stars, she paused to let her spirit sing, for even now a baby was being born.

A *baby* ushering in a new age.

57

AGNES

Hatred of women is an infectious sickness. I've seen it tear
families, hearts, minds apart.
—AGNES, EARLY WRITINGS

A gnes lit out before dawn, while the rest of their ragtag, refugee caravan slept. She'd borrowed a truck from the Captain but didn't take it all the way up the hill. For reasons she couldn't explain, she wanted to travel the last mile on foot, and tackle the final steep hill to Red Creek and its iron gates alone.

Beneath the dawn sky, the air smelled of home, of pine trees and musky forest loam. After so long in the desert, the sight of so much evergreen was sweet relief.

Yet Agnes felt jittery. More nervous about her homecoming than she'd expected. Red Creek's memories stalked her like ghosts: Father slapping Beth smartly across the face; the Prophet firing his pistol at the infected dog; the bunker stairs, so horrendously dark.

She'd never mattered here—*women* had never mattered. But now she returned as more than a woman or a man. She returned as a prophet, determined to rescue the innocent from the ravages of the Virus.

If it were only grown people Nested in the bunker, she would leave them to their fate. Every one of them was complicit in the monstrosity Red Creek had become. But the children...They'd never even had a chance.

Agnes would see to it that the twins and Sam lived again, and in a better world, even if it killed her.

As it was written in Ezekiel: *I will remove from them their heart of stone and give them a heart of flesh.*

"Amen." She was out of breath, nearing the hilltop. "Amen."

She reached the gates, iron, rusted, hateful. She put hand to metal, absorbing its cold. Through the iron bars, she saw streets eerily deserted. She gritted her teeth, preparing herself.

A stamping broke the silence. She turned to see a stag, red-hided, shining like a living gem. In wonder, not fear, she regarded it. Could it be the stag she saw, the night she and Zeke fled?

"Do you know me?"

The crimson eyes hungered. The stag quickened, hurrying to infect her as its warped biology urged. Steadying herself, she called up the prayer space.

The stag's hooves shrieked to a halt.

Agnes regarded its emaciated form. Petra had kept the animal alive, but it hadn't found its Nest. It'd been wandering in circles.

She took a step towards it, her glowing hands outstretched.

Frightened, it stumbled back.

"I'm sorry you never found your Nest," she said, and meant it powerfully.

The animal's striated neck craned.

"I'm the cure, you know. I learned that during God's test."

But the stag didn't want to be cured. It clung to its red life, as cold and hard as it was. It reared its head, snorted, and bolted into the forest.

Reluctantly, Agnes shut down. She'd come to love the prayer space's warmth and connection. She'd miss it, if she died. She didn't know much about the afterlife, but she imagined you couldn't take your gifts with you, just like you couldn't take your loves.

The nape of her neck prickled.

"*Agnes.*"

On the other side of the gate stood Beth.

She wore a baby-blue prairie dress, her hair carefully plaited. She looked lean, haunted, and more beautiful than ever.

Agnes wanted to run to her, but her legs were leaden. She felt guilty for the secrets she'd kept, for her final abandonment. What had Beth's life been like, after? What horrors had she survived alone?

"Agnes?" Beth's voice was small and uncertain, childlike.

Agnes ran. She stumbled through the broken gate, reaching for her sister, the person who knew her best in the world. They clasped each other, both shivering, quaking, murmuring.

She'd believed her sister was dead—she'd *grieved* for her—and so it felt miraculous to hold her now, miraculous as resurrection.

But who had resurrected whom?

If it hadn't been for Beth's voice mail, she'd never have known to return to Red Creek. If it hadn't been for Beth, she might've lost Ezekiel.

"I got your message," Agnes whispered into her ear. "Thank you."

"You got it? You really did?" Beth sounded amazed.

"It saved me, Beth. *You* saved me."

Beth covered her slender nose with both hands, pressed her head into Agnes's neck, and sobbed. Agnes ached, because her sister had needed her, longed for her—but never truly expected her to return. Yet somehow, they'd both made it through the tunnel into the light. They were daughters of Red Creek, but also daughters of Sarah Shiner, the girl who'd mustered the courage to run towards freedom. And they were daughters of Eve, flinging open Eden's gates and stepping into a strange new world.

The lyrics of "Amazing Grace" wove dreamily through her mind.

I once was lost, but now am found . . .

"The nightmare's almost over," she promised Beth. "We're nearly at the end."

She held her sister a long time, smelling her clean hair, feeling her warm cheek, downy as a child's. Sun warmed her neck, and a familiar breeze rustled her clothes.

In her sister's arms, Agnes came home.

58

BETH

Forgiveness is an underrated, oft-overlooked power.
—Agnes, Early Writings

Safe in her sister's embrace, Beth couldn't have pulled away if she'd wanted to. Agnes reeked of dust, sweat, and exhaust. And yet, holding her was like sinking into a dream. Her sister's warmth, her sister's eyes, were the same as ever.

Agnes pulled away first. Like a comfort-starved child, Beth yearned to be held again. She wanted to reach out and stroke the satin ribbon woven through Agnes's hair. She wanted to kiss her, thank her for the blessing she'd bestowed.

"The Prophet is here," Agnes said, shocking her silent. "I can feel him." Her eyes snapped to Beth's face, scary fast. "Why isn't he in the bunker?"

"I found him on the road." Beth shriveled under her sister's unrelenting gaze. She'd been wrong about her eyes. They were *not* the same.

"I hit him with Mr. King's truck," she explained. "We've been keeping him in the church. Cory says he's not a threat. Not anymore, anyway."

Agnes's eyes latched on to the church spire. "Take me to him."

"Don't you think—maybe, the bunker? Agnes, can you save the kids?"

"Yes. But I have to see the Prophet first," she said. "He has to answer for his crimes."

Beth wondered at the fierce sister-stranger who stood before her now. Where had she found this confidence, this decisiveness?

A cloud passed over the sun, and a dark presentiment settled in her heart.

She set her jaw, resolving to be at Agnes's side, no matter what happened next.

Cory sat in the back of the church, his feet irreverently balanced on a pew.

All week, he'd been playing watchdog and jail keep. He didn't dare let the wily Prophet out of his sight, except after locking him inside his office to sleep.

When Beth stepped into the church with Agnes at her side, Cory did a double take.

"Holy shit." He shot to his feet, then backpedaled. "I mean, holy cow, Agnes. We've been waiting so long."

Agnes's boots clicked to a stop. "Cory Jameson. I never guessed it would be you. Thank you for helping my sister. Where's Rollins?"

He jerked his thumb. "I fixed up an old rocking chair, put wheels on it. He's parked behind his pulpit."

"What has he said?"

Cory shook his head, bemused. "He hasn't spoken a word since he got here. All day long, he just...stares."

"Good." Agnes nodded like it meant something.

Cory and Beth exchanged a look.

Was it possible her sister had gone mad in the desert?

On their way to the church, she'd claimed Ezekiel was fine and that she'd brought a band of Outsiders with her. But Beth hadn't seen any people at all. Only Agnes, walking alone.

Beth snuffed out her doubts like they were a foul-smelling flame. She believed in her sister. She had to. And anyway, conspiring with God had to change a person.

My sister, a prophet. She could hardly believe it.

Agnes strode to the front of the church. Beth followed, and Cory unfroze long enough to hurry after them. Together the three of them stood beneath the dangling bronze cross, looking down at the murderer in his ersatz wheelchair.

Rollins didn't acknowledge them. Didn't even move.

Slowly and deliberately, Agnes began unwrapping the bandages that swathed her hand.

"Do you remember me?"

He darted a glance. Looked away.

Beth's shoulders tightened, remembering how furious his lack of recognition had made her on the road. She didn't want to see this new Agnes furious.

"That's all right." Agnes knelt at his side, close enough to touch the wiry hairs of his forearm. Beth felt Cory stiffen. "My name is Agnes, Jacob. My sister tells me she hit you with a car." Her tone remained gentle, almost sweet. "What were you doing on the road while your people were trapped?"

"My wives call me Jacob," the Prophet answered, his voice rough with disuse. "You can call me Prophet Rollins. I remember you now. You're the girl who ran from the Rapture."

"She ran from lies," Beth spat. "She ran from *certain death*, you miserable—"

Agnes held up her hand, marked across the knuckles with a deep purple band of bruising.

Beth sucked in a breath, and Cory put a hand on her shoulder, whispering, "Wait."

Agnes took the Prophet's hand in her swollen one. "I'm so glad you remember me. There's a lot we have in common."

Anger flared in Beth's heart. How dare her sister compare herself to that monster?

"God has made His presence known to both of us. For me, divinity manifests in sounds that only I can hear. The tenderest, most loving songs."

"You're lying," Rollins said, but uncertainly. "I could heal with a touch. I cast out demons from the body. I received direct messages from God Himself—"

"No." Agnes shook her head. "No more lies. I believe you had some power, once. But God never spoke to you. He couldn't have, because you failed the test."

The Prophet's eyes widened. "What test? What are you talking about?" He looked beseechingly at Cory, the only other man in the room. "Get this madwoman away from me!"

Rollins tried to yank his hand from Agnes's, but she refused to release her grip. The Prophet might as well have been caught in an iron trap.

Good, Beth thought. *Don't let him off the hook.*

"Jacob, I *understand*. For me, the test was terrifying. I nearly failed." Agnes stroked the ribbon with her good hand, like it soothed her. "But when you lost your power, did you take your frustration out on your people? When you sent them into the bunker, were you trying to have your revenge on God?"

She didn't sound angry, only sorrowful.

"No." His voice was hoarse. "I was trying to *get His attention*. I thought, if He saw how much I was willing to sacrifice…"

Cory hissed air through his teeth.

"God rejects burnt offerings," Agnes said mildly. "You know that."

His eyes, awestruck and terrified, were fixed on her face. She kept a tight grip on his hand and seemed to be collecting herself somehow. Watching, Beth felt a twinge of real fear.

"Rollins." Anguished, Cory exploded. "Where did my father go when he abandoned the bunker? Were you going to meet him? Do you know where he is?"

"Matthew?" The Prophet blinked at Cory. "He washed his hands of this place. Said it had all been a mistake. I was a worm, he said, I lived in the dirt, and I'd dragged him down with me. I don't know where he went."

"But then—" Beth watched Cory grappling with this new information. "Did he even try to save my mothers, my brothers?"

An indifferent stare. "He left. That's all I know."

"No." Cory sounded panicked. "That can't be *all*."

Beth touched his arm. "We may never know what was in his heart. You're nothing like him. That's what matters."

He wrapped his arms around her, holding her close. Politely, Agnes averted her eyes.

"I slept in the forest for a while," the Prophet continued dreamily. "Then, one night, I decided to leave. Seek a new fortune. See the world."

Beth wanted to kick him for the longing in his voice. The Prophet could've left whenever he wanted. He and his grandfather— they'd invented Red Creek's lethal Laws. What entitled these men to believe that they, of all people, deserved a second chance?

The dreamy look evaporated. "But what are you doing here, girl? Why did you return?"

Agnes squeezed his hand, though it must have pained her.

"I came to forgive you." Her voice dropped frightfully. "Jacob, you are forgiven."

The Prophet absorbed the words like a blow. His fish-white skin, already so pale, blanched.

Beth stared. "You can't do that, Agnes! You can't forgive what he did!"

"I could never forgive the crime." She turned on Beth, her eyes glistening like liquid stars. "But I can forgive the man. I *do*."

Even as she spoke, the air in the church shifted, changing. The light streaming through the open door imperceptibly softened, and the atmosphere became vaporous. For the first time in her life, Beth saw beauty in the church. Saw how light glowed in complex contrast with the shadows, shifting and dancing over the hardwood like leaves patterned the forest floor.

Cory's arm, wrapped around her waist, tightened.

The Prophet sobbed over his hand, still twined with Agnes's.

Then a stranger walked into the church.

An Outsider man holding hands with Ezekiel.

59

AGNES

First and foremost, love challenges the lovers.
—AGNES, EARLY WRITINGS

"*Agnes.*" Danny shouldered his impossibly heavy-looking backpack. "How could you leave without saying goodbye? And who the hell is *that*?"

Zeke also glared while Benny climbed his back like a tree. Then he noticed the Prophet.

"Oh no," Zeke moaned. "Oh no, oh no!"

Agnes hastened to him, rewrapping her hand as she ran.

Holding Zeke's head to her shoulder, she scowled at Danny. "How could you?"

Danny stood his ground. "Sorry, but we're coming with you."

Though Agnes still meant to face the end alone, she felt thankful to see their faces one last time. The sense of her death had wrapped itself around her throat like an oppressive hand. Even with Beth and Cory, she'd felt lonesome.

She glanced at the door and Danny spotted her hopeful, hesitant look.

"Max and Jazz are helping the Captain," he said gently.

"And Matilda?"

"My mother's staying with Amber and her baby." He swallowed, and she saw his recurring nightmare in his eyes like the moon reflected on water. "So, you see, it's just us."

"I came, though," Zeke said. "Max told me to stay, but I wanted to be with you."

"Ezekiel," Beth whispered, taking a hesitant step towards him.

Zeke stretched his arms up, and she lifted him like he was still little, nuzzling his nose with her own.

"You can come with me to the bunker door, but no farther," Agnes told Danny.

The discarded Prophet wept, sniffling. It was impossible to know how much he really regretted the choices he'd made, and how much he only regretted the result. But the man meant nothing to her now. He was only a blotch, a stain on the hardwood floor.

From behind her, Agnes heard a fast, whispered conversation. "Beth, I should stay. Should I stay? To make sure the Prophet doesn't—"

"Yes." Her sister sounded relieved. "Someone has to."

"I wanted to see the miracle," mumbled Cory.

"I know," Beth said sweetly. "I'll tell you all about it."

"Be careful."

Cory really loves her, Agnes marveled.

Danny stepped forwards. "I'm Danny. You must be Beth, and...?"

Cory stuck out his hand. "Cory Jameson. Welcome to Red Creek, Danny."

Agnes felt her sister's eyes seeking hers. But she avoided them. She didn't have the heart to explain her relationship to Danny now.

Her right hand throbbed, and inside her, a storm brewed.

Hurry. You'd better hurry.

She set her shoulders and straightened her spine. "It's time to go."

—⁂—

They walked through the meadows and fields, past the lake, to the grass where the bunker lay buried. This was the land of Agnes's childhood, the realm of the wide white sky and bee-spun glades. Hope lodged in her chest like a seed.

"Danny." She stopped on a weedy rise. The sun played on his hair and she thought he'd never looked so handsome. "I need you and Zeke to wait here."

His eyes darkened.

"We'll wait," Zeke answered for him. "We'll wait for the twins and Sam."

Benny jumped from his shoulders. He rolled playfully in the yellow-gold grass.

"I'll see you soon," Danny said.

Agnes opened her mouth to correct him; decided to say nothing.

She focused on the buried hatch in the ground. "Beth, you'd better wait, too."

She didn't answer right away. Agnes tore her eyes from the beckoning abyss and the sight of her sister's face, streaming with tears, shocked her.

"I thought you trusted me," Beth stuttered.

Danny pulled Zeke a short distance away, giving them their privacy. Benny followed after his boy at a loping pace, his eyes tracking a white cabbage butterfly.

"I only want—"

"To protect me, I know," she scoffed. "Agnes, how can you shut me out *again*?"

Agnes rolled her eyes up to the sky. No one drove her half as crazy as her sister.

"It's just too dangerous, Beth. Anyone who goes down into the bunker isn't coming back."

Green eyes narrowed. "How can you know that?"

Agnes shrugged. "I believe it. I suspect it."

"Fine." She crossed her arms over her chest. "But I'm still going with you."

Insufferable.

Agnes put her hands on her hips. "Do you want to die? Is that it?"

Infuriatingly, Beth smiled. "I'm not going to die."

"How do you know?" she demanded.

Beth pursed her lips, and Agnes remembered her sister as a stubborn, impish child.

"I can't die down there, because I haven't seen Outside. I haven't gotten a tattoo, I've never ridden on an airplane, and I don't know what all is out there to see. No, I'm not dying today." She shook her head emphatically. "No way."

Agnes's first instinct was to argue, but something about her sister's tone—infuriating as she was—gave her pause. After all, she knew *her* destiny. Was it really so crazy to think Beth might know hers?

"Agnes. Your *hands.*"

She looked down. Though she hadn't consciously stepped into the prayer space, her hands glowed brightly, baring every ligament and vein.

I don't have much time.

She extended her good hand to her sister, little finger stretched out. Relief swept her sister's face.

"No more secrets," Beth said.

"No more secrets," Agnes promised.

"Beth." Suddenly, it was hard to catch her breath. She was so *hot*. Feverish. "Listen. When I tell you to close your eyes, you do it. Promise me."

Beth nodded, eyes wide.

Agnes's hands glowed brighter. She shoved them into her pockets. Danny and Zeke stood stiffly, watching them.

Zeke held up a hand, like waving goodbye.

I won't see him grow up. She panicked. *I'll never know what kind of man he'll become.*

But in her heart, she knew that he'd be fine. He'd have Beth, and his Outsider family, too.

Agnes and Beth walked to the bunker's edge, turned the shrieking crank, and threw the iron hatch open. Stairs plunged downwards, disappearing into tortured shadows.

Agnes took one last look up at the sky. It was morning blue, with lavender gilding the edges. She'd seen that exact shade on thousands of mornings. This would be the last.

Descending the stairs with Beth at her back, she felt terribly glad she didn't have to go into the suffocating darkness alone.

60

AGNES

I wish I could tell you that before the end, I wasn't afraid.
—AGNES, EARLY WRITINGS

The Nest filled the bunker, a crimson forest. Overhead a single light bulb swung back and forth on its cord. Agnes smelled rotten food, human waste, and the Nest—earthy, like unwashed hair. Instinctively, she scanned for the kids. Beth dug her nails into Agnes's arm.

"What *is* this? Why are they melded together like that?"

Agnes remembered the theories of her Outsider friends, whispered around late-night campfires. Jazz believed humankind had disturbed the natural world, pushed it to extinction. Danny believed the Virus was a biological aberration science would soon control. Max simply said, "Sometimes, shit happens."

The world might never know the truth. Not understanding God's ways was where fear was born—and misinterpretations, both willful and not.

But it was also where beauty began. The burning human need for faith.

She wiped sweat from her brow. "No one knows why they Nest

together. Beth, when it's finally over, you'll have to make sense of it in your own way. Everyone will."

Agnes rubbed her temples. She felt God's thunderous voice amassing, preparing to speak in this room full of red limbs and gem-hard skins.

"I never told you about Sarah Shiner," Agnes said urgently. "But there's something in our history. Something important—"

Beth's eyes gleamed. "I know all about Sarah. I found her name in the Book of Begats. I've been wondering what happened to her after she ran."

Agnes sucked in a breath of foul air. "She had a great-granddaughter. I found her..."

In the Nest the Burn Squad destroyed.

In her mind, that little girl represented all the pain the Virus had inflicted. No matter what happened today, Petra had torn wounds that might never fully heal. But she wanted Beth to know: One woman in their family had succeeded in making a life for herself Outside.

Prayer space heat swept through Agnes's body like an arid wind. She doubled over, groaning.

"Agnes? What's wrong?"

Ashes to ashes, dust to dust.

"Let's find the kids." Her head swam sickly. "I want to say goodbye."

They inched along the Nest's perimeter, studying face after face.

Beth and Agnes both fought panic. Crystal skins bristled whenever they got too near. They had to be careful not to snag their dresses on a petrified fingernail; had to be careful, lest their horror get the best of them.

It would be all too easy to fall to the ground and never get up again.

Beth spoke names aloud, like prayers: "The second Mrs. Hearn and her son, Jacob; the little King boy, Joe; Jeremy Sayles; Patience King; Angela Rollins..." Her voice faltered. "Dear God, Agnes, all these kids!"

The prayer space pressed against Agnes's ribs like a balloon of heat, expanding in every direction. Sweat dripped down her nose. She'd never felt so oppressed. She hated this low-ceilinged room, the dark, the damp. She'd only ever wanted sky, and freedom, and Zeke—

"Oh, Agnes," gasped Beth. "Look."

At first the little huddled bodies looked the same as all the others. More red arms and legs, bowed heads, blank eyes. But two twined very tightly, not an inch of space between them, and a third bent halfway over them—as if protecting, sheltering.

She recognized that third body's shoes. They were scuffed brown leather.

They were Sam's.

The kids.

Their small bodies trembled like leaves on the outer branches of a great tree. Agnes covered her mouth with her hand.

"Sam tried to protect them." Beth knelt, tucking her prairie skirt beneath her. "Even while he was sick."

Before Agnes could stop her, Beth had wrapped her arms around the three petrified children, encircling them.

Her mind flashed to their trailer, remembering how she'd taught the twins to braid their hair; how she'd teased Sam for scuffing his shoes; how joyous it was when the breadsticks were finally baked. Small moments of happiness, winking like fireflies in their dark, difficult lives.

Now the prayer space swirled inside her like a living thing. She'd never experienced it like this before: as something separate, *alien*. But the prayer space had always been alien. A temporary gift.

God was about to speak.

Anxiety seized her. What if she fainted before she had a chance to rescue her family?

"What do I do?" she cried out. "How do I save them?"

Agnes, the voice thundered. *A kiss.*

Yes.

"Beth, close your eyes."

Her sister ducked her head against her arm. Then Agnes pressed her lips to Sam's hard, bristling cheek. She kissed him as she'd done a million times, pouring into him all her love, her hope, her heat.

Breathing out.

The prayer space left her body in a rush. Her kiss grew into a spectral wind, a shimmering heat wave. For the first time, she could *see* her power.

She heard her mother's record:

'Twas Grace that taught my heart to fear, and Grace my fears relieved . . .

The prayer space whirled chaotically around the room, weaving and caressing the gem-hard skins locked in their Nested embrace.

How precious did that Grace appear, the hour I first believed . . .

Agnes wept, watching the prayer space leave her, feeling both awestruck and bereft.

In the bunker, the Nest vibrated faster, harder. She heard teeth and bones rattling, felt the ground quaking beneath her shoes. Beside her, a face she didn't recognize dripped like over-heated glass.

"Beth," she gasped. *"Don't look."*

Skins distorted, twisted, and fell like masks, shattering on the earthen floor. People came apart and slid away from one another, shedding gemstone skins. The hanging bulb blazed brightly, picking up the electric heat. Then it broke from its chain and fell. Agnes held tightly to her family.

The bunker had become a crucible.

Beth screamed.

"Keep your eyes shut!"

It seemed to go on forever, the chaos of cracking, breaking, melting.

She lifted her head and saw the hot, shimmering wind hovering between Nest and ceiling. Then it swept gracefully up the stairs, twirling in elaborate eddies, up and out into the day.

Into the *world.*

"Thank you," she whispered to the prayer space, that force that had guided her, protected her, sustained her. "Goodbye."

It would keep going, she knew, until every Nest on earth had felt its kiss. She closed her eyes, imagining the millions of infected people and animals that dotted the world. The prayer space would race across the earth's surface like wildfire, burning away the scars of infection, preparing the land to be reshaped into something new, something better.

That was her prophecy: The world could be better.

Agnes felt tired. So tired.

She was almost glad when she finally felt herself slipping away.

A month ago, she and Zeke had escaped from their dying

home star like two shards of wayward light. It was only fitting she'd returned for a miraculous blaze, before an endless dark.

She opened her eyes one final time.

In the sunset of the dissolving Nest, she saw God.

Not heard, or sensed, or guessed—but *saw.*

Every mystery was laid bare: the reason for the Virus; the Prophet's evil; the reason, even, for those sweet slender moments of love. It was all part of the same story, the same universal fabric, twinkling with human stories like stars.

Beautiful. You're so beautiful.

She held on to Beth and the kids as long as she could, drinking deeply of her faith. Finally, calm settled on her mind like a snowdrift, blessedly cool.

"Agnes?" Beth howled. *"Agnes?"*

But she didn't hear.

For Agnes, at last, a loving silence and amazing grace.

61

BETH

What will we remember, when the red dream is done?

What lessons will we take away?

—AGNES, EARLY WRITINGS

B eth was packing up the last of her personal items: hairbrush, toothbrush, the clothes Jazz had given her for the trip.

Sexy *Outsider* clothes, which Beth hoped might one day show off her tattoo.

She was finally leaving town, for good.

She'd carefully chosen her going-away outfit: a bohemian headband, multicolored; a red tank top; denim shorts; and flip-flops. She loved feeling the air on her toes. Loved makeup, too. Mascara, eyeliner, blush. Jazz had taught her how to play with color and shadow.

The twins, both wearing T-shirts and jeans, wanted to help her pack. But every time she set them on a task, they wound up fiddling with their Nintendos.

Beth wasn't sure she'd ever be able to return home. The radio reported that the mail service continued to struggle and that trains, planes, and buses would be out of operation for years. If she wanted to go far, she must plan to be gone a long time.

And she did want to go far. She and Cory had it all mapped out. They'd drive clear across the country, stopping anywhere that struck their fancy.

Zipping up her bag, excitement pulsed in her belly.

To finally see the world beyond Red Creek...

But of course, it wasn't called Red Creek anymore. These days, the land was known as Benny's Hollow. Ezekiel had submitted his idea for a name, as did many others, for a vote. Benny's Hollow won in a landslide. People had no idea they were naming their town after a lazy orange cat.

Many Outsiders had wanted to name the town after Agnes, but the Captain decided that would lead to too many questions. People would want to hear the story of a town named after a teenaged girl, and for now, that story remained their secret.

Agnes in the bunker was something you whispered about. A legend, a myth.

"Beth!" Cory called from the porch. "Aren't you ready yet?"

Flustered, she kissed the heads of the twins.

"Can't we come with you?" Mary begged. "We want to have an adventure, too!"

"You've still got school, remember? Cory! Help me find Sam. Then I'm ready to go."

"I never can find that kid," Cory said irritably, twirling his keys on the porch. "He's got ants in his pants."

"Bees today, actually." Danny appeared on their doorstep, hanging on to the collar of one very grumpy-looking preteen boy. In the last two years, Sam had shot up like a beanstalk. Now swelling marred his bottom lip.

Beth rushed to the door. "What *happened*?"

"Got stung by one of Mr. Mullen's honeybees. Jazz brought him into the clinic."

Beth kissed the sulking boy's cheek, ignoring his protests.

Then she hugged Danny tightly around the neck. "It's so good to see you."

Danny spent every waking hour helping his mother treat patients in what used to be the midwife's hut. They'd transformed that old shack into a full-fledged medical facility with floors, beds, electric lighting.

"You're too thin." Beth pinched his wrist. "I thought we were all supposed to fatten up."

Danny smiled tiredly. "Trust me. I *am* trying."

Cory snorted. "That's true. I've seen what this guy can put away."

For months after the strange events in the bunker, life at Benny's Hollow had teetered on the edge of disaster.

There simply wasn't enough to eat.

Outsiders foraged in convenience stores, while others, like Cory and Beth, ground acorns into grain and tilled the meadows into arable land. Fearing for their lives, they'd worked their hands to the bone.

Then, in early spring, the fields turned fertile, and life mellowed. Transplanted apple trees, just now beginning to bud, lined the church road. Soon, farmers expected harvests of snap peas and corn.

Jazz claimed to have predicted it all. She'd hatched a truly magnificent crop of monarch butterflies that very spring.

Around the same time, life improved on the Outside. Cell service revived, and as soon as the social networking sites reappeared, Danny sent out a flurry of messages announcing that Benny's Hollow, a thriving safe haven, would welcome all peaceful migrants in search of home.

That, he said, fulfilled Agnes's great dream: to see the gates of Red Creek flung open.

At first, no one came. Beth had watched disappointment etch crow's-feet around Danny's eyes. He wanted people to see the new world he'd helped make. He wanted it to grow. Even in the early days, when they'd lingered on the verge of starvation, he'd always envisioned Benny's Hollow becoming a thriving desert city.

In those days, Beth had felt sick with anxiety and a tortured hope, too. But it wasn't the Hollow's long-term sustainability she'd been thinking of.

It was the children.

Of all the faithful in the bunker, only the kids had survived. No one knew why the adults had perished while the children had opened their eyes and woken up. The Kings, the Hearns, the little Jamesons, even Magda had made it out, alongside Sam and the twins. Yet their parents had died—every last one. Beth would never forget how they'd simply *melted*, like overheated glass.

She'd never been able to identify her own parents' bodies. Anyway, there'd been no time for funerals, and no time for grieving. All those orphans had needed caring for. The night air had resounded with the wails of kids who'd lost the only life they'd ever known. They'd begged for the patriarchs, for Laws to follow, for their moms and dads.

A nightmare. Beth didn't like to think about it.

Instead, she preferred to remember the first few new families to trickle into their safe haven after Danny sent out his messages. The Ventimiglias had brought five dairy cows; the Rosensteins had set up their new electrical grid; the Mullens were experts in high-desert farming; and the Boises were a family of veteran schoolteachers, perfect for a community with so many children in need of educating.

Now the town flourished, four hundred strong and growing.

"Did you catch the report today?" Danny lowered his voice so the kids couldn't overhear. "Six hundred days after, and there hasn't been a single reported new infection. Not since..."

He didn't have to finish. There had been no new infections since the day Beth and Agnes went down into the bunker. Not one.

People claimed that on that day, newly infected people—children and adults alike—became miraculously well. All over the world, fevers cooled. The sick sat up in their deathbeds.

Stranger yet, within a week of Agnes and Beth's descent, many of the Nested revived—unfreezing like in a fairy tale.

Those were the lucky ones.

Millions remained petrified, huddled in red-marbled Nests. Those Nests would be their resting places forever: The Burn Squads were decommissioned, and people could be imprisoned for harming any human Nest.

They will stand as memorials to the Red Time, a lady politician had announced over the radio. *We must never forget the many we lost, and how lucky we are to have survived.*

Beth turned to Danny. "When do you think they'll realize it's finally over?"

"Oh, it will never be over," he said. "We came pretty close to extinction. We're *still* close. Most places don't have any bird population left, and that wreaks havoc on the insect world, which wreaks havoc on—"

Cory held up his hand. "Save us the science lesson, doc. We've got to hit the road."

Beth gazed out the window at their meadow, where a handful of children played tag. It boggled her mind that with all the science in the world, no one really understood how such a strange

Virus had come into existence, or why so many were suddenly cured.

"Maybe we ought to tell someone, sometime," she wondered aloud. "Maybe someone should know who was responsible."

Danny looked pained. "Not yet. What if the world isn't ready to hear it?"

They all fell silent.

They still grappled with what they'd witnessed at the bunker. Miracles will do that—shatter a person, changing the way they see. Beth thought they'd wrestle with what they'd seen Agnes do, from their own distinct perspectives, for the rest of their lives.

She changed the subject. "Zeke." She loved calling him that. "Is he in church?"

Danny nodded. "You bet. Getting ready for Sunday. The Lord's day, or what have you."

"After all that's happened, you're still not a believer?" Beth asked, smiling.

He shook his head. "I'm afraid not."

Cory smacked his forehead in mock astonishment. "You must've put in a thousand hours helping us build a new church." He paused, growing more serious. "The things we do for love."

Danny shrugged. "The church makes people happy. That's what matters." He peered at Beth. "You're planning on saying goodbye before you leave, right?"

She bristled. "Of course."

Cory took her hand. "We'd better hurry. I want to know what Texas looks like by this time tomorrow."

Beth glanced back. Sam was crushing a bag of chips, and the twins were lost in their electronic games. So much had changed—and so little.

"Goodbye, everyone," she called. "Wish me luck."

The twins rushed her for one last hug. "Goodbye, Cory! Goodbye, Beth! Send presents!"

Wiping away tears, she let Cory help her into the truck.

It was time to go to church.

62

BETH

Sorrow can also be rich soil for those brave enough to plant there.

—AGNES, EARLY WRITINGS

B eth was dreadfully nervous, entering the church.

Even now that it had been rebuilt, renewed, she never went inside. Watching Cory nearly die had ruined churches for her forever.

If that weren't enough, there was what the Prophet had done.

The day the Nest melted, she'd hurried the stunned children up the bunker stairs, planning to shelter them in the church building. By the time she emerged, smoke curled in the distance, and Cory was sprinting towards them.

The Prophet had immolated himself at his pulpit. The fire quickly consumed the walls, the ceiling, the spire. The flames painted an image of ruination and despair she'd never forget.

She held tightly to Cory's hand. "I feel like I'm forgetting something."

"Relax," he soothed her. "It's only nerves."

Beth looked around her, taking in every change. Dozens of

windows let in the light, and no ominous cross dangled. The rescued kids had decorated the walls with murals: images of Agnes and Beth glowing in the heart of the bunker, or images of their parents, the homes they'd lost. And books—so many books!—crowded the lobby, Outsider volumes on every subject, painstakingly collected into a small but growing library.

And there at the pulpit, chewing on the end of a pencil, was Agnes.

Beth's heart swelled with pride.

Her sister wore her hair in its customary braid, woven with her scarlet ribbon. But she'd swapped out her prairie dress for jeans and a white T-shirt, her boots for white sneakers.

Agnes acted as the Hollow's unofficial preacher. Though Beth didn't attend services, she read all her sermons in the newsletter. Every week, the words amazed her. Outsiders and Red Creek veterans all left the church full of excitement, full of song.

Benny napped in a shaft of sunlight while Zeke bustled around the pews, putting out hymnals. He wore a continuous glucose monitor affixed to his arm now, reading his blood every minute of the day. When Beth first saw his blood glucose numbers appear on Agnes's phone, she wept. With the help of Outsider technology, his life was a thousand times safer than in the Prophet's Red Creek. And Zeke loved it, because he didn't have to stick his finger to check his levels anymore.

When Agnes wanted to be alone with her work, she asked Max to take Zeke out to play. The Outsider boy had been teaching him and the other kids to play soccer.

"How's this week's sermon coming?" Cory called into the sunny silence.

Startled, Agnes dropped her pencil. She grinned when she saw him.

"It's called 'The Blessings of Imperfect Faith,' Cory Jameson, and it's going very slowly, if you must know."

Her eyes found Beth's and her expression changed. She hopped down from the dais, nimble in her jeans.

They faced each other uncertainly. Agnes knew Beth didn't like to be in the church. Too many memories. She also knew Beth was leaving—probably forever.

Agnes pulled her into a warm embrace. She smelled like the inside of a Bible—where her nose was often buried—and bright sunshine.

"I worried you wouldn't say goodbye," Agnes scolded. "I thought you might slink off."

Beth frowned. "Are you sure you don't still need me here? I worry I'm letting you down, by leaving."

Cory looked sharply at Beth.

But Agnes just shook her head. "Are you kidding? It's high time you left. The Hollow is too small for you."

Words crowded her tongue. There was so much she wanted to say, yet she couldn't force a single thought into shape. Mutely, she stretched out her little finger. Her sister's sharp eyes mellowed as they linked hands.

With a start, Beth realized what she'd forgotten.

Danny.

She'd never properly thanked him for saving her sister's life.

She'd always meant to, but she hated to think of that day at the bunker. So she'd kept putting it off until it was too late.

After Beth had dragged Agnes out of that disintegrating oven—with the kids screaming, desperate to get out—she couldn't stay to watch her sister die. She had to go back for the twins and Sam and every other child who'd woken up lost, trapped, afraid. It was the hardest, most harrowing work she'd ever done.

After all the children were accounted for, she'd looked for Agnes.

Danny had hauled her into the shade and surrounded her with dozens of blue plastic bags, wafting cold. Later, Beth would learn they were disposable ice packs. They cooled her temperature, but they weren't enough to revive her. Beth shrieked when Danny put both palms on her chest, pumping hard.

"Stop hurting her!" she'd yelled. "Just stop it!"

"Beth, no!" Zeke had thrown his arms around her waist, holding her back. "It's medicine! It's medicine!"

Gray-faced, Danny struggled to start an IV line. Beth didn't like to see her dead sister pricked. Needle marks pocked her wrists, hands, arms. Finally, a line took, and Danny's face cleared.

"This will hydrate her," he'd explained.

The rest of the story she'd only learned later. Beth had gone to comfort the hysterical children, who were screaming and threatening to run back into the collapsing bunker to find their parents. She could only pray her sister would be all right.

She wasn't all right—not for a long time. Agnes's heart stopped after Beth left her. Danny gave her an adrenaline shot in the thigh. When it stopped again, he gave her another one.

He never gave up.

Eventually, Matilda and the Captain arrived in a military vehicle. The nurse took over.

But, in her heart, Beth always knew it was tireless Danny who'd saved Agnes's life. With medicine, not prayer. With shots, ice, and skills he'd learned in books.

On that day, the Outsider boy who loved her sister had worked his own kind of miracle.

—ⱷ—

Beth hopped into the passenger seat of Mr. King's truck.

"Let's go see it," she said. "The great Outside."

Cory shifted the truck into gear. She took one last look at the cloudless sky of her home.

"What do you think it'll be like?"

She shrugged—an Outsider habit she'd picked up. "I don't know. I'm embracing the mystery."

As the familiar landscape rolled by, she thought of Agnes. She wondered what her sister had seen in the bunker, what she'd *learned*. There was a look in her eye just after, a secret hanging on to her lips like the memory of a kiss. If something had been revealed, Agnes had never mentioned it to Beth or preached it in her sermons. Maybe she didn't even remember it.

And really, as they drove down the hill towards Holden, Beth thought forgetfulness might be better. Personally, she'd take mysteries over miracles any day. There was beauty in mystery—in faith set free of doctrine's iron trap.

Excitement fluttered in her belly once more.

They were going *Outside*.

"Drive faster, Cory, please. There's so much I want to see."

"You got it," he said.

They accelerated into the light.

63

AGNES

To create a just society, we must never lose sight of the vision. Never forget the dream.
—AGNES, COLLECTED WORKS

Shortly after Beth and Cory drove away, Agnes left the church to watch at the gates.

The wind caressed her face, her bare arms. Overhead, a healthy hawk swooped, wings outstretched as if to grip the sky.

In the bunker, she'd lost the prayer space, her direct connection with God. She couldn't hear the earth humming or the pines whispering anymore. Couldn't hear anything. And though she'd glimpsed His face, hard as she prayed each night, she couldn't conjure it now. The loss was a fathomless ache that never ceased, like an arthritis of the soul. Late at night, when tears came, she'd curl into Danny's side. Half-asleep, he'd hold her, murmuring, reminding her of all the beauty that remained.

New life…new home…freedom, he'd whisper. *Agnes, you're finally* free.

But sometimes, she received little intuitions. Like the one burrowing into her now.

Beth had gone, but someone new was on their way. She knew it with crystal certainty.

She looked down the bright road, watching, waiting.

A small figure appeared on the horizon, picking its careful way towards her. A child, nine or ten years old.

Agnes cupped her hand over her eyes. The girl carried a walking stick whittled from a branch. A backpack dwarfed and stooped her. She walked alone.

Agnes hurried down the road to meet her. The child stumbled to a stop, teetering under her pack's weight. Her cheeks were deeply sunburned, her forehead smudged with dirt. Her ponytail was matted, uncombed. Nevertheless, her intelligent brown eyes glittered, dewdrop clear.

"I know you," said the little girl.

"Yes." Agnes reached tentatively for her hand. "I know you, too."

The girl took her hand. Together, they walked slowly uphill. Agnes wasn't exactly surprised to meet this child, but she wondered how she'd survived.

"My name is Olivia," the girl said. "I had a dream you kissed me. Saved me from a fire."

Agnes stopped walking. "Did you?"

She nodded earnestly, her eyes deep set from malnutrition. "Your blessing protected me when the others burned. The stars told me so." She paused, hesitant. "I'm sorry it took me so long to come. A family took me in. They didn't understand when I said I had to find you. I don't think they believed you were *real*."

Agnes dropped to her knees, the better to see Sarah Shiner's great-granddaughter.

"Olivia." Her pulse raced. "You said the stars told you about me. What—what did they sound like?"

She tilted her head, considering. "Silver, like bells. They sing all night. Everything sings, you know."

Agnes was not aware of the moment when she began to cry. Tears streamed in rivulets down her face, and it was like they'd always been streaming. "Yes, I know. I used to hear it, too. I called it the prayer space."

Olivia touched Agnes's cheek. "Don't be sad, Agnes."

"You know my name?"

She nodded gravely. "I know an awful lot of things."

Agnes's mind worked quickly. Everything was about to change. A new prophet had been sent into her care. A prophet not of destruction as she herself had been, but of renovation. Agnes had witnessed the end of the world; this child would play a role in its rebirth.

But first she must grow up. She would need education and protection, nourishment after years of deprivation. She'd need a haven free of judgment—a safe place to laugh, play, and listen to God's eternal songs.

Agnes hid a smile behind her hand, thinking how startled Danny would be when he learned they were about to become guardians.

Parents.

Olivia watched her closely, exquisitely sensitive to any hint of disbelief or rejection. Agnes wrapped her arms around her small, bony frame, pressing her close. Slowly, the child relaxed in her embrace.

"Welcome to Benny's Hollow, Olivia," she whispered, amazed at this new and unexpected grace. "Welcome home."

Agnes squeezed her eyes shut, swept by searing winds of mingled hope and grief.

In her arms, she held the promise of the prayer space, and of the faith she preached every Sunday. Worlds might end in fire or in rivers of tears, but there was always a new world waiting, rising—and inhaling a great breath, to sing.

AUTHOR'S NOTE

E zekiel is a young child with type 1 diabetes, an autoimmune disease entirely distinct from type 2. A type 1 diagnosis is a life-changing event for children and their families, and most parents are deeply engaged in their child's care. It is unlikely that Agnes would be able to safely keep Ezekiel's condition a secret; luckily, in the real world, it should never be necessary. I have done my best to represent type 1 as faithfully as possible without firsthand experience. It was a true privilege to learn about the remarkable kids and teens who manage their type 1, with grace and aplomb, every single day. According to beyondtype1.org, approximately 1.25 million people in the United States have type 1 diabetes.

Agnes's Red Creek was most directly inspired by Carolyn Jessop's portrayal of her life under the Fundamentalist Church of Latter-day Saints (not to be confused with the Church of Jesus Christ of Latter-day Saints), in her excellent memoir, *Escape*. Agnes's cult is a distillation of key elements that fundamentalist cults have in common: a desire to undermine and control the humanity of their followers, and a vicious ability to turn a human being's natural impulse for faith against them.

We must all be aware of who authors our beliefs, and it is our duty, and our right, to ask as many questions about our received belief systems as we are able. Young people are especially adept at this—Agnes's story is for them.

ACKNOWLEDGMENTS

First, thanks to my partner, Bill Mullen, for being the best support a writer could ask for. This book would not exist without his unflagging faith. I also want to thank my mother for her words of wisdom, and Clara, for napping when Mommy needed to work.

To Jodi Meadows, I am forever indebted. This YA author extraordinaire helped guide this project to fruition with expert mentorship and friendship. I have We Need Diverse Books to thank for the opportunity of working with her through their mentorship program. The world is a better place for the existence of such an organization.

Heartfelt thanks to my marvelous early readers: my dear friends Katia Cota and Vanessa Weiss. Also, to Padma Venkatraman, for her priceless vote of confidence. Eternal thanks to the wonderful Sarah Glenn Marsh for her sensitivity read. Her dedication to type 1 diabetes representation is an inspiration.

I'm unutterably grateful to the brilliant Alvina Ling, my editor at Little, Brown Books for Young Readers, who saw the potential in an extremely messy draft and guided this project with such care. Thanks also goes to Hannah Milton, for the close edit that pushed me to make this book better; Ruqayyah Daud, for keeping me on schedule; and the whole team at LBYR.

A thousand thanks to my agent, Michael Bourret, for being such a safety net throughout this process.

Lastly, I must acknowledge my textual inspirations for this

work: Carolyn Jessop's memoir, *Escape,* for insights into life in a fundamentalist cult—Red Creek's motto, that "perfect obedience produces perfect faith," and the injunction to "treat the other sex like snakes," come directly from her reporting of her experience. Also, passages about prophecy in the Old Testament sense, and about the prophetic life, are inspired by the exegesis of Abraham Heschel's *The Prophets.* Finally, Leland Ryken's *Words of Delight* was an invaluable resource and guide to literary aspects of the Bible.

In the text, quotes from Psalms originate from the King James Bible. For quotations from other books of the Bible, I primarily used the New International Version, the King James Bible, the Contemporary English Version, the English Standard Version, and the New American Standard Bible.